Believing in Tomorrow

Rita Bradshaw was born in Northamptonshire, where she still lives today. At the age of sixteen she met her husband – whom she considers her soulmate – and they have two daughters, a son and six grandchildren. Much to her delight, Rita's first novel was accepted for publication and she has gone on to write many more successful novels since then, including the number one bestseller *Dancing in the Moonlight*.

As a committed Christian and passionate animal-lover her life is busy, and she loves walking her dog, reading, eating out and visiting the cinema and theatre, as well as being involved in her church and animal welfare.

BY RITA BRADSHAW

Alone Beneath the Heaven
Reach for Tomorrow
Ragamuffin Angel
The Stony Path
The Urchin's Song
Candles in the Storm
The Most Precious Thing
Always I'll Remember
The Rainbow Years
Skylarks at Sunset
Above the Harvest Moon
Eve and Her Sisters
Gilding the Lily
Born to Trouble
Forever Yours
Break of Dawn
Dancing in the Moonlight
Beyond the Veil of Tears
The Colours of Love
Snowflakes in the Wind
A Winter Love Song
Beneath a Frosty Moon
One Snowy Night
The Storm Child
The Winter Rose
Believing in Tomorrow

RITA BRADSHAW

Believing in Tomorrow

PAN BOOKS

First published 2022 by Macmillan

This paperback edition first published 2022 by Pan Books
an imprint of Pan Macmillan
The Smithson, 6 Briset Street, London ECIM 5NR
EU *representative*: Macmillan Publishers Ireland Ltd, 1st Floor,
The Liffey Trust Centre, 117–126 Sheriff Street Upper,
Dublin 1, DOI YC43
Associated companies throughout the world
www.panmacmillan.com

ISBN 978-1-5290-4986-2

1 3 5 7 9 8 6 4 2

A CIP catalogue record for this book is available from the British Library.

Typeset by Palimpsest Book Production Ltd, Falkirk, Stirlingshire
Printed and bound by CPI Group (UK) Ltd, Croydon, CRO 4YY

Visit **www.panmacmillan.com** to read more about all our books
and to buy them. You will also find features, author interviews and
news of any author events, and you can sign up for e-newsletters
so that you're always first to hear about our new releases.

For Gabrielle, who put up such a brave fight for so long. Reunited with Joe and Hannah in that place where death is just a memory and tears are no more.

And dear Yoke, an amazing mother and beautiful person. No words could convey what you've gone through and with such courage and strength. We pray every day that the God of Ages will be your comfort and peace until you're all together again.

Contents

PART ONE

The Escape

1900

Chapter One

'So what are you going to do tonight then? You coming with us or what? The Michaelmas Fair's only here once a year, Moll.'

Molly McKenzie looked at the group of girls, her big blue eyes fastening on the one who'd spoken, her best friend, Fanny Howard. Softly, she said, 'You know I want to, it isn't that. It's – it's him.'

The others knew who Molly meant. Him, her da, Josiah McKenzie. Molly was terrified of him, everyone was. A tall, muscled man with thick black hair and hard eyes the colour of pewter, Josiah was well known for his quick temper and penchant for settling even the mildest of disputes with his fists. No one, not even the blacksmith in the next village who was a huge man with hands the size of cannonballs, got into an argument with Josiah. At harvest time, when all the farmworkers for miles got together in a gang and made a contract with each farmer to be paid a lump sum based on an agreed price per acre, rather than the usual weekly wage, it was an accepted fact that Josiah acted as the gaffer. There was an innate viciousness about him, something primal that made every man, woman and child anxious not to cross him.

Fanny, her voice scarcely above a whisper, drew closer to Molly. 'He wouldn't know, lass. I heard me da telling me mam that now the harvest's in, Farmer Roach has invited all the men to the farm for a drink an' bite to eat tonight. Me mam's right put out. She thinks the women and bairns should've been invited too. I mean, we do our bit same as the men, don't we?' she added, raising her voice as she included the other girls.

Everyone nodded. For eight to nine months of the year every available woman and child was pressed into service alongside the men in the fields, working on the local farms scattered on the outskirts of Newcastle and Gateshead and Sunderland. On the whole, whether the farms were large or small, there were few cottages attached to them. The farmers relied on labour from the villages and hamlets that stretched along the country lanes and highways.

Up at earliest dawn, whole families would make their way to their designated farm in all weathers where they would divide into groups, the men to their work and the women and children to theirs. A few women and older girls would be fortunate enough to be taken on in the dairy on the larger farms under the instruction of the farmer's wife, but most would work in the fields. Pulling weeds, lifting potatoes and other crops, topping beets, hoeing, stone picking, clod beating, turning hay or whatever the season demanded would be their lot. Most of the work involved continual stooping or kneeling on damp soil, and from a toddler Molly could remember regularly getting soaked to the waist when hand-weeding a standing crop of corn. In the winter they left home in the dark and returned in the dark, six days a week. When work was available, that was.

Fanny, her voice low, went on, 'Me mam says that farmers like old Roach think more of their dogs and horses than they do the women and bairns who work their fields. Scum to them, we are.'

The group nodded in silent agreement. They knew it to be true, but it was dangerous to voice such sentiments. The farmers had the whip hand. Every penny they earned was needed at home to supplement the wages of the menfolk, and it could mean the difference between food being on the table or going hungry.

At eleven years of age, Molly and Fanny were the oldest in the little group of friends, the youngest being Bertha, a red-cheeked child of seven who had a continually dripping nose. None of them could read or write, but then, no one in their hamlet of ten cottages situated a few miles west of Ryton could. Schools were attended by farmers' children and those who didn't live hand to mouth. This was never questioned. It was how things were.

'So . . .' Fanny returned to the matter in hand. 'You'd be home afore your da gets back, lass. Me mam says they'll all be drinking and making merry till the early hours if there's free beer going.'

Mrs Howard might be right but what if she wasn't? Molly asked herself. Everyone was scared of her da but no one knew what he was really capable of, not even her brothers. Only she and her mam. The thought pressed down in her chest like a heavy weight, making the secret harder to bear. Her mam had warned her she could never speak of it or her da would be taken away and they'd end up in the workhouse, but sometimes she felt she would rather that than keeping silent.

It had been eighteen months since the night when Kitty, her sister, had broken down and told their parents she had fallen for a bairn, and her only fourteen and without a steady lad. She had heard Kitty climb out of the pallet bed they'd shared – their two brothers sleeping in a similar one on the other side of the room – and then go downstairs. Curious as to what was the matter, she had crept to the top of the steep ladder that separated the upstairs of the house from the downstairs and listened to what was being said. Their parents hadn't yet retired to their double bed to one side of the kitchen but had been sitting in front of the range. She had heard her sister tell them that she had been taken advantage of by one of the vagabonds who tramped the countryside and that he had forced her.

Kitty had cried, saying she had been too frightened and ashamed about what had happened to tell anyone, but now, some months later, she knew she wouldn't be able to hide her changing shape much longer. Their mother had sworn and carried on, but strangely Molly had heard nothing from their da.

From her vantage point at the top of the ladder she'd watched him put on his cap and jacket, still without saying a word. After he'd handed Kitty her coat they had walked off into the darkness. That had been the last time she had seen her sister. She had sat shivering and waiting for what had seemed like hours, and then her da had walked in. Alone.

She hadn't caught what he'd first said to her mam, but when her mam had let out a cry it had startled her so much she'd nearly pitched head first down the ladder. Then his voice, grim and cold, had filtered up to her. 'Be quiet, woman, you'll wake the others – and remember she's got what she deserved. You didn't think I was going to stand by and let her drag my name through the mud, did you? They'd all be at it behind me back, Stan and the rest. I can hear 'em now. Josiah McKenzie, him that likes to play the gaffer and he can't even stop his own daughter whoring.'

'But she said she was forced—'

'I know what she said and I don't care, all right? Whether she was forced or not don't matter, the end result is the same. She's got a bellyful. I've got enough on my plate without feeding some bloke's flyblow. Now here's what we're going to say . . .'

Terrified, she'd crept back to bed without hearing any more, pulling the thin blankets over her and curling into a little ball, missing the warmth of Kitty's body. Her da had hurt her sister. He'd done something bad, she knew he had.

The next morning when she and her brothers had gone down for breakfast, her da had told them that Kitty had run off in the night. He'd been out looking for her this morning, he'd added, but she'd gone. She had said nothing but when she had been in the fields with her mother she'd whispered what she'd heard the night before. Her mam had rounded on her and told her to shut her mouth, threatening her with the prospect of the workhouse if she said a word to anyone. 'Kitty ran off in the night,' she'd hissed. 'You say different an' your da'll skin you alive, you hear?'

Her parents had spread the rumour that Kitty had been hankering for the bright lights of Newcastle, but she knew that wasn't true. Kitty would never have willingly left home. Her sister had always been timid and wouldn't say boo to a goose. It had been over nine months before the body of a female had been found in thick woodland near Hendon-on-the-Wall. Animals had been at it and there wasn't much left, but according to what folk said there was still some long brown hair attached to the skull. Kitty had had long brown hair. She hadn't said anything to her mother – there was no point – but she'd been unable to eat anything for days without being sick.

'Moll?' Fanny's voice brought her out of the darkness. 'Say you'll come tonight. Your da never lets you do anything and you won't get a chance for a bit of fun for ages. They'll have shuggy boats an' coconut shies an' hoopla an' everything, and the music's grand. No one'd say anything to your da if they see you, they all know what he's like. Go on, please.'

She wanted to, so much. And it was true what Fanny said – since Kitty had gone she wasn't allowed any freedom. These days she couldn't even go for a walk with Fanny and her other friends after Sunday school in the next village like she had used to. She had been forced to miss the Sunday school picnic in the summer, an event everyone looked forward to all year, and when Mrs Howard had knocked on the door and said to her da that she would keep an eye on her if he'd let her go and deliver her home safely, he'd sent Fanny's mam away with a flea in her ear. And yet Fred and Caleb could do anything they wanted. She could understand that to some extent where Fred was concerned – he was thirteen, after all – but Caleb was only nine years old.

The feeling of being hard done by, which had been growing steadily for months, brought a spark of reckless-ness with it. Molly looked into Fanny's small bright eyes and nodded. 'All right, I'll come.'

Fanny gave a squeal of pleasure. She was a replica of her mother, being stout and round-faced with a wide smile and rather forceful personality, but she had a deep affection for Molly and Molly for her. In the early days of Kitty's disappearance Molly had relied heavily on her friend. Kitty had always been more of a mother to her than a sister – their mam had little maternal affection to spare – and even now she still missed her badly.

The six girls were working together in Moat Piece, which was one of Farmer Roach's fields, and they were busy hoeing the ground. The rural naming of fields went hand in hand with an intimate knowledge of the local terrain, fed by a continuing presence in one place of generation upon generation of country folk.

The field names often gave a clue to the field's history – Fishpond, Cuckoo's Clump, Lark Hill, Bee Meadow – and Moat Piece was no exception as it was surrounded by a narrow boggy ditch. One name was as good as another to most of the workers; what really mattered about the field in which they happened to be working was whether it was comparatively sheltered. In some of the more open ones the wind would hurtle through, driving the rain into clothes in minutes. It was better if the soil was easily workable too; sometimes it could be of back-breaking heaviness or so bound together that a ploughshare could scarcely get through it.

Moat Piece was one of the more exposed fields and could be a miserable place in the depths of winter but today, although cold, an autumn sun was shining and it made the work pleasant enough. Now that the harvest had been gathered in and the corn was safely in the stack or barns, more mundane jobs could be done again, but already it was the end of September and soon the weather would change. Molly and the others knew they had to work while they could. Winter, when unemployment for the women and children for three or four months was the great bugbear, often meant empty bellies. The men usually found work of some kind but as the most they could earn was eleven or twelve shillings a week, the loss of the few shillings the women and children brought in was sorely missed. Josiah McKenzie was normally first in line for any jobs going. Besides sheer muscular strength, Molly's father had much dexterity and knowledge of how each of the many operations of farm work should be done – even if it was only how to pull turnips and lay them out in such a way that their tops could be cut off more easily. The farmers knew they could rely on him too; Josiah got things done and if he had to tread on his fellow man to do so, it didn't worry him.

'Are you going to tell your mam you're coming with us?' said Fanny, straightening her aching back and pushing her hair out of her eyes.

Molly looked across to where her mother and a couple of other women were working at the far end of the field. It had only been after Kitty had gone that she had realized she didn't like her mam. Her mam had never bothered with her and Kitty – she only ever had time for the lads – but it wasn't that so much that had caused the resentment and dislike to fester, or the clips round the ear her mam dished out for the slightest misdemeanour. It was the knowledge that whatever her da said or did, her mam was on his side, and him doing away with her sister was proof of it. Her mam had carried on as though Kitty had never existed. Sometimes when she was lying awake on her pallet bed with the lads snoring on the other side of the room, she could hear her mam and da talking and now and again her mam would laugh, a silly girlish giggle. It always caused her stomach to knot. How could her mam do that when she knew what her da had done?

Molly looked at Fanny, and her voice was flat when she said, 'No, I shan't tell me mam owt.'

Fanny nodded. She would never say it out loud because Mrs McKenzie was Molly's mam, after all, but she didn't like her friend's mother. Mrs McKenzie had a way of looking at you that made you think you'd got a dirty nose or something. She had said that once to her own mam, and her mam had said that Mrs McKenzie had a lot to put up with being married to Josiah McKenzie, but her da had been listening and he had shaken his head. 'Birds of a feather there,' he'd said soberly. 'Birds of a feather, lass, an' no mistake.'

Fanny kept her voice low when she said, 'Shall I wait for you at Whistler's Corner after dinner then? There's a bunch of us meeting there. How are you going to get away without your mam knowing, though?'

Molly thought for a moment. 'I'll go to bed and then climb out of the window.' Their small stone cottage was built against a sharply rising bank on one side and when the window was open you could virtually climb up on the sill and step out onto the bank. The bank was covered in briars and thorn bushes, but she would manage.

'What about your Fred and Caleb? Would they tell on you?'

'Fred's going to the fair with his pals and he's taking Caleb with him, so they won't be there.'

'What if they see you at the fair, though?'

'They wouldn't say anything to me da.' She wasn't as close to her brothers as she had been to Kitty, but the three of them were united against their father.

'Me da said he's going to give me some pennies for the fair and I'll share them with you,' Fanny promised. She knew Molly's parents never gave her so much as a farthing to spend on herself.

Molly smiled gratefully. 'Ta, thanks.'

'An' we can buy some jujubes or a bag of gingerbread to eat on the way home,' said Fanny, warming to the theme. 'Some of us did that last year and it was lovely.'

'There's toffee apples an' cinder taffy an' roasted chestnuts an' all,' piped up one of the other girls, a little too loudly for Fanny's liking.

'Shut up, Clara,' she said crossly. 'Molly's mam'll hear. You've got a voice like a foghorn. And don't forget Molly coming is a secret, all of you, all right?' She glared round the small group and they all nodded.

A thick autumn twilight had been gathering pace as the girls talked, and now, as their mothers called, they joined the group of women and children who had gathered to walk home, some to the hamlet and the rest to the nearest village a couple of miles beyond. Everyone was tired after a long day in the fields, but tonight a faint sense of excitement pervaded the air. They only had fairs come to the area twice a year – one was at Easter, but the Michaelmas Fair was much larger and grander. These two events were the highlight of the year, along with the Sunday school picnic in July.

When they reached the hamlet, those who lived there called goodbye to the villagers who walked on. On the whole, the dwellings in the village were vastly superior to those in the hamlet; most of the cottages had two rooms downstairs and two up, and quite a few even had a wash house next to the privy at the end of the garden. Those who had enough room kept a pig and chickens and had a fenced-off area where they grew their own vegetables. The well in the centre of the village provided pure, clear drinking water, and there was a small general shop and a public house, the Croaking Frog.

In the hamlet, everyone had to fetch their water from the stream which ran a hundred yards behind their dwellings, and the small bit of ground near each cottage hardly deserved the grand name of a garden, although vegetables were grown in the hard, unforgiving earth. None of the cottages had an oven, merely an open fire which served for warmth and cooking. Vegetables and meat, such as rabbits and pigeons caught in the fields, were boiled in big black pots hanging from a hook in the ceiling over the flames, and sometimes dumplings in small homemade bags would be added to the mix. In the winter a lot of 'sparrowing' was done. The men in the hamlet took the nets that their womenfolk had made and captured the small birds by beating the hedges in the dark evenings. Of food that had to be bought for cash, bread was far the most important. A two-pound loaf from the village shop cost two pennies; milk and butter and cheese could be purchased too, but no one in the hamlet could afford butter. Lard, made from pigs, was much cheaper, as was skimmed milk, a big crockful of which could be obtained for a ha'penny. In the spring, birds' eggs were stolen from nests and taken home, but occasionally at other times eggs were bought from the nearby village from cottagers who had hens.

Molly couldn't remember a time when she hadn't gone to bed hungry, and now, as she entered the cottage in the hamlet with her mother, Ada McKenzie said, 'It'll only be us an' the lads eating. Your da and the other men are going to Farmer Roach's straight from the fields for supper.'

Pretending this was news to her, Molly said, 'Why?'

''Cause the harvest's in,' her mother said shortly.

From her mother's sharp tone, Molly suspected she was as put out as Fanny's mam about the matter, but she said nothing more. When her mother was in a mood about something or other it didn't take much for her to lash out and give her daughter a stinging slap across the side of the head which sometimes made her ear ache for days.

She went about the evening routine quietly, pouring some water from the bucket by the door into a tin basin, washing her hands with the slab of blue-veined soap which never lathered and leaving the basin on the stool for the lads to use when they came in. She then placed four bowls, spoons and mugs on the rough wooden table and poured more water from the bucket into a large jug which she put in the centre. As she finished doing this her two brothers walked in, and immediately her mother's persona changed as she turned from stirring the rabbit stew and smiled at them, saying, 'There you are. Wash your hands an' come and sit down, lads.'

Once her sons were seated, Ada dished out the stew into the four bowls before cutting up the remains of a stale loaf and placing a large chunk beside each of the boys' bowls and her own. She didn't offer one to Molly and Molly hadn't expected her to. Her mother had always seen to it that she and Josiah and the lads were fed first. From babyhood, Molly and Kitty had got used to going without.

Once the simple meal was over, Fred looked at his mother. 'Me an' Caleb'll be off now.' And then he surprised Molly by adding, 'We can take Molly with us, Mam. I'll see she comes to no harm.'

For a moment Molly's hope soared. This would solve her having to sneak out.

'All the bairns are going to the fair,' Fred continued, 'and—'

'No.' Ada's voice brooked no argument. 'It's getting dark already and you know your da wouldn't allow it. If he came home before you brought her back there'd be hell to pay.'

Fred cast a glance at his sister as if to say, *Well, I tried*, before pulling Caleb to his feet. 'I'll bring you back a taffy apple,' he promised Molly, surprising her further. 'All right?'

She smiled at him and nodded, warmed by the unusual show of brotherly thoughtfulness.

Once the lads had gone Molly washed the dishes and emptied the basin outside, before fetching more wood for the fire from the stack of kindling and logs stored under the tin-roofed lean-to next to the wall of the cottage. She put some to one side of the brick hearth and then swept the stone-flagged floor. That done, she picked up the empty bucket and made her way along the narrow path at the back of the cottages to the stream.

She stood for a moment in the soft darkness. A bird trilled briefly in the hedgerow bordering one side of the stream and in the distance a fox barked harshly. Although the day had been cold the sunshine had brought out the rich smell of vegetation and she sniffed appreciatively. Now the sun had set there was a definite bite to the air which announced that winter was round the corner. It always came early in the north, which ensured everyone made the most of the late summer days.

The enormity of what she proposed to do swept over her and she shivered. Sneaking out to accompany Fanny and the others to the fair was daring, but her mam and da would never know, she reassured herself in the next moment. Farmer Roach brewed his own beer, umpteen gallons a year in old rum puncheons, which he dished out to the labourers working at his farm with their lunchtime meal. It was one of the perks on the Roach farm, and the reason men vied with each other to work there. The beer would be flowing freely tonight for sure and, according to what folk said, it was potent stuff. The men would make a night of it and she would be home long before her da returned. Aye, it would be all right, she told herself again, even as her stomach turned over at her temerity.

Once back at the cottage she said goodnight to her mother, who was sitting in front of the fire, half-asleep in one of the two tattered armchairs the room boasted. Neither Molly nor her siblings had ever sat in them; it was an unspoken rule that they were purely for their parents' use.

Once she had climbed the ladder to the upstairs room, she opened the window as far as it would go and climbed onto the sill. That was easy enough, but a mass of briars protruded over the edge of the bank and by the time she had climbed out she had scratches everywhere. Trying to ignore the smarting pain, she established a firm footing and then silently made her way along the back of the cottage, only climbing down to the ground when she was some distance away. She stood in the lane, panting and smoothing her dress and smock before detangling her long hair, which had got caught in the thorns.

She had done it, she thought with a dart of excitement and fear, and she'd worry about getting back in when she had to. She just hoped Fanny and the others were waiting for her at their meeting place or else all this would have been for nothing. She would never dare to try and find the fair on her own.

She needn't have worried. As she neared Whistler's Corner, Fanny came running to meet her, her round face alight. 'I told the others you'd come,' her friend said as she reached her. 'Clara said you'd chicken out but I said you wouldn't. An' me da's given me six pennies. Here—' She thrust three into Molly's scratched and bloodied fingers. 'We're gonna have a grand time, lass. You wait and see.'

Chapter Two

Molly stared in silent awe at the scene in front of her. Naphtha lamps spluttered and flared, and candles flickered wildly on the fronts of the larger amusements – the swing boats, merry-go-round with its gaily painted horses, shooting galleries, hoopla and boxing rink among others – and smaller lights glimmered along the stalls selling toys and sweets and ornaments. Booths were illuminated with thousands of tiny glittering lamps, sapphire and amber, emerald and ruby, arranged in the form of crowns, stars and feathers. It all made for a rich kaleidoscopic array of changing colours that threw their glamour over the men, women and children milling about. Pleasure-seekers from the villages and hamlets for miles around had come to the Michaelmas Fair, and the noise from the crowd along with the thudding steam organs was deafening to ears normally tuned to the quiet of the countryside.

'Grand, isn't it,' said Fanny, as proud as if she had orchestrated the whole event herself. 'I told you, didn't I?

Come on, we'll walk round for a bit and see everything first.' She thrust her arm through Molly's and they set off with the other girls trailing behind them.

They hadn't gone far when they came across Mrs Howard and another woman from the hamlet, both of whom stared at Molly in surprise. 'Is your mam here, Molly?' Sarah Howard glanced around. She was aware of the way Molly was treated by her parents – Fanny was often very vocal about the matter – and she was amazed they'd allowed her out for the evening.

It was Fanny who said, 'Her mam an' da don't know she's here. Don't let on, will you?'

Sarah looked at the child she always thought of as 'that poor bairn'. Molly was as pretty as a picture with her sandy gold hair and great big blue eyes, but her little face was always so sad, and no wonder with Josiah McKenzie as her father. 'Me lips are sealed, hinny,' she said with a smile. 'An' I'll make sure the word's out for no one else to say owt either, all right? Now off you go and enjoy yourselves. It'll be a while before the fair's here again.'

The two girls walked on together – the others had disappeared off somewhere while they had been talking to Fanny's mother – and Molly drank in the sights and sounds and smells of the fairground. The odour of burning coal mixed with hot oil and steam, along with the delicious smells of baked potatoes and roasted chestnuts, was heady, and she felt as though she had stepped into an enchanted world. Everyone was happy and smiling, the cares of the day forgotten. It was wonderful, magical.

After buying a cone of gingerbread each, they wandered to the back of the fair where the quaint ornate living wagons stood. Horses were grazing and there were several dogs tied to the wagons. They didn't venture too close – it was darker here and the horses were huge brutes – but as Molly gazed at the little houses on wheels she found herself wishing that she was a child of the fair folk. Travelling from place to place and not working in the fields from dawn to dusk must be lovely, she thought wistfully, and to live in one of the beautifully painted wagons would be heaven on earth after their dark, dingy cottage. Anywhere would be better than home, if it came to it.

The thought wasn't a new one but in the next moment she brushed it aside; she wasn't going to let anything spoil this evening, she told herself as they strolled back towards the lights and clamour. After a ride on the swing boats and then the merry-go-round, they bought a toffee apple each and sat eating them on the steps of one of the rides.

She had a ha'penny left and decided to spend it on the hoopla before she went home; it was getting late and she was growing increasingly worried about climbing back in the window now the first thrill of the fair had lessened.

She and Fanny paid their ha'pennies and received three rings apiece, and on her third throw she was beside herself with excitement when the hoop landed over a little cloth doll clad in a gingham dress and tiny pinafore. Her delight was so transparent that the elderly stallholder grinned at her as he handed her the doll, saying his wife made most of the items and she'd be pleased to know one of her creations had given such pleasure.

Molly held the doll close to her thin chest as they walked away; she had never had a toy before and couldn't believe her luck. She would have to hide it from her mam and da but that was all right; her da never climbed the ladder to the room above, and her mam hadn't for the last few years since they were old enough to change the straw in their mattresses themselves and wash their thin blankets a couple of times a year in the stream. She would call the doll Daisy, she decided, and she could sleep with her each night. Already she loved her more than anything in the world.

After a few minutes she and Fanny joined Fanny's mam, who had marshalled the rest of her brood together and was preparing to leave the fair. They walked home singing hymns they'd learned in Sunday school and laughing and talking, and although the night had turned decidedly nippy, no one noticed the cold. Molly was glowing with happiness, a blissful happiness she would have thought herself incapable of before this night. And then, when she was only a couple of hundred yards from the hamlet, her name thundered on the air, cutting through the jollity like a knife through warm butter.

'*Molly!*'

She froze in fright. She had been completely unaware of Josiah coming up behind them – they all had been – but now as she turned to face her father she thought he looked like the Devil himself. He walked up to them, his face contorted with blazing anger, and as she shuddered and trembled, Sarah Howard, aiming to try and defuse things, said brightly, 'Josiah, we didn't see you there. Had a good time at Roach's, have you?'

He didn't answer her, his eyes emitting a black light as he kept them on Molly's white face. 'Where have you been?'

She couldn't speak through the fear strangling her, and it was Sarah who said, 'I took a few of the bairns to the fair, that's all, just for a short while.'

When he turned his gaze upon Sarah, stout and solid as she was, she took a step backwards, her children moving with her. As she said afterwards to her husband, 'It was Old Nick himself standing there, I swear it.'

Josiah's gaze returned to his daughter and he took her arm, his fingers like steel as he gripped her and pulled her towards their cottage. Sarah shouted something after them but he ignored her, flinging open the door of the cottage with enough force to cause Ada to leap out of her chair with her hand to her chest. 'Josiah, you scared me to death. Whatever's—' And then Ada's voice stopped abruptly as she took in Molly at his side.

'Did you know about this?' Josiah flung his daughter across the room so she went sprawling and landed in a heap on the floor. 'That damn Howard woman taking her to the fair?'

'What?' Ada didn't have to protest; it was clear she was flabbergasted. 'Of course not, I'd never have let her. She went to bed same as usual.'

'Only she didn't, did she?' He cursed, a foul spate of words as he walked to the small cowering figure and pulled her up by the hair. 'You dare to defy me, m'girl? Cut from the same cloth as your whoring sister but I'm damned if I'll be made a monkey of again. What's that?' He wrenched the small cloth doll out of her hand. 'Who gave you this? A lad? Answer me.'

'I – I—' Molly was shaking from head to foot, such terror gripping her that she could barely speak. 'I won it.'

'You won it? Don't give me that. Where did you get the money to win anything? It's a lad, isn't it, and I daresay that Howard scum egged you on an' all. What's his name? One of the Woodrow boys or Hogarth's eldest?' He turned to Ada. 'Bert Hogarth was telling me just the other day he'd caught his eldest lad with a lass – likely he was taking one at me on the quiet.' He swung back to Molly. 'Was it you? Were you the lass he was talking about?'

'No, no, I swear it. Fa-Fanny gave me half her pennies.'

'She's too young to go with a lad,' Ada began, only to snap her mouth shut as her husband glared at her.

'They're never too young if they're made that way but it's not happening twice.' He ripped the head off the doll, tearing the rest of it to pieces and flinging the shreds into Molly's face. Pulling the belt out of his trousers, he snarled, 'Come here.'

Molly couldn't move. She'd felt the back of his hand many times but he'd never taken the belt to her before. She stared at him, her face white and her eyes huge, tears running down her cheeks. 'I'm sorry, Da, I'm sorry,' she gabbled. 'I'll never do it again—' And then she screamed as he grabbed her.

'No, you damn well won't, I'll make sure of that. I'm going to teach you a lesson you'll never forget, m'girl.'

The first slash of the belt brought her screaming again, causing Josiah to swear and curse. He dragged her across the room as she struggled wildly, reaching for a piece of the old towelling they used to dry their hands, stuffing it in her mouth as a gag and tying the ends behind her head. Molly was demented with terror, attempting to lash out with her arms and legs, but her efforts were as futile as a baby sparrow's in the jaws of a cat. He flung her to the floor, leaning over to bring the belt lashing down with all his strength over and over again.

Her screams muffled by the gag, Molly tried to crawl away but he followed her. After a minute or so she couldn't do anything, such was the pain, but curl herself into a ball that jerked as the belt hit her small thin body.

That Josiah had lost control was clear to Ada, and but for her hanging on to his arm and shouting, 'No more, no more, she's had enough and you'll go down the line if she dies,' he would have killed her.

As it was, his wife's frantic voice got through to him, and his arm falling to his side he stood panting, before turning to Ada and growling, 'How did she go without you knowing, anyway?'

'I put me feet up after dinner and had a nap. She must

have crept down then. I thought she was still in bed. I got the shock of my life when I saw her with you just now.'

'That damn Howard woman was in on it, encouraging her to defy me. I'll see me day with her and her brood, you see if I don't.'

'I know, I know.' Aiming to placate him, Ada said, 'Come on, lad, you're done in and no wonder. Come an' sit down.'

'If I hadn't come back early because of that tooth that's been giving me gyp for days I might not have seen her. How many other times has she skedaddled without us knowing? I'll find out and when I do—'

'All right, but not now. I'll get her upstairs and you sit and take the weight off, lad. There's a drop of oil of cloves in the cupboard for that tooth, I'll get it in a minute.'

Molly could hear the sound of voices above her head but she couldn't distinguish what they were saying beyond the agony slicing through her. It made her nauseous, and when her mother tried to move her she vomited over the floor.

'Filthy little slut.' Josiah plumped down in one of the armchairs. 'Get her to clean that up.'

Ada made no comment. She could see Molly was in a bad way. All she wanted to do was to get her daughter out of Josiah's sight. Her voice low and harsh, she muttered, 'Get to bed, you hear me?' but she had to lift the child to her feet and then support her when Molly practically fainted away. Manhandling the slight form to the ladder, she managed to heave her up into the room above, although they both nearly plummeted to the ground a few times.

Once in the dark room she shoved her daughter onto the pallet bed. 'You've brought this on yourself. You know that, don't you? You must have known what he'd be like if he caught you. What on earth possessed you, girl? Was it the Howards like he said? Did they persuade you?'

Molly couldn't speak. She felt as though she was dying and she would welcome death if it stopped the pain.

Ada stood for a few moments more. She could barely make out Molly's shape on the pallet bed but she could hear her ragged breathing. It invoked no pity, merely rage that Molly had caused such trouble and upset Josiah.

Provoking him like that, she thought angrily. It always brought out Josiah's worst side if his authority was challenged, everyone knew that. She'd have a word with Sarah Howard tomorrow and give her a piece of her mind.

Not for the first time, Ada reflected on how much better their life would have been if they'd had no bairns, like Ralph and Flora Todd who lived at the end of the row of cottages. Flora was always bemoaning her lot but Ada had no sympathy for the woman. If it had been just her and Josiah all their days, she would have been as happy as a bug in a rug.

Of the many pregnancies she'd endured, only seven babies had been born alive and just four of them had survived past their first birthday. This was not uncommon in the hamlet. Womenfolk spent such long hard hours in the fields in all weathers, resulting in many miscarriages or stillbirths, and small babies who often died from sheer neglect and cold. Earning a wage was the important thing, everything else came second to that. Some mothers seemed to take the deaths of their bairns hard, but not Ada. Josiah was her world.

She had fallen for him the moment she had set eyes on him as a girl of fifteen when her family, Romany Gypsies, had passed through the hamlet to meet up with others of their kind for a wedding a short distance away. Unbeknown to her parents she had met with Josiah every day for a week, and after the celebrations had finished and the family had travelled on, she had run away and made her way back to the hamlet and her love. She'd known that her father would never give his blessing to a marriage with a man outside their clan and culture, but she was determined to have Josiah. They had been wed within a month. He was all she had ever wanted and still did. Josiah's parents and younger brother had died from the fever the year before she'd met him, and so it was just the two of them in the cottage before the first baby had come along. That time had been the happiest of her life.

Ada came out of her reverie as Molly moaned softly. Children spoiled things, she thought irritably, especially daughters. Kitty had forced Josiah's hand and made him do something that could have put him in danger with the law, and here was Molly following in her sister's footsteps.

Lads were different, more independent and less clingy. Bending down, she hissed, 'Stop that noise or you'll feel the back of my hand, m'girl. You've caused enough trouble the night, so think on and let this be a lesson to you.'

There was no answer from the small figure at her feet and after a few moments Ada turned and climbed carefully down the ladder into the room below. Josiah was still sitting in the armchair in front of the range and she walked over to him, putting her arms round him and kissing the top of his head. It still thrilled her that this big strong taciturn man that everyone else was frightened of was hers.

'I'll get that oil of cloves, my love,' she said softly, running her fingers through his thick hair before she moved away.

Chapter Three

Through the fog of burning pain, Molly was vaguely aware of her brothers coming home some time later and going to bed. If she moved so much as a muscle the pain became unbearable and so she lay absolutely still on one side, her knees drawn up and the corner of a blanket stuffed in her mouth to stop her whimpering.

A year ago it had been the talk of the area when a farmer some miles away had gone berserk after finding his wife carrying on with one of his labourers. He'd flayed her to the point of death and there had been a big outcry about it, Molly thought feverishly. She'd heard her mam and da talking about it and her mam had gone on about what the woman must have suffered and how terrible it was, but she hadn't tried to stop her da tonight. How could her mam care about this woman she didn't even know, and yet not her own daughter?

Scalding tears were running down her face now and she gulped deep in her throat. Her mam was as bad as her da; no, worse, because mothers were supposed to be the ones who loved their bairns more, weren't they? Fanny's mam did. She wished her parents were dead and she could go and live with Fanny, and she wasn't going to say sorry to God for thinking it even if it was a sin.

The long hours crept by in a haze of pain and tears and fitful catnaps, and her mind began to play tricks on her. One minute she thought she was back in the kitchen and her da was thrashing her again, and another time she imagined some of the boys from the village were prodding her with spear-shaped sticks. Then she was at the fair but with Kitty this time, and she clung to her sister and asked her where she'd been and if she could come and live with her, and Kitty kissed and hugged her back and said she was dead but Molly could be with her if she liked, all she had to do was to die.

When the pale light of morning filtered into the room, she heard Fred and Caleb begin to stir. It took all of her strength to move slowly and turn onto her hip, but the effort made her dizzy and nauseous and she knew she wasn't going to be able to get up. The lads pulled on their shirts and trousers over the vests and long johns they slept in, and took the couple of steps to her pallet bed, looking down at her.

'Hey, Molly, sleepyhead.' Fred's voice was jocular. 'I brought you the toffee apple like I promised. Here, take it.' And then his voice changed. 'What's the matter? You bad or something?'

In a cracked and hoarse whisper, she murmured, 'Da – Da took his belt to me.'

'Da took his belt to you?' Fred kneeled down beside her and now his gaze took in her sickly white face and the criss-cross of dark-blue weals on her legs and arms. There was no sign of blood but the weals were standing out like engorged veins ready to burst. Silently he lifted her dress and saw that the small thin back was similar to her arms and legs, and he could just see a weal that started at the top of her ear across her cheek to her mouth.

Caleb whispered, 'What did you do, Moll?' only to have his older brother turn on him and mutter fiercely, 'Whatever she did, it doesn't deserve this. He's mad. I've told you afore, he's stark staring mad.'

Weakly, Molly murmured, 'I went to the fair with Fanny and her mam.'

'You did?' There was a touch of admiration in Fred's voice. 'What about Mam? Did she know?'

'No. I climbed out of our window when Mam thought I was in bed. Da caught me when I came home.' Her face screwed up with pain as she spoke, her breath catching in her throat as she whispered, 'I'm feelin' bad, Fred. So bad. I – I can't go to the fields today.'

Fred reached out and squeezed her hand, saying softly, 'Course you can't. I'll tell 'em, don't worry.' He stood up and looked at Caleb, who stared back at his brother with frightened eyes. Walking across to the pallet bed he and Caleb shared, he dragged their thin blankets into a heap and then brought them across to Molly, covering her gently. 'You're frozen, lass, an' that won't help. You try an' get some sleep now, all right?'

Molly heard her brothers clamber down the ladder and then Fred saying something she couldn't catch. The next moment her father's voice came loud and angry: 'In bed, be damned. I'll go up there and drag her down if I have to.'

'She's bad, Da.' Fred's voice had risen. 'Real bad.'

'Don't take that tone with me, m'boy, unless you want some of the same.'

'Let me go and see.' Ada was attempting to pour oil on troubled waters, and the next minute she had climbed up into the bedroom. 'Your da wants you downstairs,' she began, pulling back the blankets, but then Molly heard her give a little gasp. Opening her eyes, Molly saw her mother staring down at her with an expression of concern. That this concern wasn't for her daughter became apparent in the next moment when Ada muttered, 'Look what you made him do, you wicked girl. Your da could get into trouble for this and then where would we be? You stay where you are for today and I'll see to you when I get back tonight.'

She was burning all over and so thirsty it even outdid the pain for a moment when she whispered, 'Can – can I have a drink, Mam, please?'

Ada flung the blankets back over her daughter, clicking her tongue irritably. She would have liked nothing more than to shake her till her teeth rattled. 'You've been trouble since the day you were born,' she hissed. 'Like your sister. And you'll end up like her, you mark my words.'

Descending the ladder, she saw her sons sitting at the table with their breakfast untouched. Josiah was eating his porridge which was stiff with salt, the way he liked it. Walking across to the table, she filled a mug with water and turned towards the ladder, only to stop in her tracks when Josiah growled, 'And what the hell do you think you're doing?'

'She's thirsty.'

'Am I hearing right? I want her down here, *now*.'

'She can't, Joe, not today. She's bad, real bad like Fred said. She'll need a bit of time.'

Josiah narrowed his eyes. He'd heard the unspoken message in his wife's voice and knew he'd be in trouble if the child snuffed it. After a moment, he said slowly, 'If she wants to eat or drink she'll come down for it or do without. Have I made myself clear?'

Ada nodded. She knew better than to argue.

'Now you sit an' eat.' His gaze took in his sons, who were motionless. 'You two an' all.'

They ate in silence after that and once finished, prepared to leave the house. Fred was longing to take Molly a drink and see how she was, but he knew better than to antagonize his father further. Nevertheless his features were tight with the anger he was feeling. If it weren't for Caleb he'd have taken to the road a long time ago, he told himself as he stepped into the cold morning. A frost had settled during the night, signalling that summer was well and truly over. Once Caleb was a bit older they could disappear together and make their lives elsewhere, like Kitty had done. He didn't blame his sister for running away except that Kitty's going had left Molly to bear the brunt of their mother's temper and now, apparently, their da's. Maybe he could take Molly with him too – anything was better than leaving her here.

His thoughts continued to centre on Molly as he and Caleb followed in their parents' footsteps to the farm where they all were working. His sister had looked so small and wretched. For two pins he'd turn round and go back but . . . His eyes fastened on his father and he felt the bile of shame in his throat. He hated his fear of the man who'd sired him but the self-loathing wasn't enough to make him do what he knew was right. And so he kept on walking.

It was a full hour after everyone had left before Molly dragged herself into a sitting position on the edge of the pallet, and all the time she was thinking, *I feel bad, I feel bad, oh, I feel so bad.* But painful though it was to move, her thirst had become a torment. She sat for a while and then stood up shakily, feeling weak and dizzy.

Somehow she climbed down the ladder without going head first. The room below was cold but rivulets of sweat poured off her and she felt sick as she clung on to the ladder for some minutes before she could stagger across to the kitchen table. There was a half-full jug of water standing among the remains of the breakfast dishes but even though her thirst was agonizing she had to steady herself for some moments. Lifting the jug made her groan as her bruised flesh protested, but it was worth it to gulp the water and soothe her parched throat.

She drank it all, and only then did she sink down on one of the benches either side of the table, laying her head on her arms on the scrubbed wood of the table. She dozed for a short while and then the empty trembling in her stomach forced her across to the cooking pot hanging from its hook over the embers of the fire. There were the scrapings of the porridge inside and she ate every morsel, even though it was black and burned.

Her heart beating against her chest like a wounded bird, she then did the unthinkable and collapsed into one of the armchairs. How long she slept she didn't know, but when she came to, the food and water had given her a semblance of strength. Through the dirty window she could see sunshine and it drew her to the door of the cottage.

After she had opened it she stood breathing in the fresh air and listening to the birds chirping. It was cold but still a beautiful day, she thought, the sunshine touching her face with a modicum of warmth. Suddenly she knew exactly what she was going to do.

She clung on to the door, the pain from her wounds radiating fiery shivers all over her body but knowing that this was her chance, a chance to escape her father. If she didn't go now she might never get another opportunity. She didn't know where she would make for or what she would do when she got there, but that didn't matter right now. The important thing was getting far away from him.

If she stayed, one day her da would kill her like he had killed Kitty. She felt it in her bones, and her mother wouldn't stop him. He'd be waiting for her to defy him again and whether his grievance would be real or imagined, the end result would be the same.

And she wanted to live. She looked up into the clear blue sky, shutting her eyes so that the sun made colours against her closed lids. She didn't want to be found dead in a wood, half-eaten by animals with only her hair bearing evidence that she had once been alive and breathing. *Kitty, oh, Kitty.*

She stepped back into the cottage and shut the door, looking at the steep ladder as though it was an insurmountable obstacle. But she had to climb it – her few belongings were in the bedroom. Her body pulsing with pain, she took the rungs one at a time, resting between each one and the next. Once in the grubby room, which was always gloomy even on the brightest summer day, she glanced about her.

The lads' pallet bed and her own were the only substantial items the room held. There were a few nails hammered into the wall for hanging clothes, and each of them had an old orange box in which they kept underwear and any possessions. Besides the clothes she was wearing, she owned one Sunday dress and smock and a coat, which she now pulled on over her working-day clothes as it would save her carrying them. All her orange box contained was underwear, a small Bible she'd been presented with at Sunday school and a hairbrush, and she made a bundle of these with one of the thin brown blankets from the bed.

Once she had climbed back down the ladder and was standing in the kitchen she felt as exhausted as if she had run miles, her heart thudding hard against her chest. She wanted nothing more than to lie down and sleep, but she knew she mustn't give in to the weakness. Time was ticking by and she had to be well gone before her da came home. She had brought Fred's toffee apple from the bedroom and now she walked to the kitchen cupboard and opened it. Besides the ingredients for the stew her mother was intending to cook for the evening meal, and a few other basic essentials like oats and barley and salt, it held a number of small apples the lads had scrumped from a farmer's orchard along with some blackberries they'd gathered from the hedgerows, a bowl of dripping, a lump of cheese and a fruit pudding her mother must have boiled the evening before which was still wrapped in its pudding cloth. Adding a couple of the apples, the cheese and the pudding to the toffee apple in the bundle, Molly felt her stomach turn over. Her mam would skin her alive for taking the food but then she wasn't going to catch her, and she needed something to eat if she was taking to the road. She had to get as far away from here as she could and stay hidden as much as possible for the next few days. She'd make her way eastwards, towards the coast, keeping to the fields and country lanes and skirting any villages and towns.

She was amazed both at the clearness of her mind and

at her temerity. Her body was bruised and battered and very tired, but her head was clear and working, motivated by the knowledge that what her father had done once he would have no compunction about doing again. It would be easy to give up and resign herself to her fate but she wasn't going to. *Had Kitty fought him?* The question wasn't a new one and now, bitterly, she told herself, 'Why ask the road you know?' Kitty wouldn't have resisted; her sister had been sweet and gentle and malleable, always thinking the best of folk. She would have gone to her death trustingly.

Hot tears stung her eyes and she brushed them away almost impatiently. She wasn't half as nice as Kitty had been, she knew that, because some of the thoughts she had about her mam and da were wicked. And what was even more wicked was that she didn't feel any remorse about them.

A small shred of material caught her eye, and as she bent to pick it up off the floor she realized it was part of the little doll she had won at the fair and had owned for such a short time. A surge of emotion brought a lump to her throat and tears pricking at the backs of her eyes, but in the next moment, after swallowing hard and blinking, she straightened her narrow shoulders. She wasn't going to think about Daisy, she told herself fiercely, not now. That could come later when she was away from here and safe. No more tears, she had to be strong.

* * *

There was no one about as she left the cottage; everyone would be working in the fields on such a bonny day. As she shut the door on the dwelling she'd lived in for eleven years, her bundle of bits and pieces tied on her back so it left her hands free, she felt nothing but an urgent need to get away.

Every bone and muscle in her body ached and her head was thudding. She had never felt less like walking in her life but walk she must, she told herself grimly, as she followed the country lane in the direction of the village before turning off along a narrow dirt track between two fields that would take her deeper into the countryside. The hedgerows were high at the side of the path and birds flitted here and there, tweeting and calling to each other. Elderberries hung loosely down in parts, touched by the same light which pricked the fruits of bryony and dotted rosehips, and tangles of blackberry brambles revealed their bounty. Normally she would have stopped and picked them – she was always hungry – but today she walked on, concentrating on putting one foot in front of the other. She was already desperately tired.

The day had warmed up and all the frost was gone, and with the extra clothes she'd put on she didn't feel cold. Shallow sparkles of sunlight glanced through the trees bordering the shaded path she was following and she had been walking for some time when she caught sight of a black-and-white flash of wing as a magpie dropped to the ground, cocking its tail as it landed.

She froze, remembering the stories about the bird she'd heard from childhood. It was supposed to be an evil omen if you saw just one because the creature was associated with Satan for not wearing full mourning at the time of Christ's crucifixion. According to the old timers, the magpie held two drops of the Devil's blood hidden under its tongue. Everyone she knew would spit over their right shoulder whenever they encountered the bird to avert misfortune. It wasn't uncommon to see a cross carved into the trunk of a tree in which magpies nested as this would force the bird to flee. And now one had come to find her, she thought, panic-stricken.

She remained still, staring at the bird which was intent on eating a large worm it had found, and when in the next instant it was joined by a second magpie she breathed a sigh of relief. Two of them meant happiness, a case of evil cancelling out evil. It was all right. She stood watching the birds squabbling and jabbering over their meal before they flew off and then sank down onto the ground. She had to rest for a while.

How long she slept she didn't know, but when she next opened her eyes twilight had fallen. She was so stiff that she cried out in pain as she stumbled to her feet, retrieving her bundle and tying it on her back again.

It was chilly now and she could smell frost in the air. Suddenly the world seemed less friendly than it had when the sun was shining and even through her layers she was cold. She couldn't spend the night out in the open. She had to find some kind of shelter, she thought, shivering as the loud, shrill shriek of a barn owl sounded in the distance.

A slip of a harvest moon hung in the darkening sky, and as she forced herself to walk onwards she stumbled now and again in the thick shadows. She had only gone about a hundred yards when the path petered out and she saw a ramshackle gate set in a drystone wall. Beyond it stretched the stubble of a wheat field which no doubt the farmer would be ploughing soon, and after climbing over the gate she continued walking, feeling much more exposed and wary in the open field. She didn't think the farmer or any of his labourers would be about at this time of night now the light had all but gone, but nevertheless she kept her eyes peeled. The field was massive, but after a minute or two she could just make out the dark shape of a building at the edge of it. She stopped, wondering if it was a farmhouse. She didn't want to be seen but at the same time she did need to find somewhere to sleep. Getting closer, though, she saw that the building was an ancient barn. As she approached it, the owl she'd heard earlier emerged in a ghostly-white flash, making her jump.

Telling herself not to be silly, she entered the ruined building. The old floor was still strewn with hay, and hedge bindweed had pushed its wiry tendrils between the barn's wooden planks. In one corner stood a forsaken haycart, its rotting ash and elm panels falling apart. Some of the rafters were missing but others were holding, and although she knew she'd be sharing a bed with mice and shrews and perhaps even rats, she pulled bundles of hay together and then sat down, undoing her bundle and fetching out the fruit pudding her mother had made. She ate half of it, along with a chunk of cheese, and then wrapped the remains tightly in the blanket, fearing rodents would come and nibble. She was very thirsty – the first thing she would have to do tomorrow was to find water, she decided – but for now all she wanted was to sleep again. She'd never felt so tired, not even after a summer's day in the fields when it wasn't unusual to be expected to work for fourteen hours or more with just a couple of breaks for a quick snack.

Settling herself down on the bed of hay, Molly used her bundle as a pillow, partly to protect her food from unwelcome visitors. She fell asleep immediately. When she next opened her eyes it was morning and it took her a moment to recall where she was. Attempting to move proved even more painful than the day before and after she'd risen to her feet she had to stand for a full minute, gulping air in an effort to quell the nausea. Her sore bruised flesh screamed at her to lie down again but stronger was the desire to put more distance between herself and the hamlet. Shakily, the tears streaming down her face, she smoothed her clothes and tied the bundle to her back once more.

Outside, the risen sun had yet to sweep the dew of dawn from the grass and a chill stabbed the fresh autumn air. Mist lingered, rolling across the harvest stubble, and a number of wood pigeons rose flapping into the sky as she left the barn. In the bright light she realized the old barn was situated on the brow of an incline. Far in the distance and little more than the size of doll's houses were a cluster of buildings which she took to be the farmhouse and newer barns and outbuildings.

Molly turned, walking across the field to the thick hedgerow, where she struggled through a gap. She found herself in a meadow thick with grass and the blooms of ox-eye daisies, and at the bottom of a fairly steep hill she could see a stream glinting in the sunshine. On reaching it she discovered that the water was crystal clear; cupping her hands, she drank her fill. Never had water tasted sweeter.

Any frost that might have settled had long since melted and she sat by the stream for some time, knowing she ought to be making tracks but soaking up the peacefulness of her surroundings. After a while she ate an apple and the last of the cheese and drank some more water. It was only when the sun was high in a blue sky that she began walking, shot through with pain but driven on by the fear of her da finding her.

She was sorry to have left Fanny, she thought as she plodded on. Fred and Caleb too. It would be lovely if Fanny were here with her now. Everything would be an adventure then. But Fanny was happy at home with her mam and da and she would never have left them to come with her. Fred and Caleb had each other too, but she had no one now that Kitty was gone.

She stumbled, her bruised legs making it difficult to walk. When she fell over it wasn't the jolt to her sore flesh that brought the tears but an enormous feeling of aloneness. She sat and had a good cry and then picked herself up and continued walking eastwards, telling herself not to think any more but just to keep going. That was all she had to do.

Chapter Four

By the third day the food was gone. Progress had been slow. Molly found she couldn't walk far before she had to take a rest and more often than not she fell asleep as soon as she sat down. Every part of her body hurt. The second and third nights had been spent sleeping under hedgerows, but at least the dry weather had held, though it was cold. Then, on the morning of the fourth day, she was awoken to drops of rain and dark clouds raging across a dull charcoal sky. Before long she was wet through and the temperature had dropped; in the space of a few hours it felt as though winter had declared itself.

She reached the outskirts of Newcastle in the afternoon, skirting round the town and keeping to lanes and byways to avoid coming into contact with folk. That night she slept in her sodden clothes huddled inside a dilapidated, leaky hut on an allotment, and the next morning began walking again before it was light, munching on an old turnip she had found in a corner of the shack.

It was another two nights of sleeping rough before she

reached North Shields. By then she had developed a racking cough and a fever and was walking in a daze most of the time, barely aware of her surroundings but knowing she had to keep moving. She had lost the contents of the blanket at some point, probably when she had slept with it over her for a little protection and had then forgotten to pick up her belongings when she'd begun walking again. Now she pulled it round her as a shawl, although it offered scant protection from the raw wind.

No one glanced twice at the small thin figure walking through the wet streets. Fishing from the River Tyne, and North Shields in particular, had been taking place for hundreds of years, and in that time the sight of unkempt ragamuffins and waifs hadn't raised an eyebrow – there were too many of them. The town originated on a narrow strip of land alongside the river because of the steep bank that hemmed it in, but as it eventually became over-crowded, buildings were erected above the old and insanitary dwellings alongside the river. Businessmen and shipowners occupied the new town, whereas working people remained in the lower part. The two areas were connected by a labyrinth of stairs and passageways with a public house at every corner, and in the lower section the occupants waged a constant war against disease, dirt and poverty. Nevertheless, it was a close-knit community with its own rules and customs, and many fishermen's families had lived in the same cottages for generations. Mining might be a dangerous occupation, but for seamen and fishermen the chances of death were twice as high.

The North Sea was not known for its clemency and it could be a vicious and capricious adversary, loath to give up its bounty easily.

The town had grown rapidly northwards in latter years and as Molly walked on it seemed never-ending, but as she grew closer to the Shield's quay the noise and dirt and stink of fish penetrated her dazed mind. There were forty-seven public houses round the quay, and the fish market was in operation practically twenty-four hours a day. It was late afternoon and already dark, but despite the bitter wind and rain men, women and children, horses and carts, sailors and fishermen crowded the area and the harbour was full of boats.

By now Molly was walking like a clockwork toy that was running down. Her chest was on fire and her breathing laboured and she had no idea where she was going or even where she was, but still she staggered on. When she slipped on something foul-smelling and slimy and fell backwards, cracking her head on the cobbles, she saw lights behind her eyes, heard a rushing sound that grew deafening, and then . . . nothing.

Some time later Molly became vaguely aware that she was being carried, but the pain in her head was such that she didn't fight the darkness that dragged her down again. When she next surfaced it was to hear a woman's voice saying, 'It's not only the lump on the back of her head that's the size of a goose egg an' the cough an' fever, though – she's been flayed, Jed. When I undressed her I've never seen owt like it in all me born days. To do that to a little bairn, it beggars belief,' but then she went to sleep once more.

And this sleep seemed to have taken over, because although she floated in and out of it and at times felt gentle hands on her as she was fed broth and on occasion a spoonful of something that tasted bitter, she couldn't rouse herself enough to open her eyes or speak. Along with the woman's voice she heard others; a couple were deep and clearly men's and the first time this happened she was frightened, thinking her father had found her. But nothing happened and she drifted off to sleep yet again.

It was nearly a week before she came fully to herself one morning just as it was growing light, and it was the wind howling like a banshee that woke her. She lay for a few moments before slowly moving her head but found the blinding pain had faded into just an ache. She was lying on a low platform bed set in an alcove to one side of a kitchen range and she was snug and warm. Seated in an armchair with a blanket over her knees a few feet away was a woman whose eyes were closed and who was snoring softly. Molly stared at her. She was plump and homely-looking, with a red-cheeked face and grey hair pulled into a tight bun on the top of her head.

She looks nice, Molly thought. There was something about her that brought Fanny's mam to mind.

In the next moment it was as though the woman had heard her because she snorted loudly and then sat up with a slight jerk. 'Ah, hinny, you've come back to the land of the living,' she said cheerfully. 'Given us all a scare once or twice, you have. You feelin' a bit better?' She stood up as she added, 'Now you lay quiet an' I'll get you a drink, lass.'

'Where – where am I?'

'You're safe and sound an' that's all you need bother your head about for the time being. You've been right poorly, I don't mind saying. Death's door, old Dr Price said, but you're clearly tougher than you look.' She had put a big black kettle on the hob as she had been speaking, and as the wind screeched again and gusts of rain slammed against the window, she said, 'Hark at it, worst storm all year, this is. The boats haven't been able to get out for days now. You're in the best place, sure enough.'

'I – I'm sorry.' Her voice sounded like a croak to herself.

'And what have you to be sorry about, hinny?' the woman said as she bustled about. 'Strikes me, the one who beat you to within an inch of your life should be saying that.' She bent over her, her voice soft as she said, 'Who was it, lass? Who hurt you?'

Molly stared into the kind face, fear washing over her. If she told this woman, this stranger, about her da and that she had run away, would she be taken home again? Weakly, she whispered, 'I don't know. I – I can't remember.'

'Aye, well, that's likely the bang on your head done that. Nasty, it was. But don't worry about it, it's early days. You'll be back to your old self in no time.'

Molly doubted that was true; already the urge to sleep again was so strong she couldn't fight it. She was vaguely aware of the woman murmuring, 'That's it, hinny, you sleep. Best medicine there is,' but then the soothing voice faded.

When she next opened her eyes it was to the sound of low conversation. The woman who'd tended to her earlier was sitting at the kitchen table in the company of a man and three youths, and they were eating a meal. She lay watching them, taking in her surroundings. In front of the open black-leaded range there was a long steel fender and a conglomeration of fire irons, and on the floor was a clippy mat on which a tabby cat was sleeping. The table and chairs were positioned in the centre of the room and standing against the wall opposite the range was a long wooden settle with a tall thin dresser squeezed in next to it. Along with the battered armchair there was an equally old rocking chair with flock cushions. There was scarcely any room to walk between the pieces of furniture – you would have to edge round the table to reach the back door, Molly thought – but everything was clean and the steel fender and fire irons shone. There was a very strong smell of fish permeating the air but she didn't mind that.

Her gaze returned to the five individuals at the table just as the woman looked her way. 'Ah, you're awake again, hinny,' she said cheerfully. 'I dare say you could manage something to eat now? You need to get your strength back after the time you've had.'

The man and boys were all looking at her now, and Molly found herself blushing. The oldest youth looked to be about seventeen or eighteen but the other two were nearer Fred's age. All four were smiling and she smiled back nervously. Highly embarrassed, she managed to squeak, 'Aye, yes, please,' in answer to the woman who had got up from the table and walked over to the range. She sat up as the woman brought her a bowl and spoon, saying, 'It's fish stew, lass. You like fish stew?'

Molly had never tasted it before but she nodded anyway, staring at the somewhat colourless concoction in the bowl that had bits of this and that floating in it. She discovered it tasted much better than it looked, in fact it was delicious, and once she had eaten the last morsel she wanted nothing more than to lie down once more and shut her eyes, but the woman had pulled the armchair closer and sat down. 'Now you're feeling a bit better I think we need to have a little chat, eh, lass? I'm Enid by the way, Enid Mallard, and that's me husband, Jed, and those three are Harry, Rory and Matthew. What's your name, hinny?'

She had to tell them; she didn't want to but it would be rude otherwise. 'Molly,' she said quietly.

Enid leaned further forward, her voice soft as she said, 'An' how come a little bairn like you was wandering along the quayside? How old are you, lass? Eight, nine?'

She knew she looked younger than her age but her voice was firmer and slightly indignant when she said, 'I'm eleven.'

Enid smiled. 'Eleven, is it? Right. But I haven't seen you before so do I take it you're not from round these parts?'

Suddenly Molly wanted to cry. She didn't know if it was because the woman was talking so gently to her, or because the four faces at the table were staring at her very intently, or because if she told them the truth they might insist on taking her back to her da, or simply that she felt so tired, but as she bit down hard on her quivering bottom lip, Enid said, 'Don't get upset, there's a good girl. You're not going to get wrong but we need to find out what's what, hinny.'

'I don't want to go back.'

'Back where, pet?'

'To – to my da.'

'Was it your da who did that to you? Whipped you?'

She nodded, her blue eyes huge in her pale face.

'What about your mam? Did she try to stop him? Did she know?'

'She – she didn't care.'

The man at the table shifted in his seat and muttered something that ended with '. . . make her damn well care', but the woman ignored him. 'And so what happened after your da' – she paused – 'after he did what he did?'

'I ran away.' Tears were trickling down her face but she made no effort to brush them away, and then she began coughing, harsh coughs that hurt her chest.

Enid cast a helpless glance at her husband before she said, 'That's enough talking for now, you snuggle down, pet, and keep warm, but don't you worry, all right? We'll sort something out.'

'I don't want to go back,' Molly said again, scrubbing at her eyes with her fists. 'He'll kill me if I do, I know he will, like he did Kitty.' She began crying in earnest then, and when in the next moment she was gathered up in a pair of comforting arms and held close to a motherly bosom, it made the storm of weeping worse. She had never been held like this, never known a mother's embrace, and although it was lovely it made the fear of being sent back to the hamlet worse.

When Enid knew the child had gone to sleep she lay the small form down and covered her, and then looked at the tear-stained face for a moment or two before joining the others at the table again. Sitting down, she said soberly, 'What do you make of all that then?'

'The bairn's terrified of her da, that's for sure.' Jed rubbed his bristly chin, his weather-beaten face grim. 'And who's this Kitty she mentioned?'

'I dunno but I'm going to find out. One thing's for sure, the bairn's staying put for the time being. She's not out of the woods yet, not by a long chalk. She's skin an' bone for one thing, and the whipping she took along with the fever and the bang on the head, it's a wonder she's pulled through.'

'Aye, well, that's down to your nursing, lass.' Jed smiled at his wife. He'd been their Harry's age – eighteen – when he'd first clapped eyes on her down on the quay one evening, he reflected. Enid's people had been fisher folk from across the water in South Shields but after some bother at home she'd come with some pals to the north side to work in the pickling factory. Her mam had been widowed the year before and had just got wed again to a bloke Enid couldn't stand. She'd only been fifteen but was already a woman, tall and well built with a ready smile and laughing eyes. He'd courted her and married her on her sixteenth birthday and it was the best day's work he'd ever done. She was the best of women and had borne him five bairns, all of whom had survived unlike most babies round these parts. The eldest two girls had married local fishermen so there were just his lads at home, and already Harry was courting a lass who worked in the salt-pans. Life never stood still, that was for sure.

Glancing at the sleeping child, Jed said quietly, 'I dare say we'll get the full story soon enough, poor little mite.' He'd nearly tripped over the bairn the night he'd come across her lying on the cobbles, a scrap of nothing. He had carried her back to their two-up, two-down terraced house in Beacon Street, fearing he'd be presenting Enid with a corpse by the time he reached home. Remembering this, he added, 'She looks a darn sight better than she did, love. Thanks be to God.'

Enid nodded. What the child had said about her father and the mention of this Kitty had disturbed her greatly.

Seeing his wife's expression, Jed put his hand over hers for a moment. 'Don't fret, we'll sort it, all right? If we need to keep the bairn here for a while, that's what we'll do. Once she can be moved, Harry can go back in with Rory and Matt and the littl'un can have that room.'

Harry grimaced but said nothing. Before his sisters had left home they'd occupied the other bedroom that he was in now, and he'd enjoyed the luxury of his own room the last three years. His parents slept downstairs in the front room. Still, the pallet bed they'd made up in the kitchen close to the warmth of the range for the bairn had made the already overcrowded room more jam-packed, so he couldn't very well object to topping and tailing with his brothers again.

'Do you think she'll pull through, Mam?' It was Matthew, the youngest lad at thirteen, who spoke. Like Harry and Rory he was good-looking in a rough-hewn way and as yet the life of a fisherman hadn't aged him prematurely. In their community boys went to sea when they were tall and big enough, not old enough, and like his brothers he had had little schooling. Not that this worried him. He had joined his father and siblings on their boat when he was ten years old and fishing was in his blood, like all the Mallard menfolk. He loved the sea as much as he feared it. The minute their craft left the protective banks of the Tyne and he felt the growing swell he seemed to come truly alive. The swell was an early warning that the boat was heading into one of the world's harshest seas with very little between man and the elements. He knew they might fish all day and return with barely half a boxful, or that a lost or ripped net could wipe out more than a day's hard labour and income, but on the good days, when the North Sea was kind and they returned to harbour with a hefty haul, the satisfaction was indescribable.

Their boat, the *Seahorse*, was a large coble ideal for the north-east coast. Clinker-built from larch on oak, the distinctive shape of the boat – flat-bottomed and high-bowed – meant it allowed launching from and landing upon shallow, sandy beaches, an advantage in an area where the wide bays and inlets provided little shelter from stormy weather. Powered by a lug sail and long oars, the *Seahorse*, like all cobles, needed an experienced skipper in choppy seas, but Jed, like his father and grandfather before him, felt more at home on the water than on land, as did his three sons. That wasn't to say that the nasty boils caused by salt water finding its way inside boots and oilskins weren't a trial, along with coping with a constant heavy swell and often driving rain.

Enid smiled at Matthew. If her life had depended on it she would never have admitted to having a favourite among her brood, but from the first her youngest had held her heart in a way the others hadn't. There was something – a deep kindness and innate gentleness – about the lad, and her own father had been the same. That had made it all the more difficult after he had died, when her mother had replaced him with a man whom she had considered a bully and a drunkard. Now she said, 'Do I think the bairn'll get better? I hope so but it'll be no thanks to the brute who flayed her to within an inch of her life.'

'You wouldn't take her back home? Back to him?'

Enid didn't answer this directly. What she did say was, 'We don't know where her home is yet. Anyway, like your da said, we need to get the full story first. Don't worry your head about it, son. All right?'

Matthew nodded but he wasn't happy. He and his brothers had agreed that they'd like five minutes alone with the individual who'd inflicted such injuries on a bairn, and a little lassie at that. He knew fishermen had a reputation for being hard and rough, and they were, but no man he knew would flay a small child. A cuff round the ear or a smacked backside was one thing, but that . . .

'It's blowing itself out and not afore time.' Jed inclined his head towards the window where the lashing rain had lessened in the last hour. 'We'll be out the morrer.'

The three lads nodded. They needed to get out on the water. No fishing meant no income and it had been three days now. Their mother was a dab hand at making a penny stretch to two but even she couldn't work miracles. There had been the occasional dirty British coaster with salt-caked smoke stacks going by but none of the local fishermen had been able to venture out to sea. They had a small smokehouse next to the privy in the yard and the last of the split herrings Enid had hung there had been eaten. They needed to catch enough both to sell and to build up their reserves for winter. Fresh sprats and herrings were plentiful in the autumn, likewise the cod that their mother split, salted and hung outside on a line to dry. Fortunately they'd had a good summer and there was a full sack of potatoes and turnips stored in the front room at the end of their parents' bed, along with another containing flour. They'd often be hand to mouth in the winter when the fiercest storms hit.

'I'll make another pot of tea.'

As Enid spoke, Harry stood up. 'Not for me, Mam. I'm off to see Alice for an hour or two.'

'In this weather?'

'Like Da said, it's blowing itself out.'

Enid shook her head but said nothing more. Harry had been courting strong for over eighteen months and she didn't doubt he'd be asking Alice to marry him before long. And she didn't mind the girl herself – Alice was a strong, sturdy lass with wide child-bearing hips – but her family were a different matter. They lived near Low Dock and Harry had told her the two-roomed dwelling was filthy. It was well known the lass's mother had a liking for gin and her tribe of unwashed ragamuffins ran around with their backsides hanging out. To be fair, though, Alice was always clean and presentable and the lass wasn't responsible for her family. The father was a sailor and gone for long periods at a time but she couldn't blame him for that; why would he want to be at home? Especially if the rumours about Alice's mother 'obliging' gentlemen callers were true.

As Harry left the house a minute or two later Enid sighed heavily, and Jed, reading her mind as he often did, said softly, 'He'll go his own road, lass.'

'I know, I know.' And it was only right, she supposed. She sighed again.

Jed glanced over at the sleeping form of the child in the alcove. It'd do Enid good to have a little lassie about the house, he thought. The bairn needed mothering, that much was obvious, and she'd be company for Enid when he and the lads were out at sea. And if Molly stayed, and it was only an if, she could help Enid with the household chores and gutting and cleaning the fish and other jobs when they had a catch. Harry had told him on the quiet that he intended to be married before too much longer, and he knew Enid would take it hard. She'd missed their daughters when they had got wed and no doubt the lads would go one by one over the next years. It was only natural. The bairn would cushion the blow and it was clear his wife had taken to her. But he was jumping the gun here, he cautioned himself in the next moment. First they were duty bound to find out the whys and wherefores of what had happened to the bairn. Littl'uns were great ones for embroidering the truth, although the marks on her body couldn't lie, he told himself soberly.

Now it was Jed who sighed. He just hoped he hadn't cast a spanner in the works bringing the child home to Enid like he had, because something told him his wife was already overly fond of the lass. Still, what will be, will be. His mam, God rest her soul, had been a great one for saying that but it was true, sure enough. Worrying and whittling couldn't change anything.

He watched as Enid got up and checked the little girl, pulling the covers up further over the small figure and stroking strands of sandy-gold hair from her forehead. Matthew leaned across the table, speaking in a low voice as he murmured, 'You wouldn't send her back to them as did that, would you, Da? Mam don't want to, I can tell.'

Like his wife had said, so Jed now repeated, 'We don't know where her home is, lad. Let's just take it a day at a time for now, eh?'

And with that Matthew had to be content.

Chapter Five

It was some weeks later. Quite a lot had happened in the intervening period and Molly was now established in a bedroom of her own with the knowledge that she wasn't going to be sent back to the hamlet. She'd told Enid and Jed the full story, including her suspicions about her sister's demise, and the couple had agreed that Josiah McKenzie was an evil so-an'-so and the child was well rid of both her parents. Molly hadn't been able to tell them the location of the hamlet. All she knew was that she had walked for days before she had reached North Shields and that her home was in the countryside. Due to the fever and her weakness most of the journey had become a blur and there was no way she could retrace her steps. Enid and Jed had been satisfied the child was telling the truth, and Enid in particular was relieved.

'The decision of whether she stays or goes is out of our hands,' she'd told Jed firmly. 'Unless her da comes looking for her there's no way we can return her to them.'

'And what if he *should* turn up?'

'There's still no way she's going back. A mention of her sister should be enough to put the wind up the beggar and send him packing. If not, then you and the lads might have to give him a taste of what he gave the bairn.'

Jed had stared at his wife in astonishment. He and the lads had been thinking along the same lines, but for his normally easy-going and law-abiding wife to suggest such a thing had shocked him. But then she loved the bairn like one of theirs, he had told himself in the next moment, and she could be a tigress where her children were concerned. And so Harry had joined his brothers in the lads' bedroom and Molly had been told she was staying with them for good – if that was what she wanted? The expression on the little girl's face had been answer enough. Even Jed, tough and cynical as he was, had had a lump in his throat at the child's transparent joy.

As though to make up for its chary behaviour at the beginning of the month, the weather turned unusually mild and settled in the following weeks. Jed and his sons brought in several exceptional hauls of cod, mackerel and herring, and once Molly was well enough Enid began to initiate the child into the life of a fisherwoman.

Fishing was an all-male preserve, but that didn't mean that wives and young lassies didn't work just as hard as their menfolk. Besides the normal household tasks of cooking and washing and cleaning, they were ex-pected to do a range of jobs: mending the nets with big wooden needles for heavy work down the side, and little bone needles for lighter work; gutting fish and washing the offal; selling what they could at the fish market and round the streets; collecting driftwood along with any coal or coke that had been washed up on the beaches for fuel for the range and smokehouse; and making excursions into the countryside to obtain oak leaves and twigs for the smokehouse, which gave the fish a nice taste. Any items found on the beach that could be sold for a few extra pennies were a bonus, and in the evenings Enid mended clothes, sewed calico jumpers for the menfolk, smeared oil on their boots to keep them waterproof or knitted thick boot stockings. Her hands, like those of all the women in their community, were never idle.

While Molly was still recovering, Enid made her a change of clothes and knitted some thick socks for the second-hand boots she'd obtained at the market. Although they weren't new, they were a hundred per cent better than Molly's old boots, which had been falling apart. Some of the fisherwomen made their underwear from bags that grocers kept rice or flour in and their children often didn't wear underwear at all, but Enid had always made her own and her family's from old clothing she bought cheap and cut down. For the first time in her life Molly found herself wearing a warm vest and knickers, and she had toasty feet in the cold weather thanks to the socks and boots without holes in. It made walking outside a pleasure.

She had surprised Enid and the others by taking to the work that was expected of her like a duck to water, unusual for someone who hadn't been born into the harsh life. In truth, Molly found it no harder than the long, exhausting days in the fields in all weathers, but now she felt happy, which made all the difference. She was well fed too, and already, as October and November passed, had lost the white, pinched look that had been habitual to her.

December brought thick snow, ice and gales, and in the evenings, once the meal was over and the dishes had been washed, Molly would settle herself beside Enid, who taught her to knit and sew. She would work away at anything she was given while she listened to the family talk over the day. If the menfolk had been able to fish the atmosphere was always cheery and the lads would often tease her to see her blush, something lassies in their community weren't prone to, being as rough and hardy as the lads. If the weather had prevented Jed and his boys getting out on the water the mood in the kitchen was more sombre, but even then Matthew would always smile and joke with her.

She liked Matthew the best of the brothers. He would sit with her sometimes and tell her stories of what went on in their community. Of the old fishwife who lived near Union Quay and sat on her doorstep summer and winter with a parrot on her shoulder who called out things that would make a sailor blush; of Mrs O'Leary at the end of the street who regularly chased her husband with her huge iron frying pan and beat him about the shoulders when he came home inebriated; of little Septimus Stamp, a wizened dwarf of a man who, nevertheless, at over ninety years of age still went out fishing in his coble, and many, many more stories about the characters among the fishing folk.

Molly felt like less of an outsider when Matthew related the goings-on in the area, and he made her laugh like no one else could. When the family retired at night she would climb the stairs to her own room, something that still created a feeling of wonder, and snuggle down under the heaped covers, her feet on the brick that Enid baked in the oven each evening to warm her bed, wrapped in an old towel.

The only fly in the ointment was the terror that surfaced in her dreams that this state of affairs was too good to be true, that it wouldn't last. She woke sometimes after a nightmare that she was back in the hamlet, lying shaking for long minutes before she could relax into sleep. During the busy days she could push the fear to the back of her mind, but at night when her subconscious took over it manifested itself and there was nothing she could do about it. As the weeks passed, however, she began to dream less about the man who was worse than any fairy-tale monster, and by Christmas she could go for days without a nightmare.

The day before Christmas Eve, Molly and Enid walked into the countryside and brought home a large canvas bag full of holly they had cut, bright with red berries. They decorated the kitchen together as a surprise for the menfolk, and Molly's almost ecstatic delight touched Enid deeply.

'That little bairn's never had a proper Christmas,' Enid said later that night when she and Jed were in bed. 'She's never helped her mam stir a plum pudding or put up a stocking for Father Christmas. Poor as they obviously are, you can't tell me they couldn't have done something for their bairns. We only put an orange and apple and a few sweets in ours when they were little, and maybe an old picture book from the second-hand stall at the market or something I'd made for 'em, but she's had less than nowt all her life, Jed, except harsh words and good hidings.'

'I know, lass, I know.' His wife had loved Christmas when their bairns were little nippers, and although they'd never had two pennies to rub together they'd made the day special. 'Well, Molly can hang up a stocking this year, can't she? She's not too big for that. And when you pick up the turkey from the butchers tomorrow, you could have a look round the market and get her a couple of bits.'

'Aye, yes, I'll do that.' Enid turned in to the bulk of him, putting her arm across his chest. Christmas was the only time they paid out for a turkey; the rest of the year if it wasn't fish for their evening meal then it was scrag ends or rabbit and occasionally a piece of brisket. But Christmas Day was different. She'd do a cooked breakfast of bacon and eggs and black pudding, and later in the morning, when the public house on the corner opened its doors, one of the lads would take the big stone jar along and return with it full of beer so they all had a tipple. Last year Mary and Cissy had come round with their families in the afternoon and there hadn't been room to swing a cat, but it had been nice. Bedlam, but nice.

'The bairn'll enjoy herself, you know, stocking or no stocking,' Jed said softly. 'Just being here with you and the rest of us.'

Enid didn't speak for some seconds. Then she said, her voice low and troubled, 'I pray every day that her da won't come looking for her.'

'Now look here, lass.' Jed turned on his side, drawing her into his arms. 'Let's knock this on the head once and for all. I don't believe for one minute that man would bother himself to search for her, but if he did, and if he came here, I would deal with him. Your mind can be at rest about that. The bairn's here and here she'll stay now, and we're going to have a grand Christmas. All right?'

Enid had always loved her husband but never more so than at this moment. She nodded in the darkness, her mouth finding his, and then as she pressed herself in to him and her hands moved over his body she felt him respond. It was rare she made the first initiative in their lovemaking and he always deeply appreciated it when she did, his voice revealing this when he murmured, 'Oh, Enid, Enid, you're me sun, moon an' stars. You know that, don't you? Sun, moon an' stars.'

She knew he meant it and that she had always come first with him since the day they had wed, but she couldn't in all honesty say the same. From the moment Mary had been born and she'd held her first child in her arms, she'd felt a love so powerful, so consuming it had taken her breath away. It had been the same with all of them, especially Matthew, and now Molly. She might not have given birth to the bairn but she couldn't love her any more if she had. Jed was right, they would have a grand Christmas. She would make sure of it.

On Christmas Day Molly woke early. Outside the house, the snow was packed hard on the ground and a fresh fall was adding to it, making the pavements treacherous. She climbed out of bed, shivering as she emerged from the warm cocoon, and peered at her window. There was ice on the inside of it but after she had breathed on it and worked away with her fingernails she cleared a circle big enough to peep through. It looked to be a white hushed world; for once the town was taking its ease and all the normal sounds from the docks and industry were absent.

Downstairs in the kitchen it would be warm – the range was kept going day and night – and she hurried into her clothes, glad of the thick woollen socks and sturdy boots. In the hamlet her feet had always been cold in the winter months and sometimes her chilblains had been so bad they had reduced her to tears, often earning her a hard slap from her mother and the command to 'stop snivelling'.

She pushed the thought away. She didn't want to think of the hamlet and the people in it. That was her old life and she wanted no part of it to intrude into the new. She sometimes thought about her brothers and Fanny and wondered what they were doing, mostly when she was in bed and falling asleep, but although she had missed Fanny, and also Fred and Caleb to some extent, when she had first come here, she no longer felt that way. Her new family – and that was how she thought about Enid and Jed and the lads – more than made up for those she had left behind. She wasn't quite so keen on Mary and Cissy when she had met them shortly after she'd arrived at the house – the sisters seemed standoffish – but she didn't see much of them anyway.

Enid was already downstairs when Molly walked into the kitchen, her eyes going immediately to the stocking she'd hung up the night before on the mantelpiece, and in answer to the glance, Enid said brightly, 'Aye, he's been, hinny.'

Her stomach fluttering with excitement, Molly watched spellbound as Enid unhooked the big knitted stocking which would have fitted a giant's foot and brought it over to the table. It was no longer limp and flat but bulging. Hardly able to speak for anticipation, she looked up at Enid with huge eyes. 'Should I wait for the others to come down?'

Enid smiled. Molly's reaction was everything she could have hoped for. 'No, lass,' she said gently. 'I think we'll have a sup together, just the two of us, while you see what he's brought you, eh? Sit yourself down, hinny. I won't be a tick.'

Once a plate of Enid's gingerbread and two mugs of tea were in front of them, Molly emptied the stocking.

It contained a bright blue woollen bobble hat and matching gloves and scarf; a book with dancing dolls and a party scene to cut out along with a set of crayons to colour everything in; a bag of assorted confectionery – a gobstopper, Ogopogo eyes, liquorice bootlaces and a pink sugar mouse – and down the side of it all was a barley sugar squirrel on a long stick which when held to the light proved to be magical, glowing a deep amber.

Utterly overcome, Molly flung herself on Enid and as they hugged, she whispered, 'I love you.'

The family weren't ones for outward shows of affection – none of the fishing folk were – and from infancy the children tended to follow the same pattern of behaviour as their parents. Enid knew her children loved her but it had rarely been said out loud.

She gathered Molly onto her lap and as thin arms went round her neck, she nestled the child close. The lump in her throat making her voice husky, she murmured, 'An' I love you, me bairn.'

It was nearly midnight. The rest of the household had long since been asleep but despite being warm and snug and tired, Molly was wide awake. It had been a wonderful day and she had enjoyed every minute – at least, she corrected herself in the next moment, until Mary and Cissy arrived in the afternoon. Although neither woman had said anything, she could tell they hadn't liked their mother putting up the stocking for Father Christmas, and they didn't like her either. She wasn't imagining it. But – she buried herself deeper under the covers – she didn't have to see them very often, so that was all right.

She lay picturing in her mind's eye the events of the day. After a cooked breakfast – an occasion in itself as the normal fare was porridge and slices of bread and dripping – she had helped Enid prepare their Christmas dinner before going outside with Matthew and having a snowball fight with some of the neighbouring children. It was strange, she thought, because although Rory was only a year older than Matthew at fourteen, he seemed as old as Harry and quite grown up. Matthew, on the other hand, was full of fun and had a sense of humour that saw the comical side of everything.

They'd returned to the house rosy-cheeked and with bright red noses, and she'd helped Enid dish up their Christmas dinner. Her mouth watered as she imagined it. She'd had her first taste of beer, which she hadn't liked, and she'd made Matthew laugh at the face she had pulled. In the afternoon they'd sung carols with Jed accompanying them on his mouth organ and she had shared her sweets round, and later the two daughters had arrived with their husbands and children and they'd all had tea together before they had gone home.

Tomorrow it would be just the six of them most of the time, until Harry's sweetheart arrived for tea. She'd met Alice a few times and she liked her, although she was very quiet and barely spoke more than a word or two. Matthew had told her that he suspected Alice was nervous of his mother because she sensed his mam didn't approve of them courting. His brother had said that Alice was quite different away from the house. She had felt sorry for Harry's lass after that and had tried to overcome her own natural shyness and talk to her more. She wasn't sure if she believed Matthew was right; Enid was lovely, the best person in the whole world, and she always made Alice welcome as far as she could see.

Molly nodded to herself in the darkness. Yes, Matthew must be mistaken. She was lucky, she was so, so lucky to have found this home and Enid most of all. She wanted nothing more than to live here for ever and be with her. Her da wouldn't turn up now. If he had been going to come and find her he'd have done so before now. She was safe.

When the nightmare came it was the same as the ones that had gone before it but more intense: a big black figure chasing her through the cold darkness where her feet wanted to run but were bogged down so she could barely walk. She knew she had to escape before it caught her and sheer terror had her screaming and crying for someone to help her, but now she felt hot breath on her neck and she knew it was just behind her . . .

'Me bairn, oh, me bairn, it's all right. Molly, it's all right, I've got you. Open your eyes, hinny, that's right. Look, you're in your own bed and I'm here. Nothing's going to hurt you.'

She gazed up into Enid's face and as Jed appeared in the doorway holding an oil lamp, she saw that she was indeed in her room in the fisherman's cottage.

Enid gathered her into her arms and shaking uncontrollably, Molly choked out, 'It – it was behind me.'

'It was just a bad dream, lass,' said Jed from the doorway, and then as Matthew and his brothers came onto the landing he added, 'She's all right, it was just a dream. Get back to bed, the three of you.'

'It was going to catch me this time.'

'Nothing and no one is going to catch you, me bairn.' Enid hugged her tightly. 'You hear me?'

'I think it was me da.'

'I daresay, but it's just a dream. It's not real.'

'But what if he does come here? What if he finds me?'

'If he came here Jed and the lads would deal with him, pet, and so would I. No one is going to take you from us, hinny, I promise you that. Not your da or your mam, no one. You're here for good, you're family, just as much as me other bairns. And listen to me, lass, no court in the land would make you go with him after me an' Jed had had our say. You're our daughter now, all right? This is your home and we love you, all of us.'

For the first time since she had escaped the hamlet, the tears that came were ones of release and deliverance. Enid wouldn't let her da take her, she'd said she was their daughter now. This was her home. And she believed Enid; if she said it, it was true.

'Now you snuggle back down and go to sleep, and this time you'll dream about nice things, me bairn.'

As Molly slid down into the bed again Enid tucked the covers more closely round the small form. She and

Jed had decided to tell everyone – even Mary and Cissy – that Molly's family had died of the fever and the child had been going to be sent to the workhouse when they had stepped in and said that they would have her. Only the lads knew the real circumstances of how they'd found her, and they were sworn to secrecy.

Not that other folk were overly interested anyway, Enid thought. The fishing community had enough troubles to contend with, and earning sufficient money to put food on the table and pay the rent was their main concern.

She bent down and dropped a kiss on the smooth forehead. 'No more tears, hinny,' she murmured, stroking the silky blonde hair for a few moments. And it was like that, with the feel of the kiss still on her face, that Molly drifted off into a deep and dreamless slumber.

PART TWO

The Next Beginning

1904

Chapter Six

Sometimes she found it hard to believe that she had only been living with the Mallards for three and a half years, Molly thought as she walked back towards the town from the countryside where she had been gathering oak twigs for the smokehouse. It seemed there had never been a time when she hadn't woken up in her little room in the fishing cottage and gone downstairs to help Enid prepare breakfast for Matthew and the others. Enid had been meant to accompany her today – they rarely did anything apart – but the older woman had been suffering with indigestion recently and a particularly bad bout had laid her low. Matthew had gone out early before breakfast to buy his mother some of the peppermint cordial she favoured.

Dear Matthew. Molly smiled as she pictured his tall figure in her mind's eye, but then the familiar feeling of confusion took hold. Did Matthew feel the same way about her as she felt for him? Sometimes she thought so but then she wasn't sure. He was always joking and teasing her, and his voice on occasion was deep and soft and quite unlike how he spoke to anyone else, even his mother, but he had never said in so many words that he cared for her in *that* way. The way a boy cared about his sweetheart. Did he look on her as a sister?

She knew several lassies hereabouts had been giving him the eye because his brothers ribbed him about it. Bess McCabe in particular had apparently been quite brazen in her advances, but when his brothers encouraged Matthew to take up with Bess he merely shook his head and said he was saving himself for someone special and wouldn't be drawn any further.

She hated Bess McCabe. Molly's lovely face fell into a scowl. She was always flaunting her voluptuous figure and making cow's eyes at the lads, her with her long black hair and flashing blue eyes. Bess had no shame, that's what Enid said, and she agreed with her.

She had been so lost in brooding about the girl she was jealous of that it was a few moments before she realized her name was being called. She looked up and Matthew was striding up the lane towards her, a big grin on his face.

'Mam said where you'd gone and I thought I'd come and meet you,' he called as he got nearer, taking her basket from her and tweaking her nose gently as he said, his voice changing, 'What's up? You look like you've lost a penny and found a farthing.'

'Nothing, I'm all right.' If he didn't feel the same, she would die if he suspected how she felt about him. She wished her figure was more curvy like Bess's; perhaps then he would see her as more than a little girl? She was fifteen now, after all, and some girls of her age had a lad.

'You're not.' He stopped, taking her arm and turning her to face him. 'Has someone upset you? Said or done something?'

She shook her head.

'Tell me, Molly, 'cause I'll sort them out,' he said quietly and now there was no laughter in his eyes. 'I said to Mam you shouldn't have gone into the fields alone. You're too bonny and some lads . . .'

'What?'

'Some lads don't respect a lass the way they should.'

'It's nothing like that, Matthew.'

'So there is something?'

'Not really.'

'This is like pulling hen's teeth.' He put the basket down and placed his big hands on her shoulders, looking down into the face that was so lovely it sometimes took his breath away. He had loved her for years, ever since she had first come to live with them as a young lass of eleven, but as his love had changed and matured into what a lad felt for his sweetheart, she seemed to continue looking on him as a brother. He didn't want to do or say anything that would spoil their relationship but he'd made himself a promise he would wait until she was sixteen and then declare himself. Whatever transpired after that he would accept. He cleared his throat and said, 'What's troubling you? Tell me.'

'I was just thinking about Bess McCabe.'

'Bess McCabe? Why? What's she done to put that look on your face?'

'She hasn't done anything. She's just so pretty and – and all the lads like her.'

'Well, here's one that doesn't.' Her blue eyes flickered and for a moment he saw something in their depths that caused his heart to leap. 'I don't like her,' he said again, more strongly.

'You don't?' Her voice was low but like her eyes it betrayed an emotion that gave him the courage to speak out.

'There will only ever be one girl for me, Molly, and I'm looking at her right now. I adore you, lass. I love you with all my heart and I know I'm no catch and you could do better than me but I can't help what I feel, what I've always felt for you. I don't want to be your brother—'

Her eyes were soft and shining with a light from within as she stopped his words by reaching up and putting her arms round his neck. As his lips took hers he pulled her tightly in to him, kissing her with a kind of gentle wonder at first and then, as he felt her response, more deeply and harder. They clung together, lost in the thrill of their first kiss and the knowledge of what it would mean for their future.

When finally they drew apart they stood staring into each other's eyes for a long moment before they smiled. 'You're so lovely,' he murmured huskily, reaching up and brushing a strand of sandy gold hair from her forehead. 'I can't believe you love me too.'

The dull March day that was overcast and threatening rain was filled with joy as she whispered, 'I do, so much.'

'You'll marry me as soon as you're sixteen?'

She nodded, then laughed as she almost sang, 'Yes, yes, yes, Matthew Mallard, I'll marry you,' and then squealed as he swung her off her feet and twirled her round until she was giddy.

When he set her down he kissed her again and his voice was soft as he said, 'I'll love you all the days of me life, I promise you that, and into eternity.'

They walked home hand in hand, Matthew carrying the basket of twigs, so completely wrapped up in each other that neither of them noticed Bess McCabe when they passed her shortly before they reached the house.

When they entered the kitchen where Enid was knitting in front of the fire, she knew instantly what had occurred even before they told her. She opened her arms to them, her face beaming. 'Oh, me bairns, me bairns,' she murmured. 'I couldn't be any happier than I am right at this moment. You're made for each other and that's a fact. You'll have a grand life, you mark my words. A grand life.'

'We're getting wed as soon as Molly's sixteen,' Matthew said, grinning like a Cheshire cat at his mother's reaction.

Enid nodded, hugging them again. 'And we'll have a nice little do here,' she said happily, 'after the service, all right?' Turning to Molly, she added, 'Nearer the time we'll go into town and buy some material for your wedding dress, hinny, and make it together when the men are on the boat.'

Molly smiled, her heart too full for words. How could someone be as happy as she was right at this moment and not burst? The months and years ahead were going to be wonderful, just wonderful, nestled as she was in the bosom of this family. Her family. She would never be unhappy again now she knew that Matthew loved her.

It was four weeks later, and as Molly stood with her head bowed the words she had thought that day when she and Matthew had confessed their love came back to haunt her. The April day was bright with a blue sky overhead and that seemed wrong; it ought to be stormy and grey because that was how she felt inside.

She looked up to see the simple wooden coffin being lowered into the ground, her mind gabbling, *Oh, Mam, Mam, what am I going to do without you?* It was after her first Christmas with the Mallards that Enid had suggested she call her Mam like Matthew and his brothers, and although it had seemed a little awkward at first it had soon become natural. She addressed Jed by his Christian name but that was different; she didn't have the bond with him she'd had with Enid. And it was this same bond that had strengthened the animosity Enid's daughters felt about her. Even today, when they were burying their mother, the sisters had made their dislike and resentment plain.

Through her tear-streaming eyes, Molly glanced to where Jed was standing, his daughters and their husbands either side of him. Mary and Cissy hated her and nothing she said or did made any difference.

When the first clod of earth fell onto the coffin she felt Matthew jerk. He was standing with his arm round her and she knew he was struggling not to break down. It had been such a huge shock when a massive heart attack had taken Enid where she'd stood at the kitchen sink a week ago. The doctor had told them that the supposed indigestion had been heart trouble all along.

Molly gulped hard. She needed to be strong for Matthew. Together they'd get through this awful day as best they could.

The pastor from the mission church had just finished speaking. He unnerved her somewhat. The Mallards weren't churchgoers as such but if they went anywhere it was to the mission church. Pastor Croft was what Jed called 'a fire and brimstone' preacher, but he lived what he taught and for that reason Jed respected him. Pastor Croft didn't get drunk as regular as clockwork like Father O'Kelly, or look the other way and plead ignorance when folk needed assistance like the well-spoken vicar at St Matthew's.

The gravedigger was shovelling the earth more rapidly onto the coffin now, and the hollow sound turned her stomach. Enid was trapped in that narrow box and she'd hated confined spaces. Molly had to fight the desire to call out for the man to stop and to tell Matthew that they had to get his mam out of there. She took a deep pull of salty air as she fought the rising panic, telling herself not to be silly. What had to be, had to be.

A flock of seagulls flew overhead, squawking harshly. Molly raised her blurred gaze to the birds as they circled round in the deep blue sky before disappearing. She hoped Enid was flying in heaven right now. Matthew's mam had once told her that flying was the thing she was looking forward to when she died – having a pair of big white wings that would take her wherever she liked. 'God can keep his mansions,' she'd smiled, 'nice though they'd be. A pair of wings and a sunny sky will do for me, hinny.'

Perhaps it was right after all that the day was a sunny one, Molly reflected. Perhaps Saint Peter himself was standing at the pearly gates right now with Enid's wings, ready to welcome her? One lone seagull suddenly swooped out of nowhere right past her, its huge wings catching the sun. A brief moment of comfort warmed her heart. *Enjoy your wings, Mam . . .*

Matthew turned her away from the grave and they walked towards Jed and his daughters, Rory just behind them and Harry and Alice making up the rear. They'd been married for nearly three years now and had twin boys. A neighbour was looking after the toddlers; Alice never left the children with her mother.

Without saying a word the small group left the cemetery along with several friends and neighbours. They'd all come back for refreshments. Molly knew Mary and Cissy would pick fault with what she'd prepared if they could, and to that end she had been baking and cooking for days as well as cleaning every inch of the house. She'd even scrubbed the stone flags in the back yard. The privy was as clean as a new pin with fresh ashes down the hole that morning.

She mentally pictured the food she'd got ready for the mourners. Mrs Fairley from next door had brought round an egg-and-ham pie to help out, and one or two other neighbours had contributed something too. There had been nothing forthcoming from Mary and Cissy, but Alice had provided a large plate of sandwiches and Harry had dropped off a flagon of beer on their way to the church. They rented a house in the next street and Alice had popped round most days since Enid's passing.

Just before they reached the house, Matthew stopped and put his hands on her shoulders. 'Don't you stand no truck from them two, lass. I mean it. All right?'

She knew he was referring to his sisters and she nodded, even as she knew she wouldn't retaliate whatever Mary and Cissy did. Not today. But in the future it'd be different. She had put up with a lot over the last years for Enid's sake but now she was gone there was no need for her to bite her tongue. And then she shook her head mentally at herself. Mary and Cissy were still Jed's daughters and Matthew's sisters; of course she would carry on trying to keep the peace as far as she was able. Where would she be without this family's great kindness to her? Dead, most probably. She owed Jed and Enid a debt that could never be repaid and if keeping her mouth shut was part of that, so be it.

* * *

It was later that evening. The mourners had left, Jed and Rory had gone to bed and Molly and Matthew were sitting in the kitchen, loath to say goodnight. Apart from a snide comment or two when they could be sure no one else was listening, Mary and Cissy had behaved themselves on the whole and the afternoon had gone smoothly.

'I'm glad we told her about us,' Matthew said after they had kissed and cuddled for a while, Molly sitting on his lap in the old armchair to one side of the range. 'Properly, like.'

'She knew anyway. I think she knew before we did.'

'Not me. I've loved you from the first minute I saw you.'

Molly didn't think that was quite true but it was nice of him to say it and so she let it pass. Nestling in to him, she whispered, 'I still can't believe it's happened,' before her voice choked up.

'I know, I know.' Matthew raised her face to his with the tip of his finger. 'But she wouldn't want us to grieve and be sad. We will be, of course, but she'd want us to get on with our lives.'

Molly nodded, her azure blue eyes glittering with unshed tears. It reminded him of the sun glinting on a calm sea and as he did umpteen times a day he thanked God that she was his. She was beautiful on the inside as well as the outside and all he wanted to do was make her happy for the rest of his life.

If he had but known it, Molly was thinking the same thing. Matthew was so different to the other lads and she wanted nothing more than to be his wife one day. Tomorrow he'd be out on the *Seahorse* again and she would be doing what was needed in the house as well as all the other jobs a fisher girl had to do, but Enid had taught her well and she knew she could manage. It was rare she was able to sit like this with Matthew but today was a special day. She'd thought when they were wed that they would probably rent a little cottage like Harry and Alice, but now – although not a word had been said – she knew they'd stay here for Jed's sake. He was like all the men in the community: he went out to work and that, in his mind, was enough. The house and all in it was the woman's task and it lowered a man's prestige if he so much as washed a cup. Jed would let his clothes go rotten on his back before he'd wash them and slowly starve rather than cook a meal, even if he'd known how to. It was the same with collecting the wood and coke for the range and their small smokehouse, and the myriad other endeavours that were now commonplace to her. Women's work. If things had been normal and Enid hadn't passed away, right now she would be sitting knitting or sewing or mending nets.

It was nearly midnight when they retired to their separate rooms, but although she knew she'd have to be up at five o'clock to begin heating the big pan of porridge she'd left soaking on the hob, Molly found she couldn't sleep. She was tired, exhausted emotionally as well as physically, but the events of the day spun in her head like a kaleidoscope of constantly changing images.

She would never see Enid again, not this side of heaven. Never again would the two of them work together, talking and laughing with light hearts which made the heaviest, most dirty, taxing jobs enjoyable. Enid's heart had broken and it had killed her, and now her own heart was broken but in a different way.

Turning over and burying her face in the pillow to muffle the sound, she let the storm of weeping she had been fighting all day for Matthew's sake overwhelm her. She had loved the kind, gentle fisherwoman with every fibre of her being and for the first time had known what a mother's love was. She had never imagined being without her, none of them had. Enid had seemed so strong, so robust, so full of life and vigour, and then it had all stopped in a few moments of time in the kitchen. *Oh, Mam, Mam, don't leave me. I can't go on without you. Nothing is the same now.*

She had wrapped herself into a ball, the pain within consuming and more terrible than even the agony she'd experienced when her father had used his belt on her. How long she cried she didn't know, but when it was over she lay for a long time without moving, her misery too deep now for tears.

When a tentative dawn began to steal across the dark sky she still hadn't slept, but she rose wearily and made her way downstairs after pulling on her clothes and boots.

'*Life goes on, lass.*'

She could almost hear Enid saying it as she stood in the kitchen looking out of the window into the yard. And yes, life would go on, but it would be all the poorer without Enid in it. Nevertheless, she couldn't let her grief take over and impinge on Matthew; she must do her weeping at night when she was alone and be strong for him in the day. Enid would expect that of her. And with that thought the last remnants of childhood, along with the trust and belief common to all children that everything comes right in the end, fell from her never to return.

Chapter Seven

It was the middle of July and the weather had been capricious for weeks; spells of baking hot sun followed by violent summer storms and rain and then sun again. 'Have you seen the sky out there?' Matthew said as he walked into the kitchen, smiling at Molly before sitting down at the table. 'Doesn't look good to me.'

'It'll be fine.' Jed was halfway through his breakfast and didn't look up from his porridge as he spoke. 'Get your grub down you and let's be away. Time's money.'

Matthew said nothing to this but he glanced again at Molly and made a face. She smiled at him, but in truth she was worried about Jed these days. He was a changed man since Enid's death. Never one for conversation, he was now snappy and dour, rarely speaking except to criticize one or another of them.

Rory, seated on the opposite side of the table to his father, said quietly, 'It looks like another storm to me. You sure you want to take her out this morning?'

'I said, didn't I?'

Yes, he had said, Molly thought, but she didn't trust Jed's judgement any more and she didn't think the lads did either. They'd all expected him to mourn Enid but since her sudden passing it had become clear he didn't care if he lived or died, and ignoring the signs of bad weather today was testament to the fact. But if their da said they were taking the *Seahorse* out she knew the lads wouldn't argue.

They finished eating in silence but as Molly cleared away the dirty dishes she looked out of the window. The sky was heavy and low with grey rain clouds scudding across it. Not like a July day at all.

Jed and the lads left the house just as Harry opened the gate from the back lane, and Molly followed them and stood watching until they reached the street. Matthew looked back and blew her a kiss and then they were gone. For a moment she had the desire to run after him and beg him not to go out on the boat that day, and she'd actually taken a step before she came to her senses. Not only would everyone think she'd gone doolally but it would be pointless anyway. Matthew would no more let his father and brothers go out on the *Seahorse* without him than he would fly.

She retraced her steps into the house, her stomach churning. A strange feeling had taken hold of her and no matter how she tried to fight it, it grew stronger as the day progressed.

She busied herself preparing the herrings that the men had brought back the day before, having sold most of their catch on the quay. As she walked into the narrow, single-storey wooden smokehouse next to the privy it began to rain and then hail. The smokehouse had a brick floor for the fire and a tiled roof with holes, and as she went about her business of hanging the fish on the wooden rods to cure she was aware of the wind getting up. She had long since become used to the smell of smoking fish, but today it made her feel nauseous.

She was being silly, she told herself as she returned to the kitchen. Matthew and the others would be all right. None of them would take chances or be careless; they all knew their lives depended on being alert at all times when they were out on the boat. Matthew had assured her often that he never relaxed his guard for a minute when he was at sea.

She had been planning to go round the doors in the town selling the split herrings that she had smoked the day before – she could get between thruppence and sixpence for twelve in some quarters – and, the rain having lessened, she put on her oilskin cape and apron and followed the normal route that Enid had taught her. She returned home just before midday four shillings richer, which would help with the housekeeping, but once back in the house her worry returned tenfold.

After doing her normal household jobs she sat down in Enid's rocking chair and picked up her knitting. She was in the process of making new woollen jumpers for Jed and the lads; she'd mended their old ones until they were little more than threadbare patches, and they needed new socks too. The salt water which found its way down the top of their boots meant socks didn't last long, and you could only darn the same pair so many times.

By three o'clock in the afternoon it was so overcast and gloomy that she lit the oil lamp; the wind was gusting and rattling the kitchen window so hard it made her jump more than once. They were having baked haddock for dinner, and after filleting and cleaning the fish she made the stuffing with stale breadcrumbs, suet, chopped onions and herbs. After stuffing the haddock she secured it with needle and thread and put it in a baking tin with a little dripping and another scattering of breadcrumbs. After scrubbing the potatoes she was going to bake with the fish she popped the lot in the range to cook slowly.

The dinner sorted, she found she couldn't keep the anxiety she'd been battling all day from taking over. They should never have gone out today, she told herself for the umpteenth time. Jed wouldn't like it but the next time something like this happened, she would speak up. She knew exactly what he would say if she challenged him, of course – his timeworn adage of 'No fishing, no money, and a whole horde of empty bellies, lass' – as he had done with Enid in the past if she had objected, but whereas with his wife he'd have accompanied his words with a fond pat on her bottom or a quick hug, with her it was more likely to be a scowl these days. Nevertheless, she would do it. It had been foolish to go out on the boat today, pure and simple.

* * *

Matthew was thinking the same thing. The whole day had been a harsh battle for survival, and although he knew that was a fisherman's life, coming out when the weather had been so poor didn't exactly enhance their chances of a good haul. Having said that, he supposed to be fair to his da theirs hadn't been the only boat that had ventured out, but in the last couple of hours the rest had given up and gone back to shore.

He glanced up at the sail stretched like a tent across the *Seahorse*'s bow, and then at his father, who had his hand on the long tiller handle which was the size of an elephant's trunk. It used to fascinate him when he was a bairn, the tiller.

It had been raining when they set off at six o'clock this morning with the wind straight from the north, perhaps force five or six, and a choppy sea. That in itself hadn't been too much to worry about – they'd sailed in similar before – but the signs that it was going to get worse had been there to see. And it had got worse, by, it had, he thought now. For the last few hours the waves had had white tops and now the rain was pelting down, the sky as black as coal.

He heard Harry shout to his da, 'Head for home?' but couldn't hear their father's reply. They'd only caught a few fish all day, and once had been in danger of losing the net but still his da had pressed on. Stubborn as a mule. But then he smiled ruefully. Most fishermen were the same. He supposed you had to be pig-headed to do a job where you rose at dawn, battled a dangerous and formidable enemy every day of your life, sometimes didn't earn enough to keep a sparrow alive, and were constantly cold, wet and exhausted for a large part of the year. Molly had asked him if he'd ever wanted to do anything else and his reply had been, 'Like what?' He knew he wouldn't be able to stand being cooped up in a factory or down a mine – the mere thought gave him the skitters – and from the small amount of schooling he'd had he was aware he was no academic. Even reading and writing were beyond him. No, he was where he wanted to be, sure enough.

Harry's nudge to his father must have worked because Matthew became aware that Jed was heading for North Shields. Because of the difficulty of navigating ships and boats into the mouth of the river past the dangerous Black Midden rocks, buildings had been erected in the sixteenth century with lights permanently burning to be used as a guide by the mariners. Both these lights – High and Low – were rebuilt a hundred years later and then these were replaced by buildings situated at the top and bottom of the steep bank alongside the river. It was these lights that Matthew saw far in the distance as the *Seahorse* moved through the angry sea. Cobles offer virtually no protection and although their design gives them a 'grip' in the water and they're built to be launched in the face of breaking seas, Matthew was acutely aware that waves such as they were experiencing today could capsize them. Never had he been so relieved to see the lights. Molly had told him it was baked haddock for their dinner that night and he could almost taste it. She was a grand little cook, he thought tenderly. As good as his mam had been.

He was still thinking about Molly and his dinner when he heard Harry and Rory, who'd been getting ready to row once they were a little nearer to shore and the sail was furled in, shout frantically. He turned, and saw a monster of a wave bearing down on them broadside on, and it was breaking as it came.

He was aware of several things in a split second of time: his father pulling the tiller hard over in an effort to get the *Seahorse* into the wind; Harry and Rory's panic-stricken faces as they yelled something else to his da; his stomach coming up into his throat as he realized they were in big, big trouble, and a roaring in his ears – whether from the wind or inside his own head he didn't know. And then the boat was picked up as though by a giant hand and tossed onto its side. Icy-cold water hit him full in the face as he tried to hang on to anything he could because the *Seahorse* was filling up fast, but then another wave, every bit as vicious as the first, knocked the boat clean over and he was flung out like a rag doll.

He had never learned to swim, none of them had. His father had always maintained that if you were unlucky enough to find yourself in the North Sea it was time up anyway, but now he kicked his way to the surface, his boots and his clothes trying to drag him down. He could see no sign of his father or Rory but Harry was flailing about in the water some thirty yards away, his arms desperately thrashing.

There were bits of deck board and other debris in front of him but when he grabbed at them they were too light to take his weight and he went under the water again; as he did so he managed to kick off his boots but it made little difference. The temperature of the North Sea was icy cold even in summer and the shock of it was numbing.

He surfaced for the third time and now there was no Harry. He'd gone, like his da and Rory, he thought incredulously, and now he was going to die too. *Oh, Molly, Molly.*

As the sea closed over his head he still tried to kick and struggle, but a relentless, powerful force was drawing him down and an iron band was squeezing his chest. His lungs bursting, he had to take a breath, and as salt water filled his mouth and throat again he thought, *Molly, oh, Molly,* in the few moments before his heart stopped beating.

Chapter Eight

It was eleven o'clock the same evening and Molly was frantic. She had made several trips to the quayside over the last hours and had then begun to knock on some of the other fishermen's doors. They'd all said the same, or those who had braved the poor weather and taken their boats out did. The last time they had seen the *Seahorse* was when they were heading for home and they had expected Jed and his sons to do the same. She'd been to see Alice twice, and the second time Alice's older married sister and her husband had been there and their faces were grim.

The rain was still lashing down outside as Molly sat in the kitchen, and the wind was howling. In contrast, inside the house the range was glowing and the oil lamp in the middle of the table cast a mellow light over the room. Normally the atmosphere would have been one of comfort and security, but today she didn't feel that. The dinner was cold at the side of the range and she hadn't been able to have a bite of it; she didn't think she would ever be hungry again.

Lost at sea. The words haunted her. How many times had she heard that said since living in the fishing community? Too many. And now, if what she feared was true, it applied to Matthew and the others.

One of the old fishermen she had spoken to earlier had said there was a chance the *Seahorse* had been swept off course in the storm and that Jed and his sons would be biding their time before they attempted to navigate the mouth of the river. She didn't believe that and she had been able to tell Jed's pal hadn't believed it either. Another man had suggested the boat could have ended up coming ashore further along the coast, which would mean it could be a while before the Mallard menfolk made their way home. He had been no more convincing than the first.

Molly jumped to her feet and began pacing up and down. Something terrible had happened. The foreboding she'd had on her all day had been right. What could she do? *What could she do?*

By the time the kitchen clock struck midnight, in spite of telling herself she had to believe Matthew was alive and well she'd given up hope. She wanted to scream and shout and run through the streets demanding folk go out looking for them. Instead, as the long night hours ticked away, she sat in the rocking chair in silent misery, asking herself how she could face living in a world that didn't have Matthew in it. He had been part of Enid and besides loving him for himself, she'd loved him for that too.

Did love him, she corrected herself fiercely at one point. She didn't know for sure that he was gone. Nevertheless, the sick hollow feeling inside strengthened with every passing moment and she hadn't slept a wink by the time a tentative dawn began to steal across the sky. The summer storm had burned itself out and the new day was fresh and clean. Everything in her wanted to take a boat and go out to sea looking for the *Seahorse* herself, but of course that was impossible. She knew a search would begin with the light but it was too late . . .

When there was a knock on the back door at just after six o'clock her heart jumped into her mouth. She wanted news of Matthew and the others but at the same time she dreaded what she might be told. Her heart thumping so hard it hurt, she opened the door to find Alice standing there, looking as though she'd had a sleepless night too.

'I've left the bairns with me sister,' Alice said when they were seated with a cup of tea. 'I had to come and see you, lass. I thought in a while we could go down to the quays and see if there's any news?'

Molly nodded. She had been going to do that anyway.

'Molly . . .' Alice hesitated. 'Do you think they might be stranded somewhere?'

Molly didn't answer but her face spoke for her. And then, as Alice began to cry, she quickly said, 'Aye, they might be. They might be, lass,' but it was too late and she knew it.

'Our Hilda and Walter are already talking as though Harry's dead and gone,' Alice sobbed. 'They've driven me mad all through the night. Oh, I know it's nice of them to come round and all that, but Hilda's been going on about how I wouldn't be able to stay in the house and says I'll have to move in with them. She says she'll look after the bairns and I can go out to work to pay our way. She's got it all worked out.'

Molly patted Alice's hand. Matthew had told her that Harry couldn't stand Hilda, Alice's older sister. Apparently she and her husband had been married for years with no sign of a bairn, and Hilda was always popping in and trying to take the twins out somewhere and discouraging Alice from going with them. She spoiled them with sweets and never said no to them, so of course the boys thought Auntie Hilda was the bee's knees. When Enid had died and Alice had asked a neighbour to take care of the twins for the funeral, Hilda had apparently been incandescent with rage. In the row that had followed Hilda had accused Alice of 'taking the bairns away from her', for all the world, Harry had told Matthew, as though they were Hilda's boys rather than theirs. Remembering this, Molly said, 'We don't know what's happened yet but if it is the worst, Hilda can't force you to do something you don't want to, Alice. You are the twins' mam, not her, and it's up to you where you and them live.'

'But what else *could* I do? Whatever job I got it wouldn't pay enough for me to keep our house and feed and clothe

the twins. And who'd look after them while I worked? A neighbour might but they'd want paying if it was on a regular basis. I couldn't leave them at me mam's. As much as Harry couldn't stand our Hilda, he'd prefer her to Mam. I'm in a cleft stick, lass.'

Alice wiped her eyes with her handkerchief, shaking her head miserably before she added, 'And what about you? What'll you do?'

Molly hadn't thought about it. Her mind had been so focused on Matthew and the others, nothing else mattered. Now she shrugged her shoulders. With all Alice had said it had dawned on her that she wouldn't be able to pay the rent on this place no matter what job she might be able to pick up. Women's work was poorly paid at the best of times. 'I don't know.'

'Well, you'd better start thinking about it. And perhaps we ought to let Mary and Cissy know?'

'Aye, I suppose so.'

The two women stared at each other. Mary and Cissy had made it plain in the past that they considered their brother had married beneath him when he had wed Alice, so there was little love lost between Alice and her sisters-in-law. Both Molly and Alice were well aware that there would be no help forthcoming in that direction.

And so it proved in the days that followed. Once the storm abated, the other fishermen went out looking for the *Seahorse* and her crew, but to no avail. Alice waited for a week and then moved in with Hilda and Walter, and by then Molly had come to terms with the fact that she would have to leave the little home she still thought of primarily as Enid's house. The fishing community had rallied round and been kind to her while she'd waited for news. Every day someone or other had arrived on her doorstep with gifts of food – fish, potatoes, vegetables, a loaf of bread or bowl of dripping – but she knew that couldn't continue. She had enough money left in the kitty to pay the rent that was due with a little left over, but that was all.

It was on the evening of the day on which Alice had moved in with her sister that Mary and Cissy and their husbands came knocking on the door. She hadn't seen hide nor hair of the sisters since she and Alice had called on each of them to break the news that their father and brothers were missing, and on those occasions both women had kept them on the doorstep rather than inviting them into their homes.

She stared at the four individuals standing in the back yard with dour faces, and it was Mary who said, 'We've come to tell you what needs to be done,' before pushing past her and entering the kitchen followed by the others.

Once the four were standing facing her, Molly said quietly, 'Well?'

It was clear she had taken them aback by her tone, which although quiet had been self-assured. She had been expecting a confrontation at some point and had already made up her mind that with Matthew gone she wouldn't be bullied by his sisters. She was done with trying to placate them.

Mary and Cissy exchanged a swift glance before Mary said, 'It's clear Da and the others aren't coming home and you won't be able to stay here by yourself, but don't think you can lay claim to any of the furniture or other bits. We're aware of exactly what Mam and Da had and we'll know if there's so much as a spoon missing, all right? You won't be able to pay the rent and Blackett will want you out sharpish.'

Molly had raised her chin as the woman had spoken but other than that had shown no reaction.

'You'd be best clearing off back to where you came from.' Cissy's eyes were narrowed and there was real hate evident on her flat face with its pug nose. 'Your type don't belong round here.'

'Have you quite finished?' Molly's voice was like the crack of a whip.

The two men had been shuffling their feet and looking somewhat sheepish, and now Mary's husband said uncomfortably, 'There's no need for any unpleasantness. We just need to sort out—'

'Oh, believe me, I know exactly what your wives want to sort out.' Molly glared at them all, her upper lip curling back from her teeth as though she was smelling something rancid. 'How proud of you both your mother would be if she could hear you now,' she said cuttingly. 'How you two came from such a decent, kindly woman I don't know.'

'You leave our mam out of this—'

'She would have given away her last farthing to

someone in need, and here you are sniffing about for what you can get when your da and brothers' bodies haven't even been found. You disgust me, the pair of you, and you would have disgusted her.'

Mary had taken a step forward, her hand raised and a ferocious look on her face, but her husband caught her arm and jerked her back.

Molly hadn't moved an inch, and her eyes sparking, she bit out, 'Don't worry, I have no intention of taking anything but what belongs to me when I leave here, so you can put your nasty little minds to rest. Not everyone is like you.'

'You dare talk to us like that, you! You're scum, that's what you are.' Cissy's voice was a shriek and her cheeks were scarlet with rage. 'Me an' Mary could see through you from day one, even if you pulled the wool over Mam's eyes and sweet-talked Da and the lads. You made sure you got your hooks into Matthew and you imagined you'd be sitting pretty here for life, didn't you. Well, you've caught your toe and it serves you right,' she finished with a satisfaction that caused both the men to look down at the floor in embarrassment.

'Don't you even care that your da and brothers are gone?' There was a note of real amazement in Molly's voice. 'Are you so eaten up with spite and resentment against me that you are actually glad how things have turned out?'

It was clear she had hit the nail on the head, and suddenly Mary's husband said, 'We're leaving. I didn't want to come in the first place, did I' – he had turned to his wife and now he was as angry as her – 'and this is the last time you persuade me to do something like this.' Turning back to Molly, he said, 'I'm sorry, lass. We should never have come the night.'

'No, you shouldn't.' Terrified she was going to break down and determined not to, she said, 'Get out, all of you.'

'You can't talk to me like—'

Mary's words were cut short as she gave a gasp of shock at her husband manhandling her past Molly and out the back door; Cissy's husband following suit a moment later. Molly could hear both women remonstrating with the men as she banged the door shut behind them, and then the sound of a full-scale row going on as the four disappeared into the back lane beyond the yard.

She stood leaning against the door for some moments before she could move, her legs beginning to tremble. Horrible, horrible women, and she meant what she had said – how could such harridans have come from Enid? Well, she'd burned her bridges with them now for sure, not that they hadn't been well and truly alight for some time.

Wearily she made herself a pot of tea and then sat down at the kitchen table. The sisters' visit had confirmed it was time to leave this house and the first thing she had to do was to find work of some kind and somewhere to stay. A room would do, but where?

Her head was throbbing and she felt desolate, but after finishing the tea she made her plans. Tomorrow morning she would start going round the factories and shops in the town. She *had* to get a job. She wouldn't mind what she did. Maybe she could work in the kitchen of a hotel or in a big house or even – she swallowed hard – as a barmaid in a public house? She knew Matthew wouldn't have wanted that – he considered all such girls no better than they should be – and that would be her last resort, but she had to be able to earn enough to eat and lay her head somewhere. Enid had taught her to cook and keep house and she knew all about what it meant to be a fisherman's wife, but that seemed of little use now.

Over the next forty-eight hours she began to despair. No one, it would seem, wanted a fifteen-year-old girl who was as slim as a reed working for them. Several times she'd been openly eyed up and down but it was a man at a laundry who'd said what she realized the others must have been thinking. 'The work'll be too hard for you, lass. You're not built for it.'

She had tried to persuade him that she was stronger than she looked but he was having none of it, and neither was anyone else. There were so few jobs to be had anyway; it seemed employers could pick and choose and they wanted strong, hefty women who were built like fairground wrestlers.

When help came it was from the most unlikely source. Cyril Blackett, the rent collector, had given her three days' grace before she had to be out of the house after she had told him she was looking for work, and when he called in on the evening of the second day she thought he'd come to tell her she had to be gone by the following evening. No one liked Blackett – he was a rent collector for the landlord, wasn't he, and as such the lowest of the low in the fisherfolk's opinion – but Enid had always been civil to him, even offering him a cup of tea on occasion when he was frozen to the marrow. Because of that he'd allowed Molly a little longer in the house.

She opened the door to him and before she could speak, he said, 'Find anything?'

She shook her head. 'I – I don't know what to do, Mr Blackett.'

Cyril nodded, and then, as Molly stood aside for him to come into the kitchen, he accepted the silent invitation. Once he was facing her, he looked at the girl who'd been the apple of Enid Mallard's eye. It was common knowledge that the lass being taken in by the Mallards had caused something of a family rift with the two daughters – neither of whom Cyril liked – but he had always been able to see why Enid had taken to the lass. Not only was she a bonny little thing with her fair hair and blue eyes, but she had a ready smile and a nice way about her. Not that the poor girl was smiling today, he thought soberly. He'd heard that the youngest Mallard lad had been her sweetheart, and if that was the case then all this would have hit her doubly hard.

He cleared his throat. 'Well, lass, it's like this. A pal of mine is the foreman at the fish factory on the foot of Brewhouse Bank on the fish quay, an' he owes me a favour, does Ivor.'

Molly stared at him. She didn't see what this was to do with her, besides which she had already asked at the factory and been told there was no work. 'I did try there, Mr Blackett,' she said politely.

'Aye, I daresay, but like I said Ivor owes me an' I had a word with him about you. He reckons if you go an' ask for him the morrer, he might have somethin' for you. Name's Ivor Duffy.'

Molly blinked in surprise. 'Thank you, Mr Blackett. Thank you very much.'

'Aye, well, you go first thing, all right? Now Ivor mentioned there's a bunch of the lassies who work for him that live in a house in Dockwray Square, an' one of 'em left a day or two ago so you might find lodgings there.' He didn't mention that the girl in question had got herself in the family way and when her condition had become obvious had gone into the workhouse to have the bairn. Some of the lassies at the factory were a rum lot in his opinion.

'Dockwray Square?' The square was a stone's throw from Beacon Street and Enid had told her that it had once been a set of elegant town houses over a hundred years ago. Due to the poor provision of water and drainage facilities, however, the square had since deteriorated into slums when its wealthy residents had moved to the up-and-coming central part of the town.

'Aye. It's none too bright but it'll be cheap, lass, which is what you need till you've had time to sort yourself out.'

Molly nodded. He was right, of course. Again she said, 'Thank you, Mr Blackett.'

'What are you planning to do with the furniture and other bits an' pieces? The thing is, I've got a family waiting to move in and they'll be bringing their own stuff.'

'The daughters want everything.'

He bet they did. Grasping so-an'-sos. No doubt they'd make sure this lass didn't get so much as a penny. 'Well, when I leave here I'll call on one of 'em and tell them they need to have the place cleared the day after tomorrow, all right? If you get set on at the factory you could be gone by tomorrow night.'

Molly was aware he was giving her a deadline but that was fair enough. She couldn't expect him to wait any longer when he had new tenants lined up. Where she would go if she didn't get the job tomorrow, though, she didn't know.

'Put the keys under the boot scraper outside if you're gone before I pop round tomorrow and I'll assume you got the job. I'll drop 'em in to the others so they can clear the next day.'

'Yes, I'll do that and thank you again.' She saw him out and then sat down at the table, looking about her. She'd been so happy here, the days had taken on a halcyon glow and she knew she would never be so light-hearted again. Now they'd all gone, Enid, Jed, the lads and Matthew. Her Matthew. Leaning forward, she put her head on her arms and gave way to the storm of grief that had been building for days. She had never felt so lost and alone, not even when she had left the hamlet. The future that had once felt so wonderful when she had thought she was going to be Matthew's wife now stretched before her dark and dismal, and try as she might she could see no chink of light in the days ahead.

Chapter Nine

'So, lass, Cyril tells me you need work and somewhere to live. Is that right?'

'Aye, yes, sir.'

'You don't need to "sir" me. Mr Duffy'll do, although sir'd go down well with Mr Taylor, the manager.' There had been an edge to the last words. Molly got the impression that Mr Duffy didn't think too highly of the manager. 'You know anything about the process of canning fish?' And then before she could answer, he said, 'Course you don't. That was a daft question.'

Molly found herself relaxing a little; Mr Blackett's friend seemed a nice man. Middle-aged with close-cropped black hair and twinkling eyes, he was less intimidating than she'd feared when she had first caught sight of him. She'd been tense and nervous when she had presented herself at the large premises on North Shields fish quay. Although she had been up before dawn she hadn't been able to eat a thing after she had brought the tin bath into the kitchen and had an all-over wash. She had washed her hair too, and once she had rubbed it dry she had woven it into one thick plait which she had coiled round her head and secured with grips. It was the first time she had put her hair up and straight away she had felt different. Older.

The sky had been high and blue with barely a cloud when she left home just before seven o'clock, and when she reached the quay it had already been a hive of activity. A number of herring girls had started gutting fish and as she walked past them she found herself hoping she wouldn't have to do the same in the factory; of all the jobs she had done with Enid, gutting was the thing she liked the least. The herring lassies came down from Scotland following the herring from place to place; they were young and single in the main, and a tough bunch. Recruited from villages around northern Scotland and the Hebrides, many of them only spoke Gaelic. They were good workers.

'I take it you're not afraid of hard work, lass?' Mr Duffy seemed to have read her mind.

'No, no, of course not.'

'That's the ticket. Mr Irvin, he's the owner, expects a good day's work for a good day's pay and no larking about. Self-made man, is Mr Irvin, so he knows all about hard graft. Began when he was just a nipper and worked up to owning his own company by the time he was a young man – and you don't do that by sitting on your backside whistling "Dixie", do you?'

Molly shook her head.

'Started off as a trawler man and by the turn of the century he'd got some thirty steam trawlers, a fish sale business and a shipyard hereabouts, as well as running a fleet of whalers based in South Georgia. He's got offices in ports all over, and seeing the way things were going, four years back he set up his East Coast Herring Drifter Company and got himself some steam drifters. Canny, you see? You don't get on in this life if you don't look ahead to the future, lass. You remember that.'

Somewhat bemused, Molly nodded. They were standing in a huge yard at the back of the buildings and the smell of fish was overpowering.

Mr Duffy didn't seem in a rush to rid himself of his captive audience as he went on, 'To make sure that his drifters never have to dump an unsold catch, like some skippers do, he set this place up. Tinned herring, that's what we do. Tyne Brand Herrings'll be known far and wide, you mark my words. The herring industry is coming on in leaps and bounds, but you don't want to be throwing away umpteen tons of perfectly good fish when there's a glut of 'em, do you?'

'No, Mr Duffy.'

'Not good business that, and Mr Irvin is first and foremost a businessman. Right' – he suddenly became practical – 'you come with me an' I'll show you what's what. Be careful where you tread, in some parts it's slippy.'

'I – I've got the job?'

He looked faintly surprised as though it had been a foregone conclusion, which it probably had been as far as he was concerned. 'Aye, you've got the job, lass. Don't you want it?'

'Oh, yes. Yes, please, Mr Duffy.'

'Come on then and like I said, mind yourself.' He led the way out of the yard that was stacked with crates and barrels and into the first of a row of joined buildings which had a main thoroughfare in the middle of them. This end one was under cover as they all were, but was open with no doors. A number of girls were standing working at long troughs, sorting the herring by size and quality, and tossing them into separate baskets.

The next section housed girls standing at similar troughs and they were dressed in long oilskin aprons and rubber boots. They were deftly gutting the fish with small, sharp knives. One small incision, a quick twist, and the gut and gills were out and dropped into a basket, while the gutted herring were thrown into a separate tub behind each worker.

Mr Duffy stopped for a moment. 'Them fish guts'll be picked up by some of the local farmers for use as manure. Nothing wasted, see? Waste not, want not.'

Molly followed him into each of the buildings and he explained procedures as they walked, before they reached the canning part of the factory where the machines stood. Some of them, each operated by two girls, cleaned the herrings before the fish were sent down the lines of girls to be packed and then sealed in cans with tomato sauce. 'They're cooked in ovens and the bones will be as soft as butter,' he said as proudly as if the finished result was down solely to him. 'Marvellous it is, and the tins'll keep for any length of time. The flavour improves with age and it's a meal that's ready in a jiffy.'

Molly was wondering where she would fit in at the factory. The girls who had been gutting the fish had all had finger bandages made from strips of cotton to protect their fingers from the sharp knives and had been working at great speed. She knew she wouldn't be able to keep up with them, and the lethal blades flashing around had been alarming. She'd got used to gutting fish with Enid and was reasonably proficient, but the rate at which the factory girls had been working was on another level. The canning part of the building was cleaner, although as hectic in a different way; Mr Duffy had told her that the fish and tomato sauce were sealed in their oval cans at a rate of one per second. The girls here all wore a uniform – a kind of long dress over their other clothes and a mob-cap with 'Tyne Brand' printed on it.

Foolishly perhaps, she admitted to herself, she hadn't expected the premises to be so big or to have so many women and girls working in it. Apart from Mr Duffy she'd only seen a few other men. And everyone had been concentrating on the job in hand; there had been no chatter, not even in the sections where knives weren't involved.

Mr Duffy crooked his finger at a tall young woman who had been standing to one side of a large container of empty cans, and as she joined them, he said, 'This is the lass I told you about, Ruth.' He turned to Molly.

'Ruth is my eyes and ears in here when I'm busy elsewhere and she'll show you the ropes. You do exactly as she tells you, all right?'

'Yes, Mr Duffy.'

'Work hard an' behave yourself and I expect punctuality. If you're late twice you'll be out on your ear, and I don't stand for none of my lassies coming to work smelling of liquor neither.'

'Yes, Mr Duffy.'

'You'll be paid at the end of each week. The hours are seven sharp in the morning till six at night, Monday to Saturday.'

'Yes, Mr Duffy.'

He turned but then swung back again. 'When have you got to be out of the Mallard house?'

'Mr Blackett wants the place cleared tomorrow. The – the sisters want everything so they'll see to that.'

'Aye, I'm sure they will,' he said drily. 'Right, well, as I understand it there's a bed for you at Dockwray Square' – he glanced at the woman standing silently beside them and she nodded – 'so I suggest you move in tonight. You got much?'

'Just a couple of bags, Mr Duffy.'

He nodded. 'I'll leave you in Ruth's capable hands and like I said, keep your head down and work hard an' you'll be all right.' And with that he walked away.

Molly looked at Ruth. She was tall and thin with dark hair strained back in a bun at the nape of her neck and appeared to be about twenty-five to thirty years old, but it was difficult to tell. She had an air of sedateness about her that made her seem older than she probably was.

'Mr Duffy tells me your menfolk were lost at sea a week or so back?' Ruth said quietly.

Molly nodded. 'They – they weren't really my menfolk. Well, they were, but what I mean is the family had taken me in some years back and I wasn't related to them by blood. But they *were* my family,' she added more strongly.

'I'm sorry.' Ruth hesitated before she said, 'I lost my da and brothers down the mine when I was a bairn and my mam died shortly after, so I know how you feel. Come on,' she said more briskly, 'and I'll find you a cap and apron an' show you what to do. You'll be stationed in here, in the canning room for the time being.'

Molly breathed a silent sigh of relief that she wasn't expected to join the girls gutting the herrings.

Once attired in the cap and dress-like apron, Ruth led her over to one of the many long tables where a number of girls were filling the cans with the washed fish faster than she could blink. 'Your job'll be to make sure that all the tables are kept well supplied with cans and fish, and you'll need to keep your eyes peeled because they're fast workers. I'll show you where the baskets of fish are left when they're brought through and the stacks of cans. See this table here? They'll need another basket in a minute or two and you'll have to make sure they aren't kept waiting. Come with me.'

They walked to the back of the enormous room and

into an area where baskets of fish had been placed on massive wooden tables awaiting collection. When Molly lifted one her knees nearly buckled under the weight, but she managed to stagger off with it and take it to the table.

'You'll get used to it,' Ruth said bracingly.

Molly nodded. There was a trail of salted water where she had walked and because she had had to clutch the basket to her because of the weight, the front of her apron was already stained.

'Another of your jobs will be to wipe up spills and keep the floor as clean as you can. And if the baskets run low from outside come and let me know so I can hurry them up.' Ruth paused. 'Any questions?'

'Mr Duffy didn't say how much I'll be earning.'

'Didn't he? Well, as a beginner it'll be about half a crown. There's different rates depending on which part you're assigned to. The gutters are the best paid but then you'd expect that, wouldn't you. It's filthy work. Mind you, the lassies here are under cover, not like in the curing yards. There you can be standing in a mire of mud, sand and offal whatever the weather, and although they get an allowance to cover their food and lodgings, the herring girls from Scotland have to wait till the end of the season for their real pay. If you think it's hard work in the factory, you ought to see what they put up with. We get an hour's break at midday an' all and know when we're going to finish each night. In the yards if there's a glut of fish they can be working under lines of naphtha flares the coopers rig up till the early hours.'

Molly nodded. She knew the Scottish lassies had it tough in the yards.

'Anyway, you get checking the tables and don't forget about the floor when you get a minute.'

By midday, Molly felt she hadn't had a chance to 'get a minute' all morning. As soon as one table was supplied with fish another needed some, along with cans. She had been flying about in a panic most of the time. When the whistle sounded and everyone stopped for a bite to eat, Ruth appeared at her side.

'Come with me, lass,' she said kindly, leading her over to a bunch of girls who looked up and smiled at their approach. They were all eating food they'd brought in. Ruth introduced her and once they had sat down, one of the girls said, 'Where's your grub, lass?'

'I didn't bring any but – but I'm not hungry.'

'Don't be daft. Have some of my mine.'

Within moments she had bits and pieces from everyone. The simple act of kindness brought the emotion she had been battling with every day since Matthew's death to the fore, and after stammering her thanks she sat, willing herself not to cry as she ate the food. She'd spoken the truth when she'd said she wasn't hungry. The over-powering smell of fish and the fact that she reeked of it herself had killed her appetite, but after she'd forced the offerings down she had to admit she felt better.

When the conversation turned to herself, she explained her position and why she needed a job. The girls were all sympathetic. It appeared that more than one of them had menfolk who had been lost at sea, and they understood how she felt.

Ruth hadn't said much as they'd eaten but when one of the girls asked Molly where she lived, she answered for her. 'She's moving into the Square tonight,' she said in her quiet, rather prim voice. 'We're going to get your things later, aren't we, lass,' she added.

Molly stared at her in surprise.

'I thought you might need some help?' Ruth smiled at her expression. 'Mr Duffy told me a little about your situation.'

The whistle to signal the end of the lunch hour blew just then and as one the others rose to their feet, but Ruth detained her for a moment. 'I've lived in the square since I left the workhouse twelve years ago,' she said softly. 'It won't be what you've been used to and no doubt it'll seem strange at first – it did to me – but it's all right. Believe me, you'll get used to it. I've got my own room now but you'll be sharing like I did when I first lodged there. I'll explain everything tonight, all right? And just remember, things will get better, Molly. They have for me.'

By that evening Molly felt as though her arms were a foot longer and muscles that she didn't know she'd got were aching. The speed with which everyone worked at their various jobs was intimidating but she'd kept telling herself it was only her first day and she would get better.

Ruth was waiting for her after the whistle blew at six o'clock. Molly had realized she was a kind of supervisor and clearly regarded with respect by the other girls, even the roughest of them.

They left the factory into brilliant sunshine and the July evening was still hot after the heat of the day as they walked towards Beacon Street. Women were gossiping on their doorsteps and bairns were playing their games in the dusty streets, many of them barefoot and dressed in little more than rags. They passed two little lads swinging on a lamp post, their backsides hanging out of their torn trousers.

Molly glanced at the pair whose hair was white with nits and her face must have expressed what she was thinking, because Ruth said softly, 'Don't feel sorry for them, they're happy enough. We were fed and clothed in the workhouse but I would have swapped places with bairns like this in a moment.'

'Was it bad?' Like everyone else, she had heard horror stories of the dreaded institution.

'Yes, it was bad,' Ruth said in her quiet way. She hadn't spoken except to say she thought Molly had done well on her first day and they had been walking in silence, a silence that Molly had been too tired and heartsore to try and break.

Ruth didn't elaborate, and after a moment or two, Molly said, 'Thank you for coming with me to get my things.'

'That's all right. Everything is more bearable when you've got company, isn't it.'

When they reached Beacon Street and turned into the back lane, passing a number of urchins playing with an old tin can, one of the little lads shouted after them, 'Phew, smelly Nelly!'

'Ignore them,' said Ruth flatly without turning round.

She supposed she did stink, Molly thought ruefully. She would dearly have loved a wash in the tin bath again but she couldn't do that with Ruth waiting.

On reaching the house, Ruth followed her through the yard and into the kitchen. After looking about her, she said, 'I'd better tell you now that Dockwray Square might come as a bit of a shock after this. Because he rents to the girls from the fish factory, our landlord's stripped the rooms of any decent furniture and floor coverings. It's the smell most landlords won't stand for, you see. It gets into soft furnishings and never goes away.'

Molly could believe it. 'But you've got your own room?'

'I have now and I've got it how I want it over the years, buying this and that when I've seen things I like. Eight years ago Mr Duffy offered me the job of overseeing the girls when the other supervisor left, which was good of him as I think they expected Mr Duffy to hire another man. Anyway, it meant quite a bit more money so I decided to pay for my own room. The rent is one an' six a room but the landlord doesn't care how many girls bed down as long as he gets his rent. I've got the front room downstairs. There's two on the first floor and the second. It works out at sixpence each if there's three of you. It's dear for what we get in one way, but like I said the stink of fish puts a lot of folk off renting to the likes of us. At least it's bug and rat free now, not like when I first went there. I waged a war against them for months. We still get mice in the kitchen, though.'

Molly swallowed hard. When she had escaped the hamlet and been taken in by Enid and Jed she had thought her life had changed for the better. This seemed like a massive step backwards.

Leaving Ruth in the kitchen, she went upstairs to her room and packed her belongings. It didn't take long. She stood looking around for a minute, the lump in her throat threatening to choke her. Then, squaring her slim shoulders, she made her way downstairs.

Ruth was sitting at the kitchen table and as Molly walked into the room she stood up. 'It's bonny, isn't it,' Ruth said wistfully. 'Homely like. I can't remember much about my mam's cottage – I was only going on seven when they put me in the workhouse – but something about this seems familiar.'

Molly suddenly felt ashamed. Here was she thinking she was hard done by, when Ruth had been incarcerated in that terrible place for years. 'They were a lovely family,' she said quietly. 'I can't believe they're gone. It's so unfair.'

'Life *is* unfair. Look at Mr Duffy. You couldn't get a nicer man than him but his wife's been an invalid practically from the day they married. Fell downstairs and damaged her spine. He pays a neighbour to come in and see to her when he's at work but when he's home he has to do everything for her.'

Molly stared at Ruth. There had been something in the other girl's voice when she had spoken about the foreman that she hadn't heard before. Under her stare, Ruth went slightly pink, and Molly thought, I didn't imagine it. She likes him. Why, he must be old enough to be her da.

'Have you got everything?'

'Aye, yes.' Molly looked round the kitchen, knowing she was standing in it for the last time. In spite of herself the tears came as her heart cried out for Enid and Matthew. She turned her head so that Ruth wouldn't see, but in the next moment she felt an arm round her shoulders.

'It will get better, Molly. I know it doesn't feel as though it ever will right now, but time really does have a way of making things at least bearable.' As Molly nodded and wiped her eyes, Ruth added, 'Isn't there anything you want to take as a keepsake from the house?'

'Nothing belongs to me. Enid's daughters made that plain.'

'But it's not just up to them, is it. Mrs Mallard and the others would have wanted you to have something to remember them by, surely? You need to do it now because you won't have a chance once everything's gone tomorrow.'

Molly hadn't looked at it that way but now that Ruth had suggested it, she knew Enid and Matthew would have wanted her to take a memento. Her gaze fastened on the little wooden ship next to the clock on the mantelpiece. She knew that Matthew had carved it for his mother years ago when he was just a little lad and it had been Enid's prize possession. He'd made a tiny red sail for the boat and although it was a simple object, it was charming. She reached up and slipped it into one of her bags. Then she straightened and composed herself. 'I'm ready to go now.'

Once they were outside, she locked the back door and slipped the keys under the boot scraper. This was it. The final goodbye. As they left the yard she looked back at the little terraced house sitting snugly between its neighbours. It had never seemed so dear to her. Then she closed the gate and walked away.

Chapter Ten

'Here we are then, lass.' Ruth opened the back door of the run-down terraced house in Dockwray Square. Molly followed her through a small scullery with a big stone sink and some shelves, into a larger kitchen. Several girls, still in their work clothes and reeking of fish, were sitting on the benches either side of the table. Molly recognized them from the factory. Surprisingly, the kitchen was clean and there was the welcome smell of something cooking in the range oven.

Although only a few minutes from Beacon Street, the square was battered and shabby and spoke of decades of decay. The privies in the back yards had been stinking as they had walked down the lane, and from open doors and windows they'd heard women screaming at children and a baby wailing fit to wake the dead in the house next door. Ruth had told her that in most of the properties whole families were crammed in just a single room and that one house was a brothel. The water supply came from a tap at the end of the yard which also housed the privy and a coal bunker.

'For those of you who don't already know, this is Molly.' The girls nodded at Molly and smiled. 'She's replacing Amy, of course, so she'll be sleeping with Maggie and Tilly,' Ruth continued. 'They're not here yet,' she added to Molly. 'We take it in turns on a weekly basis to cook the evening meal and they were going to call in at the market for a few bits tonight.'

'I hope they don't come back with mouldy vegetables like they did yesterday,' one of the girls said. 'I like a bargain as well as the next person but those leeks and carrots were disgusting.'

Ignoring her, Ruth said, 'Whoever's doing the meal either leaves it cooking slowly in the range all day or nips home at lunchtime to put it on. In the week we mostly have stews or puddin's in the corner, things like that. We don't have fish much, not after working in the factory all day. Come on and I'll show you where you're sleeping and then we'll have a cup of tea.'

'Do all the girls here work at the factory?' Molly asked as she followed Ruth into the dingy, dark hall and up the first flight of stairs.

'Aye, yes. A lot of the girls at the factory live at home of course, being local, but there's a few like you and me without families and ones who've come from further afield. Maggie and Tilly who you'll be with are twins and there's eighteen of them at home in Sunderland so they were glad to get away. They send money to their mam when they can, though. Eighteen living in two rooms and a shared tap with five houses, can you imagine? At least we have our own tap and privy here and it's a rule we keep the privy fresh with ashes every day.'

They had been climbing another flight of stairs and had emerged on a gloomy landing that smelled strongly of mould and – inevitably – fish. Ruth opened the first of two doors as she said, 'This is where you'll be sleeping.'

It wasn't a large room but a double and single bed had been squeezed into the space. The floorboards were bare, there were no curtains at the small window and the walls were distempered a dismal shade of brown. Molly's heart plummeted.

'The single bed's yours so at least you don't have to share.' Ruth had seen her face. 'And it's bug free.'

Molly nodded. Apart from a few nails hammered into the wall there was nowhere to hang clothes, and underneath the double bed were several bags clearly belonging to its occupants. She swallowed hard. But at sixpence a week for a roof over her head she couldn't complain, and she had the company of the other girls. This would be all right for the time being. It had to be.

After putting her bags on the bed, which had a thin flock mattress that had seen better days, she followed Ruth back downstairs where the other girl explained that everyone put in so much a week towards the evening meal and things like tea, milk and sugar, but any other food or snacks were bought individually by each person. 'It's simpler that way,' Ruth said. 'Avoids arguments. And the rent is due on Saturday night, no exceptions, after we get paid.'

Molly brought her purse out of her skirt pocket. She had just under a shilling to her name and today was Wednesday so she wouldn't be paid her full wage on Saturday, and she needed to give the others some money now for food. She tipped the coins onto the table and said to Ruth, 'How much do I owe you for meals?'

The girls all looked at each other, and one of them said, 'Is that all you've got, lass?'

'Isn't it enough? I can give more on Saturday and—'

The girl shook her head. 'You keep it for your lunches, all right? And it'll just be thruppence you need to stump up for rent this week, lass, seeing as it'll be half a week. We can start proper next week, once you've been paid your whack. Right, Ruth?'

Ruth nodded, smiling.

Suddenly the room upstairs didn't seem so bad as Molly glanced round the friendly faces. She bit hard on her bottom lip to stop the tears pricking at the backs of her eyes from falling, and in the next moment a steaming cup of tea appeared in front of her.

She drank it slowly, listening to the others chatter and larking on and feeling more settled than she had in days. There were worse places to be than here.

It was another ten minutes before Maggie and Tilly walked in and straight away Molly knew the twins were what Enid would have labelled 'cards'. Plump and genial, with round smiling faces and rosy-red cheeks, they immediately went into a long story about how they'd managed to persuade one of the stallholders at the market to throw in some scrag ends with the meat they'd purchased, imitating his Irish accent and their responses until the other girls were crying with laughter.

'Aw, begorrah,' Maggie, the taller of the twins, parroted, 'you'll be takin' the food out of me bairns' mouths, so you will afore you're satisfied, you hard-hearted hussies.'

'It's just a few scrag ends, Mr Finnigan,' said Tilly in such a prim tone that Ruth choked on a mouthful of tea.

'A few scrag ends, she says.' Maggie appealed to her audience, throwing her arms wide. 'Did you ever hear the like? Where would I be if I gave away scrag ends to every Tom, Dick or Harry, eh?'

'But you know us, Mr Finnigan.'

'Aye, I do that. By, I do that, an' I fair tremble in me boots when I see the pair of you, so I do.'

'That's not very nice, Mr Finnigan.'

The show ended when the twins became so convulsed with laughter themselves that they couldn't continue, and once they had put away their purchases for the next day, they introduced themselves to Molly after which the other girls followed suit.

Dinner proved to be mutton stew thick with carrots, turnips, onions, leeks and potato and big chunks of somewhat stale bread the twins had bought cheap, but it was tasty and filling, as was the Spotted Dick pudding that followed. There was much laughter and banter as they ate, but none of the girls seemed overly concerned about changing out of their fish-stained clothes or having a wash. Molly had noticed an old tin bath hanging on the yard wall but she didn't like to ask if she could use it when it clearly wasn't something the others did every day.

They all sat chatting for a while after dinner, but eventually Ruth said goodnight and disappeared to her room and one by one the others followed. Maggie and Tilly had busied themselves doing the washing-up in the scullery after they'd cleared the table and were now preparing the meal for the next day, another stew but this time with stewing steak and the scrag ends and again plenty of vegetables, and though some of them looked the worse for wear it didn't matter in a stew. Molly had offered to help the twins and had been busy chopping vegetables, and when it was just the three of them left in the kitchen, Tilly said, 'So how come you're not living with your folks, lass?'

Molly looked at the two round pink faces which, although similar, were not identical, although both were topped by fuzzy fair hair. She hesitated for a moment, uncertain of how much to say, and then decided that if she was sharing a room with these girls it was better they knew the whole story. She began at the beginning when she had left the hamlet and finished when the *Seahorse* had been lost at sea, and for once the twins were solemn-faced and silent. 'So,' she said quietly, 'Matthew's sisters are clearing the house tomorrow and the new family will be moving in at the end of the week, I suppose.'

'By, lass,' Tilly said softly, 'and you're fifteen, you say? You've packed a lot into your fifteen years thus far, haven't you.'

She supposed she had, but not by choice.

'Your da, your real da, sounds a right so-an'-so. Our da' – she glanced at her sister – 'is a bit handy with his fists which is one of the reasons we moved out as soon as we could, but he doesn't sound a patch on yours.'

'An' you were going to marry your Matthew next year?' said Maggie, her pale blue eyes sympathetic. 'Aw, lass, I'm sorry.'

Molly shrugged. 'It is what it is.'

'You're a right unlucky beggar, if you don't mind me saying so.'

She didn't mind; she'd been thinking the same thing.

'Well, you're here now,' said Tilly, suddenly brisk, 'and I don't know if Ruth's said, but we all look after each other in this house.'

'When we can.' Maggie grimaced. 'We tried to tell Amy that the lad she was courting was a wrong 'un but she wouldn't have it, and what was the result? He left her with her belly full and skedaddled. She was bonny too, like you.'

'And young,' Tilly put in.

'So you be careful, all right. Not all lads are like your Matthew.'

Molly nodded. She didn't want a lad, not if he wasn't Matthew. She wasn't sure what she *did* want, if she were truthful, but now she had a job and was living here she would have time to think. She felt heartsore and desperately unhappy but yesterday she had been completely alone and today she didn't feel like that. Which was a start.

And later that night, when she was lying in her narrow bed on the spectacularly lumpy flock mattress, listening to Maggie and Tilly compete for the loudest snore, she felt a sense of – not peace, exactly, but more of a calm deep within. It was soothing after the desperation and turmoil of the last days.

She would do anything to go back in time and be lying in her bed at Beacon Street with the lads next door and Enid and Jed downstairs, but that time had ended. Gone like the sea mist that rolled in one minute and then vanished the next. She didn't know how she was going to get through the next weeks and months without them but she would have to. As Enid had been fond of saying, life goes on. Even when you don't want it to.

PART THREE

The Metamorphosis

1909

Chapter Eleven

In the five years that had passed since the day Molly had moved into Dockwray Square, little had changed in North Shields, but the same couldn't be said for Molly herself or the country as a whole. The latter had seen increasingly bitter and hostile confrontations between the suffragettes and the police since the first women supporting the cause had been imprisoned in 1905, and although the government had dug its heels in over the matter of the women's war for the vote, there were some in high places who said it was just a matter of time before the authorities would be forced to capitulate.

When the Liberal Party swept to power in a landslide victory at the beginning of 1906, their election campaign had been notable for the participation of women. They had been much more prominent as speakers and canvassers as well as persistent hecklers demanding female suffrage, but once the new government were in place the Prime Minister informed the suffragettes that, although they had made out a conclusive and irrefutable case, they had to be patient: 'It is more likely you will succeed if you wait than if you act now in a pugnacious spirit.' It wasn't what the women had expected or wanted to hear and consequently things had worsened very swiftly.

Molly had followed these events closely, enabled by the fact that during the first year she had been staying at the house in Dockwray Square, Ruth had taught her to read and write. Most evenings and every Sunday without fail, she and Ruth had ensconced themselves in Ruth's room and Molly had had her lessons. Ruth had been a patient teacher and Molly an apt pupil given her burning desire to enter into the world of books, and indeed a whole new universe had opened up to her. Ruth had painstakingly acquired a collection of books and the first time Molly had entered her room, which Ruth had furnished and made strikingly different to the rest of the house, she had gazed in wonder at the shelves along one wall containing Ruth's treasures.

'I like to read,' Ruth had said simply. 'Don't you?' And when Molly had confessed her inability to do so, Ruth had offered there and then to teach her. Most of the books were second-hand and often musty and some were falling apart, but that didn't matter. Molly had sat with her mentor at Ruth's small table and chairs or in front of the fire on the little sofa, and by the end of the first winter had become proficient.

Ruth bought a newspaper every day and once Molly was able she had devoured that too, and they had enjoyed many discussions about the state of the country and the world. They didn't always agree, especially about the suffrage movement. Ruth considered Emmeline Pankhurst and her followers to be 'unfeminine' and shameful over the militant stance they had taken in latter years, whereas Molly was in full agreement with them.

'It's not just here in England where women are treated so unfairly, it's all over the world. Look at India, for example. They talk about "the land of hope and glory" spanning the globe, but to my mind it's the men who bask in the glory and the women can merely hope things improve for them. There they don't even regard women as important enough for census purposes,' Molly had said indignantly during one somewhat heated discussion. 'And women being urged to shun netball and the rougher sports here is rubbish. Those university types who come out with such drivel ought to spend a day at the factory or on the quays and see what women do.'

Ruth had smiled at her passion. 'It's the way things are,' she'd said with a shrug of her shoulders. 'And I for one wouldn't want to dash about trying to grab a ball in a most ungainly fashion.'

'Neither would I as it happens, but we ought to be able to do so if we want without being labelled unlady-like and mannish. Finland have got it right at last, giving women the vote and even electing them into the Finnish parliament. That ought to add credence to the suffragettes' campaign in countries like here and America.'

Ruth had shaken her head. 'It might work the other

way if men think that by giving the vote to women they'll end up in government.'

Molly had literally stamped her foot in frustration. 'How can you be so accepting of such wrongs?'

'Because I'm not like you and I don't look on it as wrong. I wouldn't want to worry myself about who to vote for,' Ruth had said with such serenity that Molly wanted to shake her. 'And why I ever taught you to read I don't know,' Ruth added with a grin to soften her words. 'I had no idea you were such a tigress under that pretty exterior.'

It had been one of many such conversations which both women secretly very much enjoyed and looked forward to, and Molly was thinking of that now as she stared at her friend. It was a sunny Sunday in late August and outside the weather was hot and sticky, but Ruth's front room was its normal oasis of cool calm which mirrored its owner's personality.

'You're going to do what?' Molly asked, wondering if she'd heard what Ruth had just said correctly. They were sitting having a cup of tea and in the kitchen Sunday lunch was in the range.

'I'm going to get married.'

'To – to Ivor?'

'Of course to Ivor.'

The foreman's wife had died in the New Year and Molly was one of the few people who knew that Ruth had been walking out with him the last month or so.

'But . . .' Molly was floundering and it showed.

Taking pity on her, Ruth said quietly, 'I know, I know, it's too soon after Prudence's passing, but he asked me and I said yes. We know what people'll say and for that reason he's transferring to Mr Irvin's Aberdeen branch and I shall go with him as his wife. We're getting married as soon as we can before we leave.'

Recovering herself, Molly said, 'Oh, I'm happy for you, I am, but I'm going to miss you so much,' and as she said the words she realized how true they were. Ruth had been more than a friend the last five years: mother, sister, confidante and teacher, she owed her so much. She got on well with all the girls in the house and the twins had become dear friends but nothing compared to her relationship with Ruth. And Aberdeen, it was so far away. She would never see her again. But she couldn't focus on that, she had to be glad for her.

'I'll miss you too,' Ruth said softly, aware of some of what was going on in Molly's mind. 'But Ivor wants a fresh start. Last year when Prudence got worse was so hard on him and he wants a normal life, he wants to be married,' she added with a tinge of pink to her cheeks. 'But there'll be talk, you know what folk are like. They'll say we were carrying on when his wife was alive and getting married so quickly will only confirm that. We weren't, of course, but that'll make no difference.'

Molly nodded. She knew that was true. Gossip provided spice in people's otherwise humdrum lives and the factory was no different to anywhere else. It didn't matter if what was whispered and chewed over was true or not; folk would cheerfully rip another person to pieces with their tongues and all under a cloak of righteous respectability.

'Ivor would like a family and so would I before it's too late,' Ruth went on, 'but here any bairns would be brought up under a cloud of scandal because we didn't wait for three or four years before we got together. Aberdeen is far enough away for us to be just another married couple.' Ruth put her hand over Molly's. 'I would have liked to stay here with you and the others close by, but you do understand, don't you?'

'Of course I do.' Molly hugged her. 'And you're doing the right thing. You both deserve to be happy, lass.' Ruth had told her of the harrowing life Ivor had led for years, working hard at the factory and then going home to work even harder caring for his wife. He had paid a neighbour to pop in several times a day while he was at work, but it had been him who had done the housework, got the meals and washed Prudence's bedding every day, as she had been doubly incontinent after her tragic accident when they had only been wed a matter of weeks. He had had to do everything for her and he had done it gladly, Ruth had told her, because he'd loved his wife, but it had aged him beyond his years. Molly had been surprised to know that Ivor was only ten years older than Ruth; he looked double that at least. And Ruth's life had been far from a bowl of cherries too. She hugged her again as she said, 'You'll write to me when you go, won't you? We will keep in touch?'

'Always.'

They continued to chat but Molly's mind was only half on their conversation. Ruth and this room had been a haven for her but now that was coming to an end. She'd really only gone upstairs to sleep; the rest of the time she'd spent with Ruth.

From her first day at the fish factory she'd been determined to save every penny she could. It was the reason she'd never aspired to renting her own room like Ruth, even though she now earned six shillings a week. The other girls apart from Ruth liked to be out and about in their leisure time, going for walks through the town arm in arm and visiting the picture houses and inns. This was mostly in the hope of catching a lad's eye and even the twins were worldly wise and free with their favours.

Molly was aware the fish factory lassies had a bad reputation but that didn't bother her. The factory paid well and that was the important thing. Money was the key to one day making a future for herself away from the town but as yet she wasn't sure where she would go or what she would do. She just knew she would make it happen.

Later that night she lay wide awake in bed, mulling things over. The nest egg under her mattress now amounted to nearly thirty pounds. It seemed like a small fortune but it would only stretch so far once she wasn't earning a good wage. She had barely bought any clothes in the last years so if she left North Shields for pastures new she would need a new wardrobe among other things. She intended to pass herself off as a respectable young woman from a good family who needed to earn her own living through no fault of her own, but that was as far as her plans had gone thus far. Now it was time to start thinking about the future more seriously.

After another couple of hours of imagining one scenario after another, she came to the conclusion that she was panicking unnecessarily. After all, Ruth hadn't even gone yet. For the time being she needn't rush to make any decisions. Even after Ruth had left there would be no hurry. She could continue at the factory and nothing would really change. Immediately the last thought mocked her. Everything would change without Ruth and the sanctuary her friend's room had been.

A day at a time. She could almost hear Enid's voice as the thought came. It had been one of Matthew's mam's favourite sayings. She was trying to cross all her bridges tonight and that was silly. Looking on the bright side, she was in a much better position than when she'd left the hamlet or even the house in Beacon Street. She could read and write now, and had broadened her mind far beyond what she could have imagined five years ago. She had a good grasp of current affairs and politics and she and Ruth had delved into history and science and all manner of subjects, along with having elocution lessons with a local gentlewoman to improve their diction and the way they spoke generally. The other girls had been tickled pink by this, even standing outside Ruth's door when they were practising at home and then mimicking them unmercifully.

'All that learning and talking proper isn't going to help you meet a lad and get wed, lass,' the twins had said on numerous occasions when the three of them were ensconced in their bedroom. 'You'll end up an old maid like Ruth and you so bonny. You want to live a little, enjoy yourself before you're too old.'

She'd just smiled and said she was happy the way things were. There was no real malice in any of the girls although even then she'd known she didn't want to end up like Ruth, truth be told. She wanted to *do* something with her life but that didn't mean marrying a lad and having one bairn after another. She wasn't like the other girls, she knew that. Not even Ruth. She was a square peg in a round hole, she supposed. She didn't really feel she fitted in anywhere and sometimes, in spite of Ruth's friendship, she felt so lonely.

Go to sleep, she told herself silently. *You're thinking too much.* And then another of Enid's sayings popped into her mind. *'Tomorrow is another day and only the good Lord knows where He'll lead you.'*

'That's all very well, Enid,' she whispered into her pillow as Maggie and Tilly's snores echoed in the room, 'but couldn't you ask Him to give me a bit of a clue just this once?'

Chapter Twelve

It was two months since Ruth had told her about her forth-coming marriage and a month since it had occurred, after which her friend and Ivor had disappeared to Aberdeen, but it could have been two years – two decades – as far as Molly was concerned. So much had changed, and not just because Ruth was no longer around. Ruth had sold her belongings and now three girls from the factory were squeezed into what had been her room; suddenly the house where Molly had lived for five years was no longer some-where she wanted to be. After returning home from the factory and eating dinner with the other girls each evening she would either stay in the warmth of the kitchen for as long as possible before going upstairs to her dismal room, or if the weather was clement she would wrap up and take a walk by herself. Her housemates had all tried to persuade her to go out with them, and she had done so once or twice if they were going to the picture house or looking round the shops, but mostly they spent time in the public houses chatting to lads and she wasn't interested in doing that.

Things were very different at the factory too. The foreman who had replaced Ivor was a younger man of around thirty who was unable to keep his hands to himself. Most of the girls laughed and giggled with him and didn't seem to mind, and a couple had apparently seen him after work and got up to all sorts, but Molly found him objectionable. Working with so many women, he clearly thought he was God's gift to the female sex even though he was no oil painting, and his arrogance grated on her. Perhaps because she was one of the few who didn't flirt with him he seemed to have targeted her more and more for his unwanted attentions. One of the older women had taken over Ruth's job but she was clearly so pleased with the promotion that she didn't want to endanger it by taking the foreman's conduct to a higher authority as Ruth would have done, merely turning a blind eye to his behaviour.

It was in the second week of November that things came to a head. Just before the whistle had blown, Mrs Casey, Ruth's replacement, had asked Molly to fetch one of the wheeled stands holding stocks of empty cans ready for the morning, and by the time she had returned with it the factory was practically empty. She put the cans in their assigned place, but as she turned to make her way out of the factory the foreman, Mr Kirby, stepped in front of her, blocking her path.

She stepped back a pace and as she did so, he smiled. 'Well, if it isn't Lady Muck all on her own,' he drawled softly. 'The nobody who thinks she's somebody. That's right, isn't it?'

Molly stared at him, her voice cool when she said, 'I don't know what you mean, Mr Kirby.'

'No?' He glanced about him. The last few workers had walked out of the door some distance away. Emboldened, he took a step towards her, causing her again to retreat. 'I think you know exactly what I mean. Think yourself too good for the lads round here, don't you? I know all about you.'

'I doubt that, Mr Kirby.'

'See, that's what I mean. Hoity-toity. Well, it don't wash with me.'

'Would you move out of the way so I can leave, please.'

'And what will you do if I don't?'

There was a knot of fear in her stomach now but she was determined not to show it. 'It's gone six and I'm entitled to leave.'

'I bet you're one of these unnatural types, these suffragettes, aren't you, eh? Men-haters?' His heavy-lidded eyes were running all over her and his wet tongue flicked over his lips in a quick, snake-like movement.

Molly repressed a shudder. 'I don't think it's any of your business. I am employed here to do a job of work and I've had no complaints thus far.'

'Well, you wouldn't, would you, being in with Duffy's bit on the side, but they've moved off to pastures new and I'm the one you have to please now.' This was an itch he'd wanted to scratch from day one. It wasn't just that she was a bonny piece, it was her aloofness, her way of talking and looking at you, everything about her that had got to him. And what was she, after all? Factory scum. But unlike the rest of them she didn't seem to realize he had the power to throw her out on her ear if she wasn't nice to him.

'If you've a problem with my work—'

'Aye, I have.'

'Oh, yes?'

'Come into my office and we'll talk there.'

There was no way she was going into his office. More than one girl had come out looking dishevelled and flushed, and last week Audrey had been crying when she'd emerged. When they'd tried to make her say what had happened she wouldn't be drawn, though. It was common knowledge her da had broken his back in a fall at the docks and she and her brother supported their parents and four younger siblings. She'd do nothing to endanger her job.

'I don't think so, Mr Kirby. Anything you've got to say to me you can say here.'

There it was again, the uppityness of her. 'You've got this all wrong, m'girl,' he said, narrowing his eyes. 'I tell *you* what to do, all right?'

She wasn't going to take any more of this. It was a Saturday night and her wage packet was in her pocket; she had nothing to lose by walking out right now. Perhaps this was the spur she'd been waiting for? 'Not from today, Mr Kirby. I don't need this job that badly. I'm leaving as of now.'

His expression of total amazement would have been funny in any other circumstances, but in the next moment he recovered himself. He caught hold of her arms, glaring at her as he hissed, 'You need teaching a lesson, m'girl. You won't be so high and mighty when I've finished with you. An' if you go telling tales it'll be my word against yours, remember that, an' who's going to believe scum like you over me?'

It was as she heard someone call her name from the other end of the factory that she reacted instinctively, bringing one knee up with all the force she could muster into Kirby's groin. The scream he uttered could have come from a woman, so high-pitched was it, and as he collapsed to the floor, his hands between his legs, she heard running footsteps behind her and turned to see Maggie and Tilly and another girl from the house, their shocked faces speaking for themselves.

'He – he tried to . . .'

'I think we know what he tried, lass. Dirty beggar.' Maggie looked at the man still rolling about on the floor, his face screwed up with pain and anguished moans coming from his contorted mouth. 'He's had this coming.'

Tilly took her arm. 'Come away, lass. You've taught him a lesson he won't forget in a hurry.'

They left him where he was as they hurried out of the factory, the twins on either side of her and Elsie, the other girl, making up the rear. It was Elsie who said, 'We were waiting for you so we could all walk home together, lass. We thought you'd been a while so we came to see what was what.'

'He wanted me to go into his office with him.'

Maggie snorted. 'I bet he did.'

It was sleeting as they walked out into the bitterly cold November day but the waterfront was as busy as ever. 'I've told Kirby I'm not coming back. I've had enough.'

They stopped walking and the others stared at her in concern. Maggie clicked her tongue. 'You shouldn't have done that, Moll. What'll you do? Look, we'll all back you and say what happened.'

Molly shook her head. 'It'd be my word against his in the final count, and guess who they'll believe? Anyway, my card would be marked whatever happened, you know that as well as me. Management sticks together. I wouldn't want you lot to lose your jobs if Kirby turned nasty — which he would.'

'But what'll you do?' Maggie said again.

Molly shrugged. 'I'm not sure but I'm ready for a change. I've got a bit saved and I've a mind to go somewhere different, leave North Shields altogether. I'm sick of fish,' she finished with a somewhat shaky grin. The incident with Kirby had frightened her and brought home just what some folk thought about the lassies who worked at the fish factory. Easy game. Up for anything. She'd heard such phrases bandied about before.

'Don't decide anything in a hurry — sleep on it.' Tilly squeezed her arm.

She didn't need to. When she had walked out of the factory she'd known she wouldn't be coming back. And she didn't want another factory job somewhere either. She couldn't tell the others because they would think she was an upstart, and maybe they were right, but she wanted something better. It was time to do something rather than just thinking about it.

To that end she bought a newspaper on the way home. She had noticed in the past that in the Saturday edition there was the occasional job advertised for the sort of woman she was going to present herself as. A housekeeper or teacher or lady's companion, things of that nature. Of course, a teacher was out of the question – she didn't have any training for that – but there might be something?

After dinner the other girls tried to persuade her to go out on the town with them to 'cheer her up' as Maggie put it, but in truth she didn't need cheering up. She felt as though she was on the cusp of something, something new and exciting. She just didn't know what.

Once she had the house to herself she settled down with the newspaper. The front page was full of the progress of the new colliery at Ellington a few miles up the coast. The colliery was going to change the face of the area, which hitherto had mainly been a farming community although it had its own school, a couple of public houses and several businesses. Two huge bridges had already been constructed to accommodate a railway system to the proposed new site from Linton, one to cross over the Ashington Road at Ellington Bank and the other a short distance away to cross over the River Lyne as it flowed into Ellington Dene. New roads were being constructed and the one-time rural village was already seeing more prosperity, the article claimed, with many more jobs and opportunities available.

There was a picture of a number of men, arms crossed and caps pulled low, with somewhat grim faces, standing at the site where they were sinking the new colliery.

Molly read a little more and then turned to the page she wanted. There were two posts advertised that would be suitable but one, for a lady's companion, ruled itself out as references from previous employers were required. The other piqued her interest immediately:

> *Housekeeper wanted for a doctor and his family in Ellington village, live-in only. Enthusiasm and the ability to deal with two young children on occasion essential. Applicants may apply in writing to: Dr Heath, Buttercup House, Ellington, Northumberland.*

Molly felt her heart racing. There was no mention of references or age, and she could always add another five years to her twenty. Buttercup House. That sounded lovely. And then she shook her head at herself. Here she was, running away in her mind and she hadn't even written a letter of application yet. She would need to buy some good-quality paper and a nice pen if she was going to make a fist of it, and get the story she intended to present to the doctor clear in her mind. She wondered why he was dealing with this rather than his wife but perhaps that was the way things were done with the middle-class? And he would be middle-class if he was a doctor. Maybe his wife was an invalid, like Ivor's had been?

She sat back, too excited to read the rest of the newspaper, and began to plan the letter in her mind. Come Monday morning the first thing she would do was to purchase the notepaper and pen. She wanted to apply promptly. He would probably have plenty of replies. The thought dampened her excitement for a few moments before she shook her head at herself. Nothing ventured, nothing gained. And one thing was certain: she was never going to set foot in the fish factory again.

She posted the letter of application on Monday afternoon. She'd kept it as brief as she could:

Dear Dr Heath,

I am writing in reply to your advertisement in the Shields Daily News *for a housekeeper. I am twenty-five years of age and until recently have been managing my father's household after my mother died some years ago. Owing to a change in circumstances I find myself in the position of seeking employment of a similar vein. I am used to children and would be happy to deal with them when required. I would be pleased to attend an interview at a time and date of your choosing should my application meet with your favour.*

Yours faithfully,
Molly McKenzie (Miss)

She had agonized over the letter, rewriting it several times. She had no idea exactly how such an application should be phrased but had decided that stating her age and experience was necessary. Of course, none of it was true.

After the envelope had slid into the post box she immediately felt guilty, but once back at the house and after a cup of tea she comforted herself with the fact that adding five years to her age wasn't exactly a crime and she *had* kept house for Jed and the lads at Beacon Street for a while after Enid had passed away. So it was more stretching the truth? And she liked children. Hardly the same as what she'd written in the letter, her conscience said primly.

She took a sip of tea and told herself that there was no need to worry because she probably wouldn't hear back anyway. And if she did, if she got an interview it didn't mean she would be successful. The bottom line was that if she'd written and said she was a factory girl of twenty years old with no experience of running the sort of establishment this doctor probably lived in, she wouldn't have stood a chance. The end justifies the means? *Shaky ground*, her conscience said again, and now she felt so guilty she ate a whole bag of biscuits she'd bought on Saturday.

During the next few days she kept herself busy. Whether she heard back from the doctor in Ellington or not, she needed to kit herself out for the new persona she was going to adopt. She was determined to leave North Shields and begin the next phase of her life sooner rather than later. To that end, she took some of her hard-earned cash from under the mattress and went off to the shops with a list of things she wanted.

A little while ago she'd spotted a suitcase in the window of the pawnshop in Church Street. Although it looked a little worn it had clearly been expensive when it was new and this made it perfect. It would look odd if she turned up somewhere with brand new luggage, besides which she intended to make every penny she had stretch into two. As the only child of a hitherto wealthy businessman she would have been used to going on holiday and things like that. She was going to say her father had made some disastrous business decisions before dying unexpectedly, after which she'd discovered he'd lost everything, leaving her with no choice but to earn her own living.

To her relief the suitcase was still there, and after purchasing it she also bought a small gold locket and chain and a lady's neat little wristwatch from the pawn-shop. These were items she felt sure her new self would have.

The Grand Emporium in Saville Street was her next visit. They had good-quality second-hand clothes that were a step up from the pre-owned clothing stalls at the market. She had wandered about the Emporium in the past with Ruth but had never bought anything. It was an Aladdin's cave of a place, and she emerged a few hours later with a smart blue-and-grey costume and matching blouse, a day dress in navy blue and another in rose pink with a lace collar and cuffs, a formal evening dress in deep mauve and two skirts and three blouses. She had also found a thick midnight-blue winter coat and hat, two pairs of shoes and a pair of black ankle boots. She knew she would have to take the dresses in at the waist and the bust but she was immensely pleased with her purchases, even though she had gulped at the total amount of money she'd spent in one afternoon.

Another visit to the pawnshop towards the end of the week yielded a mother-of-pearl brush and comb set and a set of fine lawn handkerchiefs, along with a leather handbag and purse. Underwear and a few personal items made up the sum total of her spending spree and now the suitcase was full. Matthew's little red-sailed boat she wrapped carefully in a piece of material and slid it between the clothes to cushion it from harm. She had packed everything as soon as she had got it home, hoping the smell of fish that pervaded the house wouldn't penetrate the suitcase.

The reply to her application came on the following Monday morning. The other girls had left for work some time before, and she gazed at the envelope with her name and address written in dark scrawly handwriting for a good few seconds before she could bring herself to open it. Her heart pounding like a sledgehammer, she unfolded and read the single page of thick linen paper:

Dear Miss McKenzie,

Thank you for your prompt reply to my advertisement for a housekeeper. I would be pleased if you could attend an interview at Buttercup House on Monday, 29th November at one o'clock in the afternoon. I have other applicants to see so if this date is not convenient perhaps you would be good enough to let me know by return. Otherwise I look forward to meeting you then.

I am your obedient servant,
Dr John Heath

A man of few words, she thought, excitement mingled with terror gripping her, but then her own letter had been brief. *She had an interview.* It wasn't until this very moment that she realized she hadn't expected a favourable reply.

Her legs felt a little weak and she sat down suddenly, one hand to her chest. She had committed herself to putting on a front as a well-brought-up young lady from a good home, someone who would have been protected and cared for from the cradle. Nothing could be further from the truth. *What had she done?*

She sat quite still, the letter dangling from her hand. What if she couldn't pull this off when she met Dr Heath in person? What if he saw through her and realized she wasn't who she purported to be? She would die on the spot of shame.

But what if he didn't suspect anything? she argued to herself. He might accept her at face value and even offer her the job. If she wanted a better life she had to make it happen. No one else would. She had to push this particular door and see if it opened. If it didn't, she would think again. She could perhaps go further south to a big city and look for work there? Take a room, maybe even learn to type while she did other work in the meantime in a shop or factory or something? But for the moment she would pursue the chance to be a housekeeper to Dr John Heath of Ellington. Decision made.

Chapter Thirteen

John Heath looked at the young woman sitting primly in the chair opposite the desk in his study. Miss Molly McKenzie wasn't what he'd expected. Foolishly perhaps, he admitted, but he'd had in mind a schoolmarm type rather than the beauty this girl was. And she barely looked more than a girl – seventeen, eighteen or thereabouts. Her skin was beautiful, pure peaches and cream, and that hair . . .

He suddenly became aware that he was staring and she was waiting for him to speak. Pulling himself together, he cleared his throat, aware that of the two of them it was Miss McKenzie who seemed in charge of the situation.

'So,' he said with a smile. 'Tell me a little about yourself.'

She was too nervous to smile back. 'There isn't really much to tell, Dr Heath. As I stated in my letter of application I have kept house for my father for some years after the death of my mother. Unfortunately, my father passed away recently and it was only then that I was informed by his solicitor that he was heavily in debt.

The house had to be sold and I was left with virtually nothing, hence my having to earn my own living.'

He nodded. It happened. 'What business was your father in?'

She blinked and hesitated for a moment but when she spoke her voice was quiet and steady. 'He had a rope-making works and several other interests but I was told that since my mother's death he had started gambling heavily.'

'Ah, yes. Grief affects everyone differently.' At some point the father had clearly been well off; her clothes were of good quality and she spoke well, although the north-east burr was present. 'You're an only child?'

She nodded.

'And there were no other family members, aunts and uncles and so on, that you could have turned to?'

'I prefer to stand on my own two feet, Dr Heath, rather than accept the charity of others.'

'I see.' Commendable, of course, but why did he feel that he wasn't getting the full story here? She was certainly a self-contained young woman. Not that that was a bad thing but—

His thoughts were interrupted by a knock on the door and the maid, Lotty, entering with the tea tray he'd ordered when Miss McKenzie had arrived. Telling Lotty he would see to things, he waited until the maid had left before saying, 'How do you take your tea, Miss McKenzie? Milk or lemon?'

Again she blinked, and now a faint tinge of pink flushed her cheeks. 'Milk, please, no sugar.'

After handing her the cup, he said quietly, 'I think I ought to explain my situation, Miss McKenzie. Unfortunately my wife passed away over twelve months ago and since then the household has not run as smoothly as I would have wished. My cook and maid have done a sterling job but neither of them is equipped to take charge of things. I have two children aged ten and eight and they take their lessons here at the house with their tutor, who used to be the headmaster at a private school in Durham before he retired. My son will be going away to boarding school in the summer' – he stopped as though he was going to say something more about that but then continued – 'but for the present he remains at home.'

He appeared to be waiting for her to say something but she didn't know what, so she nodded.

'Oliver and Angeline were close to their mother and her death affected them badly.'

'That is only natural, of course.'

'Quite. Unfortunately, though, their distress has taken the form of disruptive and unacceptable behaviour at times. Mr Newton, their tutor, stands no nonsense, but when he is not here and I am out I understand from Mrs McHaffie, my cook, that they tend to run wild, refusing to go to bed or tidy their rooms, things of that nature. Not, I admit, great sins in themselves but ones that create an unpleasant and fraught atmosphere nonetheless.'

'I see.'

'What I am trying to say, Miss McKenzie, is that you would need to be firm with the children from the outset.

I am tired of coming home to tears and tantrums and disorder.' He paused. 'The loss of their mother was hard for them but it has been over a year now.'

Molly took a sip of tea before she said, 'Do I take it that in your absence you would expect the housekeeper to be in charge of the children as well as the rest of the household?'

'Yes, exactly that.' He seemed relieved at how she'd put it.

'Personally, I see no problem with that, Dr Heath, but if I was offered the post I would expect your backing with any decisions I made in your absence, certainly in front of the children. It would need to be a united effort.'

He stared at her. She certainly called a spade a spade. 'Yes, of course.' He was finding himself slightly on the back foot with this young woman and he wasn't sure why. He'd felt more in control with the other two applicants he had asked for an interview but he hadn't warmed to either of them. One had told him she knew how to deal with youngsters in a tone of 'spare the rod and spoil the child', and the other had assured him that under her command the children would be seen and not heard.

Over the last year he had to admit that he'd despaired as to how to handle Oliver and Angeline. Of course, the main problem was that when Christabel had been alive she had spoiled the pair of them and his relationship with his son and daughter had been practically non-existent. His wife had seen to that. It had been part of his punishment for choosing to become a country doctor rather than what she had expected – Harley Street at least, like his brother, Lawrence. And he had understood her disappointment, he really had, but he'd wanted to work where he was really needed, among what Christabel had liked to call the common people. Like her, he came from a wealthy background and he had a generous private income courtesy of a legacy from his paternal grandparents, but it had been the unexpected death of his father and mother in a boating accident a few months after he and Christabel married that had decided him he had to follow his own star. Life had all at once seemed fragile and short. And at first Christabel hadn't objected too strongly – she had liked the idea of being a big fish in a small pond, he supposed – and he had agreed she could go and stay in London with her parents whenever she wished, but the novelty had soon worn off.

He cleared his throat. 'I'd better explain that I have a small premises in the centre of the village which my patients attend, but I can be called out unexpectedly at times. With the new colliery being sunk, and fresh blood coming into the area along with the existing farms and hamlets, my patient list has increased somewhat, and I cover the village of Linton too. I'm a busy man, Miss McKenzie, and I'm thinking of taking on an assistant in the foreseeable future but for the moment there's just me. There's another doctor's surgery in Lynemouth but I understand they're hard-pressed at times too.'

He offered her a biscuit from the plate on the tray and then took one himself, eating it in two bites before taking another.

Molly found she was relaxing a little. When she had first approached Buttercup House, set on the outskirts of the village, she'd felt somewhat intimidated. She'd had a picture in her mind of a small thatched cottage, she supposed, but the large house in mellow, honey-coloured stone certainly wasn't that. A small drive had opened on to a wide lawned area studded with ornamental trees and the house itself was covered in parts with red ivy. Semicircular steps had led to the studded front door and a maid had answered her knock.

She had stepped into a beautifully decorated hall, the pale walls displaying several fine landscapes and the wall-to-wall carpeting thick and luxurious. There was a pleasant smell, too – lavender, she thought – and a small cabriole-legged sofa with a little table beside it covered in magazines which oozed good taste.

The maid had shown her straight into the doctor's study, saying he was waiting for her, and this room was a much more masculine affair. Bookcases crammed with leather-bound volumes lined the plain white walls, and the polished oak floorboards and small blackleaded fireplace in which a coal fire burned brightly were functional.

Dr Heath wasn't what she had envisaged either. Even though his letter had mentioned young children, she had expected a middle-aged man with a fatherly air about him. Instead, she had been confronted with a tall, lean and broad-shouldered individual who looked to be in his late thirties. His wavy hair was jet black and he had keen grey eyes and a deep cleft in his square chin. His handshake had been hard and firm and he gave the impression of a man who would stand no nonsense, which made the revelations about the difficulties with his children all the more surprising.

She finished the last of her tea and then said, 'What exactly would my duties be, Dr Heath?'

'Your duties?' He looked almost surprised. 'Well, Mrs McHaffie is a fine cook and I'm sure Lotty does her best but the house needs to be organized again, Miss McKenzie. You would see to the household bills; order supplies and anything else we need like new clothes and shoes for the children, furnishings, things like that; talk to tradesmen; give Lotty her instructions every morning and liaise with Cook about meals; deal with the gardener who comes one day a week; make sure Oliver and Angeline have clean clothes each morning; check with Mr Newton that their work is satisfactory; bring to my attention anything that needs my input—' He paused and shrugged his shoulders. 'Just everything involved in running an establishment, I suppose,' he finished a little lamely. 'I simply haven't the time to concern myself about such matters.'

It sounded more and more as though they had been in a pickle the past several months and the problems with his children – which she suspected were even worse than he had let on – wouldn't have helped things.

'So, Miss McKenzie,' he said after a moment. 'Do you think you would be willing to step into the breach?'

She smiled for the first time. 'Yes, I think so.'

'Good.' He relaxed back in his chair and grinned at her. 'Then the position is yours.'

It was the grin that threw her. It was lopsided and it gave his handsome, rather stern face a boyish quality for a fleeting moment. Her breath caught in her throat as her heart gave a peculiar little leap.

'I'm aware that the position is a responsible one,' he went on, unaware of the disquiet he'd caused, 'and worthy of a salary to reflect this. I'm offering two pounds a week to begin with to be paid quarterly, if this is acceptable?'

She stared at him. Two pounds a week was more than she could have dreamed of. A miner would be fortunate to earn as much, grubbing under the earth six days out of seven. Trying to keep her amazement from showing, she said, 'Thank you, Dr Heath.'

'Excellent. How soon can you start?'

'Would the end of the week be convenient?'

'I'll look forward to seeing you then. And now I must show you the house. Most of the grounds are at the front so you've seen that already, but we have an orchard and greenhouses at the rear. Cook makes fine use of the plums and apples and other fruit.' He stood up and she followed, her head whirling.

Just as they walked out of the study into the hall there was a loud knocking at the front door.

'Excuse me a moment.'

She remained where she was as he hurried to the door, opening it a second before the maid came scurrying out of another at the end of the hall. Molly couldn't help but hear the conversation that ensued between the doctor and a distraught young man whose father had apparently fallen under the wheels of a cart.

Lotty clearly knew the drill. Even before the two men had finished speaking, she was at the doctor's elbow with his black leather bag, overcoat and hat.

Turning to Molly, he said ruefully, 'This is how it is, I'm afraid. I'm sorry, but I need to leave now. Lotty will take you on a tour of the house and I'll see you later in the week. Would Friday or Saturday suit best?'

'Friday will be fine.'

'Friday it is then.' Although he was perfectly courteous, she could sense that his mind was already focusing on his patient.

He held out his hand as he said goodbye, and as she shook it she realized that although she was considered tall for a woman at five foot seven, he towered over her by a good few inches. It was disconcerting. And then with a slam of the door he was gone.

On the train back to North Shields, Molly sat lost in thought. She was oblivious to the stare of the well-dressed plump matron stuffing chocolates into her mouth in a corner of the carriage, or of the equally rotund pug dog drooling and panting on the woman's ample lap.

She could barely take in that she was going to live

in the lovely house she'd just left. The five bedrooms had each been decorated in a different pastel colour with a dressing room attached to two of them, and there had been an indoor bathroom and closet too, the first time she had come across such an innovation. At the back of the big farmhouse kitchen on the ground floor the staff quarters had comprised a further three bedrooms, each large enough to hold a bed, wardrobe and armchair. These rooms had been utilitarian but comfortable enough.

The narrow corridor on which the staff rooms were situated had a door at the end of it leading to an outside yard, where there was a brick-built washroom complete with a coal-fired boiler and tin bath, and next to this a separate privy. The rest of the downstairs of the house was made up of a beautifully decorated drawing room, a dining room, a small breakfast room, a morning room and of course Dr Heath's study.

Lotty had proved to be a chatterbox, and she'd learned more about the family during her tour of the house. It hadn't been until she had boarded the train and sat thinking about the day that Molly had realized that in her new position of housekeeper she probably shouldn't have let the maid gossip so freely.

'Mrs Heath had the house done up from top to bottom just the way she wanted it afore they moved in,' Lotty had told her. 'It must have cost a fortune, Cook says, but Mrs Heath was never satisfied.' Here Lotty had hastily added, 'God rest her soul.'

According to Lotty, the marriage hadn't been a particularly happy one. 'They put up a front, mind, like the upper classes do, but me an' Cook knew. There were weeks at a time when she barely spoke to the poor doctor after some argument or other, and they had separate bedrooms after Miss Angeline was born. Dr Heath said it was because the mistress worried about the babby 'cause she was sickly but me an' Cook didn't think so. And the way the mistress was with the bairns – daft, Cook called it. Always buying 'em things and never saying no and if he, Dr Heath, ever objected there'd be hell to pay. Me an' Cook have had our work cut out with the bairns since the mistress passed, I tell you straight.'

'In what way?' Molly had asked quietly.

'Well, they're good as gold when Mr Newton's here, toe the line with him, they do, but once he's gone home and if the master isn't here they play up something rotten. They've gone to stay with the master's brother an' his family in London for a few days and I have to say it's been grand without them, peaceful like. Mind you, we'll suffer all the more when they're back, I dare say.'

The tale of woe had continued but when they reached the kitchen Lotty had stopped her chatter. Molly had got the impression that Mrs McHaffie, the cook, discouraged the maid's prattling. Mrs McHaffie was a big woman with a cheerful face and bright twinkling eyes and Molly took to her immediately. She had been icing a cake as they'd entered the kitchen but stopped what she was doing and greeted Molly warmly.

'I'm right pleased the master's realized we need a house-keeper, Miss McKenzie,' she'd said, wiping her hands on a dishcloth. 'I'm a cook and the kitchen's my domain – I can't be doing with seeing to other things an' all. The mistress had her faults but she kept this house running like clockwork, I'll say that for her. Lovely dinner parties she gave and she'd be in here discussing menus for days aforehand and see to it I got everything I needed in plenty of time. Every Monday I'd give her a list of what was required and she'd see to the rest and that's how it should be in my book. I didn't have to bother me head paying tradesmen an' all that palaver but everything's been up in the air since she passed, and of course the doctor's out a lot. He can't help that, I know, but it don't make for a happy house.'

Molly leaned back in her seat on the train and sighed as puffs of steam rolled by the window. She did so hope she'd done the right thing in accepting the role of house-keeper. The cook clearly expected her to wave a magic wand and have everything running as smoothly as when the doctor's wife had been in charge.

The dog on the opposite side of the carriage snuffled and snorted and his mistress slipped a chocolate into his slavering mouth. Molly looked up and smiled but only received a blank stare from the woman and an equally blank stare from the dog.

Going back to her thoughts, she told herself not to be so defeatist. She could do this, of course she could. The vast majority of it would be common sense and although she might make a few mistakes along the way, so what? It wasn't as if the doctor's house was a huge mansion with umpteen staff to oversee. She had faced worse than this in the past, after all. Success was a state of mind and she didn't intend to fail.

And Dr Heath? Her breathing quickened as she pictured him in her mind. Well, by all accounts she wouldn't be seeing much of him anyway – and for the life of her, she didn't know if that made her feel relieved or disappointed.

Chapter Fourteen

It was beginning to snow as Molly left Dockwray Square for the last time and the December day was dull and overcast.

She'd written to Ruth informing her friend about the new job and giving her the address of Buttercup House, and she knew Ruth would be pleased for her. The other girls in the house had been slightly nonplussed when she'd told them she was going to work as a housekeeper. 'But you won't have any time to yourself, not like if you got another factory job,' Maggie had said. 'They keep you at it in service, I tell you, lass. One of me sisters got taken on at a big house in the country and the tales she's told. Mind you, she's only a kitchen maid, but still . . .'

'I don't have to do it for ever.' Molly had smiled at their bewildered faces. She knew they lived for their evenings out in the town, flirting with the lads and drinking gin, but that had never interested her. Two pounds a week meant that she could add to the small amount she had left in her savings and her nest egg would grow considerably. She might be able to buy her own little property in the future, maybe take in paying guests to provide an income but one where she would be her own boss? Anything was possible.

She stood looking back at the square for some moments and then turned away, mentally shaking the dust of the last five years from her feet, but there was something she had to do before leaving North Shields for good. Carrying her suitcase, she walked to Beacon Street and into the lane at the back of the terraces. There were no bairns playing out today, no women gossiping over their back yards, just the snow falling and the occasional bark from a dog in the distance.

When she reached the back of the house she would always think of as Enid's, she stood staring into the paved yard, the snowflakes settling on her hat and shoulders. Everything looked the same but they were all gone: Enid, Jed, Matthew and his brothers.

'Thank you,' she whispered softly past the huge lump in her throat. 'Thank you for saving me, thank you for loving me. I will never, ever forget you.' This had been her real home, the first time she had ever known what it was like to be part of a family. The cottage in the hamlet didn't count. She wished she could turn back time; she'd give everything she possessed for one day with them all. She had been happy then, full of a joy that had died with them.

'Mam, oh, Mam,' she sobbed quietly. 'Matthew, my love. You should be here. I love you so much.'

She stood for several long minutes, thinking of the life that might have been, that *should* have been, and then forced herself to turn away. She had said her goodbyes and wherever they were they would wish her well, she knew that. They had loved her.

When Molly stepped out of the horse-drawn cab that had brought her from the train station to Buttercup House, the snow was falling more densely than ever, big fat flakes that were settling on the frozen ground and were already an inch or so thick.

'We're in for a packet, you mark my words,' the cab driver said cheerfully as she paid him. 'It'll be a long winter, this one.'

Although it was only early afternoon it could have been twilight, such was the lack of light. As the cab trundled off, she stood staring up at the house for some moments. This was it. The beginning of yet another new life. Taking a deep breath, she climbed the steps that had been swept clear of all but a light dusting of snow and knocked on the front door.

Almost immediately it was opened by a smiling Lotty. 'Miss McKenzie, you're here safe and sound then? By, what a day, isn't it? The master's been called out but he said to tell you to make yourself comfortable an' he'll see you later on.'

As Molly stepped into the hall the warmth hit her after the bitter chill outside.

'Here, miss, let me take your hat an' coat. Now I

daresay you'll want to get unpacked first, an' then Cook's got sandwiches an' tea an' cakes ready. You can have it in the kitchen, or in the morning room if you'd prefer? The master's said that's yours from now on. It's where the mistress used to do her accounts and see tradesmen and so on, an' he said for you to use it as your own sitting room.' Lotty's voice dropped to a whisper. 'The bairns are having their lessons in the breakfast room with Mr Newton. They use that as a schoolroom during term time.'

'Right.' She'd like to compose herself before she met the doctor's children. 'I'll have tea in the kitchen, please.'

Lotty led the way down the hall and into the corridor off which was the kitchen and scullery and the staff rooms. On reaching the first of these, Lotty opened the door. 'I've lit a fire so it should be as warm as toast,' she said cheerily. 'Makes all the difference if somewhere's cosy, don't it?'

Molly was touched by the girl's thoughtfulness. 'Yes, it does. Thank you, Lotty.'

Once Lotty had gone, closing the door behind her, Molly put down the suitcase and gazed about her. She had only glimpsed this room on her last visit but now she took in her surroundings properly. There was a thick shop-bought rug on the polished floorboards that she was sure hadn't been there before, and the pretty blue-and-green eiderdown on the bed and matching curtains looked new too. With the crackling fire in the small blackleaded grate, the little room had taken on quite a different atmosphere to the somewhat spartan one that she remembered. Had the doctor arranged this for her? Whether he had or hadn't, it was a lovely welcome, she thought gratefully.

It didn't take her long to unpack. Once she'd combed her hair and tidied herself she walked along to the kitchen where the cook and Lotty were waiting.

Again her greeting from Mrs McHaffie was warm, and they were sitting drinking tea and chatting when the door to the kitchen opened and a young girl entered. Molly found herself being surveyed by a pair of blue eyes set in a round face that would have been pretty but for its scowl. With no preamble, and whilst staring at Molly, the child said rudely, 'We're ready for our milk and biscuits and Mr Newton's tea and he said to jump to it.'

'Now, Miss Angeline, I'm sure Mr Newton didn't put it like that,' Mrs McHaffie said mildly, rising from the table as she added, 'This is Miss McKenzie. Aren't you going to say hello?'

The open hostility in the small face was amazing considering they had never met, Molly thought, her heart sinking. She didn't let her feelings show, though, saying calmly and quietly, 'Good afternoon, Angeline.'

She saw the blue eyes widen. The child had clearly expected to be addressed as Miss Angeline but Molly had made up her mind beforehand that she was going to forgo that formality. The children needed to see her in a different light to the cook and maid, besides which, the thought of being subservient to bairns didn't sit well. She would respect them as her employer's children but that was all. Not that she considered herself better than Mrs McHaffie and Lotty on a human level. She didn't, she told herself, but by Dr Heath's own admission her job carried a different kind of responsibility and his children needed to be aware of that. How the doctor would view her decision she'd no doubt find out shortly.

Angeline stared at the interloper. Oliver had said this woman was trying to replace their mother and he was furiously angry about it. She didn't know what had happened to her brother since their mother had died. Sometimes he frightened her. He hated their father but she always followed his lead because he was Oliver and she loved him. If her brother said that their father had never wanted them and his job was all that mattered, it must be so. She vaguely remembered their mother saying the same thing but her recollections were less clear than Oliver's.

'I said good afternoon, Angeline.'

She forced herself to mumble a reply of sorts. She was then further taken aback when the new housekeeper said firmly, 'I suggest you ask Cook for your refreshments in a manner that is becoming for a well-brought-up young lady, don't you?'

For a moment Angeline thought about defying this stranger. Oliver would be cross with her if she fell at the first hurdle. He had told her that they were going to make the new housekeeper's life a misery and then she would disappear back to where she had come from. She was less sure about that now, having met Miss McKenzie. 'Please could we have our afternoon snack?' she asked sullenly.

'Aye. Lotty will bring it shortly,' Gladys McHaffie responded, trying to keep her surprise at the proceedings from showing. As Angeline flounced off, banging the door behind her, the cook looked with new eyes at the woman about whom she had privately had misgivings. She'd seemed such a young slip of a thing when she had come for the interview with Dr Heath. Running the doctor's house was one thing, but with the master's bairns being the Devil's own imps at times . . . But there, she had to admit she might be mistaken. Miss McKenzie had hidden depths. Mind, from what the lass had been saying as they'd had their tea she was more of the doctor's class than the normal servant and that made a difference. They had a way of handling themselves, did the upper classes. Whatever, if the lass could manage the young master and miss and restore some sort of harmony to this house, she was all for it.

While she bustled about getting the tea tray ready for Lotty to take through, she said, 'It must have been a shock when you were forced to leave your home, Miss McKenzie. I applaud you for rolling up your sleeves, so to speak, and finding a position to support yourself. Big place was it, your da's?'

'Not as big as this one,' Molly prevaricated. She hadn't

realized how uncomfortable she would feel about perpetuating the web of fabrication she had woven to folk like Mrs McHaffie and Lotty, nice ordinary souls. But it had been necessary, she told herself. And the last years of broadening her horizons with Ruth and the elocution lessons in which she'd learned articulation and enunciation had to be for something.

As Lotty disappeared with the tray they heard voices from the hall and when the maid reappeared it was with the news that Dr Heath had returned. 'He wants coffee in his study, Cook, and could you go along when you're ready, Miss McKenzie?' Lotty said brightly, adding, 'It's getting really deep out there. Do you want me to clear the steps again, Miss McKenzie?'

Molly stood up. 'Yes, please, Lotty.' She had just given her first order but she was going to have to get used to thinking ahead and anticipating such things, she told herself. 'I'll take the doctor's coffee along,' she added to Mrs McHaffie.

'Right you are.'

When she reached the study, Molly found herself hesitating. She didn't question why. After taking several deep breaths and composing herself, she knocked firmly and then opened the door.

He was sitting slumped in his big leather chair behind the desk and he didn't look up as he said wearily, 'Thank you, Lotty.'

'You wanted to see me, Dr Heath?'

His head shot up then. 'Miss McKenzie!' He jumped

to his feet. 'I'm sorry I wasn't here to welcome you personally but I trust Cook's provided you with refreshments after your journey?'

'I've been looked after very well.'

'Excellent, excellent.'

He looked tired, she thought, drained. She placed the cup of coffee on the desk and then took the hand he was offering.

'A belated welcome to Buttercup House,' he said, looking into the beautiful face that had been at the forefront of his mind since the last time he had seen her. He had wondered if he'd exaggerated her loveliness but now saw that he hadn't. She looked so fresh and flawless, so different to the poor woman he had just left in that labourer's cottage in a hamlet north of the village. Nine children she'd had in as many years but the last one had killed her. He'd been unable to save either mother or baby and now the husband was left with eight motherless children to fend for themselves while he worked each day.

He became aware that he was still holding her hand and quickly let it go, saying, 'I'm sorry, I'm not myself. A difficult case today, I'm afraid. Do sit down, Miss McKenzie.'

Once they were both seated he gulped at his coffee. *Focus, man, focus*, he told himself. 'Did Lotty tell you that the morning room is yours?' he asked. 'Good. My wife kept a book in which she recorded any expenditure and I have placed it on the writing desk. Hopefully it will be of assistance. I will give you a sum of money every month to cover the household expenses along with things like new clothes and shoes for the children, and if you require more let me know. Large bills I pay myself by cheque but the local tradesmen prefer cash.'

She nodded.

'Any problems or questions, do feel free at any time to talk to me, Miss McKenzie. Have you met the children yet?'

'Angeline came into the kitchen to request a tea tray while I was having refreshments,' she said expressionlessly.

He hoped Angeline had behaved herself. When he had explained that he had engaged a housekeeper to take control of things, Oliver and Angeline's reaction had left much to be desired. He didn't understand his children, especially his son. He had made allowances the last months for them losing the mother whom they'd both adored, but the way Oliver had spoken to him that day had been beyond the pale and, big as his son was, he had put him over his knee and spanked him for the first time since he was a toddler. The boy hadn't fought him, neither had he cried, but when the punishment was over he had stood, his cheeks burning and his eyes flashing, defiant to the last.

Remembering this, and the hatred in his son's eyes, he said quietly, 'If you have any difficulties with Oliver or Angeline refer them to me. I won't tolerate it. I'm afraid my wife spoiled them when she was alive and I didn't take a strong enough hand in checking it. We reap what we sow, Miss McKenzie.' He smiled a smile that wasn't a smile.

'I'm sure you were extremely busy.'

'That's true but it's no excuse. If I intervened with them, Oliver in particular, the result was such discord it was easier to do nothing.' He leaned back in his chair. 'But of course it is never easier in the long run.'

'No, I suppose not.'

'Come along with me now and meet the children properly, and I can introduce you to my friend Mr Newton, who you'll be seeing quite a bit of. He's the best of fellows.'

So saying, he stood up and walked to the door, opening it and allowing her to precede him. When they entered the breakfast room they found the two children working at the table and Mr Newton sitting in a chair near the fire. He rose to greet them, smiling as he said, 'Ah, yes, Miss McKenzie. You join us today, I hear. Welcome, my dear. Welcome.'

He was an elderly man with white hair and a lined face, but his body was straight, not stooped, and his brown eyes were bright and twinkling. Molly found herself liking him straight away. 'Thank you, Mr Newton,' she said, feeling the tutor could become a friend.

'You've met Angeline earlier and this is Oliver. Stand up and say hello to Miss McKenzie, Oliver.'

Molly noticed that the boy obeyed him instantly and although his voice was a little sullen, he said, 'Hello, Miss McKenzie.'

Oliver was so like his father it was as if she was seeing the doctor at that age. The same black wavy hair, the same grey eyes and cleft in the chin, but there was something in the child's eyes that wasn't in the father's, a deep, dark emotion that was disturbing. Keeping her voice even and cool, she said, 'Hello, Oliver.'

'And what's the lesson today, Mr Newton?'

She glanced at the doctor as he spoke, wondering if he realized that his voice was too jovial.

'Why don't you tell your father what we've been doing, Oliver, and I can see how much you've learned,' Mr Newton said quietly, his manner kindly.

Oliver looked at the tutor and then turned towards his father but it was noticeable that he kept his eyes to the floor as he said, 'We've been looking at volcanoes, what causes them and where some of the major ones have occurred like Mexico and Italy and Japan.' His voice was flat, devoid of expression.

'Very interesting, I'm sure.'

'Oliver particularly liked the name of the one called Krakatoa in Sumatra,' Mr Newton put in encouragingly. 'He said it even sounds like a volcano, didn't you, Oliver?'

The boy nodded, still without glancing up.

Molly saw the two men look at each other and the slight shrug the doctor gave before he said, 'Well, we'll leave you to it,' and again his voice was too hearty.

Once outside again in the hall, John raked back his hair from his brow. 'I'm sorry,' he said quietly, wondering if she was already regretting taking the position of housekeeper.

Blue eyes looked straight into his. 'Why are you sorry?'

'For – for Oliver's behaviour.' She had taken him aback and he felt at a disadvantage without knowing why.

'Your son was perfectly civil.'

'Yes, but not' – he couldn't find the word he wanted and finished somewhat lamely – 'friendly.'

'Perhaps not, but after what you have told me, maybe that is to be expected? It must be difficult for both Oliver and his sister to accept the fact that another woman has been brought in to run the house, something their mother did very well, by all accounts. Children rarely have the veneer we adults have to cover their true feelings.'

He stared at her. Had he just been told off? It felt like it. She was certainly very direct and outspoken, which was not a quality he expected or particularly liked in women, he was discovering. Most ladies of his acquaintance were more reserved and self-effacing. Stiffly now, he said, 'I'm glad you were not offended.'

'Not at all.' But *she* had offended *him,* she thought. She could see it in his face. But standing there, in that room just now, she had felt sorry for his son, an emotion she hadn't expected to feel if she was honest. Dr Heath had told her quite openly that he'd had little to do with either of his children and that his wife had monopolized their affections when she had been alive, but she had been dead for over a year. Wasn't it time he tried to get to know them? But perhaps he had, she told herself in the next instant. Perhaps he had tried but hadn't known how to reach them? She was being too quick to judge here, but in spite of his defiance there had been something pathetic in that little figure standing in front of his father.

Her voice soft now, she said, 'Thank you for being concerned but please don't worry yourself on my account, Dr Heath. I'm sure Oliver and Angeline and myself will get on perfectly well, given time.'

The gentleness and obvious sincerity in her voice had taken the wind completely out of his sails and now he chided himself for his churlish thoughts. She had merely been solicitous regarding Oliver's feelings, and wasn't that exactly what he had hoped for when he had made the decision to employ her over the other applicants? He had felt she would be understanding where the children were concerned, as well as being strong-minded enough to bring order and calm to his house again.

What was the matter with him anyway? he asked himself; he wasn't usually touchy. But he was tired, that's what it was. It had been a long day and it wasn't over yet. He still had the early evening surgery to get through and he was finding it difficult to put the dire circumstances of Art Shawe and his eight surviving children out of his mind. It was a hell of a world at times.

He reached for the pocket watch in his waistcoat and after glancing at it, said apologetically, 'I must leave for the surgery, Miss McKenzie, and no doubt you are tired after your journey. Please feel free to rest before dinner and start your duties properly tomorrow. The children have their tea in the breakfast room once Mr Newton has left and I usually dine alone at eight o'clock, but now you are here I would be pleased if you would join me? It would be an opportune time to discuss any matters you need to bring to my attention and talk over the events of the day.'

She stared at him. Did housekeepers usually dine with their employers? She wouldn't have thought so but she couldn't very well refuse. Perhaps it was because she had led him to believe she was a gentlewoman and would expect such treatment? 'Thank you,' she said politely.

He nodded at her before turning and walking towards the study. She stood for a moment and then made her way to the morning room. She didn't feel tired and she certainly wasn't going to rest with all she needed to familiarize herself with.

Once in the room she shut the door and glanced about her. It was very much a female environment. The stamp of his wife was clear. Heavy pink drapes hung at the window and the thick carpet was a shade deeper. Two small chairs and a chaise longue upholstered in pale green velvet, along with an ornate and expensive-looking writing desk and a figured and carved walnut scroll-top chest-on-chest, took up much of the space, and the fire burning in the tiled fireplace added to the oppressive feel of the room. She wanted to fling the windows wide open but with the cold weather that would be silly.

A few moments later she heard the doctor leave the house. She walked to the window and watched him stride down the drive and turn left towards the village. She was still standing there lost in thought some minutes later when a carriage and horses pulled into the drive. A moment later Mr Newton left the house and climbed into the vehicle. He'd seemed a nice man and the children had been well behaved in his presence, she thought. Not that she expected they'd be the same with her initially, if Angeline's attitude in the kitchen had been anything to go by. There would be confrontations ahead.

The snow was turning the grounds into a winter wonderland and it occurred to her how cossetted the wealthy were. Weather like this always made life so much harder for the working class. The winter months at the fish factory had been a trial. She had been frozen to the marrow at work and then once back in the dismal bedroom at Dockwray Square she'd lain awake for hours, shivering and shaking with cold. Even buying extra blankets had made little difference; the very bricks and mortar of the house had seemed to ooze a raw chill which penetrated any number of coverings.

She turned and surveyed the room again. Now the heat didn't seem unwelcome. She was fortunate to be living here, she reminded herself. Of course there would be lots to learn and almost certainly some battles with the doctor's children, but she would persevere and make a success of things. Failure was not an option.

She walked across to the writing desk and sat down. Opening the book the doctor had left, she looked at the small flowery handwriting of his late wife. If Mrs Heath had been able to run this establishment, then so could she. It was merely a matter of taking it a day at a time and keeping her wits about her.

When she left the room some time later she felt she had a good idea of the incomings and outgoings of the household, which was helpful. The little ledger would no doubt be invaluable in the days ahead as she settled into her new role. As she crossed the hall intending to go to her room, Oliver and Angeline emerged from the breakfast room after having their tea, Lotty following in their wake.

The maid was clearly trying to reason with the children, her manner distraught. 'You know it's time for bed, Master Oliver, and there's hot water in the washstand for you. It'll get cold if you don't use it now. Go on up now, there's a good lad.'

Speaking to the maid but looking at Molly, the boy said cheekily, 'I'm not tired, neither of us are, are we, Angeline?'

'Aw, please, Master Oliver—'

Molly cut into the maid's wheedling voice, her own cool and crisp. On her previous visit to the house when Lotty had briefly shown her the children's rooms, she had been taken aback by the state of them. There had been toys and clothes everywhere, and Lotty must have noticed her expression because she had said apologetically, 'I haven't had time to tidy yet today.' Now she said to both children, 'Come upstairs and show me your rooms, please.'

For a moment she thought Oliver was going to refuse

and then he said insolently, 'Well, I might as well because I'm going to play with my fort and soldiers.'

They both went ahead of her, and she said in an aside to the maid before following the children, 'I'll deal with this, Lotty. You get on with whatever you need to do.'

The children's rooms were at the far end of the landing side by side and opposite the bathroom and indoor closet. Oliver marched in front, flinging open the door to his room so that it banged on the wall. Molly followed him inside while Angeline stood on the landing watching them. The bedroom was even worse than she remembered. It looked as though the boy had purposely pulled every toy and book he possessed off the shelves and thrown them about. In this she wasn't far wrong. If she had but known it, every evening was a battle with both children determined to still be up and about when their father got home and cause as much mayhem as possible. They regularly reduced Lotty to tears and often she would still be clearing up in their bedrooms at eleven o'clock at night.

Molly looked at the chaos. 'You're not tired?' she asked Oliver coolly.

'No.' He looked past her to his sister and sniggered.

'Then I suggest you expend your energy by tidying your room and making it habitable.'

It was evident to her, as he just stared at her for a moment, that he was taken aback. He was used to Lotty pleading with him to get ready for bed, bribing him with promises of titbits from Cook once he was washed and in his pyjamas. He recovered quickly, though, saying haughtily, 'I don't tidy my room. Lotty does.'

'Not from now on.' Molly wasn't sure where the words were coming from but at her interview the doctor had told her to be firm and she intended to start as she meant to carry on. 'Lotty has more than enough to do and you are both big enough to take a pride in keeping your rooms presentable.'

He glared at her, his eyes narrowing. 'You're not my mother, you can't tell me what to do.'

'You are quite right in that I am not your mother, but wrong in that I can't tell you what to do. When your father isn't here I have the authority to do just that.'

'Well, I won't do it. You can't make me.'

'Let me put it this way, Oliver.' She was aware that she was speaking to him almost as an adult rather than a child. 'I'm going to take the key to the door and I shall lock it from the outside. Until this room is tidied and you have put everything away, you will not be allowed out. Now it's up to you whether that means you are in here for hours or days, but you are going to get very hungry and uncomfortable if it is the latter – and you strike me as an intelligent boy?'

Oliver was truly astounded. No one had ever spoken to him like this before, not even his father, but he could see she meant it. Sullenly he said, 'I hate you, you're horrible. I shall tell Papa and he will let me out.'

Over her dead body. 'No, he won't, Oliver, because

he will agree with me that you need to take responsibility for your actions. Now, once this room is as it should be we will talk again. I think it should take you an hour or so at the most so I will return at half past seven. Your father and I will be dining at eight so if you haven't finished by then I shan't check again until much later.'

She stepped back with the key in her hand, almost falling over Angeline, who had watched the proceedings with wide eyes and a slack jaw but without saying a word, and locked the door. There was quiet for a moment and then inside the room the sound of objects being thrown about and stamping feet. Turning to the little girl, she said expressionlessly, 'Let us see what condition your room is in, Angeline.'

It was fractionally better but not much. As in her brother's room, toys and books were scattered everywhere and all the clothes had been pulled out of the wardrobe into a heap. Angeline was staring up at her with big blue eyes and looked near to tears, and now Molly said gently, 'Are you going to tidy your things and put everything away like a good girl?' She received a little nod in reply. 'Then I won't need to lock your door, will I?' A little shake of the head. 'Good. I'll come back in a while but I want you to stay in here until I do.'

Oliver was now shouting and screaming and as Angeline glanced towards the dividing wall of the rooms, she said, 'He won't do it.'

'Yes, he will, Angeline.'

'He gets himself into a temper.'

'Well, if he gets himself into it he can get himself out of it, can't he.'

'He – he misses Mama.'

She wanted to put her arms round the child and hold her close but it was too soon for that. 'And I'm sure you miss your mother too but I don't think she would want you and Oliver to behave badly, do you?'

Angeline shook her head uncertainly, her brown curls bobbing. 'Oliver says that Papa doesn't care she's dead.'

Oh, dear. Angeline's bottom lip was trembling and now Molly crouched down so their heads were level. 'Grown-ups don't show their feelings,' she said softly, 'but your papa loved your mama very much and he's sad inside, Angeline.'

'Oliver says that Papa is only bothered about his work and other people, not us.'

'That's absolutely not true.'

'Oliver says Papa never wanted us in the first place.'

It seemed Oliver was in the habit of saying quite a lot, Molly thought grimly, and this little girl had to bear the brunt of her brother's resentment against his father. She looked into the sad little face, trying to find the right words. 'Your father did want you, both of you, and he always will no matter how you and Oliver behave, but when you are naughty it makes things very difficult for him and everyone else – you must see that? He loves you both – you are his children and he would do anything to make you happy – but if you don't talk to him and tell him how you feel, how can he help you? Being naughty just makes everyone upset – your papa, Lotty, Cook, everyone. And when people are upset they sometimes say the wrong things and react badly and then that makes matters worse. Everything gets in a tangle and it becomes harder and harder to sort it out.'

'Like a ball of wool? Cook was sitting knitting the other day and her wool got tangled when Oliver started throwing it about.' Angeline paused for a moment. 'I threw it about too,' she admitted solemnly.

'Just like a ball of wool.'

'I won't do that again.'

'Good. Now make a start on your room and I'll come back later to see how you've got on.' The sounds from next door weren't abating, and Molly added, 'Ignore Oliver, please. He needs to be left alone to calm down and think about what I have said.'

She left the child beginning to pick up her story books and place them on a shelf, and walked back downstairs. Making her way to the kitchen, she found Cook preparing dinner and Lotty tackling a load of dirty dishes in the scullery. She told them briefly what had occurred, adding that under no condition was Lotty to venture upstairs, something the maid appeared only too happy to agree to.

'I'll make us all a cup of tea,' Mrs McHaffie said. 'It'll be a while yet afore the master's back. He said you'll be eating with him in the dining room, Miss McKenzie?'

The cook's voice was bland but something told Molly she was surprised at this development. Molly nodded.

'Because he's so busy he thought it would be a good opportunity to discuss any household matters and any problems relating to the children from day to day.' She didn't blame the cook; she'd been surprised herself.

'Aye, I daresay,' Mrs McHaffie said impassively, wondering if the master would have suggested the same thing for the other two applicants who had come to the house. She doubted it. They'd both been a bit long in the tooth for one thing, and for another, according to Lotty who had shown them in to the master, neither of them had exactly been oil paintings. Still, it was none of her business and least said soonest mended.

Molly sat down at the kitchen table. She was suddenly exhausted. It had been quite a day, one way or the other, and she still had dinner with the doctor to get through.

John got home at half past seven and as he opened the front door he was struck with the quietness. Nine times out of ten there would be noise from the children upstairs and Lotty coming to greet him, often teary-eyed, whereupon he would be forced to lay down the law with Oliver and Angeline, which would result in more tears and tantrums. By the time he sat down for dinner he would be so worked up he barely tasted his meal.

As he took off his hat and coat Molly came down the stairs. She looked a little flushed and before he could say anything, she said, 'Could I have a word in private, Doctor?'

His heart sank. What now? She hadn't decided to leave already, had she? All the time he had been seeing his patients he had been wondering if she would find Oliver and Angeline too much to cope with. He hadn't been totally honest with her, he'd admitted to himself, about the state of war that existed between himself and particularly Oliver. 'Yes, of course,' he said briskly. 'Come into the drawing room, Miss McKenzie. I was just going to pour myself a sherry before dinner. Would you like one?'

She had never tasted alcohol in her life and was about to say no when she realized that the young lady she had presented herself as would almost certainly have partaken of sherry and wine at dinner. 'Thank you.'

In the drawing room he waved for her to be seated, and once he had handed her the glass and sat down himself, he said, 'Problems?'

'Not really, but I feel I ought to acquaint you with what's been happening whilst you have been gone. The children wouldn't get ready for bed—'

'Ah, I see.'

'So I took matters into my own hands. I don't feel it's fair for Lotty to have to try and deal with them.'

'No, quite.'

'I told them they needed to tidy their rooms before they got ready for bed. Oliver thought otherwise.'

'Ah,' he said again. 'And Angeline?'

'Angeline was perfectly compliant.'

'Was she?' he asked in surprise.

'I told Oliver he would remain in his bedroom until the room was satisfactory and to that end I locked the door. I gave him until now to put things straight. He hasn't. Therefore I've informed him I'll check again after dinner.'

'He's still locked in?'

'And will remain so until the room is as it should be.' She looked him straight in the eye. 'I've informed Cook and Lotty he's to have no supper for the time being. I understand they usually have milk and biscuits before they go to sleep. Angeline's having hers, of course, and is waiting for you to say goodnight to her.'

His eyes widened. 'She wants me to say goodnight?' He couldn't remember the last time he had done that amid all the incessant tears and carrying-on at this time of night.

'Of course.'

He nodded, putting down his sherry glass and standing up. 'I'll read the riot act to Oliver at the same time.'

'I can't tell you what to do with your own son, Doctor, but I would prefer you didn't. I've told him I'll go and see him after dinner and until then I think it's best he's left alone.'

His eyes widened still further. He didn't know about Oliver but he wouldn't want to go up against Miss McKenzie in a battle of wills. 'As you see fit.'

Once upstairs, he listened for a moment outside Oliver's room but there was only silence. Walking into his daughter's room, he saw Angeline sitting up in bed finishing her hot milk and biscuits, her favourite teddy bear tucked in beside her. She looked very small and sweet and he suddenly had a lump in his throat. Christabel had never let him say goodnight to the children other than in the drawing room, when Lotty would bring them down for a few moments before dinner; she'd said it only disturbed them once they were in bed. She, on the other hand, had often popped upstairs for a few minutes. When he had questioned this it had resulted in more altercations and so he had shelved the matter. He'd done that a lot, he thought suddenly. Taken the route of least resistance and buried himself in his work still more. The coward's way out.

Walking across to the bed, he said softly, 'Miss McKenzie tells me you've been a good girl, Angeline.'

Big blue eyes stared into his. 'I tidied my room.'

'So I see.'

'Oliver got upset.'

'I'm sorry to hear that.' He sat down on the side of the bed. 'But he'll be all right in the morning.'

Angeline looked doubtful, as well she might. 'Miss McKenzie said we have to tidy our own rooms from now on.'

'Well, you're not babies any more and I agree with her. It's part of growing up, taking responsibility for things, and I have to say you've made a good job of it. Your room looks very nice.'

Angeline glanced about her and nodded, her small face breaking into a smile. 'I'm going to keep my cuddly toys on one shelf and each night a different one can sleep with me and Teddy. Teddy's the boss of the toys, you see.'

'He keeps them in order, does he?'

She nodded again. 'He's the boss of all of them, the dolls too, although Matilda, the one in the green dress, quarrels with him sometimes and he has to tell her off.'

He found he was fascinated by this little person whom he had to admit he didn't know. His own daughter. Quelling the feelings of pain and regret, he said quietly, 'I think it's time to snuggle down with Teddy, don't you?'

'Will you read me a story first?'

He almost said, *But you can read yourself*, and checked himself just in time.

'Mama used to do that sometimes.'

'Did she?' Christabel had never said. He walked across to the small oak bookcase in a corner of the bedroom. 'Which book would you like?'

'The one about the naughty fairy. It's that one, with the blue cover.'

He selected the book and came and sat by her as she moved to make room for him, and as he began to read she cuddled in to his side. He found himself overwhelmed by such emotion that he had to exert all his self-control to continue reading, glancing down at the small head with its riot of brown curls. He had missed years of doing this by letting Christabel monopolize the children, he thought painfully, and controlling when he saw them. True, he had been building up relationships in the community with the people round about who had been very wary of the new 'upper-crust' doctor, as one of his patients had put it, but he could still have had times like this. But he hadn't. And it was his fault more than

Christabel's; he had to face that, and the fact that he couldn't get the lost years back.

Angeline was half-asleep by the end of the story and as he settled her down, kissing her and his heart being wrenched yet again as a pair of small arms went round his neck, he vowed things would be different from now on. And somehow he would get through to Oliver. He just had no idea how.

Chapter Fifteen

As John walked down the stairs after leaving his daughter's room, he saw Lotty hovering in the hall and realized it was close to half past eight. 'I'm sorry,' he said quickly, 'I've delayed dinner, haven't I. Tell Cook we'll go through to the dining room now.'

'Yes, sir.' Lotty sped back to the kitchen to tell Mrs McHaffie that the master had been upstairs with Miss Angeline all that time and there had been no shouting and carry-on, but wondrous though that was, Cook told her she was more concerned with dishing up the dinner before it was completely frazzled.

John popped his head in the drawing room where Molly was sitting in front of the fire, her sandy-blonde hair catching the light. She really was a beautiful young woman, he thought, and Angeline at least seemed to have taken to her. Oliver, he feared, was a different kettle of fish. 'Shall we go through to the dining room?' he said as she looked up, and as she rose to her feet he found he was feeling ridiculously bashful, as though he was a young schoolboy wet behind the ears rather than a grown man of thirty-eight with a wealth of experience behind him.

If he had but known it, Molly was feeling much worse. She hadn't bargained on eating with her employer, she'd told herself while he had been upstairs with his daughter, and as time had gone on she'd become more and more nervous. As they walked into the dining room which Lotty had set for two and she glanced at the silver cutlery and fine crystal, she thanked Ruth for ever suggesting the elocution lessons with an old spinster gentlewoman who had lived in a decaying, once grand house in the centre of North Shields. Miss Gray's three-storey house had been one of faded splendour, the sofas and curtains moth-eaten and the carpets threadbare, but she had regaled them with stories of when she was young and of the fine dinners and parties her parents used to have once upon a time. As part of their lessons she had taken a delight in showing them the correct knives and forks to use for a meal of several courses, illustrating a place setting which a well-to-do family would have along with the different wine glasses and so on. They had both felt sorry for the old lady who lived in the past most of the time and had humoured her, although they'd remarked to each other that it was somewhat useless information – for when would they ever be in such exalted company? And in fact the doctor's table wasn't so elaborate as Miss Gray's, but at least Molly knew which was the soup spoon and the fish knife and so on.

She could do this, she told herself as the doctor pulled out her chair and she seated herself. And the glass of sherry she had sipped while he had been upstairs with Angeline had helped, giving her a warm glow inside that was quite pleasant.

He sat down opposite her at the table for a moment and then sprang up again, saying, 'Oh, I'm sorry, let me pour you a glass of wine.'

She hesitated and then said, 'Could I have water instead?' She had noticed a water jug next to the wine.

'Why not both?' he said jovially.

'Just water, please.' She wanted to be fully in control of herself when she went to see Oliver after dinner, and the sherry had already made her feel a little light-headed.

'Just water it is.' He poured her a glass and after taking his seat again, said quietly, the jovial tone gone, 'You're quite a miracle worker, Miss McKenzie.'

She blinked. 'I am?'

'Angeline was like a different child.'

Her cheeks turning pink, she said with a smile, 'She's a sweet little girl.'

He had poured himself a large glass of wine and now took several gulps before replying. 'Not always. Believe me, not always, although I fear my son has had a hand in that.'

Lotty chose that moment to enter the room with a tureen of soup and once she had served them and departed, they ate in silence for a few moments. Molly found she was hungry in spite of her nerves and the vegetable soup was delicious. Mrs McHaffie was certainly a good cook.

'I trust you've settled in?'

'Yes, I think so, thank you. The room is very nice.'

He had gone into town and bought the new bed coverings and curtains and rug himself after he had inspected the room that was to be hers. What had been there before had been serviceable but that was all. He would have liked to have offered her one of the bedrooms in the main house but had recognized that would be inappropriate. The fact that Miss McKenzie was so young and comely might cause a bit of gossip anyway and he hadn't wanted to add fuel to the flames.

They continued to talk generally as the dinner progressed, the fish course, the main course and the pudding all delicious. When Lotty came in to remove their empty dishes at the end of the meal, John said, 'Would you care to have coffee in the drawing room, Miss McKenzie?'

'No, thank you. If you don't mind, I'd like to go and check on Oliver.'

'Of course. Shall I come with you?'

She hesitated; she could hardly refuse.

He clearly sensed how she felt, however, because in the next breath he said, 'Or perhaps better you carry through yourself?'

'I think that would be best.'

She left him finishing his second glass of wine in the dining room and once in the hall stood composing herself for a moment or two, wondering what she would find when she unlocked Oliver's door. All was quiet when she reached the landing, the thick carpet masking her footsteps as she reached his room. Taking a deep breath, she opened the door. The faint glow from the dying embers of the fire in the grate and the flickering flame in the oil lamp at the far side of the room on a small table showed the room to be tidy and neat. His toys had been put away, books replaced in the bookcase and the small heap of clothes that had been strewn in the middle of the floor must be in the wardrobe.

A small mound was curled under the bedclothes, and thinking he must be asleep she walked across to the oil lamp, pulled up the glass chimney and put out the light. It was then a small voice said, 'Are you going to leave the door unlocked?'

She moved closer to the bed. 'Of course, Oliver, and thank you for tidying your room. It looks very nice.'

A sound like a 'huh' came from beneath the bedclothes and biting back a smile, she said, 'Goodnight, sweet dreams.'

'I never have sweet dreams.'

'No?' She had been about to walk to the door but now she paused. 'Not ever?'

'Well, sometimes, but I have horrible ones too since – since Mama died.'

'I'm sorry to hear that. Have you told your father about them?'

'No.' It was sharp, aggressive.

'Why not?'

'He wouldn't care.'

'I don't think that's true,' she said gently. 'I think he would be very concerned.'

The 'huh' came again, louder.

'What about Mr Newton, then?'

'No. Just Angeline.'

'Oliver, whatever you may think, your father does love you very much, I know that. He would want to help.'

There was silence.

'Won't you talk to him about it?'

The silence stretched and lengthened, and after a few moments, Molly said softly, 'At least think about it, all right? I'll see you in the morning.'

She left the room quietly and shut the door behind her, leaving it unlocked with the key on the inside. In the hall she found the doctor waiting for her, standing in the open doorway of the drawing room. As she approached, he said, 'How was he?' and turned, indicating for her to follow him into the room, whereupon he shut the door. 'Sit down for a minute,' he said when she continued to stand. 'Tell me.'

So she told him, starting with the fact that the room had been tidied and Oliver had been lying quietly in his bed, and finishing with what the child had confided about his dreams.

'Nightmares? He has nightmares?'

'That is what he said.'

She watched the doctor shake his head. 'I didn't know.'

She would imagine there was a lot he didn't know about both his children. 'He told me he's only mentioned it to Angeline, no one else.'

'He told you.'

'Yes, he told me.'

'And you have only been in the house for five minutes.'

An exaggeration but she knew what he meant. Softly, she said, 'Perhaps that's why it was easier for him to confide in me, a stranger.'

'My son doesn't like me, Miss McKenzie, but then you've probably gathered that much.' He stood up, walking across to the fireplace and standing with his back to her. 'And I can't reach him, I'm afraid. I confess I've made mistakes with my children. I should have been around more in the last years, given them more attention, but it's been difficult.' He turned to face her. 'And Oliver's always been such a confrontational and truculent child, at least with me.'

Molly stared at him. Like he said, she'd only been in the house five minutes so should she say what she thought or wait until she had got to know him better? To her mind, it sounded almost as though he was making excuses and holding his son wholly responsible for their lack of relationship, but he was the adult here.

'What?' His grey eyes had narrowed.

'I think Oliver is a troubled little boy.'

'He's certainly a disruptive and aggressive one.'

He wasn't *hearing* her. She shook her head. 'Angeline told me that Oliver thinks you don't want him and Angeline around, that you never have. If he has grown up believing that, it's bound to have an effect on his well-being.'

'And that's an excuse for his atrocious behaviour?'

She had touched a nerve, she could hear it in his defensive tone. 'No, but it's a reason for it.'

His shoulders went back and now his grey eyes glinted like polished granite. 'When my son is creating havoc and encouraging his sister to do the same, of course I discipline him. It doesn't mean I don't love him.'

'But does *he* know that? Have you told him?'

John was holding on to his temper by the skin of his teeth. 'Not when he's behaving badly, no.'

'And at other times?'

There were no other times, he thought angrily. Didn't she understand that? The boy had been difficult enough before his mother had died but since then he had been impossible. If a child is raging at you and throwing his weight about, the last thing you should do is to appear weak. He took a deep breath, his voice icy when he said, 'Miss McKenzie, I appreciate your concern but I think I know my son better than you do and I shall deal with him as I see fit.'

'Of course.' She inclined her head, her voice equally icy as she said, 'May I be dismissed now?'

He didn't trust himself to speak and as he nodded she swept from the room with more dignity than Christabel had ever displayed after one of their arguments.

Blasted woman. He ground his teeth, feeling he could have cheerfully throttled her. How dared she criticize him in that way? What did she know of him and his life or what he had put up with in this house? Christabel had made him feel like an unwelcome guest when she had been alive and the children had been firmly kept out of his way as though he was the Devil himself. Oliver, his son, had been a surly toddler and had grown into an even surlier young boy. He was like Christabel's father, that was the truth of it. John had never been able to stand Edgar Armstrong and the man hadn't liked him either when he'd been alive. He remembered at Edgar's funeral how, when he had refused to give an address as Christabel had wanted, she had railed at him, telling him he'd always been envious of her father and that he would never be a patch on the man he'd been. And that had been half the problem in their marriage – she was still Daddy's little girl. She should never have left their grand London house and become a married woman; she would have been content there for the rest of her life, being petted and spoiled by both her parents as though she was still five years old.

He drained the last of his coffee and then walked across to the drinks cabinet and poured himself a good slug of brandy, tossing it back in two gulps before pouring another. To hell with all women, he thought bitterly. He had imagined he was doing the right thing in hiring a housekeeper but now he wished he'd never bothered. And then he remembered Angeline's little face and how she had snuggled in to his side when he had read her the story, and groaned softly.

Flinging himself into an armchair in front of the fire, he stared morosely into the flames. He had thought he had engaged a demure young woman who would bring a semblance of peace to his home, but now he felt as though he had caught a tiger by the tail, and a very vocal tiger at that. One who certainly had no misgivings in pointing out his apparent shortcomings. And this was only the first day she'd been here. He groaned again. What had he done? What *had* he done?

Molly was sitting on her bed, asking herself the same question. She shouldn't have jumped at the first job she was offered; she should have kept on looking for something – *anything* – other than here. The way he had glared at her as she had left him, she wouldn't be surprised if he dismissed her in the morning anyway. And she shouldn't have spoken to him the way she had when she'd asked if she could leave the room, sarcastic and uppity, but he had made her so *angry*.

She put her hands to her hot cheeks and then jumped up and began to pace the small room. She had heard Mrs McHaffie and Lotty in the kitchen when she had passed the door but she hadn't gone in, fearing she might say something she would regret later. She had only been trying to help, she told herself, anger still uppermost, but he had been so pig-headed. And he called *Oliver* confrontational and aggressive. Well, all she could say was, like father like son.

She plumped down on the bed again, and as her anger began to dissipate and she went over what had been said, she began to regret being quite so outspoken. But she *had* been trying to help, she reiterated again, although he might not have seen it that way. Something had to break the cycle of harsh words and enmity between father and son. Angeline was a different kettle of fish, softer, gentler, but she was an unhappy little soul too.

But you were employed as a housekeeper, not as some kind of mediator between the warring factions in the house, and you should have kept out of it. She answered the accusing voice in her head sharply: Well, if that was what the doctor expected when he had given her the position, he had chosen the wrong person. Of course Oliver was no angel – what child was? – but the doctor didn't need to be so inflexible, did he? He had said he'd deal with the boy as he saw fit, but to her mind he had been doing precisely that for the last twelve months and it hadn't exactly yielded any results, had it? Not good ones, at least. That little boy was terribly unhappy, and no wonder with such a cold, unfeeling father. And him a doctor! Doctors were supposed to be kind and compassionate, weren't they? It was a beggar's muddle, all right, as the twins would have said, but it was the children who were suffering and they needed to be her prime concern.

This last thought caused more regrets that she had spoken so frankly to the doctor. The children needed her and if he told her to pack her bags tomorrow and leave she would have to go. She should have held her tongue.

After a while she stood up and put on her coat and hat to venture outside to the privy. She'd found this to be spotlessly clean and Lotty had told her, with some pride, that she put fresh ashes down the hole every day without fail and that a man from the village came to the house and cleared it once a week.

It was bitterly cold as she left the warmth of the house. The snow was still falling and it was already several inches deep, coating everything in a pure mantle of glistening white. Molly stood still for a moment, gazing up at the thousands of starry flakes and breathing in the clear air that made her nose tingle.

'Let things be all right in the morning,' she murmured. Considering that the occupants of the house were virtual strangers she didn't know why she felt such a burden for the children, but she did. Perhaps it was because she knew what it was like to feel wretched and helpless in a world of adults who didn't seem to care? She wanted to help Oliver and his sister and she would try to be tactful with the doctor, she promised. She would at least try.

Chapter Sixteen

John was as nervous as a kitten when he came down to breakfast the following morning. He had hardly slept, lying awake till after four in the morning with a cartload of regrets and recriminations pounding through his head until he felt as though it would burst open. He should never have been so antagonistic with Miss McKenzie, he had told himself some time after one o'clock when his temper had subsided and pangs of conscience had begun to make themselves felt. He wasn't that way normally with folk but there was something about her that made him feel . . . He couldn't find a word to describe it and after a while gave up trying. But he didn't want her to leave, he knew that much. Only because of the children, he told himself firmly. Of course only that. She had already worked wonders with Angeline and seemed to have some influence over Oliver.

He had got out of bed at that point and gone to sit in an armchair by the window, watching the snow fall. There had been an element of truth in what he saw as her accusations against him regarding the boy. More than an element, to be honest, but he was damned if he knew how to put things right. It would be giving Oliver the whip hand if he appeared weak, but Miss McKenzie's question about him telling his son he loved him had cut deep. He couldn't ever remember doing that since the child had been a babe in arms, and even then Christabel used to snatch Oliver away as though the mere touch of his father would contaminate him. This wasn't his fault, he told himself wretchedly, none of it. If she knew what he'd had to put up with.

In the next instant he had made a sound of deep irritation in his throat. He had always despised self-pity – it was one of the least attractive qualities a man or woman could have – and here was he practically drowning in it.

He had continued to sit in the quiet of the night, the house sleeping around him as he had faced the fact that his life was a damn mess. He hadn't even known that his own child, his firstborn, had been tormented by nightmares for umpteen months. What sort of a father was he? The answer to that question had brought his mouth into a grim line. He had been so concerned with building up the practice and ingratiating himself with the locals that he hadn't noticed or cared about the needs of his own flesh and blood. And so the mental self-flagellation had gone on.

He had eventually gone back to bed and fallen asleep but now, as he walked into the dining room, his head was aching and his eyes felt gritty. Was he going to have to eat humble pie and try to persuade Miss McKenzie to stay? She had looked ready to fell him on the spot when she had exited the drawing room so magnificently angry the night before.

Breakfast was not normally a meal he looked forward to. Usually, Oliver and Angeline had to be called by Lotty several times before they deigned to make an appearance, and then once they were seated, spoonfuls of porridge inevitably found their way over the floor, bread and butter would end up stuck to the table surface and their boiled eggs would be splattered down their fronts. Lotty would run around like a scalded cat clearing up after them, and he would be so thoroughly irritated that he would disappear to his study leaving his breakfast unfinished.

This morning, as he walked into the room he found his two children sitting eating quietly opposite Miss McKenzie, who looked up and smiled, saying primly, 'Good morning, Doctor. Oliver, Angeline, say good morning to your papa.'

Angeline's greeting was more enthusiastic than his son's, which was a mumble, but he noticed with some amazement that the table and floor around his offspring were devoid of spills and their clothes were clean. Lotty had scurried off to fetch his usual plate of bacon, eggs and sausages from the kitchen and returned in a trice, and once he had sat down he looked fully at his housekeeper. She appeared as fresh and bright as he was jaded and exhausted. Expressionlessly, he said, 'I trust you slept well, Miss McKenzie?'

'Very well, thank you, Doctor,' Molly lied sweetly. She had lain awake for hours tossing and turning and risen long before it was light, washing and dressing and then sitting on her bed until she heard sounds from the kitchen meaning the cook and Lotty were up. She had gone along and had a cup of tea with them, approved Mrs McHaffie's plans for lunch and dinner and then told Lotty that she would go and wake the children. Lotty's round face had been comical in its gratitude.

'I'd better warn you, miss, that they don't like getting up. Five or six times I have to tell 'em – I'm up and down them stairs like a fiddler's elbow. I lay their clothes out on a chair before I draw the curtains and put their slippers by the bed and—'

'I shall do things a little differently from now on, Lotty. At eight and ten years old they are quite capable of choosing their own clothes and getting dressed before they make their beds.'

'Make their beds, miss? I – I see to all that.'

'You have enough to do with laying and lighting the fires and so on. I would like to take them each a mug of hot chocolate first thing, though.'

'Yes, miss.'

'It's nice and cheery on a cold winter's morning, isn't it. What time is breakfast?'

Lotty darted a glance at Mrs McHaffie before she said, 'Eight o'clock but I usually start to wake 'em round half six because they take so long.'

'I'll go up at seven. That will give them plenty of time

to have the hot chocolate and get washed and dressed before they make their beds.'

Lotty looked at her doubtfully. 'Right you are, miss.'

At seven o'clock she had gone into Oliver's room first. After placing the hot chocolate on the small table next to the bed which had a couple of books on it, she gently shook the child's shoulder. He was lying fast asleep on his back, one arm flung over his head, and in repose he looked so much like his father that she caught her breath. 'Time to start the day,' she said softly, before walking across and lighting the oil lamp and then opening the curtains. Although it was still dark outside, the white light from the snow provided its own illumination.

He stirred, muttering, 'Don't wanna. Go away, Lotty.'

'It's Miss McKenzie, Oliver, and I've brought you a mug of hot chocolate to drink before you have to get out of bed. Once you've finished it you will wash and dress yourself and then make your bed before you come down to breakfast at eight o'clock.'

He was wide awake now, staring at her and then glancing at the mug. 'Hot chocolate?'

'That's right. Would you like me to move the oil lamp closer so that you can read while you drink?'

That he was completely nonplussed was abundantly clear. He nodded in a bemused fashion, sitting up and watching her for a moment before he said, 'Where's Lotty?'

'Lotty is downstairs laying and lighting the fires and she will no longer wake you in the morning – I will – and as you are a big boy of ten years old you may choose what you wish to wear from your wardrobe. After you have washed and dressed and made your bed—'

He interrupted her, his voice more bewildered than hostile: 'Lotty makes our beds.'

'Not any more, Oliver. As I said, you're a big boy. Now, let's plump up those pillows behind your back so you are comfortable. What book are you reading?' She picked up the top one from the bedside table. 'The Boy's Book of Adventures. That looks interesting.'

After a moment, he said, 'I want to be an explorer when I grow up.'

'An explorer? How exciting.'

He nodded, his voice taking on an eager note when he said, 'Did you know that two explorers are having an argument about who reached the North Pole first? One is called Cook and the other is Commander Peary. Cook says he did it last year but Peary says he didn't and he was the first when he reached the Pole in April this year. Mr Newton says he believes the commander and so do I.' He paused. 'The Royal Geographical Association asked the commander to address them last month, not Cook, and Mr Newton says that's because they don't believe Cook either.'

'I'm sure you and Mr Newton are right.'

He nodded again. 'I think so but it's a pretty bad show to tell a lie like that, isn't it? I mean, it's not a little lie.'

This conversation was beginning to prick her conscience when she thought about the lies she had told recently, but she managed to say matter-of-factly, 'I'm sure the truth will out, Oliver, and I think you would make a very good explorer when you are older.'

He smiled at her, the first smile she had seen, and the difference it made to the little face was amazing. 'That's what Mr Newton says. He thinks I have the ability to be anything I want to be.'

She felt a pang of sadness that it was the tutor and not the boy's father who was encouraging him and listening to him. But at least Oliver had a Mr Newton in his life, she thought in the next moment. That was something. She handed him the book as she said, 'Drink your hot chocolate while you read but don't be too long. I shall expect you downstairs for breakfast at eight sharp and your bed made, do you understand?'

After she had gone into Angeline's room and repeated the procedure, she had retraced her footsteps to the kitchen and questioned the cook and the maid about various aspects concerning the household. It appeared the breakfast room was used solely as a schoolroom and referred to as such, and Mr Newton arrived at the house at nine o'clock in the morning and left at four o'clock most days. 'The bairns have their lunch with him in the schoolroom in the winter,' Mrs McHaffie informed her, 'but in the summer they often eat outside so the bairns can run around and let off some steam. Mr Newton lives with his married daughter in Lynemouth and their coachman brings him every morning and fetches him at night.' She had lowered her voice as though the doctor or the tutor was in the room when she'd added, 'He's a friend of the master and I think he took on the bairns as a favour to him 'cause he don't need the money. Family's rolling in it. But the bairns had a couple of governesses before and that didn't work out. Ran rings round 'em, they did. Cor, the do's we had. Do you remember, Lotty?'

Lotty nodded, rolling her eyes.

'And the mistress blamed the governesses, but then she would. The bairns could do no wrong in her eyes. Ran riot, they did, but when Mr Newton arrived it all changed from the first day. Got a way with them, he has, especially Master Oliver.'

'He seems a nice man.'

'Oh, aye, he is. Proper gentleman. Like the master.'

Molly came out of her reflections of the morning so far and looked at the 'master' now. 'I thought I would go into the village today and acquaint myself with the local shops and so on, if that is all right?'

John felt a huge sense of relief. She wasn't going to throw in the towel after last night, then. 'Of course. I can take you when I go to the surgery at ten o'clock and bring you back when I finish? It's stopped snowing for the moment but the sky looks full of it and it's pretty deep out there. I can clear the drive and once we're on the road it should be all right for the horse and trap.'

'I don't want to inconvenience you, Doctor. I'm quite able to walk.' He hadn't used the horse and trap last night, so she doubted he usually did when he went into the village to his surgery. Lotty had told her that the horse, Dobbin, was an old boy and when the doctor didn't need him for house calls he usually spent most of the time in his stable next to the orchard. He had a paddock where he gambolled in the summer months. 'The bairns love him,' Lotty had added. 'They like animals but the mistress wouldn't let them have a dog or a cat because she said the fur made her sneeze and cough, but I think it was more that she couldn't stand any kind of animals. She said they were all dirty and spread diseases.'

'It's no inconvenience,' John said now. He found he was thoroughly enjoying his breakfast for once. 'Dobbin could do with stretching his legs.' This wasn't true. He would probably have to persuade the old chap out of his stable because the horse didn't like the snow.

Once the children had finished their breakfast, Molly told them to go and wash their hands and then wait in the schoolroom for Mr Newton. They slid off their chairs without protest and disappeared out of the room, and again John found himself staring at his housekeeper. How the dickens did she do that?

Seizing the opportunity now they were alone, he said quietly, 'I feel I need to apologize for my attitude last night, Miss McKenzie. I am not usually so boorish.' He was about to follow this with an excuse and say he'd been tired but instead said, 'To be absolutely truthful, I suppose I didn't like being taken to task.'

Molly could feel the colour in her cheeks. 'I spoke out of turn, Dr Heath. As you pointed out, I've only been here five minutes.'

'Perhaps, but you were quite right in what you said.' He sighed, leaning back in his chair.

He had left his suit jacket in his bedroom and only had a waistcoat on over his crisp white shirt. The male magnetism she'd been aware of before was accentuated this morning and the pink in her cheeks deepened. He was a disturbing man to be around, she thought ruefully.

'What was it the Jesuits said? "Give me a child until he is seven and I have him for life"? Well, Christabel had Oliver and Angeline at least that long, and she effectively cut me out of their upbringing and I let it happen. I've no one but myself to blame. I have no relationship with them and it's too late to start now.'

'It's never too late.' She leaned towards him, her deep blue eyes holding his as she said earnestly, 'Never, believe me. Children are far more forgiving than you would think.'

'Angeline, maybe,' he said slowly, wondering how he could have regretted engaging Molly, 'but not my son. He doesn't like me and – and this is an awful thing for a father to say, I know – I don't like him. I love him – I would cheerfully give my life for both of them – but Oliver and I are like oil and water.'

'You've just said you don't know him so how can you say you don't like him? He's shown one side to you, his bad side, admittedly, but we're all multifaceted, Dr Heath. He's a very bright and intelligent child and although his mother's influence has directed him in a certain way towards you—' She stopped abruptly, realizing she was in danger of speaking too frankly again.

'Yes?' The skin at the corners of his eyes crinkled for a moment as he smiled. 'Don't hold back, Miss McKenzie. I promise I won't take umbrage.'

Her cheeks pink again, she said, 'I was going to say that although Mrs Heath's influence was strong you didn't, and haven't, done anything to make him change his mind.'

Yes, definitely he'd caught a tiger by the tail but this morning it didn't seem so disastrous. 'What do you suggest?' he asked drily.

'Did you know he wants to be an explorer when he grows up, that he's interested in the North Pole and so on?'

'No, I didn't.'

'Mr Newton does. Perhaps you could have a word with him in private and find out more about Oliver's interests? You could engage in conversation with him about such things, maybe buy him books on subjects he particularly likes?'

'Try and bribe him for affection?' he said disapprovingly.

'Not at all. It's surely normal for a parent to take an interest in their child's likes and dislikes?'

'I suppose so.'

'Apparently the children would very much like a pet of their own, a cat or a dog, something of that nature.'

'How have you gathered so much information in such a short time?' he asked, the expression on his face so like Oliver's when she had presented the child with the mug of hot chocolate that Molly could have smiled. Instead she said simply, 'I asked.'

* * *

It was seven o'clock that evening. Molly had gone into the village and had a good look round, getting her bearings, and then walked home. She had persuaded the doctor not to force poor Dobbin out of his warm stable before he had to do his rounds later, and they had walked into the village together, and on a couple of occasions when the ground had been treacherous with packed snow he had taken her arm to assist her. Both times she had felt the contact down to her toes and been painfully aware of the height and breadth of him at the side of her. She had been relieved when he had left her outside the newly built Co-op shop and gone to his surgery, a small single-storey cottage on the main street.

He had told her a little about the origins of the village as they had walked. Apparently, Ellington was an old Saxon settlement and the name meant 'Ella's River Town', Ella being a Saxon leader. Lin was a Celtic word for river and a tun was a Saxon dwelling place, he had told her gravely. It had been an old farming community until the advent of coal and the sinking of the Linton colliery fifteen years before, and the Ashington Coal Company owned and farmed much of the land.

'It's been good for the locals on the whole,' he said as they passed the Plough Inn. 'The dairy just outside the village gives employment to local women and to local lads who deliver bottled milk by horse and cart to households in the mining villages – and they're only going to expand as Ellington Colliery gets going – but overall, life is hard. The places the farm labourers and miners are forced to live in are poor and mortality is high for many reasons.'

Molly thought of the hamlet and nodded. The coal owners and gentry regarded their workers as expendable, she knew that well enough, and it was always the women and children who were least thought of.

'There's a school here but education is still considered relatively unimportant when able-bodied lads and lassies are needed to bring money into the home, I'm afraid. Until change happens from the top down, I fear child labour will be ever present.'

'I think few of the propertied classes are prepared to consider change. They are too comfortable with things as they are which is why the People's Budget was thrown out by the House of Lords.'

He had stopped in his tracks, staring at her. 'You follow the political situation, Miss McKenzie?'

She didn't see why he was so surprised, in fact she found it insulting, and her voice reflected this when she said coolly, 'Yes, I do. Social reform is desperately needed in our so-called civilized country but it will be fought against tooth and nail by the privileged few.'

He eyed her quizzically. 'You're not a suffragette, are you?'

'Would it be so terrible if I was?'

'No, not at all, in fact I thoroughly agree with women being given the vote. I was asking because I'm interested.'

Telling herself not to be so prickly, she moderated her tone when she said, 'If you are asking if I agree with the cause and find it abhorrent that women like Mrs Pankhurst have been incarcerated in Holloway simply for marching for their beliefs, and lately even been force-fed in prison, then yes, I suppose you could call me a suffragette, but I've never joined a rally or anything like that.'

'Why not?'

Because I've been too busy working and keeping myself fed and clothed. 'It's never been possible.'

'Your father would have disapproved?' he asked gently.

Not for the first time in the last twenty-four hours she found herself bitterly regretting that she hadn't told the truth at her interview but it was too late now. Anyway, she wouldn't have been offered the position of house-keeper if she had. A girl from the fish factories, the lowest of the low, being in charge of his household and his children? She would have been shown the door so fast it would have made her head whirl.

She shrugged. 'Most men do.'

They had begun walking again and after a moment he said, 'I would like to say you are mistaken but in all honesty I cannot.'

She was brought out of her reverie about the events of the morning and her conversation with the doctor by Lotty popping her head round the morning-room door. 'It's nearly seven o'clock, miss, and you said you wanted to take milk and biscuits up to the bairns then?'

Molly put aside the ledger she'd been looking at before her mind had wandered. 'Thank you, Lotty.'

Once Mr Newton had left earlier that afternoon and after Oliver and Angeline had finished their tea, she'd taken them into the garden and the three of them had built a snowman, the lights from the house windows illuminating their effort. It was a fine snowman, complete with hat and scarf. By the time they'd re-entered the house they'd all been rosy-cheeked and glowing.

She'd asked Lotty to run each of the children a bath and once they were in their nightclothes she'd told them they could play nicely together for a while upstairs. Apart from the occasional sound of laughter she'd heard nothing, which she took to be a good sign.

In the kitchen, Lotty had termed the children's behaviour a miracle to the cook. 'They were as good as gold having their baths and Miss Angeline even let me wash her hair without the normal carry-on,' she said, a note of wonder in her voice. 'If Miss McKenzie weren't so bonny I'd say she was a witch, the difference she's made – I would straight.'

At seven o'clock Molly took milk and biscuits upstairs, going first into Oliver's room. She found him reading by himself in bed and the room was tidy except for the boy's fort and soldiers which were set out in intricate patterns on the floor. He saw her glance at it and said quickly, 'I didn't forget to put it away but I wanted to leave it like that for morning, if that's all right?'

Molly smiled. 'I don't see why not, the rest of your room is in order.'

'It's the battle of Rorke's Drift, you know, when the British defended the mission station against the Zulus,'

Oliver said eagerly. 'There were a hundred and fifty of us against three or four thousand of them but we won. That's pretty amazing, isn't it?'

Molly nodded. Oliver's face was so bright and animated as he spoke, she felt that she was seeing yet another side of the boy.

'The commanding officers were very clever in their strategy of defence and didn't panic,' he said earnestly. 'They arranged a defensive perimeter constructed out of mealie bags. Look there' – he pointed to the fort – 'but I've had to use socks. This perimeter incorporated the storehouse, the hospital and a stone kraal. That's an enclosure for cattle and things,' he explained very seriously. 'They knocked firing holes through the external walls and the doors were barricaded with furniture. Some soldiers still died, though, but only about seventeen, I think, and hundreds of Zulus were killed. Eleven Victoria Crosses were awarded, *eleven*, and some other decorations and honours.'

'How do you know all this?' Molly asked, fascinated by the animated little face.

'Mr Newton told us. We're covering the Anglo-Zulu war. He said the Zulus were brave too – all they had were short spears and shields made of cowhide and a few old muskets and rifles.' He paused. 'I think Mr Newton feels sorry for the Zulus,' he said with an air of bewilderment. 'He said they were only trying to protect their land from us, the invaders.'

'And you don't feel that?'

Oliver shook his head. 'If you go round killing people then you have to expect to be killed yourself,' he said with a child's logic. His tone changing, he added, and this time with a tinge of scorn, 'Angeline just doesn't understand about fighting strategy in a battle. She kept putting her soldiers where they shouldn't go and saying things like they were hungry and wanted dinner. In the end I made her bring her little dolls from her doll's house to be the Zulus, but two of their heads fell off when my soldiers attacked and she didn't want to play after that.' He grinned. 'It was funny, though.'

Ah, hence the laughter. 'I'm sure Angeline didn't think so,' Molly said drily.

'You can push the heads on again.'

'Oh, that's all right then.'

She left him reading and went into Angeline's room. The child was sitting sandwiched between her teddy bear and a stuffed toy giraffe and looked as angelic as her name. Molly gave the little girl her milk and biscuits and went downstairs. As she crossed the hall the front door opened and the doctor came in, brushing snow from his coat. 'It's coming down again,' he said, stating the obvious, as Lotty came through from the kitchen and took his hat and coat. 'And I saw a magnificent snowman standing guard outside.'

'Oliver and Angeline have named him Mr Winter,' she said solemnly.

'Very apt.' And then, as Lotty asked him if he wanted a hot drink, he shook his head. 'Miss McKenzie and I are going to have a sherry in the drawing room, thank you, Lotty,' he said as though it had previously been agreed, leaving Molly with no choice but to follow him as he walked into the room. She sat down in one of the chairs and took the sherry glass he gave her with a nod of thanks.

'Are the children still awake?' he asked as he seated himself, taking a gulp of his sherry.

For a moment it crossed her mind that they could have been a married couple, such was the ease of his manner, and, infinitely glad that he couldn't read her thoughts but flustered just the same, she said a little stiffly, 'Yes, they're reading in bed. I said I would go up when it's time for them to go to sleep.'

'I'd like to do that.' He had made up his mind that a new routine at bedtime would include him saying goodnight to his own children and settling them down; he should have done it years ago. He didn't fool himself about the reception he'd receive from Oliver but nevertheless, he intended to push ahead. All day he'd been chewing over the conversation he'd had with Miss McKenzie that morning, and had come to the conclusion that it was up to him to make any overtures of reconciliation with his son because they certainly wouldn't be forthcoming from Oliver. She had said Oliver was a troubled little boy rather than an aggressive and awkward one, and he needed to find out for himself if that was true. He had to admit the revelation about the child's nightmares had bothered him more than a little.

Molly nodded. 'As you wish.'

He had finished his sherry before she'd barely had a sip of hers and as he stood to his feet, he said, 'Wish me luck.' She didn't question what he meant because she knew.

'Underneath all that bravado he's just a boy who needs his father,' she said gently, aware that he was actually nervous.

John stared at this woman. She was so young in spite of her twenty-five years – at least, she looked it, he corrected himself – and so beautiful, but there was something about her eyes that gave the lie to the fact that she'd been sheltered and cossetted all her life. Behind the deep blue that was as clear as the sky on a cloudless summer's day there was a kind of knowledge, an intensity that he could almost imagine spoke of pain and grief and something else, something undefinable. But of course she had lost her father, he told himself, and not only that, had suddenly found herself thrown on her own resources. It must have been a terrible shock for her, a gentlewoman, to be put in such a precarious situation.

Suddenly aware that he had been holding her gaze too long, he nodded, forcing a smile as he said, 'I hope you're right, Miss McKenzie.'

Once on the landing he went first into Angeline's room, and in a repeat of the night before read to her before tucking her up in bed with her toys. This time she lifted her face for his kiss, and on the landing again he had to take a minute to compose himself and wipe his eyes. Then, steeling himself, he opened the door of his son's room. Oliver looked up from his book, his face changing and taking on the blank mask he often presented when in his father's company.

'I've come to say goodnight.'

The boy made no reply, merely staring at him with narrowed grey eyes.

He walked across to the bed and sat on the end of it, glancing down at the fort and soldiers as he said, 'That's quite an elaborate set-up you've done there – I'm intrigued. Is it a battle of some kind?'

Oliver shrugged, still making no reply.

As it always did in his son's presence, John's temper rose before he reminded himself to take it easy. Keeping his voice offhand but pleasant, he said, 'Your Uncle Lawrence and I had a fort when we were young and used to enact all kinds of battles with our soldiers. It was a fine fort with inside rooms you could get to by taking the roof off, and battlements and so forth.'

He saw a flicker of interest on his son's face. After a moment, Oliver said, 'What happened to it?'

'The fort? Well, when your uncle and I were away at boarding school our mother got rid of it, along with some other toys she considered needed to go, as she wanted to redecorate the nursery.'

'Without asking you?'

He nodded. 'I was very upset at the time.'

'What about Uncle Lawrence?'

'He didn't mind too much but he's a few years older than me.'

'How old were you?'

'About your age.'

'I wouldn't like it if you got rid of any of my toys.'

'I wouldn't dream of doing that, Oliver. They are *your* toys to do what you want with. Maybe you will want to keep them and pass them down to your own children in the future.'

Oliver stared at him as though he was trying to work something out. 'Would you have liked to have done that? With – with me?'

'Very much. You're my son and I love you. I would have enjoyed seeing you play with my toys.' He found he was holding his breath as he waited for Oliver's reaction to the words 'I love you'.

The moments stretched silently on and John could almost see the cogs whirring in his son's little head. 'Mama gave Angeline some dolls she'd had when she was a girl,' he said after another few seconds. 'She said she had saved them specially in case she had a daughter.'

Immediately, John wondered if Christabel had insinuated that he, the boy's father, hadn't cared enough to do the same; but perhaps he was being paranoid? 'Like I said, I would very much have liked to do that too but I'm afraid my mother disposed of everything, even my books, when I was away at university some years later. Your grandmama liked things just so.' In fact, he had long since realized that his mother was the type of woman who should never have had children to mess up her perfect home and interfere with the serenity she liked to create around her. She and Christabel had got on like a house on fire from day one; maybe that should have told him something about his wife?

Oliver frowned. 'That wasn't very kind, was it.'

'No, it wasn't.'

'Didn't she care about your feelings?'

He thought about lying for a moment, passing the question off and changing the subject, but instead found himself saying, 'I don't think she did, Oliver.'

'And your papa?'

His father had always been too busy to take an interest in his sons. As the thought came, it hit him like a ton of bricks that the same charge could be laid at *his* feet. 'Your uncle and I never saw much of either of our parents when we were young – the nanny and nursemaid took care of us.'

This time the silence was even longer but something told John not to break it. At the end of it, Oliver said flatly, as though he was expecting a rebuff, 'You can always play with my fort and soldiers when you want to.'

Swallowing against the lump in his throat, John said quietly, 'I would like that if you'd play with me.'

Oliver eyed him warily and John could see the child was trying to work out if he really meant it. 'All right.' He nodded, and in an offhand manner, added, 'Angeline isn't very good at war games.'

'Girls aren't,' John said solemnly. 'So, *is* this a battle of some kind?'

Oliver nodded again. 'It's the defence of Rorke's Drift.'

They spent the next few minutes discussing wars and battles, and John had to keep reminding himself that this was Oliver talking, his son who previous to this night had barely said two words to him except in anger.

Eventually he stood up and extinguished the oil lamp, saying it was time for sleep, and as the boy settled down under the covers everything in John wanted to gather up the small thin body and tell him he loved him again, but he knew it was too soon for that. Instead, he contented himself with bending and depositing a swift light kiss on the top of the black hair and then exiting the room with a 'Goodnight, son.'

It was a start, he told himself as he walked down the stairs to the drawing room where Molly was waiting. It was a start and more than he deserved.

PART FOUR

The Real Miss Molly McKenzie

1914

Chapter Seventeen

Just over four years had elapsed since Molly had arrived at Buttercup House, and they had been ones of mixed blessings. After a few weeks of her living there John had insisted they do away with the formality of 'Dr Heath' and 'Miss McKenzie' and that they address one another by their Christian names. She had found this uncomfortable at first, partly because she felt it had introduced an intimacy into their relationship, but one that merely blurred the edges. She was neither fish nor fowl, as Enid would have put it. But then would she ever feel entirely comfortable living in close proximity to John Heath? He was a man of many contradictions. Compassionate, warm and highly intelligent on one hand, and narrow-minded, reserved and stubborn on the other. She knew he thought she was too outspoken and strong-willed for a woman because he had told her so in one of their disagreements. She hadn't taken offence at the outspoken and strong-willed part – she regarded such attributes as virtues rather than shortcomings – but the qualification that because she was a woman these were unacceptable had made her furious at the time.

One of the happier results of working for John was that through her input his relationship with his children was much improved. Father and son still clashed now and again, but mainly because they were so alike. Oliver had baulked at being sent to a boarding school where he'd be away for months at a time when he turned eleven, and so on her prompting Mr Newton had recommended a good public school in Durham from where the boy could return home each weekend, an arrangement that had worked out very well. Angeline now attended a small and very select establishment for young ladies in Morpeth as a day student and was happy there. She liked coming home each night and seeing her two cats, Mops and Minty, and would play with them for hours with their toys. Unlike her bright and quick-witted brother, Angeline was no academic. Her chief interests seemed to be the latest fashions and hairstyles and spending time with her friends. Oliver had labelled his sister a flibbertigibbet, and John and Molly had to admit the boy was spot on.

Molly's savings had grown substantially over the years. Her wage was a generous one and apart from clothes and the occasional personal item she had little to spend it on. She'd opened a bank account shortly after arriving at Buttercup House and continued to put money away for the future. What this future would entail she hadn't been sure about, not until fifteen months ago when an unpleasant incident had occurred which prompted her to begin making plans.

It had happened at Angeline's eleventh birthday party. A number of guests had been invited, including Angeline's best friend, Rebecca Havelock, and her family. The Havelocks could loosely be termed neighbours, having a large estate on the edge of Longhorsley as well as a London residence. John knew them fairly well both socially and professionally. When they were in residence at the estate, which was a large amount of the year, he was often called to attend Rebecca's grandmother. The woman fancied herself an invalid, although John thought she was as fit as a flea. Nevertheless, the old lady was approaching eighty and had been thoroughly cosseted all her life, so he indulged her hypochondria. As he'd remarked to Molly, the autocratic matriarch wasn't going to change at this late stage of her life.

The October day had been an unseasonably warm one and the country had been in the grip of an Indian summer. After a fine lunch, the guests had spilled out into the grounds at the front of the house. The ladies had sat under their parasols, big hats shading their delicate complexions, and games had been organized by the men. Molly had gone along to the kitchen to thank Mrs McHaffie for the excellent food and ask Lotty to take jugs of lemonade outside for the women and children, and beer and cider for the men, and was just crossing the hall when Cuthbert Havelock, Rebecca's father, waylaid her.

'There you are. I've been looking out for you,' he'd said, his smile showing stained teeth, probably because of the amount of red wine he'd poured down his throat with the meal.

'What can I do for you, Mr Havelock?' she'd asked pleasantly, although she couldn't stand the man. He had a way of looking at her that made her skin crawl, and whenever he came to the house she tried to make herself scarce.

'Now that's an offer I've been waiting for.' He'd grabbed at her, making a clumsy attempt to kiss her, but she'd extricated herself and stepped away, saying sharply, 'Don't do that.'

He'd grabbed her again and this time she had slapped his face hard, but it hadn't seemed to deter him. He'd stood grinning at her, rubbing his cheek. 'Like to play hard to get, do you, my beauty?' he'd drawled. 'Well, that's all right, I like the chase as much as the next man.'

'I think you've had too much to drink,' she said icily, turning away, but he'd caught her arm and swung her round.

'Don't play the injured innocent – we both know what you are,' he'd said thickly. 'I'm only asking for a bit of what you give John readily enough.'

'I've no idea what you are talking about, Mr Havelock, but I suggest you go back to the others now.' She had jerked her arm free as she'd spoken, her eyes blazing.

'My, we can put on the airs and graces when we want, can't we, but you needn't keep up the pretence with me.

Everyone knows you serve old John in more ways than one, m'dear.'

The words had hit her like a blow to the solar plexus and for a moment she was unable to speak. Whether Cuthbert had taken this as compliance she didn't know, but when he had lunged at her for the third time she had pushed him so violently he'd gone sprawling backwards, landing in an undignified heap on the floor.

She had gone into the morning room, locking the door and standing with her back to it, trembling from head to foot. She had half expected him to bang on the door and try to enter but when all was quiet, she had sunk down on the chaise longue. So everyone had assumed she was John's mistress? Did John know what people were saying?

She covered her face with her hands. She would die if he knew. It was bad enough that she was attracted to him. But that was all it was, a physical attraction, she told herself in the next moment. It didn't mean anything. And she sensed he liked her in that way too but he had never said or done anything to make her think he felt anything more. It was unfortunate that he was the only man she had ever met who could make her heart beat faster even when he was at his most annoying, but she could cope with that. And thinking about it, she doubted if even Cuthbert Havelock would presume to suggest to John that she and he were lovers. John could be very much the autocrat when he wanted to be and he had a natural reserve that discouraged familiarity.

She had stayed in the morning room for some time and when she had emerged most of the guests, including the Havelocks, had left. She hadn't mentioned the incident to anyone but from that day forth she'd made herself scarce if Cuthbert called to see John, letting Lotty wait on them. Mrs McHaffie had told her that there were over twenty inside servants at Havelock Hall and more outside, and that Christmas, when the cook was a little tipsy after freely imbibing the cooking sherry, she'd confided that at least two maids had been dismissed in the past for being in the family way.

'The word is that they both blamed the master, Havelock, for their condition but he denied it, of course. The lassies got packed off to the workhouse and that was that. Same in all these grand houses, isn't it, lass. The master thinks he owns his servants body and soul. Meself, I'd never work for such as Havelock. He thinks he's special and that the good Lord Himself placed him where he is. Never mind his ancestors were the same as all the upper class – traitors, thieves and murderers, most of 'em – but they've got the money and power now and the rest of us are scum to them.'

Molly had agreed with Mrs McHaffie in principle. She didn't know about the masters in all the grand houses but she did know Cuthbert Havelock, obnoxious, nasty little man that he was.

But that incident on the day of Angeline's party had had a profound effect on her. In her naivety, she'd imagined that the veiled glances from some folk in the village and the conversations that stopped at her approach were because the villagers on the whole saw her as different to them. She was a servant but she dressed and spoke like someone from another class. It had taken Cuthbert to awaken her to the realization of the gossip that she was the doctor's mistress.

For some time after the truth had dawned she'd avoided the village, but then her natural fighting instinct had kicked in. Embarrassment had been replaced with a sense of injustice and a determination to 'show them'. To that end she'd held her head high and started to go about her business as usual again. People would always gossip and assume the worst, and what they didn't know for sure they would make up. She didn't intend to have her freedom curtailed by such nasty little minds.

At the same time she had started to think seriously about her future. Oliver and Angeline were growing up fast and she wasn't needed in the same way she had been. The house ran on oiled wheels and, with a little input from John, could continue to do so even if she wasn't around. The assistant he had taken on at the practice two years ago was a nice young man and had proved to be a great help. Although John was still busy, he no longer worked all hours and had every other weekend off.

That was what she told herself in the cold light of day. At night it was a different matter. Lying awake for hours on end she was forced to face the fact that she would find it hard not to see him every day, to sit and share dinner and discuss the events of the day. Even the arguments they frequently had she'd miss, she realized, but that was silly. He persisted in seeing women as delicate flowers to be protected and wrapped up in cotton wool, grown-up children if you like. And she *didn't* like. One thing was for sure: now she had found out what folk were saying, everything was different.

It was at the beginning of that new year that the idea had come to her, and through Lotty of all people. The maid had returned from a visit to her mother on her half-day in tears. It appeared her father was ill and the family were in danger of being thrown out of their tied cottage. As in Ellington, the Ashington Coal Company owned the Linton colliery where Lotty's father worked, and the company had built rows of houses for their employees as they were doing in Ellington. The first coals from the pit had been drawn some eighteen years before and Lotty's father had been one of the miners who'd gone down then, but that meant nothing to the company. No work, no pay. No pay, no rent money. No rent money, no home.

'It isn't as if the houses are anything much,' Lotty had sobbed. 'They're infested with black clocks.' She'd gone on to explain that what they called black clocks were big shiny black beetles that loved to hide in the cupboard next to the fireplace, ugly great things with a hard body armour that made a crunching noise when stood on. 'Me mam has a constant battle with them with sprays and powder but no sooner are they gone than they come back and bring their sons and daughters and aunts and uncles and anyone else who wants a warm home,' Lotty said with unconscious humour. 'They come out at night an' many a time me da's come home after working the night shift and they've bin everywhere. Still, home's home, isn't it.'

Molly had agreed, home *was* home, and she knew that several of Lotty's brothers and sisters were still at school and money was always tight. She'd told John about the possible eviction of Lotty's family and he had immediately gone to see the manager at the Linton mine, who lived in a nice cottage some distance from the rows of colliery houses. He had attended the man's wife when she'd had complications giving birth to a long-awaited child six months before, and the manager had been fulsome in his praise when John had saved mother and baby. The upshot of that conversation had been that the manager had agreed to keep Lotty's father's job secure, and until Lotty's father had recovered from the severe bout of pleurisy that had brought him low, John had paid the family's rent and provided food and free medicines.

Months had passed by, but the whole episode had set Molly thinking. In the past she'd considered eventually using her savings to buy a property by the sea, a fine house that would be conducive to taking in paying guests and thereby providing an income for herself. But the plight of folk like Lotty's family had struck a chord. The mine-owners and landed gentry were ruthless landlords. Whether their workers were miners grubbing away under the earth or labourers working on the estates and farms, the same rules applied. If the rent wasn't met for what-ever reason, families would be evicted be it summer or winter, leaving them with the choice of living rough or the workhouse.

She had a large pot of money sitting in the bank now. She could buy a parcel of land and build low-cost affordable housing to let, over which she'd have control as landlord. She'd have the right of discretion if families fell on hard times, as well as who she accepted as tenants to her properties.

She had begun investigating the possibilities of such a scheme, and had soon found that another idea had been birthed. Buying bricks and having them delivered was expensive. Why couldn't she start her enterprise off by building a brick-making factory first, and then use her own bricks to build the houses?

The more she'd thought about it the more excited she had become. She had gone along to see the bank manager and put her proposal in front of him, knowing that she would need a loan sooner or later. He had given the matter some thought over a number of days and then announced that he thought the undertaking was a sound one, recommending a solicitor he knew and also the name of a building firm in Ashington who were trustworthy and reliable.

'The bank considers you a good investment, Miss McKenzie,' he had said with his thin smile. As she'd expected that he would throw up all sorts of reasons why she – a single woman – shouldn't even be thinking of doing what she intended, the meeting had been a happy and successful one. She didn't, for one moment, imagine that John would react in a similar way.

She had gone to see Weatherburn & Sons, the builders, on one of her days off after the bank manager had kindly made an appointment for her, and although the tough-looking middle-aged man had initially been somewhat doubtful, the bank manager's backing of her had persuaded him to take the job. 'Old Cunningham's a canny gent,' he'd said over a cup of very strong tea in his cramped little office. 'There's not much gets past him and if he says I won't be left chasing the wind for me money, that's good enough for me.'

Molly had assured him that he most definitely wouldn't be left chasing the wind, and after she had met his two burly sons who were the very image of their father, she'd left them scratching their heads and saying that times were changing if a woman was now building a factory and houses, and not necessarily for the better. But her money was as good as any other and so . . .

Two weeks ago she had bought a parcel of land on the outskirts of Ellington and deposited the paperwork with the solicitor. She was now investigating what kind of bricks she wanted to produce; she'd had no idea of the variances before beginning her research. The factory would need brick and tile kilns, drying flats, an engine and a clay house, a machine house and other kinds of equipment, but all that would come once Mr Weatherburn and his men had built the factory. She hadn't mentioned her purchase of the land to John yet, or what she intended to do with it, mainly because work couldn't start with the weather being so bad. It was the second week of January and there had been savage snowstorms and howling winds since the beginning of the month. Oliver had been forced to stay at his school the previous weekend because the roads had been impassable in places, and Angeline had been home all week with a head cold.

Molly gazed out of the morning-room window at the winter wonderland outside. It had stopped snowing in the last couple of hours, and she had seen Cuthbert Havelock arrive on his big black stallion a little while ago. She had remained where she was and let Lotty answer the door and deal with him. No doubt he'd come with a summons to the Hall for John, regarding his mother; the woman really was a pest, she thought uncharitably. Cuthbert had left a short time later and she had seen him stand and look at the house for a full minute before mounting the horse and riding off. She had kept herself out of sight behind the thick drapes. The less contact she had with the man the better; just the sight of him made her flesh crawl. His nature was written all over his florid face.

John was thinking much the same thing as he sat in his study, the late-afternoon light reminding him that he would have to leave for his surgery soon. The cold weather always increased the number of patients who would be waiting for him, along with the after-surgery visits he would have to make.

He just couldn't take to Cuthbert Havelock, he told himself, however friendly the man tried to be. The fellow was something of a womanizer, from what he had heard, and he disliked such men on principle. Which made the invitation which Cuthbert had come to deliver even more unappealing. Apparently Rebecca was desperate for Angeline to join the family as their guest when they visited France for several weeks in the summer.

He moved restlessly in his chair, pulling his tie undone and flinging it on the desk before undoing the first three buttons of his shirt. Lotty had recently been in to see to the fire, heaping it with wood and coal, and now the room was stifling.

It was unfortunate that Angeline and Rebecca were such good friends, but the fact that they were both somewhat empty-headed and frivolous no doubt contributed to that. Nevertheless, his daughter was growing more lovely by the day and he didn't like the idea of her being so far away from home in the company of the Havelocks, despite Cuthbert's assurance that the girls would have a chaperone with them at all times. He could just imagine the scene which would occur if he refused the invitation for Angeline, though; his daughter would never forgive him and would make life impossible at home. And what excuse could he give? Hardly the real one.

There was a tap at the study door and Molly entered with a cup of tea. 'Just a reminder that time's getting on,' she said coolly, her voice disguising the fact that her heart had speeded up as it had the annoying habit of doing in John's presence.

He nodded his thanks, thinking how beautiful she was. The firelight turned her hair to molten gold and made the blue of her eyes almost black. He tormented himself most nights wondering how those silky tresses would feel running through his fingers. She always wore her hair in a demure chignon at the nape of her neck and he'd often wondered what she would say if he asked her to loosen it, not that he would dare. She would most likely give him a piece of her mind and he had learned to his cost that she didn't hold back, the more so if she suspected she was being treated as 'the little woman'. He didn't doubt that if he confided the reason for Cuthbert's visit and his own reservations about the invitation, Molly would dismiss them out of hand, saying Angeline was just as capable of looking after herself as Oliver.

'What's the matter?' She stared at him. She knew by now when he was out of sorts and she didn't think she had done anything to ruffle his feathers today.

He shrugged. 'Just something on my mind, that's all.'

'Do you want to talk about it?'

He did, desperately, but he really couldn't take one of her lectures about misogyny today.

'Well?' she said impatiently. 'Do you?'

He sighed. 'Cuthbert called earlier with an invitation for Angeline to accompany them when the family holidays in France in the summer.'

'You don't want her to go?'

'No, I don't. Those two boys of his are out to sow their wild oats and Angeline is an innocent and beautiful young girl. I wouldn't want her put in a situation she can't handle.'

'I agree.'

'You do?'

His amazement was so transparent Molly had to smile. 'Your duty as her father is to protect her from harm.' If the sons were anything like the father then they most certainly weren't to be trusted.

John nodded, leaning back in his chair and putting his hands behind his head as he sighed. 'You know that and I know that, but once Angeline hears about the invitation she'll set her heart on accompanying Rebecca. You've seen how close the pair are. We'll have tears and tantrums galore.'

'We'll weather them.' She wished his shirt hadn't pulled tight over his muscled chest. It was distracting.

'But how do I explain my refusal, not just to Angeline but the Havelocks too? It's bound to cause offence.'

She thought for a moment. 'Actually, I think you have the perfect excuse for keeping Angeline close to home this summer. The prospect of war is looming larger every day, if the newspaper reports are to be believed, and the future is so uncertain – everyone agrees on that. The last thing one wants is to be in a foreign country if war does break out.'

'Now that's very true.' John had brightened. The European arms race had been fuelling rumours of imminent war for a while and in Germany Admiral von Tirpitz had admitted that his navy was growing fast, with new warships entering service this year. Those of his friends and acquaintances who were in the know agreed with Winston Churchill, the first Lord of the Admiralty. War was coming. It was simply a matter of how soon. It could be weeks or months, but it was on the horizon. He'd tried not to dwell on it himself – he had his patients to attend to and his practice to run – but in all honesty he *wouldn't* want either Angeline or Oliver far from home for the time being.

He straightened in his chair. 'Thanks, Molly. I think Angeline will see the sense of that argument even if she doesn't like it.'

'Perhaps,' Molly said drily. Angeline was still a sweet girl some of the time, but since she'd attended the school and mixed with the likes of Rebecca Havelock, she'd developed a few airs and graces. John had taken the children on a visit to London in the autumn to stay with his brother for a few days, and on her return Angeline had waxed lyrical about the wonderful shops and theatres and eating places in the capital, and not least her uncle's beautiful London residence, expressing her dissatisfaction with the North-East and her own home. Molly had taken the girl aside when this had gone on for a few days and tried to talk some sense into her, but Angeline had refused to listen.

'Uncle Lawrence said he would love to have Papa as a partner in his practice and then we could live in London too,' Angeline had retorted, her pretty face petulant. 'But

Papa said he'd never do that and it's not fair. Rebecca says they always have a lovely time when they're down in London and it's the place to be. I hate it here.'

'You have a beautiful home, Angeline, you know you do, and you are a very fortunate young lady. You like your school and have lots of friends – you've so much to be thankful for.'

Angeline had huffed and puffed at this before flouncing off to her room, and Molly could have shaken the girl. Her attitude of late was even more of a reason for not allowing the child to accompany the Havelocks; their influence was strong enough as it was.

'I'll see Cuthbert tomorrow and explain,' John said. 'I'm due at the house after morning surgery to attend his mother anyway.' The old lady had had a cold and had decided, yet again, that she wasn't long for this mortal plane.

Molly nodded. Hopefully Rebecca's father would have had the sense not to mention anything about the holiday until the matter was decided, but she doubted it.

She left John drinking his tea and made her way to the morning room. It had been on the tip of her tongue to tell him about the land purchase and her plans when she had taken in his tray, but she'd wait until he had seen the Havelocks and his mind was clear. He would react badly, she knew that, but if she was able to put over her vision for the future in a reasonable way, surely he would see the advantages for folk like Lotty's family? She knew John had come to the North because he felt he was needed here rather than in the affluent South, and she would appeal to the altruistic side of him.

She sat down at her desk but instead of dealing with the household accounts which she always presented to John every week, although he had not requested this, she looked round the morning room. She had never liked it. Perhaps because it reflected the personality of its previous occupant so strongly? Christabel Heath's presence made itself felt in the rest of the house, of course, but nowhere so powerfully as here. It was fussy and ultra-feminine and almost claustrophobic.

She wouldn't have liked John's wife and Christabel wouldn't have liked her. She had often wondered why he'd married her because from what he had said when she had first arrived at the house, almost from the start the marriage hadn't been a happy one. He had not discussed his late wife since, and of course she had never asked about her. She suspected Christabel would have fitted nicely into John's image of how the 'weaker' sex should look and behave, though. In spite of his insistence that he agreed with women having the vote, he was scathing about the militant attitude which Emmeline Pankhurst and her followers had taken in recent years, declaring it unwomanly and unseemly.

Unseemly. She bit on her bottom lip, telling herself not to get annoyed. They'd had many heated discussions on the subject, especially around the time six months ago when Emily Davison had dived under the rails and dashed into the path of the King's horse at the Derby. Her protest was the last in a series that had led to her imprisonment and force-feeding on numerous occasions, and when Molly had pointed out to John that Miss Davison must have been desperate about the way the movement had been let down by the government to do such a thing, he had shaken his head in a supercilious way that had made her want to slap him.

'She gave her life for something she believed in,' Molly had protested vehemently. 'Can't you give her any credit for that?'

'She was foolhardy and undignified,' he'd replied calmly, 'and her actions won't have furthered the cause an iota. The government will come round all the quicker if the women show restraint and decorum.'

She had told him he was as bad as the Home Secretary and his cat-and-mouse strategies against the movement and moreover a hypocrite too, and left the room with her cheeks burning and her eyes blazing. The atmosphere between them had been frosty for a week after that.

Molly sighed. He could make her more mad more quickly than anyone she'd ever known. And what would be, would be. It was no use worrying over it now, there'd be time enough for that when the worst happened.

She didn't have long to wait. John came back fuming from seeing Cuthbert Havelock, and initially Molly thought that was because their meeting hadn't gone well. He knocked on the morning-room door while she was busy making a list of what she needed delivering by the butcher's boy that week, and on entering said curtly, 'I would like to see you in my study if that is convenient?' Without waiting for a reply he marched off, slinging his hat and coat onto one of the hall chairs as he passed.

Molly finished the last item on the list and followed him, wondering what had happened. She had never seen him in such a temper. One of the things that got under her skin about him was his ability to remain calm and collected when they disagreed about something, whereas she knew she got too heated too quickly and would say things she'd later regret.

When she entered the study he was sitting at his desk, his face glowering. 'Shut the door, please.'

She did as he asked and sat down, and with no preamble he said, 'I saw Farmer Baxter on my way back from the estate.'

Her heart sank. This was the man she had bought the land from.

'Is there anything you would like to tell me?'

His tone brought her chin up even as she warned herself not to counter-attack. 'You mean about the land?'

'Yes, I mean about the land,' he said, his voice dripping with sarcasm.

'Well, you clearly know I've bought a few acres on the outskirts of Ellington.'

'And you were going to mention this to me . . . when?'

'I nearly told you yesterday but I thought you had enough on your plate about Angeline and the holiday.'

'How considerate.'

Don't retaliate, don't retaliate, he's got every right to be angry. Quietly she said, 'There was no point mentioning it until everything was signed and sealed.'

'I disagree, but let's put that to one side for the moment. I presume you had a purpose in purchasing it?'

'Of course.' Molly's tone was now as cold as his.

'May I be privy to it?'

This wasn't how she had wanted it to be. 'I intend to build a brick-making factory.'

Whatever he had imagined, it clearly wasn't this, because he stared at her as though he couldn't believe his ears. 'You intend . . .'

'To build a brick-making factory, yes, and then after that, a number of houses to rent out at a reasonable price to the folk hereabouts. Lotty's parents' situation gave me the idea.'

'Have you taken leave of your senses?'

Her eyes were steady, her voice equally so, as she gazed back into his infuriated face. 'It's a perfectly viable undertaking. I have the backing of the bank. I will be able to get so far with my own money but I will need a loan at some point.'

John found himself lost for words. He had listened in amazement when Farmer Baxter had stopped the horse and trap and congratulated him on his housekeeper's enterprise. The man had clearly been digging for information on what was happening, and John had got the impression the farmer had assumed that although Molly had been the mouthpiece in the purchase of the land, it was he himself who had been the instigator of the scheme.

He had said little and continued homewards, his rage increasing with every turn of the trap's wheels. She had bought a piece of land? With what intention? He had known she had an independent streak and didn't conform to the usual social niceties, but this? This was something else. He had thought of various scenarios regarding why she had purchased the land but never in his wildest imagination had he suspected the real reason.

A woman going into business? Competing with every Tom, Dick and Harry in a male-dominated environment was unthinkable.

'Why?' he brought out on a growl. 'Why are you doing this?'

'I've told you.'

'Because Lotty's parents were going to be turned out of their cottage?' he said incredulously.

'Mainly because of that, yes, but I had been wondering for some time what to do in the future.'

He had thought she was happy here. Yes, they had their ups and downs but never for one moment had he thought she would willingly walk out of his life, that she would leave him. And without discussing anything beforehand. Or did she think he would countenance her continuing to live here while she built her damn factory and houses? She would be the talk of the county and he would be a laughing stock. Bitterly, he said, 'I don't know you. You have lived here for four years and I don't know you. What would your father have said at you behaving in such a scandalous way?'

She looked into the granite face and her next words came out of their own volition. 'My father, if he's still alive and I pray he's not, is a beast of a man. He killed my sister and nearly killed me before I ran away when I was a child. So I don't care what he would think, or anyone else for that matter. I have to look after myself. I've always had to look after myself.'

For a moment there was a deep, cavernous silence between them, a silence so profound it was as though the world was holding its breath. His voice, when it came, was quiet and flat-sounding. 'What are you saying?'

'I'm – I'm not who I said I was, apart from my name.'

He shook his head, like a boxer after a heavy blow. 'Explain.'

And so she did. She started her story from when she was born into the one-up, one-down cottage in the hamlet; the days working in the fields; Kitty's death; the attack on her; her escape to North Shields and the Mallards saving her; their deaths and her being forced to work in the fish factory to survive – all of it, even the long evenings with Ruth and their thirst for knowledge and the elocution lessons with Miss Gray. He listened without interrupting but she didn't fool herself that this was because he felt any empathy; his face was as hard as nails and his eyes black with rage. 'And so I came here,' she finished, keeping her voice from shaking with enormous effort, 'but I always knew one day I would need to be self-supporting. I had considered buying and running a guest house in the future but then Lotty's family nearly lost their home and the idea came to me to provide housing for such as they.' She shrugged. 'Whether you believe me or not, I *was* going to explain when you came home today.'

'So it's all been a lie, that's what you are saying.' She had never intended to stay with him and he had thought— What had he thought? The answer came back loud and clear. He was a fool, that's what he was. There he'd been imagining that when the children were off his hands he would ask her to marry him and make a new life somewhere in a different part of the country, where the scandal of him marrying his housekeeper wouldn't intrude on their life. Yes, they met head on at times and he knew marriage to Molly would never be a tranquil affair, but he had thought that under all their disagreements and different ways of looking at things she felt for him what he felt for her, even if it had never been spoken about. But he had clearly been wrong. He meant nothing to her. Not only that, but she was a completely different person to the woman he'd thought he knew – she had fooled him for years. He could strangle her with his bare hands.

'My background is different to what I told you but I'm still the same person as I was yesterday.'

'*No, you are not.*' He saw her jerk, her hand going to her throat, and knew he had frightened her but he didn't care. He wanted her out of his sight. 'No, you are not,' he repeated more quietly. 'You are a stranger.'

'I see.' She stood up, her face chalk white but her back

straight. 'Then there's no more to be said. I'll leave immediately.'

'I think that would be wise.'

'What – what will you say to Oliver and Angeline?'

'I don't think that is any concern of yours, not any more.' He wanted to hurt her just as she had hurt him. He wanted her to feel desolate and betrayed and torn apart inside, but there she stood, as cool and contained as usual. 'I will pay you to the end of the month,' he said stonily.

'Keep your money, I don't need it.'

And she certainly didn't need him. 'I pay my debts, Miss McKenzie.'

'Then give it to Lotty for her family.'

'As you wish.'

She left the study feeling physically sick and went straight to her room, closing the door and sitting down on the bed. He hated her. Hated and despised her; she'd seen it in his eyes. Pressing her hands against her chest, she swayed back and forth, moaning softly. She should have told him the truth about her beginnings before now, she knew that, so why hadn't she? Why hadn't she confessed that she had come from humble beginnings and hadn't been born the gentlewoman she now portrayed?

The answer was stark and clear. Because she loved him and she hadn't been able to bear the thought that if she revealed the truth about herself he would look at her the way he had just done in the study.

She became quite still, her hands dropping limply into her lap. *She loved him*. In spite of John seeing her merely as a servant, his housekeeper, she loved him as she had never done Matthew. Matthew had been her first love and it had been a sweet, innocent, happy feeling. She had felt safe and secure with him and his family and she had been eternally grateful for their care and affection for her, and her love for Matthew had been an extension of that. But John . . .

She shook her head, her despair too great for the relief of tears.

She loved John as a woman loves a man, knowing he wasn't perfect, that he could drive her to wanting to hit him on occasion, that he was stubborn and narrow-minded and saw things totally in black and white, but still, in spite of all his faults, she loved him. And he despised her, which was her own fault. It was all her fault. She had put the final nail in her coffin with her plans for the factory and houses. He would never forgive her for any of it and as he'd said, he saw her as a stranger.

After a while she pulled herself together. She had to remain strong, at least until she had left Buttercup House and found somewhere to stay. She'd go and see the landlord at the Plough Inn first and see if he had a room available. If not, he might know someone who could take in a temporary paying guest. Failing that, she supposed she would have to travel to Morpeth and find accommodation there. Once she had somewhere to stay she'd decide what her next step would be.

She quickly packed her things – it didn't take long – and then left her suitcase and bags on the bed and went along to the kitchen to say goodbye to Mrs McHaffie and Lotty. She told them she'd had a disagreement with the doctor and had decided to leave, but hopefully would find somewhere to stay in the village and would let them know when she did. They were shocked and horrified, and when Lotty insisted that she would accompany her and help carry her bags, Molly didn't argue. In truth, she was feeling quite shaky.

As she and Lotty walked into the hall a few minutes later, John came out of his study. 'Where are you going?'

She almost said, *What do you care?* but, conscious of Lotty and wanting to keep things as civil as possible, she said curtly, 'Into the village.'

'Now? Today? In this weather?'

'You agreed I should leave immediately.' She didn't look fully at him; she couldn't, because she knew she would break down.

'I didn't think you meant this immediately. Lotty, take Miss McKenzie's things back to her room.'

'No.' Molly stopped Lotty with her hand. 'Now is as good a time as any and it's for the best. Lotty is helping me with my things and if I find somewhere to stay in the village she can tell you where to send any correspondence that might come addressed to me.' Ruth's letters arrived at regular intervals and one was imminent.

'This is ridiculous.' His voice grated with anger and frustration.

Still she didn't look fully at him as she reached for the front door and opened it. 'Goodbye, Doctor,' she said flatly, hoping he wouldn't detect the misery in her voice. 'Everything should run perfectly well without me. The records of regular orders for food and coal and so on are listed in the ledger in the morning room, along with other information pertaining to the running of the house.'

She thought she heard him mutter something which ended in '. . . damn the house', but by then she had stepped outside into the bitter cold. She took care not to slip on the steps, which were covered in a layer of ice; the last thing she needed was to fall flat on her face. That would nicely finish off what had turned into the worst day of her life.

She set off down the drive carrying her suitcase, with Lotty trotting along behind her with the other two bags. She didn't look back.

Chapter Eighteen

'So, where is she?' Lotty had just walked in through the back door of the house which led into the scullery and then the kitchen, and Mrs McHaffie had almost pounced on her.

'Well,' said Lotty, feeling important for once, 'she's at the Plough for the moment but one of the barmaids said she knows of a cottage that's coming up north of the village on the way to Cresswell. Lilac Cottage or Rose, somethin' like that. The old lady who lives there has been ailing for years and her son's saying she's got to go and live with him in Ashington. The girl didn't know if it'll be for sale or rent but the son always calls in the inn for a drink when he comes to see his mam and he's due in a day or two. The barmaid wouldn't be surprised if he says his mam's got to go home with him there and then, the weather being what it is.'

'What's it like, this cottage?'

Lotty shrugged. 'Dunno.'

'Well, you'd better take your hat an' coat off and go

and tell him she's at the Plough but I wouldn't mention this cottage for now. If that comes off the lass'll tell us and that'll be soon enough for him to know. I don't know what's gone on but it must have been quite a barney for her to walk out like this. And here was me thinking that the two of 'em might—'

'What?'

'Nothing, it don't matter. Go an' tell him and don't get upset if he bites your head off. He's all worked up.'

John was worked up. He was beside himself. He had been mad enough when he'd learned she'd bought a piece of land without so much as mentioning it to him first, and then even more furious when she'd told him the plans of what she intended to do with it; but all that paled into insignificance besides her calmly stating, in so many words, that he wouldn't feature in this future she was building. He was expendable; he had served his purpose and she was going to move on. And then she'd further compounded what he saw as a deep betrayal by revealing that everything she had told him about herself was a lie. If ever a man had been taken for a fool, he had.

And just to leave as she had, as though she couldn't wait to be rid of him. He ground his teeth, his stomach churning. *Damn woman. Damn and blast her.*

He slumped down in the chair behind his desk and put his head in his hands, his elbows resting on the wood. When had he first admitted to himself that he loved her? He couldn't say. Perhaps he'd known it from the first week she had been here but had hoped that if he didn't acknowledge it the feeling would fade and die? It was so soon after Christabel, for one thing, and for another they were like chalk and cheese, oil and water – any damn definition you wanted to put on it. But as time had gone on it was as though she had inveigled herself into his bones and blood. He didn't understand what it was about her, that was the thing. If he could have put a name to it, identified it and pigeonholed it, he could have dealt with it better.

He pressed his fingers against his temples as though he could force the knowledge out. How long he sat there he didn't know, but when Lotty knocked on the study door and then opened it, it took him a moment to focus. 'Yes?'

'I'm sorry, sir, but I thought you might like to know, Miss McKenzie found a room at the inn.' Lotty's voice was hesitant. She had never seen the master looking like he was now, not even when the mistress had died and that had been a terrible shock for everyone. One minute she'd been as right as rain, although complaining she'd got one of her headaches, and then she was gone. A bleed inside her head, they'd said, and for months afterwards every time Lotty got a headache she panicked.

'Thank you, Lotty. So she's quite comfortable?'

'Yes, sir.'

'Good.'

'Can I get you anything, sir? A cup of tea or coffee?'

He shook his head. 'I'll be leaving shortly for the surgery. Can you see to Miss Angeline when she gets home from school?' It was his daughter's first day back after being unwell and he hadn't been looking forward to seeing her that evening. Cuthbert had admitted that he'd mentioned Angeline accompanying them on holiday to Rebecca, and by now Angeline would no doubt be expecting his blessing. Curse the man – he hadn't got the sense he was born with, John thought irritably. He didn't need aggravation from Angeline on top of everything else. Cuthbert had said he understood his reservations in view of the current uncertainty; whether he did or not, John didn't know and right at this moment he didn't care.

'Of course, sir,' Lotty said flatly. It had dawned on her that she would be left to deal with Miss Angeline's tantrums now Miss McKenzie had gone. She left the study, closing the door quietly behind her, and went to report to Mrs McHaffie how the master had seemed.

Molly sat in the window seat of her room at the inn, gazing down into the courtyard outside but without really seeing it. It had started to snow again in the last few minutes, feathery white flakes falling from a leaden sky that promised more. The room held a double bed, dressing table and wardrobe, and it smelled of smoke from the small fire in the leaded grate that one of the barmaids had lit. She suspected there was something wrong with the chimney because every so often a gust of smoke billowed into the room. It was cold too, very cold, and after taking her coat off she had put it on again.

The landlord, a big cheery fellow with hair that stuck

up like bristles and a bulbous red nose, had told her she could have meals in her room if she wished, to which she'd thankfully agreed. The thought of going downstairs to eat was beyond her. In fact, the thought of eating a meal altogether was beyond her at the moment.

She had made such a mess of everything, she told herself wretchedly, and there was no way back. He was lost to her. From living in his home and being part of his life for four years, eating with him, laughing, arguing – oh, yes, arguing – he now saw her as a stranger, and a stranger he would probably cross the street to avoid. She could blame no one but herself for what had happened and that made it all the worse.

When the tears came she cried for a long while to the point of exhaustion, and she must have dozed off sitting on the window seat because when there was a knock at the door she came to with a start that nearly saw her falling onto the floor. For a breathtakingly hopeful moment she thought it might be John come to tell her he was taking her back to the house, but then a female voice called out, 'Miss McKenzie?'

She got up slowly. Her right arm had gone to sleep and was sending painful pins and needles down into her fingers. She also realized it was almost dark outside and before long she would have to light the oil lamp on the dressing table.

One of the barmaids was standing on the landing when she opened the bedroom door. 'Sorry to bother you, Miss McKenzie,' the girl said brightly, 'but Mr

Palmer was wondering if you'd want dinner tonight and if so what time?'

'Nothing for tonight, thank you, but could I order breakfast in the morning?'

'Right you are. It won't be much – lunch and dinner are the main meals – but would cold ham an' cheese an' crusty bread be all right?'

'That's fine.'

The barmaid nodded, her round brown eyes bright with curiosity. She looked as though she was going to say something else and then thought better of it, merely smiling and walking away.

Molly had seen the girl out and about in the village before and knew she would be aware she was the doctor's housekeeper. She sighed as she shut the door. Now the rumours and gossip would start.

In the days that followed, Molly's fighting spirit rose up in her. She could do nothing about restoring whatever relationship had existed between John and herself, and she had to come to terms with the fact that she had ruined the friendship she believed had existed between them. That being the case, she had two options. She could either sit in this little room and cry and chastise herself all day, or she could get on with salvaging something out of the tangled mess her life had become and hope that one day he wouldn't hate her so much. The first course of action wasn't viable, not with her nature, and so that left the alternative. This didn't stop her pacing the floor for hours at night, dissecting the last ugly scene with John until sheer exhaustion caught up with her and she slept for a few hours, but it did convince her she needed to be doing something and that being incarcerated in the inn wasn't good for her either mentally or physically. She'd been worried that if she ventured outside she might run into him but she had to get over that, she told herself on the third morning at the Plough.

And it was that afternoon that salvation appeared in the form of a small, middle-aged man with bushy hair and a face like a rosy apple. May, one of the barmaids, knocked on her door and said that there was a Mr Donald Stefford downstairs in the bar who wanted a word with her. 'It's him, miss, the man I told you about the first day you came,' the girl added in a whisper. 'The one whose mam is ailing. I said you might be interested in the cottage.'

Molly thanked the girl, quickly tidied her hair and went downstairs. Mr Stefford was waiting for her and conducted her to a table by the fire, ordering two coffees from the barmaid and then coming to the point immediately. 'May tells me you're on the lookout for somewhere to stay. Temporary or permanent, like?'

'Preferably permanent but either. I – I recently left my employment and want to make a new start somewhere.'

He nodded, and when he didn't question her further she surmised – rightly – that he had been told of her circumstances. The whole village was no doubt buzzing about it.

'Well, me mam's agreed to come and live with me an' the missus,' he carried on, 'an' not before time, I must say. She's been right poorly for the last few years since me da died but she's a stubborn old biddy and wanted to stay put. Worried me to death, she has.'

'I'm sorry,' Molly said, liking Mr Stefford immediately. There was something about him that reminded her of Mr Newton although the two men were poles apart.

'Anyway, I must say at the start that I'm no landlord, miss, and I'll be looking to sell the place rather than rent. It'll be a bit of a tug at me heartstrings, truth be told, cause it were me great-granda who built the cottage for his bride well over a hundred years ago an' there's been Steffords there ever since. He built it well, mind – it's stood the test of time – and I wouldn't mind living there meself but it's a bit out of the way and me missus is an Ashington lass, born an' bred, an' don't like the country.'

'I see.' Molly nodded. 'Well, I would love to view the cottage, at your convenience, of course.'

'It's nothing grand, miss. Not like you've probably been used to, I mean.'

She thought of the hamlet and the room at Dockwray Square. 'I'm sure it will be fine, Mr Stefford, but I'd like to see it before I decide?'

'Oh, aye, of course. Well, I'm going to take me mam back home today. I've come up with a horse an' flat cart for the bits she wants to take but there'll be plenty left which might or might not suit. Shall we say tomorrow morning about elevenish?'

He clearly didn't want to let the grass grow under his feet but that suited her too, Molly thought, as she smiled and agreed, feeling a flicker of something akin to excitement pierce the abject misery of the last few days.

Molly was up at the crack of dawn the next morning. For the first time since she had arrived at the inn she managed to finish her breakfast, her thoughts occupied with the forthcoming visit to the cottage as she ate, rather than the last caustic scene with John.

Mr Stefford was true to his word and arrived at the Plough just before eleven o'clock in a small horse and trap. It was a bit of a squeeze on the plank seat for both of them but Molly didn't mind. She was doing something positive and it felt good. She had made up her mind during another long night that once she was settled in permanent accommodation, be it Mr Stefford's cottage or something else, she would go and see Mr Weatherburn and find out when he and his sons could begin work on the factory.

The morning was bright but bitterly cold as they drove out of the village and along the country road to Cresswell, which was two or three miles as the crow flies. There had been no fresh snowfalls over the last three days, and although in the village the snow had become impacted in certain places, either side of the road they were following the drifts were five feet tall or more at some points. It was a beautiful day, the sky high and blue, and although the winter sun was devoid of heat, it was still nice to feel it on your face, Molly thought.

When they arrived, Molly realized the cottage was nearer to Ellington than it was to Cresswell. It lay just off the road and had a bridle path stretching away towards woodland at the back of it. The roof was thatched and it had a small square of cultivated garden neatly enclosed with a picket fence at the front and what appeared to be a large paddock and outbuildings at the rear, although she couldn't see this clearly from where she was standing. 'There's a well at the back for water,' Mr Stefford said as he helped her down from the trap, 'and a stream runs at the bottom of the land over there' – he pointed – 'before the ground rises up into the wood. Keeps you in fuel, the wood does. I put a new roof on the old barn for me mam no more than five years ago so that's sound, an' the stable's still good although she didn't get another horse after old Bessie died. Same with the chicken run – she got no more hens as the old ones died off. Me an' the missus used to bring her groceries and anything else she needed once a week, winter and summer. I shan't be sorry not to have that journey at the back of me mind in the bad weather, I can tell you.'

'I can imagine,' Molly said politely, gazing around her. It was so peaceful, tranquil.

'When I was a lad we had a cow and pigs an' all sorts,' Mr Stefford went on. 'Right little smallholding it was. Me da kept everything hunky-dory outside and me mam on the inside. House-proud she was in those days but of late things slipped a bit, although she struggled on, bless her. All her memories of me da are here, you see, an' they rubbed along right well together. I've said to her, she'll be with me and the grandkids now and though it won't be the same for her we'll make things nice.'

'I'm absolutely sure you will, Mr Stefford,' Molly said warmly, touching his arm. He had tears in his eyes and her heart went out to him. Selling the cottage was the end of an era for him too. 'Your mother is lucky to have such a caring son.'

'Don't know about that,' he said huskily before pulling out a big red handkerchief and blowing his nose hard. 'Come an' see inside – but like I said, don't expect too much.'

He opened the stout, unpainted front door with an enormous key which he took from his coat pocket. 'First time in umpteen years this door was locked, yesterday. Me mam an' da never bothered although once she was on her own we kept saying. She didn't take any notice, though. They don't, the old ones, do they.'

Molly stepped straight into a sitting room and stood still, her heart thumping. It was small, admittedly, but not dark as most cottage interiors were. The stone walls had been whitewashed and reflected any light from the mullioned window. Two armchairs upholstered in a faded tapestry material stood either side of the open fireplace, and a carved oak settle with a thick cushioned seat in the same cloth as the armchairs sat against one wall. An oak bow-front corner cabinet with shelves above and drawers below and a chest of drawers made up the rest of the furniture in the room, and on the stone floor were two brightly coloured thick clippy mats.

'Me mam re-covered the armchairs and settle to match when Da was still alive,' Mr Stefford said, his tone apologetic, 'and everything could do with a good polish, as you can see. Likely you won't want to keep anything and I could borrow me pal's flat cart again and take away anything that's not needed.'

Molly couldn't speak for a moment for the lump in her throat. She felt as though she had come home – that was the only way she could explain the feeling that had risen up in her the second she had walked into the house. The cottage had been loved. It radiated out from the walls, the furniture, everything. She wouldn't change a thing, from the small wooden clock ticking away over the mantelpiece to the flowered curtains at the window. Whatever Mr Stefford wanted for it, she had to have it.

'Come through and see what you make of the kitchen,' Mr Stefford said, his voice still apologetic. He had clearly assumed that her silence was down to disappointment. 'It's about the same size as this room and there's a small scullery attached with a sink and some shelves.'

The kitchen was – to Molly – as perfect as the sitting room. The fireplace was a large open blackleaded range with a massive four-foot-long steel fender and a conglomeration of well-used fire irons in one corner. A bread oven still smelled of fresh bread and a big black kettle stood on the hob. A row of copper saucepans along with a black frying pan stood on shelves at the side of the range, and a well-stocked dresser holding crockery and dishes and cutlery was to the left of the kitchen door. An oak refectory table with a three-plank top and two long benches either side of it took up the centre of the room. On the floor, along the length of the fender, was a huge clippy mat and on this, one at each end, stood two beechwood rocking chairs, the cushions of which matched the curtains at the small window.

'Well, what do you think so far, miss? I know the furniture an' that is getting on now – me granda and his da before him made most of it – and everything needs a good clean but–'

'It's perfect, Mr Stefford.'

'Really?' he said, brightening. 'Well, come and see upstairs.'

There were two bedrooms, both with small fireplaces. The one overlooking the front garden above the sitting room held a double bed, wardrobe and dressing table and had clearly been Mr Stefford's mother's room because it still smelled faintly of a mixture of old woman and lavender. The other one was at the back of the cottage. When Molly looked out of the little window the view was of the paddock and old barn and beyond that a sloping field and then the woodland. Although this room was slightly smaller than the other one and only had a three-quarter-sized bed and wardrobe, Molly liked it better.

Both bedrooms had varnished floorboards and clippy mats and there were faded curtains at the windows. There was no bedding in either room that she could see, and she assumed – rightly – that Mr Stefford had taken all the linen and towels home with him the day before. That was not a problem because she would have wanted to buy new anyway, she thought, and replace the flock mattresses in both rooms.

Once she had finished inspecting the interior, Mr Stefford took her outside via the back door from the scullery. This led on to a paved yard holding the brick-built privy, a coal bunker and a wash house. The latter boasted a coal-fired boiler, deep stone sink and a tin bath propped against one wall.

The yard was enclosed with a five-foot wall, and through the gate leading from it was the old chicken house and run. Beyond that was the enclosed paddock with the barn standing to the left of it, along with a stable large enough for just one horse.

By the time they left Lilac Cottage, Molly had agreed to pay Mr Stefford the hundred and ten pounds he wanted for the place. She knew she would have to buy a pony and trap; the walk from the village would be pleasant when the weather was clement but if it was raining or snowing then transport would be a must. But that was all right – she could do that, she told herself. True, she'd never had anything to do with horses, but she could learn.

Mr Stefford had said that all the furniture that was left, along with pots and pans and other bits and pieces like crockery and cutlery, was included in the price if she wanted it, and she'd gladly accepted the offer. It would mean she had little to buy initially apart from a new mattress and bedding for the bedroom she intended to use. She could replace things as she went along and buy new curtains and so on, but for now the cottage was perfectly inhabitable.

They arranged to meet at a solicitor's that Mr Stefford knew of in Ashington at the end of the week, and he told her of a shop there where she could buy a new mattress and anything else she needed. 'They'll deliver it for you and take the old one away. They're most obliging – me an' the wife have used them ourselves. Now, there's a good stack of dry logs and kindling in the barn that I chopped for Mam for the winter but you'll need to get coal delivered – that bunker's nearly empty, if I remember rightly. The well won't freeze whatever the weather so you'll always be all right for water but I'd keep yourself well stocked up with food once you move in. You never know if the weather might turn and you can't get out for a week or two.'

Molly listened and thanked him; Mr Stefford seemed to have taken a fatherly attitude once he knew she was buying the cottage. She was finding it hard to concentrate as they made their way back to the Plough, her mind buzzing with the knowledge that she'd just bought her own home. And Lilac Cottage *would* be a home, not just a house: it had welcomed her the moment she'd set foot inside. That might sound fanciful to some folk but it was true. The hundred and ten pounds was a big chunk of money to come out of her savings, but the bank manager had assured her he'd be willing to provide her with a loan in the future so she wasn't going to worry about it.

And if she met any difficulties in the next months she'd deal with them, one by one. She didn't need anyone else.

Immediately, a mental image of a tall dark man with slate-grey eyes flashed across her mind. Her chin rose as she recalled the look in those same eyes the last time she had seen him, and she told herself that that chapter of her life was over and done with. If her heart ached, only she would know. From this moment forth she was Miss Molly McKenzie, businesswoman and builder of houses. Not even Ruth knew how she felt about John; she'd given no hint of her feelings in their correspondence and she was glad about that now.

Maybe she was destined to live her life alone? It seemed that if ever she got close to anyone it ended badly. But she would have her own home now and that was more than she could have imagined years ago. Her own home and a career. That would be enough for her, it would have to be.

Chapter Nineteen

Cuthbert Havelock stared at his daughter in amazement. He couldn't believe his ears. He glanced at his wife, who was calmly eating her breakfast and showing no reaction whatsoever to the news Rebecca had just imparted. 'Were you aware of this?' he asked sharply.

Gwendoline raised perfectly manicured eyebrows, her delicate nostrils flaring slightly at his tone. 'Why would the actions of a servant interest me, Cuthbert?'

'She's John Heath's housekeeper, or was.'

'Quite.'

The three of them were sitting in the breakfast room at the Hall. The table could easily have accommodated twenty or more people, and three staff – a footman and two maids – were attending them.

Rebecca, delighted to have her father's attention for once, continued, 'Angeline said Miss McKenzie left without even saying goodbye to her.'

'And you say the woman's going to build a *factory*? Are you sure Angeline isn't mistaken?'

Rebecca shook her head, her blonde ringlets bobbing. 'Her father said that's why Miss McKenzie had to leave, because she is going to be too busy to be a housekeeper too, but Angeline thinks he's cross about it although he hasn't said that.'

'When did all this happen?'

'Two weeks ago, I think. Angeline has been longing for me to get back so she could tell me.'

Rebecca had been ill with the same virus Angeline had had but in Rebecca's case the cold had gone to her chest and she had been confined to bed, only returning to school the day before.

Cuthbert leaned back in his chair, reaching for his coffee cup and taking a loud slurp. *Well, well, well*, he thought. Miss High and Mighty certainly intended to make a name for herself in one way or another. First as John's mistress and now this. He could imagine how John had reacted to the undertaking, which was no doubt why she'd found herself out on her ear. No man in his right mind would approve of a female behaving in such a disgraceful fashion and the shame would have reflected on him if he'd kept her in his employ.

He speared a sausage on his fork, chomping on it like a pig at a trough, partly to annoy Gwendoline, who was looking at him with distaste, but also because he couldn't be bothered with the niceties of taking his time over a meal.

'Did Angeline say where this supposed factory is going to be and what it's for?'

Rebecca shook her head. 'I don't think she knows.'

He would find out. If it was somewhere round here maybe the McKenzie woman had taken lodgings in the vicinity. With John's patronage gone she'd be more inclined not to look a gift horse in the mouth and he'd be happy to oblige.

He began to shovel scrambled egg into his mouth, bits dropping out onto his plate and the fine linen tablecloth. Where the hell did she get the money to build a factory? he asked himself. She'd have needed to purchase a plot of land too. She must have known a lot of tricks in the bedroom for John to dig that deep into his pockets, something he was no doubt regretting now. She'd got whore written all over her – he'd thought that the first time he saw her. But a high-class whore, he'd give her that. If he were able to come to some sort of arrangement where he set her up somewhere, she could carry on with this factory notion as long as she was discreet about him. He'd had a fancy for a while now to see how she performed between the sheets. There was something about her, something he couldn't put his finger on, but she was like an itch that needed to be scratched.

He glanced at Gwendoline, who was dabbing the corners of her thin mouth with her napkin. Who would have thought she would have dried up into such a thin old stick just years into their marriage? Once she'd given him the heir and the spare and then Rebecca, she'd moved out of their marital suite and into her own set of rooms before their daughter was a year old. That sort of thing was over, she'd told him. He was at liberty to find satisfaction elsewhere but outside the home; if there was any more trouble with maids in their employ, then she would go home to her parents and take the children with her. He didn't think she would have followed through on the threat – Gwendoline was too conscious of their social standing to cause a scandal – but nevertheless, since then he'd confined his needs to various brothels. He could have taken a mistress, of course, but he'd found he liked variety, and the more earthy and vulgar the wench, the better. He'd make an exception with Molly McKenzie, though; a small house where he could visit at will would suit him very well, and she'd be a fool to turn down such an offer.

Excitement caused the blood to pound through his body and he felt himself harden. It had been a week since he'd had any relief. He'd call and see John today on the pretext of his mother needing another visit and find out what had gone on, but he'd be circumspect about it. John could be a funny fish at times, something of a closed book.

Gwendoline stood up. She dropped her napkin onto the table as she said, 'It is nearly time for school, Rebecca. Come along.'

She didn't look at her husband as she ushered the child out of the room; she rarely did unless it was absolutely necessary. She knew exactly what he was thinking, though. Did he realize how transparent he was? she asked herself as she walked into the hall. She had no doubt that later that morning he would decide to take Midnight for a gallop and she knew just where he would go. And if he didn't find out what he wanted to know from John Heath, he would gain the information in some other way. She had noticed the McKenzie girl when they'd visited Buttercup House before – tall, beautiful, dignified, a servant but cut from a different cloth to most. She had also noticed the way Cuthbert had eyed the housekeeper, nauseating man that he was.

Once the maid had helped Rebecca into her hat and coat and fetched her school bag, Gwendoline watched one of the footmen assist her daughter into their chauffeur-driven car which would take her to Morpeth. Much as she liked the Rolls-Royce, she still preferred to use the horse and carriage when the weather permitted in the warmer months, but today the motor car came into its own.

She waved Rebecca goodbye and walked into her private sitting room, shutting the door behind her. Settling down on the chaise longue in front of the roaring fire, she sat straight-backed as she had been taught by her governess as a child – ladies never slumped in their seats or curled up on a sofa to read. She could almost hear Miss Smyth's voice all these years later.

She reached for the book of poetry she had been reading the day before but after a few moments laid the volume on her lap. Her thoughts were taken up with the conversation at breakfast and particularly her husband's reaction to the news about the McKenzie girl. She knew what he intended and for the girl's sake she hoped

McKenzie had left these parts. She had no personal feelings about Cuthbert's infidelities, but there was something about the girl – an elusive quality she couldn't quite put a name to – and she wouldn't want McKenzie marred by intimacy with him.

She herself had been marred, she knew that. She gazed into the leaping flames of the fire, her pale blue eyes pained, and then, realizing that her hands were clenched into fists, she forced her long white fingers to relax.

She had been as innocent as a lamb when she had married Cuthbert but that had ended on their wedding night. He'd taken no account of her inexperience and that it was her first time with a man. By the morning she had known she'd made a terrible mistake in marrying him. He had filled her with revulsion at some of the more unnatural acts he had demanded, things that she doubted were normal between a man and a woman.

When they'd returned from honeymoon she had tried to speak to her mother but her mother had thought her indelicate and made her feel ashamed. If 'that' side of marriage held no appeal, she had said coldly, then Gwendoline had best provide Cuthbert with an heir or two as quickly as possible and then encourage him to seek pleasure elsewhere.

'All men have mistresses for that side of things, Gwendoline,' she had said calmly, shocking her still further, 'from the royal family down. I dare say there's not a man of our acquaintance who does otherwise. One simply turns a blind eye, darling. It's the done thing.'

It had been the thought of the 'done thing' that had enabled her to get through those first years of marriage, Gwendoline thought as she heard Cuthbert's voice bellowing in another part of the house. Why was everything he did loud, coarse and unpleasant?

She sighed, nipping at her lower lip with her teeth. She should have perceived Cuthbert's true nature during their courtship, but as a chaperone had always been present she hadn't got to know her future husband at all. Her father had been keen on the match – the Havelock name carried some weight and the family's social standing was good – and so, silly little girl that she had been then, she'd meekly gone along with what had been arranged. The proverbial lamb to the slaughter.

She heard the sound of voices outside. Putting down the book, she walked to the window in time to see Cuthbert cantering off down the drive on Midnight. Their groom stood looking after him for a few moments before turning towards the stable block at the rear of the house.

Gwendoline's gaze narrowed. It hadn't taken Cuthbert long, she thought, her lip curling in contempt. What a thoroughly dreadful individual he was. She did so hope that in this instance with the McKenzie girl he would be thwarted.

John looked up from the papers on his desk as a tap on the study door was followed by Lotty opening it. 'It's Mr Havelock to see you, sir,' the maid said a trifle nervously. 'I've put him in the drawing room.'

John stifled a groan. The last person he wanted to see this morning was Havelock. Nevertheless, he smiled as he thanked Lotty and told her to say he'd be along shortly. He was aware that his maid had been practically creeping round the house since Molly had left and after apologizing to her for his bad temper, had of late tried to mend his ways. The fact that he was more miserable than he'd ever been in his life made that difficult. And now that damn man was here, no doubt with a summons to Havelock Hall from his neurotic mother.

And then his professional side kicked in. The old lady was his patient and had every right to call on his services, he knew that. What was the matter with him? It was a silly question – he knew exactly what was the matter. She had left him for pastures new without a backward glance and anything he had thought – hoped – he'd meant to her had been purely a figment of his imagination.

When he walked into the drawing room Cuthbert was standing with his back to the fire, holding up his coat-tails and warming his fleshy backside. 'Enough to freeze your innards out there,' he said conversationally. 'I've asked the girl to get me a coffee laced with brandy, trust you don't mind?'

John did mind. He didn't want Cuthbert to settle himself down but he couldn't very well say so. He smiled thinly. 'Your mother under the weather again?'

'Isn't she always? Would appreciate a visit when you've got a minute, old man. Keeps her happy.' Cuthbert plonked himself down into an armchair, stretching out his legs as Lotty entered the room with the coffee tray.

John saw there were two cups and a plate of Cook's shortbread and sighed inwardly, sitting down and resigning himself to one of Cuthbert's inane conversations which normally featured two topics: hunting, and how all the ills in the country could be laid at the feet of the Labour Party. He liked a good discussion as much as the next man but Cuthbert had neither the intelligence nor the grasp of even the most elementary political situations to make this possible. Now Molly—

He stopped himself sharply, taking a sip of the scalding hot coffee and burning his mouth. His eyes watering, he said in as friendly a tone as he could muster, 'How's the rest of the family?'

'Fine, fine. The boys are away at school, of course, and Rebecca's recovered well from that nasty cold now and happy she can see Angeline again. Thinks the world of your girl, she does.'

This last was said with an edge. Cuthbert had accepted John's explanation of why he was going to keep Angeline at home in the summer but he didn't like it. In his opinion, John ought to have been gratified that such an offer had come his daughter's way.

Seizing the opportunity, Cuthbert continued, 'Talking of the girls, Angeline mentioned something to Rebecca about your housekeeper taking off and proposing to build a factory somewhere? I told her it was nonsense, of course.'

'No, it's true,' John said stiffly.

'Is it, be damned? Well, I never. Has the wench no sense of propriety? Can't have a woman meddling in such things. What's it all about then?'

'I have no idea,' John said even more stiffly.

'No?' Cuthbert's tone made it clear he didn't believe him.

'No.' John's tone made it clear he didn't care, and wasn't going to discuss the matter further.

'Well, it's a rum do, that's all I can say.'

'I see no reason why women can't begin to venture into commerce and other areas in the future. The world is changing.'

Cuthbert stared at him as though he had taken leave of his senses, which he probably had, John thought ruefully. Why he was defending her when she had cast him off so arbitrarily, he didn't know.

'Thin end of the wedge, that sort of thinking, if you don't mind me saying so. It's like the working class – give them an inch and they'll take a mile. Women are the same.'

What a stupid, crass individual he was. Hot as it was, John finished his coffee and stood to his feet. 'I'm sorry, Cuthbert, but I've a visit to make and I don't want to be late. I'll call and see your mother later this afternoon if that is convenient?'

'Perfectly, old man. Perfectly.' He wasn't going to get anything out of him, he could see that. 'All right if I just drink this before I leave? I can let myself out.'

'Of course.' Seething inwardly, John left the drawing

room and fetched his black bag from the study. He was putting on his hat and coat when Lotty appeared from the direction of the kitchen. 'I'm leaving for Robson's Farm to check on Mrs Robson's ankle,' he said shortly. Dora Robson had taken a nasty fall on the ice a couple of days ago and broken her ankle. 'Mr Havelock is still in the drawing room and will be leaving shortly.'

'Very good, sir.' He was in a fit again, Lotty thought. This house was all at sixes and sevens since Miss McKenzie had left. The master walked around with a face like thunder and Miss Angeline had thrown a massive tantrum last night when she had come home from school. Something her friend Rebecca Havelock had told her about a holiday or something. Even Master Oliver had been upset when he'd come home the first weekend and found Miss McKenzie gone. She wouldn't have thought he would have bothered unduly but it just showed, you never could tell. He clearly thought a bit about the lass.

She closed the door after the doctor and once the sound of the horse and trap had disappeared, stood biting her thumb in the hall. She ought to go and make sure Mr Havelock was all right but she had to admit she didn't want to be alone with him. He had a way of looking at you that made you feel you didn't have any clothes on. She'd said this once to Mrs McHaffie and the cook had nodded, saying, 'Aye, he's one to watch, lass. Have your drawers down afore you could blink, that one. You steer well clear, all right?'

She was still standing there two or three minutes later, dithering, when the door to the drawing room opened and he exited. 'My hat and coat, girl.'

She hastened to obey, but after she'd helped him on with his coat he turned and looked at her. 'So I hear Miss McKenzie has left?'

Lotty blinked. The likes of him didn't usually engage the likes of her in conversation. 'Aye, yes, sir.'

'Still in the vicinity, is she?'

'Sir?'

'Still around these parts,' he qualified impatiently. The girl was an imbecile.

Flustered, Lotty stammered, 'Aye, I – she – aye, sir.'

'Where exactly?'

'I do-don't know, sir.'

'You must have some idea if you know she hasn't left the area.'

'She's ta-taken a cottage somewhere, sir. That's all I know.' Instinct told her to say no more.

He nodded. So she was renting somewhere round here, was she? He considered asking the maid about this factory business but the girl appeared so dim-witted he changed his mind. 'I'm leaving,' he barked. And when she just stared at him, wide-eyed, he hissed, 'Open the door, girl.'

'Yes, sir.' Lotty nearly fell over her own feet in her haste to obey. Once he'd left, she stood with her back to the door for a few moments, her cheeks burning and her bottom lip trembling. He had made her feel so small and stupid.

A saying of her mam's came into her mind, lifting her spirit. *You can dress a pig in fine clothes but it's still a pig at the end of the day.*

That's what Mr Havelock was, she told herself, a pig in fine clothes. A gentleman like the doctor was worth a hundred of him.

When she entered the kitchen and told Mrs McHaffie what had occurred, the cook narrowed her eyes. 'Sniffing about after Miss McKenzie, is he?' she muttered. 'You didn't tell him where her cottage is, did you?'

Lotty shook her head. Miss McKenzie had let them know via the butcher's boy where she was and invited them for tea a week on Sunday. 'I made out I didn't know.'

'Good lass. Well, you can bet he asked the doctor and got no joy there or else he wouldn't have questioned you.' She had told the doctor about Lilac Cottage, ostensibly when she had asked him if she and Lotty could have their half-day off together when they visited the lass, but also because she'd hoped that once he knew where Miss McKenzie was he might go and see her and ask her to come back. There were no signs of that happening, though.

She had to admit she'd been shocked when she had learned what Miss McKenzie intended to do, and the lass had certainly made a name for herself hereabouts. Everyone was agog. It was one thing being the doctor's housekeeper and fancy woman, they were saying, but quite another for a young woman to have the effrontery to think she could step into a man's shoes.

Gladys shook her head to herself at the way the gossip-mongers had blackened Miss McKenzie's reputation regarding her relationship with the doctor. She'd told them in the village until she was blue in the face that she'd never seen hide nor hair of the lass being anything other than the doctor's housekeeper, but of course they weren't inclined to listen, not when there was a juicy titbit to chew over. Even her best friend, Sybil, who ran a grocery shop with her husband, didn't believe her. The last time the subject had been mentioned, Sybil had nudged her in a knowing way and said how nice she was to be so loyal but the writing was on the wall. 'Writing on the wall?' she'd snapped back irritably. 'How can you and the rest of them say that when you're not living there like I am?'

But there you are, she said to herself now. Women didn't like another woman who was different, and Miss McKenzie was definitely that. But she was a nice lass at heart, a good lass, and if Mr Havelock tried it on with her she would put him in his place, no doubt. She could wither you with a look, could Miss McKenzie.

Chapter Twenty

Molly shut her front door and walked down the garden path, opening the little gate and stepping out onto the bridle path and then the lane beyond. The February morning was crisp and dry, a thick frost coating the ground, hedges and trees. There had been a brief thaw at the end of January that had seen off the snow, but then it had turned bitterly cold again and heavy frosts had made the world white once more.

She had been living in the cottage for two weeks now and although there was masses to do, both inside and out, she had been concentrating on her plans for the factory and what type of bricks it would produce when it was up and running. She had been to see Mr Weatherburn several times and he had proved most helpful, going through the various grades with her and mentioning the different bricks produced by firms in Durham and Northumberland. Shaped bricks, standard bricks, enamel ones glazed in dark green, white, coffee brown and deep yellow, engineering and facing bricks – he was a fount of knowledge on them all. 'You hire a good manager right from the beginning and you won't go far wrong, lass,' he'd assured her. 'Meself, I like a nice red brick made from shale, but let's get the factory built first, eh?'

The only changes she had made to the interior of the cottage were to give it a good spring clean from top to bottom, and buy a nice mattress for the bedroom she'd chosen along with new bedding and curtains. Everything else could wait. The coal bunker was now full, she'd had a big sack of potatoes and another of flour delivered which stood in the scullery, and when the butcher's boy brought her weekly order to the cottage she paid him to bring eggs, milk and cheese too. Any other groceries she needed she fetched from the village herself.

She had realized the necessity of owning a horse and trap within a day or two of moving in, and here Mr Stefford had proved helpful. He'd called the week before to check how she was settling in, and over a cup of tea he'd mentioned a pal of his who wanted to sell a pony and trap as he had bought himself a motor car. 'Wouldn't catch me in one of those things,' he'd grunted. 'Noisy, smelly monstrosities. But Arthur was always up for anything new. Anyway, he's got this little mare, nice animal with a sweet nature, and a small trap if you're interested?'

She'd said yes, she was very interested. He'd called back yesterday and told her the price, which she had agreed, and Arthur was due to deliver the horse and trap after lunch today. Since first talking to Mr Stefford she had cleaned out the stable before putting down fresh straw and making it cosy. It had taken her a full day but at the end of it she was satisfied that it was a suitable home for its new occupant. In the summer the horse would be in the paddock most of the time, but in winter it would need protecting from the worst of the cold.

She had stored more bedding straw and hay in the barn, along with sacks of chaff, oats and beans, and a big tin of molasses. She'd even bought a hand-turned chaff cutter for the mash which Mr Stefford had told her how to make. Everything was ready, and she was off to the village to do a little shopping.

Either side of the lane, white frozen branches of elm and hawthorn hung overhead and the hedgerows were silent, devoid of birdsong. It was as though the world was holding its breath, Molly thought as she walked along, her boots crunching on the frost beneath her feet. But she liked it. The landscape was still beautiful in its stark bleakness, and from within the barren tangle of briar and hawthorn, minute specks of scarlet shone and beckoned her eye with a glint of rosehip or the gleam of leathery haw. She didn't mind the solitude of Lilac House's setting – in fact, she welcomed it. Once she reached the village she would have to endure the veiled glances and whispers once again.

She had only walked a couple of hundred yards when she heard the sound of horse's hooves from the direction of the village. She moved to the edge of the lane and in the next moment a rider came cantering round the bend on a black stallion. Her heart sank when she saw who it was but she continued walking.

Cuthbert Havelock had reined in the horse on seeing her and now he watched as she approached. He was eyeing her up and down but she ignored his lascivious expression, hoping that if she simply inclined her head and walked past he would take the hint. It was too much to ask. As she reached him he moved the large animal in such a way that she was forced to a halt.

'And how are you, my beauty?' he drawled. 'It took me a little while to find out where you were hiding but I persevered.'

'I'm not hiding anywhere, Mr Havelock, as you can see,' she said coldly.

'Just so, just so. Staying in a cottage down the lane, I hear? Couldn't you have got something in the village?'

She didn't say she had bought the cottage – it was none of his business. Neither did she answer his question. She kept her voice expressionless as she said, 'Could I pass, please.'

'You were wasted on someone like John, a provincial doctor. You know that, don't you? But of course you do.'

'I beg your pardon?'

'The fellow's got no ambition, that's the thing. Oh, I'm not saying he isn't a good doctor. He is – one of the best – but John'll be content to live his life in this backwater and from what I can see that wouldn't suit you.'

'Where Dr Heath lives is up to him and him alone.'

'Yes, but it tells you something about the man, m'dear. That's what I'm saying. Now, I'd be willing to treat you as you deserve. Set you up in your own place with trips to town to show yourself off whenever you had a fancy. You'd be the toast of London, I promise you. I'm not a mean man with those who please me – clothes, jewellery, whatever you liked, it'd be yours. We'd have some high old times.'

'I don't think so, Mr Havelock,' she said icily.

'Playing hard to get? Well, that's all right—'

'I'm not playing hard to get. Now would you let me pass, please?'

'What's your hurry?'

To Molly's dismay he slid off the horse's back. Holding the reins of the huge animal in one hand, he lifted the brim of her hat with the other.

'Mmm, much too delicious to be wasted on John Heath,' he murmured in the instant before her hand knocked his away. 'And fiery too. I like a filly with spirit. We'd get along just fine, m'dear, and I'm making you a damn good offer. What you would do in your spare time would be up to you. If you wanted to stay in these parts and carry on with this factory idea I've heard about I wouldn't object. As long as you were discreet about us, of course. But I'm sure a woman like you has had a lot of practice in being discreet. Had old John panting after you, I'll be bound. It's a wonder his patients have seen anything of him the last few years.'

Did he seriously think that speaking to her like this would entice her to become his mistress? Molly thought in amazement. The man's ego was colossal. Not only did he resemble a slug but he had the brains of one. 'I find your suggestion offensive, Mr Havelock, and your assumption about my relationship with Dr Heath insulting. He was my employer, that is all.'

'Come, come, m'dear. Do I look stupid?'

He was sweating slightly in spite of the bitter cold, his fat face moist. Repressing a shudder of distaste, she said steadily, 'Mr Havelock, I see I need to make myself plain. I wouldn't take up your "good" offer if you were the last man on earth. Is that clear enough for you? Now I repeat, let me pass.'

'Hoity-toity.' His face had darkened, his eyes narrowing. 'Think you're special, don't you? Well, all cats are grey in the dark, my fine lady, and they all squeal the same. I could make you squeal some – oh, yes. I've tried to do this the nice way but you're not having it, are you. No matter, but just remember you've brought this on yourself.'

Before she had time to realize his intention he'd dropped the reins and grabbed her with both hands, pulling her in against his protruding stomach with a jolt that jerked her neck. Thick wet lips clamped down on her mouth and the thrust of his tongue made her want to gag, but in the next moment he found himself tottering backwards as she wrenched herself free with a ferocity that took him aback. She hadn't worked in the fields, or toiled in the fish factory, to no avail. She might look as slender as a reed but there was steel in her limbs.

With a growl that could have come from an animal he slapped her hard round the face, stunning her for a moment, and then his hands were at the collar of her coat. He ripped it open so that buttons pinged off as his leg pushed at the back of her knees, causing her to lose her balance. As she fell he was on top of her, and he clearly thought he'd won because he mumbled, 'It'll be here and now then, in the open.'

Molly didn't have to think about what she was doing; her instincts kicked in and she fought him like a wild cat. She'd seen women in the fields fight when she was a child and some of the fishing girls would go at each other hammer and tongs if they'd had a falling-out, and such incidents were stored in her psyche. Lying as she was with his bulk on top of her, she couldn't bring her knee up with the force she'd used with the foreman at the fishing factory, but it was enough for him to groan as her nails raked at his face. She managed to scramble from beneath him on all fours and then jump up just as he came at her again.

With every ounce of her strength she pushed him. It was just enough for the momentum to send him off balance and he fell against the stallion's flank, startling it. It reared up in the air with a shrill neigh, its front hooves flailing, and as it thudded down it knocked him off his feet whereby it reared up again and this time the great hooves stamped down on his left leg.

Cuthbert's scream sent a number of hitherto silent birds squawking out of the trees lining the lane, the air turning blue with his curses as he rolled out of the path of the agitated animal and onto the spiky white grass of the verge.

'He's broken my leg,' he moaned, dragging himself into a sitting position. 'Damn it, help me, woman.'

She wasn't going anywhere near him. She was shaking from head to foot, the savagery of the violent assault and the force he'd used bringing back memories of the beating she had endured at the hands of her father, wiping away the years in between as though they'd never been. For a few moments she'd felt like a small child again, but she wasn't that little girl any more, she told herself as she straightened. And she wouldn't be manhandled by anyone ever again, not while she had breath in her body.

'You try and touch me again and I'll kill you,' she said harshly. 'Do you hear me? I mean it.'

He was in agony with his leg but he didn't doubt she meant it; her voice had vibrated with hate. And it was in that moment his own hate was born. That she, a skivvy, a nothing, had treated him like this brought a red mist behind his eyes. His rage enabled him to struggle to his feet despite the searing pain, and as he stood swaying on one leg he made a clicking sound with his tongue which brought the horse to where he stood. It took him several attempts before he was in the saddle and twice he came close to passing out, and all the time she stood stiff and straight, watching him. If he could have murdered her there and then he would have – oh, yes, he would have, he told himself. But his time would come.

'I'll see you driven out of these parts with your tail between your legs if it's the last thing I do,' he ground out, once he was on the animal's back and looking down at her. 'You won't get the better of me, not scum like you.'

Molly's face was aching and burning where he had slapped her and she could taste blood in her mouth where she had bitten her tongue with the impact, but she could have been carved in stone as she faced him. And her voice was as hard as stone too when she said, 'You, to talk of anyone being scum. You might have been born with a silver spoon in your mouth but everyone from the oldest to the youngest knows what manner of man you are. Your servants might have to touch their forelocks and pay lip service but they despise you, do you know that? Behind closed doors you are spoken of with disdain for the disgusting, odious creature you are.'

Never in the whole of his privileged, pampered life had he been spoken to like this, and that this chit of a girl, this *whore*, dared to speak thus made him incandescent with fury. If he had had a gun in his hands he would have used it. Spluttering with rage, he hissed, 'You'll pay for this, m'girl. I'll have the law on you.'

'For what?' she said with withering scorn. 'Because you had an accident on your horse? You do that, you tell the constable to call and I'll tell them what really happened and I won't hold back. I'm not one of your servants or housemaids that you force to keep quiet, I'll shout your behaviour from the rooftops. I would enjoy the opportunity, so do your worst.'

He glared at her from maddened eyes and for a moment she thought he was going to ride the stallion straight for her. Instead he turned the horse's head so that it was facing the way it had come as he growled, 'You'll live to regret this day. I'll see you ruined,' and then, swearing and cursing with the pain from his leg, he urged the animal into a trot.

It wasn't until he had gone out of sight that Molly's own legs gave out. She sank down onto the ground, frosty as it was, and sat there for some minutes amid the silence that had fallen. She didn't feel the inclination to cry, which was strange, but her whole body seemed to be trembling. However, when she looked at her hands they were steady; the shaking was within. After a while she rose to her feet and one by one picked up the shiny brass buttons that had been torn off her coat.

Why did things like this happen to her? First Kirby at the factory and now Cuthbert Havelock. Was there something about her that suggested to a certain type of man that she wanted to be molested? Did she invite it, in some way?

She looked down at herself. She couldn't go into the village like this; she would have to return home and mend her coat and anyway, she needed a hot, strong cup of tea.

She walked home slowly, like an old woman, and once inside the house the first thing she did was to bathe her face in cold water. Next she made a pot of tea but when she came to drink it, her sore tongue pained her. Nevertheless, she had two cups before fetching her sewing basket and setting about restoring her coat to its former glory. It was a bonny new coat in a gold-and-brown tweed material with a big fur collar and fur cuffs. That done, she had another cup of tea.

She wouldn't have time to go into the village now. She wanted to make sure that she was here when Mr Stefford's friend came with the horse and trap. Apparently the little mare's name was Gracie and she had been looking forward to owning her first pet. Well, not a pet exactly, she corrected herself, because the pony would be a working animal, but still a pet in a way. But now, after the ugly scene outside, the anticipation and excitement were gone.

By the time Mr Stefford – who was going to give his pal a lift home – and Arthur Briggs arrived she was feeling much better, partly because she had decided on a course of action over the incident that morning. It had been someone passing by the cottage on a horse that had told her she had to do something about Cuthbert Havelock. She'd heard the sound of its hooves and her heart had shot into her mouth, her stomach churning. In the event it had been a youth riding a big farm horse but the occurrence had shown her how jumpy she was and the sick feeling it had induced had remained long after the boy had gone.

She had sat looking round her little home and it hadn't appeared like her sanctuary any more; she was frightened, she'd realized, and she wasn't going to have that – Havelock making her afraid to be in the cottage. So she needed to do something about it. She would go to Havelock Hall once she had her own transport and make it clear that if she was attacked, if anything befell her, it would be laid at his door. She would leave a letter with her solicitor to be opened in the case of her being hurt, stating what had happened that morning and detailing his threats against her.

And so when the two men arrived and she met Gracie, a dear little piebald mare with big, soft, heavily lashed eyes and a velvet muzzle, she was able to enjoy the moment to the full.

Chapter Twenty-One

Gwendoline stared at her butler. Winters had just informed her that a Miss McKenzie was here seeking an audience with the master and that he had told the young lady that the master was indisposed. Miss McKenzie had become most insistent, almost – the butler had hesitated in his ponderous way – impertinent.

'Impertinent?'

'She stated that she would not leave without seeing the master, ma'am.'

'I see.' Gwendoline could imagine how that had been received. Winters wasn't used to his authority being challenged. He was as old as the hills and had been with the family in Cuthbert's father's day. She had been somewhat in awe of the steely-eyed, stiff individual when she'd first come to Havelock Hall as a young bride.

'Do you wish me to see that Miss McKenzie is escorted from the premises, ma'am?'

Gwendoline thought rapidly. Cuthbert had arrived home the day before in a great deal of pain and a foul temper after apparently being thrown by Midnight. He was now ensconced in his suite of rooms upstairs with a badly broken leg and orders from John Heath, who had tended to him, that he was to remain in bed for some weeks. She'd been sure her husband's purpose in going out yesterday was connected with the young woman who was now waiting to see him. A coincidence? She didn't think so.

Her curiosity piqued, she said coolly, 'I will see Miss McKenzie myself, Winters. Show her in here.'

'Very good, ma'am.' Winters's tone suggested it wasn't good. It wasn't good at all.

Gwendoline allowed herself a smile when he left. No one could accuse Winters of failing to express how he felt.

A few moments later the door to her sitting room opened again. 'Miss McKenzie, ma'am.' There was disapproval evident in every syllable.

Gwendoline looked at the young woman and her first thought was that she was lovelier than she recalled. She remained seated – one did not stand for a menial – and said quietly, 'How may I help you, Miss McKenzie?'

Molly hesitated. It was Cuthbert Havelock she had come to see, she'd had no intention of disturbing or upsetting his wife. Mrs Havelock must have enough to put up with being married to a man like him. 'It was your husband I wanted a word with, Mrs Havelock.'

'I am aware of that but Mr Havelock is confined to bed – an accident when he was out riding yesterday.' As she spoke, Gwendoline saw the girl's great blue eyes flicker. It was all the confirmation she needed that something had happened between Cuthbert and this young woman the day before. Aware of the butler standing like a sentinel, she said, 'Thank you, Winters. That will be all for now.'

The old man drew himself up and with an almost imperceptible nod of his grey head, said, 'Very good, ma'am.' Again his disapproval was palpable. He turned, shutting the door behind him.

Molly remained standing where she was. She almost felt as though she was in the presence of royalty. The woman sitting surveying her was beautifully dressed and coiffured and still pretty in a faded kind of way, but it was her manner that was so formidable. She seemed like a true lady, Molly thought, and yet she was married to Cuthbert Havelock.

'You may speak freely, Miss McKenzie.'

Again Molly hesitated.

'Well?'

'I think it is better if I come back another day and speak to Mr Havelock.'

'You appear to be in some distress, Miss McKenzie. Has my husband upset you?' And when Molly stared at her without speaking, Gwendoline said gently, 'If it helps you to express what you came to say, I am aware that my husband is not what he should be. Sit down, please, and tell me.' She pointed to a chair. 'And as I said before, speak freely.'

Molly perched on the edge of the cream satin-upholstered

seat and after a moment began to relate what had happened the day before. She kept nothing back, finishing with the reason she had come to Havelock Hall and the letter she intended to lodge with her solicitor.

Gwendoline listened without interrupting. From a child she had been taught not to show her feelings – it simply wasn't done in good society, her governess had instructed her – but behind her cool facade she was angry and disgusted. And ashamed, yes, ashamed, because she might have prevented the grievous assault if she had confronted Cuthbert yesterday about his intentions regarding this woman.

When Molly finished, there was silence for a moment. She had no idea how Cuthbert's wife was going to react. The upper classes thought that they could do whatever they liked in most cases, after all. And the woman might not believe her. It would be his word against hers. One thing was evident, Mrs Havelock was a cold fish.

And then she had to retract that thought when in the next moment Gwendoline leaned forward, putting her hand on one of Molly's. 'I am truly sorry, Miss McKenzie,' she said with a catch in her voice. 'To attack you like that, it is unforgivable. He is a wicked and debauched man but to try to force you . . .' She hesitated. 'Do you wish to take the matter further?'

'With the police?'

Gwendoline inclined her head.

'If he had managed to achieve what he set out to do then I would have done so, but he would deny it. It would be my word against his and I think we both know who the authorities would favour too.'

'I fear you are right.' Gwendoline felt a dart of relief in spite of herself. It would have been a messy affair. 'But may I offer you some recompense for the ordeal you have suffered, Miss McKenzie?'

Molly's head shot up and she removed her hand sharply. 'I didn't come here for money, Mrs Havelock. I want nothing from your husband but an assurance that he will stay away from me in the future.'

'I can promise you that,' Gwendoline said grimly.

'I don't mean to be rude, Mrs Havelock, but can you?' Molly looked the other woman straight in the eye. 'He seems to be a man who thinks he can do exactly as he likes.'

'Yes, that is so, but I think together we can accomplish what you want.' According to what John Heath had said in the past regarding his housekeeper, the girl had come from a good middle-class background but the family had fallen on hard times and Miss McKenzie had been forced to earn her own living. Cuthbert had been convinced she was the doctor's mistress, but then he would be, Gwendoline thought. The man had a mind like a cesspit. She cleared her throat. 'I understand that you have left Dr Heath's employ?' she said, careful to keep her voice expressionless.

Molly nodded. She had no doubt that Mrs Havelock would be aware of the gossip surrounding John and herself.

'But you are still living in the area?'

'I have purchased a small cottage outside Ellington. It is rather isolated, which is why I came here today. I am not prepared to live in fear, Mrs Havelock.'

'Nor should you be.' Gwendoline made up her mind. Winters would be horrified and Cuthbert would be livid, but she wanted to find out more about Miss McKenzie. 'Can I offer you some refreshments?' she said gently. 'I normally have something about this time.' She rang the bell by the fireplace and when a uniformed maid appeared requested a tray for two, realizing instinctively that if Winters had anything to do with it the tray would only hold one cup. For the first time in a long, long while she was interested in another human being.

It was an hour later and Gwendoline watched Molly McKenzie drive away in her small horse and trap. She was still standing at her sitting-room window a minute or two later when a very disgruntled Winters tapped on the door. 'The master would like a word, ma'am,' he said stiffly.

She turned and looked at the old man, knowing he had been to see Cuthbert to report on the morning's happenings. She had fully expected him to. Winters was Cuthbert's man through and through. Never mind his master was a rake and an adulterer of the worst kind and a thoroughly obnoxious individual, the butler would remain faithful to Cuthbert to his dying breath. It had been Winters who had packed first one housemaid and then another off to the workhouse during her first years of marriage, keeping all mention of the incidents from her on the orders of his master. She probably would still be none the wiser but for the second girl's father arriving at the Hall some weeks later, brandishing an axe and threatening to use it to make sure Cuthbert didn't father any more children. She had known her husband was unfaithful to her, of course, and she had chosen to turn a blind eye to his philandering; but to find out that he had committed fornication in their very house . . .

'Tell him I will be up shortly.'

'The master said immediately, ma'am.'

'And I said I will be up shortly.' She hadn't raised her voice but she didn't need to. When Gwendoline spoke thus she was every inch the grand lady. The Havelocks' ancestry could be traced back for generations but so could hers, and the family she came from had a superior pedigree even if in recent years their wealth had declined. The thought had often crossed her mind since her marriage that her parents had been aware of the sort of man Cuthbert was, but because of his affluence and properties had decided to marry her off anyway. It had changed the way she regarded them.

Winters looked at his mistress. Although she showed no outward signs of it he felt she was more than a little annoyed and no doubt it was to do with the young woman who had been with her for over an hour. What had the master done this time? When he had told him that a Miss McKenzie had called and was cloistered in with the mistress in her sitting room, the master had become apoplectic. He would never say so to a living soul but he often wished the master had just a little of the mistress's dignity and propriety.

Once Winters had left, Gwendoline gathered her thoughts. She liked Miss McKenzie, admired her even. Of course, she was not of their class and could never become a close acquaintance, but the last hour had been refreshing in an existence which carried few such interludes. When she had learned that the reason for the factory, a brick factory, was because Miss McKenzie intended to build an estate of houses she had been both shocked and intrigued. She had been brought up to look down on business people in any realm. It was necessary, of course – the infrastructure of the country depended on such folk doing whatever it was they did – but they were rarely included in the circles she had inhabited. And now here was a woman, a *single* woman, entering what was very much a man's domain. She had asked lots of questions and the time had flown by; she had almost forgotten the reason for Miss McKenzie's visit. But she remembered it now.

Her pale blue eyes with their fair lashes narrowed. That a man like Cuthbert, an uncouth, coarse and odious individual for all his lineage, could dare to think that he had the right to force such a woman, that he was superior to her, was obnoxious.

There were a few desultory snowflakes drifting in the wind and the white sky looked full of them. She turned from the window, walking across to the fire and warming her hands. She was aware that her conversation with

Miss McKenzie had challenged some of the convictions and concepts she had accepted without question all her life, and it was sobering. She felt almost as though she had been asleep and was just beginning to wake up. Had she given a thought to what had become of those two housemaids and the babies they would have borne since she had learned of their plight? Not really. To her shame, not really. The matter had been swept under the carpet as such things always were. As Cuthbert had said at the time, 'My dear, I don't know why you are so upset. These things happen in every big house in the country and one doesn't concern oneself with the result. The workhouses are packed with young girls and their brats and always will be.'

She shook her head. And so she had taken the easy way out, the acceptable path. When she had mentioned the matter to her mother she had been made to feel very gauche and graceless. 'Good heavens, Gwendoline, if you pursue this you'll make Cuthbert a laughing stock. In every county in the country the workhouses, along with the surrounding farms and cottages, are bespattered with the results of the gentry sporting with only-too-willing servant girls.' Her mother's words had been a reflection of her husband's and so she had concurred. But now, in the shape of Miss McKenzie, the victims of such practices had become all too real.

She waited another ten minutes before going upstairs. Cuthbert's suite of rooms was in the west wing, hers in the east. She had made sure she was as far away from him as possible when she had announced that any marital intimacy was over.

He was sitting up in bed when she entered the bedroom via the small sitting room, a half-empty bottle of brandy on the table beside the bed and a full glass in his hand. It was the first time since she had moved to the east wing that she had entered what had once been their shared rooms and she shuddered inwardly. She had been so dreadfully unhappy in those days and she had lost count of the number of times she had contemplated walking into the deep, dark lake in the grounds and ending her misery.

'You took your time.' He downed the whisky and, grunting with pain, leaned across and poured himself another glass.

Gwendoline did not reply to this, merely standing at the foot of the grand four-poster and surveying him coolly, her face impassive.

'Well? What have you got to say for yourself, woman?' He straightened, shifting his position, and then swore as the movement disturbed his injured leg.

She still said nothing but now her expression was as though she was smelling a foul odour.

Cuthbert pulled his head back on the heaped pillows behind him as if to survey her better. He was holding on to the remnants of his temper with some effort. Standing there in her regal way, looking at him as though he was scum! He'd like to damn and blast her to hell but he had to be careful here. He needed to find out exactly what the other one had said to Gwendoline. He could still hardly believe that the McKenzie chit had had the effrontery to come here, to his home, but as soon as Winters had told him he'd known what the girl was after – money. They were all the same.

When it became apparent that Gwendoline had no intention of breaking the silence that had fallen, he cleared his throat. 'I hear you've had a visitor?'

She inclined her head.

'So? What was John's whore after?'

Now Gwendoline moved so swiftly that she startled him. Bending over the bed, she ground out in a voice unlike her own, 'Don't call her that.'

His eyes narrowed. 'Well, well, well. So that's the way the land lies, is it? Well, my dear, whether you agree or not that's what Miss McKenzie is – or was – I gather John has got shot of her for good.'

'So that is why you propositioned her yourself, is it?'

'Is that what she said? Rubbish. I did no such thing.'

Ignoring this, Gwendoline continued, 'And when she refused you, you attacked her and tried to force her. Don't deny it.'

'I most certainly do deny it. I—'

'You are the most vile, disgusting man. I wish I had been barren when I look at you. It makes my flesh creep to think that my sons have your blood in their veins but I shall do everything in my power to see that they respect women as the weaker sex, something you have never done.'

His face had gone puce with rage but before he could speak, she carried on, 'Miss McKenzie is lodging a letter with her solicitor detailing everything that happened yesterday so that if you approach her, or if any harm befalls her, you will be held responsible. And I have written a document also which I have given to her to place with the letter saying that every word she's written is the truth. My paper also mentions the two housemaids you took advantage of in this very house, and that you are known to visit places of ill repute.' This last she hadn't been altogether sure of but from the look on his face she knew she had hit the nail on the head.

He gazed at her, his lips slightly apart. His whole attitude spoke of incredulity. He could not link the coldly angry figure standing in front of him with his cool, regal wife, who had chosen to withdraw from him and look the other way rather than engage in protests or arguments about his activities. She valued their good name more than he did, he knew that, and it was this that made him say, 'I don't believe you, you wouldn't do that.' He didn't include Molly McKenzie in this; he wouldn't put anything past the woman but even if she had written such a letter it would carry little weight if it ever came to light. It would be his word against hers, after all.

'You are wrong, Cuthbert. I have done exactly that.' He couldn't mistake the ring of truth in her voice and as she watched his face darken, she continued, 'In talking to Miss McKenzie I realized I had reached a crossroads in my life.'

'What the hell are you talking about, woman? Have you gone stark staring mad—'

'I could either continue down the same path I've trodden for years, the easy path if you like, or tread a new one. I chose the latter.'

'You've gone doolally. I'll have you put away—'

'A path where your threats and intimidation won't wash any more. I have my sons and Rebecca to think of, I see this clearly now, and to the best of my ability I will show them what is right and what is wrong. They will, of course, make their own choices in life but where I can influence their actions and decisions, I will.'

'Do you realize what you've done, writing a letter like that and putting it in her hands? She'll be after money all the time now, she'll think she's got me over a barrel.'

Her words seeming to come from deep in her throat, she said, 'Don't judge everyone by your own contemptible standards, Cuthbert. Miss McKenzie doesn't want a penny from you.'

He snorted. 'I can see she's done a work on you. Got you eating out of her hand, hasn't she.'

'I suggest you think long and hard about what I have said. You will have plenty of time to do so lying here.'

She turned, and now his voice came as a growl: 'That's what you suggest, is it? Well, you know what you can do with your suggestion.' And when she carried on walking, he bellowed, 'Come back here, I haven't finished talking with you.'

She shut the door on his curses, walking through the

small sitting room and out onto the landing where Winters was hovering. She passed him without moving a muscle of her face, descending the stairs at a measured pace. Once in her sitting room, she sat down in front of the fire and the long breath she let escape seemed to deflate her body. She had nailed her colours to the mast, there was no going back. Whereas before she and Cuthbert had existed in a state of mutual dislike, from this moment on it would be war. She knew that. Perhaps this knowledge should distress her but it didn't. The worm had turned.

She rose from the chaise longue and rang the bell, and once the maid appeared, asked for coffee and one of Cook's delicious pastries. Of a sudden she felt hungry.

Chapter Twenty-Two

It was the beginning of May and during the last months the suffragettes' campaign to gain the vote for women had become more and more violent. In February a church in East Lothian had been burned down, shocking even some loyal supporters, and in March one of the nation's most famous works of art, the Rokeby Venus, was slashed with a foot-long meat chopper by one of the militant followers of Emmeline Pankhurst, protesting at her leader's imprisonment. Things escalated in April with a bomb being thrown at a London church and more acts of vandalism, including another bomb which destroyed Yarmouth Pier. Whether the suffragettes' actions added to the bad feeling surrounding the building of a factory by a woman, Molly didn't know, but she was aware that many of the villagers were outraged and offended by what they saw as her temerity.

Mr Weatherburn and his team had begun work at the site of the factory at the beginning of March, clearing the ground and then starting to dig the foundations. The thick frosts of February had abated, but in their place a steady icy rain made itself felt. By April, when truckloads of bricks were delivered, the weather had picked up, and although it was a windy, cold month it was dry on the whole and the actual building could start. It was then that the first real threats and intimidation by certain of the locals began.

She had just been climbing into the trap after buying some shopping when one of the farmers had stopped his horse and cart and told her she ought to be ashamed of herself. ''Tisn't right, a young lass giving working men their orders,' he said grimly, 'and what are you building a factory for anyway? You ought to be wed at your age and lookin' after bairns – that'd keep you out of mischief. It's a crying disgrace, that's what it is.'

More of the same had followed from other folk over the next weeks as the building work had progressed. Even Barney, the butcher's boy, who had loved to sit and have a piece of fruit cake when he delivered her order, had begun to keep his head down and scoot off as though any contact with her would contaminate him. She was a scarlet woman, but worse than that she was an independent one too.

When she had taken Gracie to be shod at the local blacksmith's after the little horse had thrown a shoe, the man had made a point of talking to the youth who assisted him about the sinfulness of suffragettes and the wicked way some women behaved, making sure his voice was just loud enough to reach her. 'Unnatural, that's what they are,' he had said gruffly. 'Men under the skin, if you know what I mean, lad. A woman's place is in the home. That's God's order of things and no good can come out of them meddling in matters that don't concern 'em.'

She had remained calm and collected each time something was said but she could feel the animosity growing, and today, the first Sunday in May, she was feeling weary of it all as she sat in the cottage waiting for Gladys and Lotty to call. She had been working outside that morning, clearing some ground near the paddock for a vegetable patch, and she was tired. When she had been John's housekeeper they had all gone together to the small parish church every Sunday morning, but since she had left his employ she hadn't ventured through its doors, partly because she didn't want to run into him but also because some of the worst gossipers in the village would be sitting in the pews. She could just imagine the avid interest should she and John meet.

Oliver and Angeline had accompanied Gladys and Lotty twice since she had been living at Lilac Cottage. The first time they had come she hadn't been expecting it and had been worried that their father might not know. However, within the first moments Oliver had said their father sent his good wishes. She didn't know what John had said to the children about her sudden departure and she hadn't asked them; some things were best left alone. It had been nice to see them, particularly Oliver. He was bright and humorous and had a warmth his sister did not possess.

Angeline had been polite enough but clearly unimpressed and within a short while had been fidgeting to leave. The second time they had visited, Molly rather thought Oliver might have taken his sister to task, because Angeline was more sociable and made an effort.

A thud at the window suddenly made her start, and thinking that a bird might have flown into the glass she hurried outside. Standing on the bridle path outside the front gate were two rough-looking men, and she saw a big clod of dried earth under the window. Realizing they must have thrown it, she said sharply, 'What do you think you're doing?'

The taller of the two leered at her. 'Just come to see where the builder lady lives, that's all.'

'And now you have, I'll thank you to leave.'

'We've got every right to stand here,' he began, only to turn and look to where Gladys and Lotty had just appeared round the bend in the lane.

It was Gladys who called out, 'Hey, you, get out of there. What are you about?'

The two shifted their feet, looking uncomfortable, and as Gladys got nearer, she said, 'These two bothering you, lass?' Before Molly could speak, Gladys added, 'I know you lads, don't I? Your da's the gamekeeper at Havelock Hall and you work on the estate an' all.'

'Might do.'

'No might about it, I used to go to school with your da an' I know your mam an' all.' Glancing at Molly, she said again, 'They bothering you?'

Molly pointed to the lump of earth beneath the window. 'They threw that.'

'Did they, by jingo.' Gladys glared at them. In spite of the young men looking to be in their twenties, they now had the appearance of naughty schoolboys caught out in a misdemeanour. 'Well, I'll have something to say to your mam an' da when I see 'em next. I'm sure they didn't bring the pair of you up to harass young ladies.'

'It was just a bit of fun.'

'Oh, no, lads, there's nothing funny about it. How would you feel if it was your mam or sister living here and the same had happened to them, eh? I think an apology is in order, don't you?'

The two shuffled their feet and then in unison, said, 'Sorry, Miss McKenzie,' the taller one adding, 'We didn't mean owt.'

Molly inclined her head. They didn't seem aggressive: if anything, merely somewhat dim-witted.

As they shambled off with their heads down, Gladys and Lotty walked up the garden path, Gladys clicking her tongue at the clod of mud. 'Thick as two short planks, them two,' she muttered as they all walked into the house and through to the kitchen, where she deposited a large slab of fruit-and-cherry cake on the table. 'Bit simple, I reckon.'

Molly nodded. When Gladys had mentioned Havelock Hall she'd wondered if Cuthbert had had anything to do with it, but it was probably just that the young men had been influenced by the general gossip and bad feeling against her. She hadn't mentioned any of this to Gladys and Lotty, but now as they had their tea and cake she told them about some of the things that had been said, though she mentioned nothing about Cuthbert Havelock.

They were both shocked and up in arms on her behalf, but in Gladys's case Molly thought she detected an underlying sentiment of 'What can you expect?'

'The men round here are set in their ways, lass, that's the thing,' Gladys said soberly as she finished her second slice of cake. 'It's not like a big town or a city, and even there a woman doing what you're doing would ruffle a few feathers.'

'But it'll be a good thing for everyone when I build the houses,' Molly protested. 'And the factory will provide work for folk.'

'Aye, I know, I know.'

She might know, Molly thought to herself, but at the bottom of her Gladys didn't approve of what she was doing either. If she had been a young man doing this she would have been applauded. It was so unfair, but if women just accepted the status quo nothing was ever going to change.

It was later that night when there was a knock at the front door. A heavy twilight had descended early with storm clouds gathering, and she had lit the lamps two hours ago. As she walked to the door she felt a fluttering in her stomach. Not more trouble? She really didn't feel she could take much more today.

'Hello, Molly.' John's voice was soft.

She stared at him, utterly taken aback.

'Can I come in?'

'Of course.' Flustered, she stepped back and let him pass, the colour flooding her cheeks. He brought the smell of the wind and cold in with him and as she shut the door the first raindrops began to fall.

He stood in the small room, making it even smaller with his presence, and her heart seemed to be trying to get out of her chest as she looked at him. Somehow she managed to say, 'Can I take your hat and coat? Please sit down, won't you.'

'Thank you.' He smiled ruefully. 'I didn't know if I would be allowed over the threshold in view of our last meeting.'

'Don't be silly.' Her composure was returning. 'Would you like a hot drink? It might be May but it's bitterly cold when night falls.'

'What I really want is to talk to you.'

Same old John, she thought, *straight to the point*. She motioned with her hand for him to sit down, taking his hat and coat and putting them on the pegs to one side of the front door, but he didn't seat himself until she had and then only on the edge of the armchair, leaning forward with his hands clasped between his knees. His black hair was ruffled and his face had been newly shaved. Had he done that because he was coming to see her? she wondered as her heart leaped again. He'd nicked himself on his chin . . .

'This is nice, cosy.' He waved his hand to take in the

room but kept his eyes on her. 'You are renting it, I presume?'

'No, I've bought it. I felt it was right for me the first time I saw it so there was no reason not to.'

'I see.' Was that a polite way of telling him that she had no intention of returning to Buttercup House or having anything more to do with him? But then he had known that, hadn't he, so why did it feel like a slap in the face? 'And are you happy here, now that you have settled in?'

'Very.'

'It is rather isolated for a young woman living on her own, if you don't mind me saying.'

So that was it. Gladys had clearly told him about the young men who had been here, maybe even the rest of what she had confided. He wasn't here because he wanted to be, simply because he felt obliged to be, which was completely different. She knew what John was like – anyone in difficulties or struggling he wouldn't be able to ignore. It was the doctor in him, that and his innate sense of responsibility. He still despised her and wouldn't choose to have anything to do with her in the normal way of things.

Her voice cool, she said, 'Do I assume Gladys has been speaking to you?'

'Mrs McHaffie?' He nodded. 'She did mention that certain folk have been a little unpleasant.' More than unpleasant, and when he'd heard what his cook had related his blood had boiled. As for those two louts who had dared to try and intimidate her in her own home, he could have strangled them with his bare hands. Not that she seemed intimidated, far from it. He had expected to find her distressed and upset, crushed even, but there was no sign of that.

'I am quite capable of dealing with it and have no intention of being swayed from my plans.'

Molly's chin had gone up a notch. He recognized the stance from his dealings with her in the past. She had dug her heels in. 'I didn't think for a minute you would be.'

'Good. Progress is often challenged and never more so than if it's perceived that a woman doesn't know her place.'

'And do you? Know your place?' he shot back, goaded by her air of autonomy and superciliousness. As soon as the words were out of his mouth he regretted them. He didn't even really mean them, he told himself, but she had the knack of making him *so* mad.

Her blue eyes narrowed. 'Oh, yes, Doctor.' In contrast to his heated voice, hers was icy cold. 'I know exactly what I want to achieve and I won't be deflected by narrow minds that refuse to accept that society needs to come out of the Dark Ages. Women are every bit as intelligent as men and more than capable of engaging in business and commerce and politics if they so choose, and science too. Look at Madame Curie winning an unprecedented second Nobel Prize. She is not an oddity or a one-off, there are plenty of other gifted, intelligent women who could rise to great heights given the chance. But society, especially in certain countries, feels threatened by this.'

'I take it you mean men when you say society?'

'Yes, men. We are governed by men, are we not? Men who insist women should "know their place",' she added acidly.

'You sound bitter.'

'And that doesn't fit your image of womanhood?'

He stared at her. 'I didn't come here tonight to argue with you,' he said after a few seconds of screaming silence.

'Why did you come?'

Because I love you. 'To see how you are.'

She inclined her head. 'Thank you. As you can see I am quite all right.' It had never been further from the truth.

The rain was lashing against the windowpanes now, the wind whining like a lost soul down the chimney. The storm had hit in earnest.

He rose to his feet, his voice clipped as he said, 'I won't impose further.'

'You're not going in this?' she said involuntarily, and then blushed hotly. She didn't want him to think that she was angling for him to stay.

'A drop of rain never hurt anyone.' If he stayed another minute he was going to make a prize fool of himself. He wanted to beg her to— *To what?* he asked himself as he walked across and lifted his coat and hat from the pegs. To come home with him? She had just told him she had bought this cottage, so that was never going to happen. To ask her if he could call sometimes? What was the point of that? She had made it clear she neither wanted him nor cared about him in a romantic sense. In fact, she seemed to see him as the enemy when all he wanted was to take her in his arms and tell her he loved her – he could just imagine how that would go down. But he had been desperately worried about her after Mrs McHaffie had related what was going on. He still was.

As he turned to face her this last thought prompted him to say, his voice stiff now, 'If any further incidents like the one today occur, or anything untoward, I hope you know you can come and see me. You might not work for me any more but we were friends once.'

She stared at him across the room, the firelight turning her hair into a blonde halo. Friends. So this thing she had sensed between them, this feeling that had nothing to do with friendship, had all been on her side? But of course it had, she told herself, holding on to her composure by the skin of her teeth. Look how he had reacted when she had told him about her past. He could have revealed anything about himself, *anything*, and she wouldn't have thought any the less of him but he hadn't been able to wait to see the back of her. She knew that – she'd had to come to terms with it, hadn't she – so why did it feel as raw as ever at this moment?

She didn't answer him – she couldn't, for fear of breaking down – and merely moved her head in a little nod. *Go, just go*; all she had left from this disastrous relationship was her dignity and she was in danger of losing that if he didn't leave.

'Goodbye, Molly.'

It sounded very final and it closed her throat still more. She inclined her head again and then he opened the door and stepped out into the storm, closing it behind him with some difficulty as the wind tried to snatch it from his fingers.

And then she was alone.

PART FIVE

Friends and Enemies

1915

Chapter Twenty-Three

It was fifteen months since Molly had become the owner of Lilac Cottage and much had happened in that time. War had been declared the year before as Britons had returned from their bank holiday. In the resulting euphoria, thousands of young men had beaten a path to the recruitment centres. They had been anxious to do their bit for King and country in view of the prediction that the war would be won by the Allies by Christmas. The reality proved more grim. The enemy had prepared well for the conflict, and seemed invincible.

At first Molly had lived in dread that she would hear through Gladys that John had joined up. As time had gone on, however, it had become clear that he felt his place was in Ellington caring for his patients. His assistant had gone off to war within weeks and John was now the only doctor for miles around.

'Working all hours of the day and night, he is,' Gladys frequently grumbled on her Sunday visits. 'Thin as a beanpole and his clothes are hanging off him. This war will be the death of him as surely as if one of them Germans put a bullet in him but he won't listen to rhyme or reason.'

Oliver visited her often now, usually without Angeline. They had become close enough for Molly to take the boy to task when he kept saying that he wanted to join up and fight the enemy, regardless of the fact that he was only sixteen.

'Plenty of lads lie about their age,' he had protested when she'd admonished him. 'Hubert Whitely at school said the recruitment officers ask no questions even if they suspect you're younger than you say.'

Molly knew that was true. She had heard lots of reports about young lads of fourteen and fifteen joining up. Some wanted to escape the prospect of the pits and factories for what they saw as the glory of a uniform in the King's army, taking no account of the hell they would be plunged into, like the bloodbath at Mons. 'Your father would be devastated if you did that,' she told Oliver, 'and he's got enough on his plate trying to cope with his workload as it is. And war isn't noble, Oliver. It's dirty and bloody and horrific. Promise me you won't do anything foolish. You'll get called up when you are old enough, wait till then.'

'What if the war's over by then, though?'

She prayed it would be. 'That's in the future and no one can foresee it. Now promise me you will wait.'

He had promised. Reluctantly. But she still worried about him. There was so much propaganda going on and even though as many men and youths were joining up in a few days as had done in a year before the war, the government still said it wasn't enough.

The number of training centres all over the country had been rapidly expanded, with local authorities providing accommodation in public buildings where they could, but many raw recruits were under canvas. Some British regiments were honing their skills for war camped around the Cresswell area, with a number of officers being housed in Cresswell Hall. This gracious residence of twenty-four rooms also boasted a separate building for servants and a state-of-the-art stable block which the army was making use of. According to Gladys, who knew the cook at the Hall, garden parties were still being held in the grounds so that some of the dashing officers could meet wealthy local families, particularly those with marriageable daughters. She knew from Gwendoline Havelock that Cuthbert was resisting all efforts for Havelock Hall to be used in the same way. When Gwendoline had said she felt it was their duty to offer accommodation to the army he had had a blue fit.

Molly still wasn't quite sure how her friendship with Gwendoline had come about. Shortly after her visit to Havelock Hall and about the time Mr Weatherburn and his sons had begun work on the site of the factory, she had been there one day discussing things with the builder when a grand carriage and horses had pulled up a short distance away and Gwendoline had alighted. She had hurried over to Cuthbert's wife, expecting trouble of some kind, but instead Gwendoline had told her that she'd wanted to see the site of the factory for herself.

Gwendoline had looked somewhat incongruous in her exquisite clothes stepping daintily over mud and rubble but had expressed a genuine interest in the proceedings, and since that occasion had called at Lilac Cottage several times, taking tea and cake with Molly in her little sitting room. Molly had been extremely uncomfortable at first, wondering – perhaps unfairly – if Cuthbert's wife had an ulterior motive in seeking her out, although she couldn't think of a single thing; but as time had gone on she had realized that, for all her wealth and riches, Gwendoline was lonely and unhappy. Furthermore, in spite of their different backgrounds and standing in life, the two women had found in each other a kindred spirit. By unspoken mutual consent Cuthbert was rarely mentioned, although Gwendoline had intimated that her husband was spending a lot of time in London whereas she preferred the country these days. Reading between the lines, Molly felt Gwendoline's championing of her hadn't gone down too well.

Due to men enlisting at the outbreak of the war, including Mr Weatherburn's sons, work on the factory had ground to a halt the previous September. However, the old builder had called on some of his equally old pals and between them they'd finished the job before the worst of the winter. Molly knew she'd need many more hands to the plough if the estate of houses was going to be built and she had no intention of letting that dream be put on hold because of the Kaiser. The war had turned everyone and everything topsy-turvy; all the old codes and values were up in the air with the government urging women everywhere to quit their homes for the factories and all kinds of work that would have been considered highly unsuitable just a couple of years before. The aim was to get as many women as possible doing vital jobs so that the men could be freed for fighting the Germans. Women were desperately needed in trade, industry, agriculture and armaments – any job that had been done by a man could be done by a woman, the government had declared in a complete about-face that had been warmly welcomed by leaders of the women's movement, including Emmeline Pankhurst, who had said that women were only too anxious to be recruited.

The winter had been hard in the north with continuous deep snow and blizzards that had seen villages and farmsteads cut off from the outside world for weeks on end and drifts that could swallow a horse and cart whole. But by the middle of March, when the government decided to set up an official Register of Women for War Work Service and over fifty thousand women had entered industry, the snow disappeared and after the resulting floods the weather became milder.

With the idea of women working outside the home becoming more acceptable – even patriotic – Molly's position had changed in the community. True, some men still held her in suspicion, but overall she met with less hostility. In April she secured her second, larger parcel of land some few hundred yards from the factory and set about the idea she had been mulling over all through the long winter days: to recruit women to build her houses.

She had begun her campaign by going to see Gladys's best friend, Sybil McGuigan, at the grocer's shop, and asking her to put a notice in the shop window. It read as follows:

> *Ladies of Ellington, Cresswell and further afield.*
> *Are you healthy and fit and willing to work in the*
> *building trade to provide affordable rental housing*
> *for your local community? Full training will be*
> *given on the job and your wage will be equal to*
> *that of a man doing the same work. If you are*
> *interested in hearing more, come to a meeting at*
> *the Ellington village hall in a week's time on*
> *Monday, 19th April at six o'clock.*
> *Molly McKenzie*

Sybil had read the notice and then stared at her open-mouthed, handing it silently to her husband, who had come over when he'd seen her stance. It wasn't often his wife was lost for words. *More's the pity*, he thought.

'By, lass, this'll cause a stir,' was his only comment before he passed the notice back to her and went to serve a customer.

And now it *was* April 19th and Molly had no idea if the small hall would be empty when she arrived. She had felt sick to the pit of her stomach all day and now, as she climbed down from the trap and tied Gracie to one of the posts outside, she stood for a moment in the weak evening sunlight. The village hall was never locked, the same as most of the houses and cottages in the village along with the parish church, and the old oak door was slightly ajar, but that didn't mean anyone was inside, she told herself. Folk might have mellowed a little towards her in the last months, but she knew her reputation was still that of a scarlet woman who had compounded her sin of being the doctor's mistress by leaving him and starting up in business on her own.

A number of men and older youths from hereabouts had enlisted when war had broken out, and she had heard that already there were some tragic cases of deaths at the front. That might sway one or two women with hungry mouths to feed to work outside the home, but she just wasn't sure. Women and girls who had been in service at big houses all over the country had left in droves for the factories, especially the armament ones where they could earn the sort of money they had only dreamed of before the war, but married women with families in the villages and hamlets weren't in a position where they could just up sticks. Neither would they ask for what they saw as charity – northern folk were proud – and many would rather quietly starve than enter the workhouses.

She let out a long, silent breath and stroked one of Gracie's velvet ears, and the little mare stared at her with her big liquid eyes. She had fallen in love with

Gracie and all through the winter had spent hours in the stable, grooming and petting the little horse and just talking to her; Gracie had rewarded her devotion by nuzzling her with her soft mouth and snorting with pleasure when she came to see her in the morning. 'Right, girl, wish me luck.' She patted the mare's back, squared her shoulders and walked through the partially open door into the hall.

Over twenty women turned their heads as she entered and watched her as she walked to the front of the hall, her heart beating fit to burst.

Gladys had told her she would try and come to support her – Molly had wondered if that was because her friend suspected no one else would turn up – and sure enough, there she was in the front row, smiling and nodding as Molly walked by. Overwhelmed, Molly took a moment to compose herself as she turned and faced the women, some of whom had brought their children with them.

She cleared her throat, her cheeks flushed. 'Thank you all for coming. It's lovely to see so many of you.'

'Me sister would have come,' said a sharp-faced woman dressed in black who was sitting next to Gladys, 'but her youngest is down with the measles and right poorly with it, but she wants to be included.'

Molly nodded. 'That's fine.'

'So, lass, what's it all about?' said another voice from the back of the hall, whereupon Gladys turned round and called, 'If you shut up, Nelly Parker, she'll tell you, won't she.'

'I'll try and explain the best I can – I know some of you have got bairns you want to get home to.' Molly cleared her throat again. It seemed as if hundreds of pairs of eyes were fixed on her. 'We all know that the war has changed everything. Lots of men and older lads are already at the front and still more will follow. That means that all over the country women have had to step up and take on men's jobs, and I have to say that they are doing well at it too. We are stronger, more capable and intelligent than most men give us credit for. Would anyone disagree with that?'

Several of the women looked at each other and shuffled in their seats but no one said anything. Molly glanced at Gladys, who winked at her encouragingly.

'I'm sure you are all aware that I have recently finished building a brick-making factory?'

Again there were a few glances and shifting in seats.

'The factory is a means to an end. I decided to build it because I intend to construct low-cost and affordable housing which will be comfortable to live in and provide families with a nice home. As I will own the houses, I will make sure the rent is reasonable and conditions are good. They will be very different to most colliery housing or agricultural cottages, having three bedrooms upstairs and a kitchen, dining room and sitting room downstairs along with an indoor bathroom. They will be erected in blocks of twelve, with a back garden of fifty feet by twenty feet and trees planted twenty yards apart between the blocks and the road. Does anyone have any questions thus far?'

'Aye, I do.' It was the woman Nelly Parker again, and her voice still carried the slightly confrontational note it had before. 'When you say these houses are for families, does that mean the pit officials and shop owners and the like, them with a bit of money?'

'Not at all. They will be for everyone.'

'If they can afford 'em,' Nelly responded with a sneer.

'I can promise you that the rent will be no more than some of you have to pay to the Ashington Coal Company or other landlords, but the accommodation will be vastly improved. Furthermore, if the breadwinner in the house falls ill or loses his job through no fault of his own, or her own, it won't mean that families will immediately be turned out on the road. That is not to say I will prove a soft touch – I can assure you that I am not – but genuine hardship will be met with understanding and a wish to help.'

Nelly's eyes narrowed. She was a big, tough woman dressed in an old coat and hat with a shawl about her shoulders and looked formidable. 'And what's in it for you, then?' she challenged.

There was a ripple of consternation. You didn't ask them who were a cut above something like that. Miss McKenzie had been the doctor's fancy bit and now was in business for herself, and it was no secret that Gwendoline Havelock paid her visits too, although no one could quite work out what that was all about. Nevertheless, it added to the mystery that was Molly McKenzie. She wasn't like other women, that was for sure.

Molly raised her chin. 'I don't intend to lose out financially in the long run, if that is what you mean, but neither do I believe that looking the other way when someone needs help is morally justifiable. I've seen families sitting by the side of the road with all their belongings beside them or sheltering in broken-down barns or huddled in doorways, like I'm sure you all have. Bairns reduced to scrambling for mouldy fruit in the gutter or old folk dying in one room without heat or food or hope. It's wrong that certain landlords crack the whip and blackmail men and women into not daring to protest about wretched living conditions or rates of pay for fear of ending up in the workhouse. It's a sin before God and man but most people are unable to do anything about it. In some small way I can. That's all.'

The two women looked at each other steadily for a moment. Then Nelly said quietly, 'Aye, well, that'll do for me.'

The atmosphere in the hall lifted. Nelly Parker was the undisputed queen bee among the women, although most of them were a little afraid of the rough miner's wife. Nelly's first husband had been killed down the Linton pit when they'd only been married for eighteen months, leaving her with a babe in arms. She'd come to Ellington to work in the East Moor Dairy which gave employment to local women, working with her son tied to her back with a shawl and lodging with a poor family where she slept on a pallet on the kitchen floor. She'd married her second husband when he'd arrived to work at the new colliery five years ago but to date there had been no children from that union. He had joined up as soon as war had broken out and some unkind souls had said it was to escape Nelly's acid tongue. Certainly she had been furious with him; the separation allowance of fifteen shillings a week that the army paid was only a third of what he had been bringing home from the colliery.

Molly nodded to the dour-faced woman and continued speaking. 'What I need to ascertain tonight is how many of you would be prepared to learn the aspects of the building trade like bricklaying, carpentry, plastering among other things? My builder, Mr Weatherburn, and a friend of his would teach you these skills on site, but first all the groundwork would need to be done, which will be hard, dirty work. I'll provide working clothes and boots and machines and so forth, but it won't be easy.'

'My old mam, God rest her soul, knew all about hard work,' a woman who looked to be in her fifties said from the second row. 'Down the pit she was, from a bairn, an' she used to say the only difference between the pit and hell would be that hell'd be a darn sight cleaner, an' she weren't just talking about coal dust. Animals are cleaner than humans, she said, and their muck smells better an' all. Fire damp and falls and being in stinking water up to your knees an' the dark an' rats didn't bother her like human muck. Twelve-hour shifts she did when she was knee-high to a grasshopper and sometimes didn't see the sun for weeks on end, so whatever you've got in store for us, it won't be nowt like that.'

Molly stared into the lined face before saying softly, 'No, it won't be like that.'

'What about those of us who want to work but have got bairns at home?' asked another woman.

Molly nodded. 'I've been thinking about that. How many of you would be in that position?' Several of the women raised their hands. 'Well, why don't you get together and delegate one of you to stay at home with all the children and you each pay a certain amount of your wage to that person? You could even work out a rota so that it's a different woman each week if you prefer?'

'How much are we talking about, pay wise?' It was Nelly again, her voice interested now rather than confrontational.

'I've taken advice from Mr Weatherburn on that and he informs me that there are different rates of pay for labourers and those men with skills like bricklaying and plastering and so on. As we'll all be in this together I shall do away with that. I'm sure every one of you will pull your weight regardless of the job you do and so everyone will be paid the same, thirty shillings a week. A man's wage and you'll be doing a man's job. It's top whack, I might add, so for anyone who is employed by me, Mr Weatherburn will expect absolute commitment.'

'For thirty shillings a week, lass, I'd dance naked for him,' said the irrepressible Nelly, causing everyone to laugh.

Molly smiled. 'I don't think that will be necessary. So, any questions?'

'When would we start?'

'Next Monday. That should give those of you who have children time to make arrangements. The hours will be from eight in the morning until six at night, five and a half days a week. Saturday afternoons and Sundays will be for family.'

'Some of the men won't like it,' a sallow-faced woman sitting next to Nelly piped up. 'My Neville for one.'

'That's for you to sort out with your menfolk, not me,' Molly said firmly. 'I am offering you work but I'm not forcing anyone to take it.'

'Did your Neville ask your permission when he upped and joined up?' Nelly asked the woman, who shook her head. 'No, I thought not. All very well to do his bit for King and country but what about doing his bit for his wife an' bairns?'

'Isn't that the same thing?' the woman asked meekly.

'Not in my book.'

The woman didn't argue. No one argued with Nelly.

'He's left you to cope with the bairns and feed 'em and clothe 'em as best you can, so he can't object about the way you do it.'

The woman looked doubtful but still said nothing.

'My Frank was a bit funny about me coming tonight,' another woman proffered, 'but I said to him the government's saying everyone has got to work now if they can. You tell him that, Gertie. Things are changing.'

And not before time, Molly thought. A woman should be able to choose whether she worked outside the home or not but some of these women had been dictated to by society, and not least their menfolk, all their lives. A marriage should be a partnership, surely, with neither one controlling the other, but was it only her that thought like that? She and Gwendoline had had some interesting discussions on the topic and it had caused her to realize that although the constraints and restrictions regarding upper-class women were different to those of the working classes, there were social limitations nonetheless. Imposed, on the whole, by men. For men.

'In my world,' Gwendoline had told her, 'girls know from birth that they are second-class compared to boys. I don't think any of my friends ever questioned the distinct roles of men and women. We all knew that our sole purpose in life was to marry well and then secure an heir with a spare for the family name to continue. Two of my friends, for example, were married off to men old enough to be their grandfathers for this reason.'

'Didn't they object?' Molly had asked, amazed.

'I don't think so. One doesn't.' Gwendoline had shaken her head. 'You have to understand that we are conditioned from babyhood to embrace our place in society. My mother would organize shooting parties for my father and his male friends but wouldn't have dreamed of asking to attend them, and there were many other such things. She would put on wonderful dinner parties and see to every little detail, but on the night present herself as decorative and somewhat empty-headed because that was the way my father liked it.' Gwendoline had leaned forward and taken her hand for a moment. 'I confess, before I met you I never questioned such matters.'

'And now?'

Gwendoline's mouth had pulled tight. 'Now I do. Oh, yes, now I do. I feel as though I have walked through life with my eyes closed and am seeing properly for the first time.'

Coming back to the present, Molly glanced over the assembled women. Some were dressed in widow's black. It was unfortunate that because most of the men who had joined up from the four villages of Lynemouth, Ellington, Cresswell and Linton had done so together, they had been put in the same regiment as their pals and therefore had died together in the bloody battles that had ensued in France. There were still plenty of miners who had remained at home, unlike Nelly's husband, but a good number of the farm workers hereabouts had gone off to war, and those in other jobs. 'Let me say again, I am not here to cause trouble between man and wife or persuade you to do anything you don't feel is right, but for everyone who wants to work for me I would ask you to write your name and address on this piece of paper tonight so I have some idea of numbers. I shall purchase hard-wearing dungarees and boots too, so let me know your sizes for both or a rough approximation.'

She paused. 'Can I say one last thing, ladies. Every single one of you is strong and courageous. You've had to be, growing up where you have and carving out a life for yourselves and your families amid poverty, disease and the uncertainty of day-to-day life. Your menfolk work hard and those at the front are there because they believe in fighting for their families and country, but every single day of your lives you fight just as hard. I know that. Running your homes and making a penny stretch to two, endeavouring to put food on the table for your children and clothes on their backs, sometimes going without so your family's fed and always the worry of paying the rent man at the back of your minds. And sometimes that rent is for properties that in all honesty you wouldn't house an animal in.'

The hall was completely silent; you could have heard a pin drop.

'Every woman who works for me will have an option to rent a house on my new estate before I open it up to other tenants, I promise you that here and now. And the second phase of the build will incorporate shops, run by locals for locals and with no extortionate prices or inferior produce. This estate will be what you make it, for better or worse. It's up to you.'

There were a few seconds of absolute quiet and then Gladys rose to her feet and turned to look at the assembled women. 'Well?' she said loudly. 'Have you lost the use of your feet?' And as one the occupants of the hall rose and came in a rush to sign the paper Molly was holding.

Chapter Twenty-Four

Cuthbert Havelock sat in his book-lined study at Havelock Hall, red in the face with anger.

It was the middle of May, and he had returned from his London house where he had been residing since early February after Zeppelins had carried out their first air raid on the capital a couple of days before. He had been terrified, hightailing it back to the country as fast as he could. He had been pretty shaken earlier in the month when the huge Cunard liner *Lusitania* had sunk after being torpedoed without warning by a German submarine. One of his cousins had been on board on a return voyage from New York, and had been among the one thousand and four hundred men, women and children who had perished. Cuthbert had comforted himself that he was safe enough on dry land and he had no intention of leaving terra firma any time soon, and therefore the attack on London from the air had shocked him profoundly.

He had been relieved to arrive back at the Hall the night before and had slept well, but this morning Winters had informed him of two happenings that had made his blood boil. The first, that the McKenzie woman had an army of local women working on land where she intended to build a housing estate, and the second, that it had come to the butler's ears that Gwendoline had been known to call on the wench.

He had stared at Winters, unable to believe his ears. 'You are saying that the mistress . . .' Words had failed him.

Winters had nodded solemnly. 'I heard one of the maids talking and so I made it my business to have a word with the coachman, sir. Apparently the mistress has called on Miss McKenzie several times. When I asked Tollett why I hadn't been told of this, the man said he hadn't known that he was expected to report on the mistress's comings and goings.' Winters had been unable to keep his anger at what he saw as the coachman's insolence out of his voice. Tollett, like the rest of the outdoor staff, resented his authority. He knew that. He was in no doubt that the man had imagined he was getting one over on him by keeping the mistress's visits to the McKenzie woman quiet.

Cuthbert had dismissed the butler and then sat brooding about what he had been told for an hour or so, the large measures of brandy he'd taken with his morning coffee adding fuel to the flames of his temper.

'What the hell is Gwendoline playing at?' he murmured to himself, throwing back another tot of brandy. Since his wife had told him about the document she had written and placed in the care of McKenzie, they had barely exchanged a word unless out of necessity. He was still furious with her.

He'd made it his business to spend as much time lately as he could in London. He enjoyed the pleasures the capital had on offer. He'd found a tasty young whore in a brothel in Soho who continued to tickle his fancy even though he had visited her many times. Jinny had been on the game since she was eight years old and her father had sold her to Madam Neill. Now, at sixteen, what Jinny didn't know about pleasing a man wasn't worth knowing. She had even taught him a trick or two and he'd imagined nothing could surprise him. The girl was like a drug; he couldn't get enough of her. Just thinking about her now was making him excited. Nothing was out of bounds with Jinny.

Bringing his mind back to Gwendoline and the McKenzie woman, he ground his teeth, his fingers itching to wrap themselves around his wife's neck. Did she have no sense of propriety? he asked himself angrily. But he knew what this was about. She was trying to get at him, damn her. He'd like to see the pair of them rot in hell.

He poured himself the last dregs of brandy, swirling the amber liquid round in the glass as he frowned into it. He'd thought he might see the back of Molly McKenzie after he'd bent a few ears to her goings-on. The local blacksmith had been a willing listener when he'd taken Midnight to be shod and given the man a hefty gratuity for his trouble, and a few casually spoken words to one or two others hereabouts had stirred up a host of bad feeling. Of course, those two louts from the estate that he'd paid to go and give her a fright had been a mistake but he'd got away with it without anyone suspecting him. When they'd admitted what had occurred he'd frightened the life out of them as to what he'd do if they mentioned his name. With the war and all, he had to admit he'd thought she would move on to pastures new, but apparently not. And now she intended to build *houses*? No doubt with bricks from her damn factory. And his own wife was encouraging the enterprise? Well, he'd see about that.

Standing up, he nudged his chair with the back of his legs so violently it almost tipped over and strode out of the room. He had no doubt she would be in her sitting room; she tended to stay out of his way when he was here and it suited both of them. Flinging open the door, he saw the room was empty, and slamming it shut he stood in the hall and bellowed at the top of his voice, 'Winters!'

As smoothly as if he was on wheels, the butler appeared. 'Yes, sir?'

'My wife. Where is she?'

'I believe Mrs Havelock is in the kitchen garden talking to the head gardener, sir.'

Cuthbert stared at his butler. Life at Havelock Hall, like many great houses, tended to revolve around farming the land and he had over a dozen tenant farmers on his estate as well as several gardeners for the grounds of the house. The kitchen garden and greenhouses and orchard were tucked well out of sight of the ornamental pleasure gardens and he had rarely walked that way; up to this moment in time he would have sworn Gwendoline hadn't either. His wife would discuss menus with their cook and food would appear on the table, it was as simple as that. 'The kitchen garden?'

'Yes, sir. Due to the war there have been some families who have lost their breadwinners and fallen on hard times, and of late the mistress has seen to it that baskets of produce have been distributed to needy folk.' Winters took a perverse pleasure in his next words. 'I understand Miss McKenzie is involved in the undertaking, sir.'

Cuthbert pushed the old man out of the way so savagely he almost fell, his voice a growl as, striding from the hall, he bit out, 'And you didn't see fit to inform me of this before?'

Winters stood looking after his master for some moments, his stiff face unreadable, and then made a sound in his throat that even he wouldn't have been able to translate into words.

Gwendoline stood at the end of the huge kitchen garden under the shelter of a large lean-to which housed several gnarled and battered oak tables. Along with all sorts of different vegetables the tables held some fruit, of which nectarines and peaches were the prize products. The brick wall of the sheltered spot where they grew was heated with fires all along, stoked through the night by the youngest of the gardeners so that the fruit would ripen sooner and long before the normal season. One table consisted of a number of plucked and headless chickens wrapped in muslin and an enormous pile of wicker baskets. Gwendoline was filling each one with a chicken and vegetables and fruit as Cuthbert appeared through the door at the other end of the garden, and she didn't stop what she was doing as he approached, merely glancing his way for a moment as she said, 'Good morning.'

'The hell it is.' One of the kitchen maids had been helping in the task and now he clicked his fingers at her. 'You. Get back to the house.'

'Stay where you are, Margaret,' Gwendoline said in a cool, clear voice as she raised her head and looked him fully in the face. 'She is assisting me and we haven't finished yet.'

His eyes widened slightly. In all their years of marriage she had never countermanded an order from him and it had taken him aback. They stared at each other and he saw steel in the pale blue eyes which further disconcerted him, causing his voice to be less forceful than he would have liked it to be when he said, 'Assisting you doing what?'

Gwendoline didn't doubt for a moment that Winters would have already informed his master, but she said calmly, 'I am making up baskets of food which will be distributed to those in need in the surrounding area.'

'And what prompted this? Or should I say, who?' he bit out tightly.

'Circumstances have prompted it, Cuthbert. There is a war on or haven't you noticed?'

The anger inside him was acting like a fire stoking an engine and if they had been alone he might well have lashed out at her, but with the kitchen maid and head gardener hovering close by he contented himself with growling, 'Yes, Gwendoline, I am well aware there is a war on, having nearly been bombed out of my bed in London.'

This was an exaggeration but it suited his purposes.

Gwendoline raised her fine eyebrows. 'Then you will understand we have to help where we can, and on that note we have received a further request to make the house available for the army.' It had actually been more of a command this time but she would let him read the notification himself. 'The papers are on my desk in my sitting room as I wasn't expecting you home.'

His gaze returned to the baskets. 'Who collects and delivers these?' he barked.

'Atkinson' – she nodded at the head gardener – 'sees to it that they are taken to the village, where they are distributed by Miss McKenzie and some of the other women.'

Apoplectic now at the casual way she had spoken of McKenzie, he didn't trust himself to reply, glaring at her with maddened eyes before turning and walking back the way he had come. At the end of the kitchen garden he wheeled round and watched her a moment. She was serenely carrying on with the job in hand and looked happier than she'd done in years. Practically foaming at the mouth, he made his way back to the house, and once in the hall yelled for Winters to get him more brandy. His mother had chosen to remain at the London residence, so the slight constraint he applied to his drinking when she was present wasn't necessary.

Slumping down behind his desk in his study again, he stared across the room; his countenance looked evil. So McKenzie thought she was calling the tune, did she? he thought. Inveigling herself into Gwendoline's good books and the locals hereabouts by all accounts, and snubbing her nose at him while she was about it. And now, with his dear wife's help, playing the lady of the manor. Didn't Gwendoline realize she was being used for McKenzie's own ends? Was she really that stupid? It would appear so.

A tap at the study door announced Winters with the brandy. He glared at the old man as Winters set it in front of him, saying, 'Is there anything else I can get you, sir?'

'There are going to be changes here, Winters. By hell there are.'

'Yes, sir.'

'The one thing I demand is loyalty. Do you understand that? From the lowest to the highest in this house. *Loyalty.*' The crash of his fist as it hit the desk made the old man visibly jump. 'I expect to be kept informed of everything that goes on inside and outside this house. I thought you knew that?'

'Yes, sir.' Winters had stiffened.

'Then why wasn't I told about the McKenzie woman – the visits my wife has made to her and this matter of the damn food baskets?'

'I only recently became aware of both issues, sir.'

'Not good enough. Do you hear me? Not good enough by half. You've let things slip, Winters. What is it? Too old to carry out your duties? Is that it?'

'Not at all, sir.'

The old man had begun to tremble but rather than invoking any pity it made Cuthbert crueller. Like most bullies, he fed on fear. 'No one is indispensable, Winters. Remember that. Now get out of my sight.'

The colour had drained from the butler's sallow face, leaving it grey. He stood for a moment, clearly bewildered by the attack, and then turned and left the study.

Cuthbert settled further in his chair and poured himself a brandy. The venting of his rage and frustration had restored his equilibrium to some extent. He'd make Gwendoline pay for her behaviour, he promised himself. Not only had she sided with the McKenzie woman against him in the matter of the letter, but she had further compounded the betrayal by apparently championing her ever since. And now the matter of these food baskets. He could understand why McKenzie had pressed Gwendoline to assist her; not only did it give her a certain amount of prestige to be associated with his wife but the doling out of the baskets furthered her power and influence among the locals.

His eyes narrowed. She was a wily one, all right. Scum,

of course, but clever with it, building what she saw as her small empire. But empires could be toppled.

He took a large swig of the brandy. No one thumbed their nose at him and got away with it, least of all a mere woman. She'd rue the day she crossed him, but he'd have to go about things carefully and make sure that nothing could be traced back to him.

He finished the glass of whisky and relaxed fully in the chair, shutting his eyes and resting his hands on his big belly. Revenge was a dish best taken cold, wasn't that what they said – or something to that effect? Anyway, the thought behind it was appropriate. Nothing impetuous or spur-of-the-moment. He'd deal with her; he'd crush her and bring her to her knees when he was ready and after that he'd bring his wife to order. He had been a fool to acquiesce to her demand for separate bedrooms, he saw that now. Not that her scrawny body held any interest for him but imposing his conjugal rights was a means to an end. She'd learn who was master all right.

One of the housemaids had opened the window and the scents of the May morning wafted in. Although it was still a little cool the promise of summer was every-where and in the grounds of the house horse chestnut trees, lush with foliage, displayed their pyramids of bloom, whilst huge oaks were decked in green and gold. There were worse places to be, he told himself, and although he would rather be in London with Jinny at hand he could tolerate the country for a few weeks or longer if the air raids continued in the capital. It would give him time to concentrate on the matter of the McKenzie woman, if nothing else.

Replete after the gargantuan breakfast he had consumed served to him in bed, and not least the amount of brandy he had poured down his throat, he drifted off to sleep to dream that he was squeezing the life out of Molly McKenzie with his bare hands. It was very satisfying.

Chapter Twenty-Five

'There's a couple of nice girdle scones to go with your coffee, Doctor. Make sure you eat 'em, mind.'

John glanced up from the notes he was writing and smiled at Gladys. She was like a mother hen with one chick these days, he thought, always trying to feed him up. 'Thank you, Mrs McHaffie,' he said as she placed the tray in front of him and then stood back, her arms crossed. The stance told him she wouldn't leave till he had tried one of the scones and dutifully he picked one up, oozing with butter, and ate it.

'And the other one,' she said as though he was five years old.

It was easier to eat it than argue. 'There,' he said as he finished the second scone. 'Satisfied?'

'I'll be satisfied when you look more like yourself. All them hours you're working, it's too much for one man if you don't mind me saying.'

She had been saying the same thing for months now but he didn't remind her of that, merely nodding. 'I know, I know, but needs must.'

'And there's still no word of an assistant to help?'

'I promise you, Mrs McHaffie, you'll be the first to know.'

'This war,' Gladys said angrily. 'It's turned everything upside down.' She reached for the empty plate and left the room, saying over her shoulder, 'Drink your coffee while it's hot. I've made it with milk.'

It wasn't the way he liked it but when he had objected before he'd been told it was more nourishing this way. Sighing, he took a sip, wincing at the amount of sugar she'd put in. The woman would drive him mad before she was finished.

No, that wasn't fair, he admonished himself in the next moment. She was only being kindly, and it wasn't Mrs McHaffie or even the war and the fact that he was the only doctor for miles around that had culled his appetite and zest for life.

He stood up abruptly, angry with himself. He despised self-pity but he'd expected that the ache in his heart would get better in the last months. Time was supposed to be the great healer, wasn't it? He stared morosely out of the window, the clear blue sky and bright sunshine mocking his inner turmoil. Since the day he had gone to Molly's cottage he'd seen her in the distance once or twice but that was all. He knew she'd bought the piece of land on which to build her houses; Mrs McHaffie had filled him in on the meeting in the village hall when Molly had inspired her female workforce, but he hadn't ventured near the site himself. She'd made it crystal clear how she felt about him and he had to accept it. He knew that was the only course of action, but how did his head convince his heart? It didn't help matters that Oliver had taken to visiting Molly when he was home at the weekends and was always full of her doings on his return, the proverbial salt in the wound.

Oliver . . . His frown deepened. His son was already set on joining up as soon as he was eighteen rather than going to university; he seemed to have no concept of just how horrific war was, and Angeline was a problem in a different way. The girl grew more feather-brained by the day. He didn't understand either of them. He slumped down in his chair again, wincing as he finished the sweet coffee, and then applied himself to the paperwork in front of him. He was working sixteen to eighteen hours a day, sometimes more, but still his patient notes and other correspondence had suffered. The receptionist he'd had at his surgery in the village had taken care of a certain amount of that side of things, but Belinda had left for factory work in Newcastle before Christmas and her replacement was straight out of school and a mouse of a girl. She could just about show the patients in and out and make a cup of tea.

When he heard the doorbell ring he groaned softly. He hadn't been back long from morning surgery and he had been hoping for an hour or two of peace. If it was Cuthbert Havelock again he would have to make it plain he didn't have time for the man's inane chatter. In the six weeks since Cuthbert had returned from London he'd regularly called at least twice a week – three times last week. He'd been furious that the army were going to use Havelock Hall to house some of their officers. When John had said he thought it was a good idea and that perhaps Cuthbert could get involved in the war effort, the man had left in a fit and he had rather hoped he wouldn't return for a while.

Within moments Lotty knocked and put her head round the door. 'There's been an accident, sir. Miss McKenzie—'

He shot to his feet. 'Miss McKenzie's hurt?'

'No, no, sir.'

'Then who?' he asked, pulling on his jacket from the back of his chair.

'The man who works for her, Mr Weatherburn. He's in charge of the women and something's happened. I couldn't make head nor tail of what.'

John hurried out to find an older man standing in the hall, twiddling his cap in his hands. 'Hello, Doctor. Miss McKenzie asked if you could come to the site as quick as you can. It's my pal, Bert, Albert Weatherburn. We were on our way in this morning when a couple of blokes stopped us, saying they wanted directions to Lynemouth. The next thing we knew they'd pulled Bert off the horse an' trap and were threatening him, saying he shouldn't be working for no woman and it was a disgrace an' so on. I got down and it ended up in a bit of a set-to – nothing much, just a few punches thrown and then they skedaddled. Me an' Bert carried on and I thought he was all right and then just a while ago he keeled over.'

'How long after the attack?' John asked, taking his bag from Lotty and opening the front door.

'Three hours or more.'

The man's horse and trap was waiting outside and John said, 'I'll come with you and you can fill me in more on the way.'

'Right you are, Doctor.'

In the event the man couldn't add much more to what he had already said, but it was enough to worry John more than a little. Clearly the two men who had attacked Bert and his pal Lonnie had lain in wait along the road they'd known the builders would use with the sole intention of using physical force to warn them off working for Molly. Were they just random individuals with a grievance against men working for a woman, or part of a bigger group? Possibly even husbands or menfolk of some of the women Molly employed? If such men were prepared to use violence, what was next? Attacking Molly herself?

When he arrived at the site his first impression was that it was much larger than he had expected. No houses had yet been built but extensive groundwork had been done and building materials, small mountains of dirt, several horses and carts and groups of women clad in dungarees and hobnailed boots were all over the area. It was a hive of activity.

Lonnie stopped the horse and cart outside a wooden hut on the outskirts of the site. There were a couple of other smaller structures some distance away which John took to be temporary privies by the look of them. The door to the hut was open and on entering it he found it to be a tiny office of sorts, with a table and chairs and several boxes piled in one corner. His patient was sitting on the floor with his back to the wall of the hut, his legs stretched out in front of him and a scowl on his face. Molly was sitting on one of the chairs at his side, her face pale and anxious. Of the two of them, John thought Bert Weatherburn looked in better shape.

Before John could say anything, the builder growled, 'I've told her I'm all right now, I don't need no doctor.'

John's heart had leaped into his throat at the sight of Molly but drawing on his professional experience, he said quietly, 'Let me be the judge of that, Mr Weatherburn. I hear you've been involved in an altercation through no fault of your own.'

'I told her I can get up but she's insisted I stay here.'

'Quite right. Now tell me in your own words what happened when you collapsed. Did you lose consciousness?'

'I didn't collapse, I just had a bit of a turn, that's all.'

'He was out for a minute or so,' Lonnie said firmly. 'One minute we were discussing getting a small-gauge railway to move building materials round the site once building proper starts, and the next he was flat out on the ground. That's right, isn't it, Miss McKenzie?'

Molly nodded. Seeing Mr Weatherburn black out and crumple to the ground had shaken her but having John in such close proximity was worse. 'I'm sorry,' she said to the disgruntled builder, keeping her gaze on him rather than John, who was now kneeling at the side of his patient taking his pulse. 'But you really weren't with us for over a minute or so, Mr Weatherburn.'

'Did you get punched in the head?' John sat back on his heels, reaching into his bag for his stethoscope.

'Aye, but we saw the beggars off atween us, didn't we, Lonnie.' Bert Weatherburn was determined he wasn't going to lose any more face. He was mortified to have passed out. Bit lassies fainted or had an attack of the vapours, not grown men of sixty-five. 'They got the worst of it.'

'I don't doubt it but nevertheless at—' John stopped abruptly. He had been going to say 'at your age' but sensing how that would go down with the disgruntled man, he changed it to, 'at any time a punch in the head can cause problems for a while.' He listened to the builder's heart and then straightened up. 'Your heart seems sound enough, Mr Weatherburn, and your pulse is strong, but I'd like you to rest for a couple of days. Delayed shock probably caused the episode but you can't be too careful with things like this. If you start to feel unwell in the next little while, call your doctor, all right? You live in Ashington, don't you? There's a doctor you can call?'

'Aye, aye, but I told you I'm as right as rain now. I can carry on here today. It's a lot of fuss about nothing.'

'Please, do what the doctor says.' Molly leaned forward and squeezed Bert's arm. 'Go home and put your feet up. I feel responsible for what happened and I shall be worried sick if you continue working. Lonnie can see you back home and we'll be fine here for a few days.'

'There's nowt for you to feel responsible about, lass.' Bert Weatherburn had come to like and respect the young woman who was his employer. As he had said to his wife on several occasions, she was as straight as a die and had more in her noodle than most men he knew. 'But if you're going to fret I'll take the rest of the day off and see you in the morning.'

'Only if you are well enough,' Molly cautioned.

'Aye, only if I'm well enough.' From his tone of voice he might as well have said that wild horses wouldn't stop him turning up tomorrow.

Once John and Lonnie got him up and on his feet, however, he confessed to being a little dizzy and didn't protest when they helped him into the horse and trap.

Molly and John stood looking after the two men as they drove away, an awkward silence enveloping them for a few moments before Molly broke it by saying softly, 'Thank you for coming straight away. I panicked, I suppose.'

'To see a stout fellow like him drop to the ground in front of you would unnerve anyone.'

They turned as one to look at each other as they spoke and again the silence descended but this time it throbbed with emotion. Molly realized Gladys hadn't been exaggerating when she'd said how thin he had become. He looked gaunt, in fact. The words came out of her mouth by their own volition: 'You're not eating enough.'

He blinked. 'No.'

'You should look after yourself better.'

'Yes.'

'Gladys is worried about you.'

He smiled one of his rare smiles and her insides fluttered. 'Believe me, I have been left in no doubt about that,' he said ruefully. 'She is a dear soul but once she gets a bee in her bonnet . . .' He shrugged. 'And you?' His voice gentled. 'How are you? You didn't really mean what you said about feeling responsible for those ruffians, did you?'

He had taken her hand as he spoke and the feel of his warm flesh prevented any prevarication she might have made, melting her defences. 'Yes,' she said simply, willing herself not to cry.

'Oh, my dear.' All around them was the hustle and bustle of the site but they were oblivious to it. 'You cannot blame yourself. You building these houses and employing local women and the rest of it is a good thing, anyone can see that.'

'Perhaps.'

'There's no perhaps about it. The last year has shown us that the country needs to adapt to a new way of going on, but unfortunately there will always be those who resist change. Some men are ignorant through no fault of their own, having not had the chance of an education, but others are ignorant by nature, as I suspect is the case with the two miscreants who attacked Mr Weatherburn and his friend.'

Molly stared at him. He had changed his tune, hadn't he?

She hadn't realized that her thoughts were mirrored on her face until John said quietly, 'I was wrong to object about your housing scheme, Molly. It is no excuse, no excuse at all, but in part it was because you hadn't discussed it with me beforehand. I – I was hurt, I suppose. I had thought we were friends, perhaps more than friends, but also I have to confess it was part prejudice too. For a well-brought-up young lady to compete in a male-dominated environment seemed terribly wrong.'

'And then you discovered I wasn't a well-brought-up young lady,' she said equally quietly, her voice soft but conveying something of the agony she had felt when he had rejected her so arbitrarily. 'You were disgusted when you learned of my beginnings.'

'What? No. No, that wasn't it at all. Is that what you thought?'

'You made it very clear,' she said, withdrawing her hand. 'You told me I was a stranger and wanted me to leave your house.'

'Molly, listen to me. I was foolish and proud and angry that you didn't feel for me what I felt for you but I never, not for one moment, thought any the less of you because of what you revealed about your past. I was bitterly disappointed you hadn't trusted me enough to confide in me until you were forced into it, I suppose. I had imagined we—' He stopped, shaking his head. 'I'm sorry, you don't want to hear this. I know how you feel and the last thing I want to do is to make things awkward for you.'

She couldn't take in what he was saying. She wanted to, she wanted to hope that somehow, against all the odds, he cared for her as she cared for him, but if she believed that and then she was wrong she wouldn't be able to bear it. Not for a second time.

'I should go. This isn't fair to you, I know that.'

Still she couldn't speak. The pain she had felt that night when she had left his house, the way he had made her feel, as though she was nothing, was as raw as ever. She had fought so hard to get to where she was but that day he had made her feel as helpless and worthless as the child in the hamlet. She couldn't let him do that again, she couldn't take the risk. He had the power to hurt her like no one else.

Aware that he was making a fool of himself and prob-ably making her highly embarrassed into the bargain, John stepped back a pace. He shouldn't have brought up the past, it would have been better to let sleeping dogs lie. It was the nearness of her that had done it. He swal-lowed deeply and attempted to defuse things when he said, 'Well, I must be off. I hope Mr Weatherburn suffers no ill effects from the incident other than what occurred today. I'll make enquiries at the surgery and on my rounds and ask if anyone saw these fellows loitering but I would think they're long gone. I'm sure you won't see hide nor hair of them again.'

She stared blankly at him, so consumed in the turmoil of her thoughts that for a moment his words didn't fully register.

'Molly, are you all right?' She was deathly pale and still, not like herself at all. 'You're not worried about these ruffians, are you?'

'No.' She wasn't, not at this moment in time when he was going to walk away from her. 'I'm – I'm fine.'

'Just remember, this has been upsetting for you too, seeing Mr Weatherburn collapse the way he did, so go easy today. Doctor's orders.'

He smiled and she attempted to smile back, desperate to say something to stop him leaving but too frightened to speak. Which was ridiculous, she told herself feverishly. She gave instructions on site and made decisions and dealt with deliveries and all kinds of things every day, so why couldn't she open her mouth and just talk naturally to him?

'It was nice seeing you again.' His voice was warm and soft. 'Oliver often speaks of you – he's very fond of you, you know, and rightly so. He was an angry little boy before you came to stay but you seemed to understand him right from the start and worked quite a transformation.'

'I'm fond of him too.'

'Well, goodbye then.' He didn't attempt to take her hand again, aware of the covert and not so covert glances that were coming their way from the various women scattered about, but simply nodded and turned away.

He walked swiftly but had only gone some twenty yards or so when her voice called after him, 'John? You're not walking back, are you? Where's your horse and trap?'

He swung round to see she had taken some steps towards him. 'I came with Lonnie but I can easily walk home – it's not far.'

'I can't let you do that. I have my own horse and trap over there.' She pointed to a small square of field that had been fenced off and where a small piebald mare was grazing on thick grass. 'I'll run you back. The girls are stopping for their lunch break now anyway.'

He thought about being polite and saying he wouldn't dream of bothering her, but only for a moment. He wanted a few extra minutes with her, it was as simple as that. 'That's kind of you, thank you.'

She didn't return his smile, merely inclining her head before she called to one of the women he recognized as Nelly Parker that she was taking the doctor home and would be back in a short while. He noticed the knowing look Nelly sent his way and in spite of himself felt hot colour flood his neck and face.

Cursing the fact that he always seemed to be put on the back foot in any contact with Molly, he drew his dwindling dignity about him like a cloak and turned his back on Nelly, and once the small horse and trap reached him climbed up on the vehicle's narrow seat with as much stateliness as he could muster, aware of many pairs of eyes boring into his back.

'This is Gracie.' Molly inclined her head at the pony. 'She's a darling, isn't she.'

'She looks a sweet-tempered animal.'

'Oh, she is.' Molly felt more relaxed now that she

was – quite literally – in the driving seat, the sun on her face and a warm breeze ruffling her hair.

It was the last day of June and the month hadn't been a good one for the Allies. The Russians had lost Lemberg to the enemy after the ancient fortress town of Przemyśl had been captured by the German army shortly before, and what with the Zeppelin raids and sinking of British liners and boats off the Cornish coast the war suddenly seemed very close to ordinary men and women. Three more of Molly's workers had suffered bereavements, including Nelly, whose husband had been killed at the Western Front. It was a harrowing time for everyone but right now, in the fresh warm air and with John sitting by her side, the war was furthermost from Molly's mind. She let Gracie trot along comfortably at her own pace and once they were clear of the site, took a deep breath and said quietly, 'I'm sorry I acquired the job of housekeeper under false pretences. I'm not proud of that.'

He looked at her but she kept her eyes on the country lane in front of them, her profile calm but her cheeks flushed. She was beautiful; everything about her was beautiful, even her voice which held a slight catch of huskiness that added to its charm. He had been fooling himself in hoping he would ever get over her, he realized suddenly. She was in his blood, his bones, his soul. Clearing his throat, he said earnestly, 'I understand the situation you were placed in, truly I do. I just wish that once we had got to know each other a little you would have been able to have the confidence to confide in me, but since I have thought about that I see why you hesitated. I can be set in my ways and—'

'No, please, John, it wasn't your fault, it was mine.' Her face had taken on a sadness which conveyed itself in her voice. 'I ruined everything, I know that.'

'I was monumentally pig-headed. *I* know that.' He was of necessity pressed against her on the seat and as the breeze blew, her hair smelled of apple blossom. 'And like I tried to explain earlier, it was all down to pride and self-pity and other attributes I despise. I had thought, in the future, that we—' He hesitated. 'But you were happy to walk away from me.'

'You had thought that we . . . what?' Her heart was beating so fast it was painful but the words had to come from him first. She didn't have the courage to declare herself without knowing exactly how he felt, she just didn't.

'Molly, I didn't feel that you cared for me at all, not in the way I'd hoped you might, but if I was wrong, if I hurt you, then I'm more sorry than you'll ever know. Could – could you pull over for a moment so I can say what I want to say?'

Once Gracie was standing obediently by the side of the dirt road he took her hands in his. Her face was unsmiling and tense, his equally so. They were so close on the little seat that he could see each eyelash. 'I don't want to distress you by saying something you would rather not hear but I need to declare myself this once and then if you do not want to refer to it again, I will understand.'

She stared at him, unaware that she was holding her breath.

'I love you. I love you in a way that transcends anything I have ever felt for anyone before and without you in it my life is empty, barren. You are the finest person I know and—'

His words were cut off as she leaned in to him and took his mouth with such passion, such longing, that no more words were necessary. For a second of wonder-filled time he froze and then his arms went about her, crushing her to him as their hearts pounded and everything faded away but each other. How long the kiss lasted they didn't know – it could have been minutes or hours, so lost were they in each other – but when eventually their lips parted it felt as though there had never been a time when they hadn't been together like this.

'My darling girl, my love, do you know what you mean to me?' he murmured, his lips moving over her face in swift kisses. 'Will you marry me, Molly? Soon?'

She drew back slightly and took his face in her hands. 'Tomorrow if you like,' she said softly, smiling.

'Say it. Say you love me.'

'I love you, I love you so much.'

'The children will be thrilled.'

Oliver yes, Angeline perhaps not so much. She rarely came with her brother these days on his Sunday visits to the cottage and often Oliver said Angeline was at Havelock Hall.

'We'll tell them together when Oliver gets home for

the weekend on Friday evening, and after they know we can tell everyone,' he said eagerly.

'Yes, all right.' He seemed to have shed ten years in the last few minutes and appeared almost boyish.

'I can't believe this.' She did not answer but leaned against him, touching his cheek with her fingers. 'This morning the world was as it's been every day since you left – grey and dark – and now . . .' He pulled her in to him again, kissing her long and hard until they were both breathless.

The country lane was tranquil in the hot June day, wild flowers scenting the air whilst in the distance hills were obscured by a trembling heat-haze. It was as though they had stepped out of time into a world of beauty and light; the war with all its ugliness had never seemed so far away. Gracie was cheerfully munching the thick grass dotted with flowers at the side of the road and above them towering elms and oaks cast heavy shadows over the leaf-bound lane, birds twittering away in the branches.

She wished this moment could last for ever, Molly thought as she nestled in his arms. Just the two of them with no one else to think about or consider. But of course, life wasn't like that. John's days were long and heavy with responsibility and she needed to get back to the site, especially with Mr Weatherburn and Lonnie gone.

'I shall bless Mr Weatherburn all the days of my life,' John said throatily, his voice gruff with emotion. 'Oh, my darling, how can you love a fool like me?'

'Don't.' She kissed the corner of his mouth, the mouth that could appear so stern at times. 'We've both been foolish.'

'Not you, never you.' He covered her mouth with his again and all thoughts of the site faded away.

Chapter Twenty-Six

'Yes!' Oliver leaped up, grinning like a Cheshire cat. 'I knew you two should be together.'

It was Friday evening and John had brought the children to Lilac Cottage, where he and Molly had just broken the news of their engagement. John had gone into Ashington the previous day and returned with a beautiful ring set with an emerald and two diamonds. It still felt heavy and strange on her finger but every time she glanced at it she felt a rush of joy spread through her that made her tingle.

'Did you think that?' John looked at his son in surprise.

'Definitely.' Oliver reached out and gave Molly a big hug.

He was as tall as her now at only sixteen, having had his birthday in January, Molly thought with a stab to her heart. She prayed every day that the war would be over before Oliver was old enough to fight. She felt she loved him as much as if he had been her own son.

'Miss McKenzie is good for you,' Oliver said, grinning. 'She'll keep you on your toes and stop you from becoming too staid and stuffy. Actually, can I call you Molly now instead of Miss McKenzie?' he added to Molly, resuming his seat by the fireplace. 'I always think of you as Molly anyway.'

'Of course you can.' Molly opened her arms to Angeline, who had followed her brother's example, but although the girl was polite her body was slightly stiff and her voice carried none of Oliver's enthusiasm when she offered her congratulations.

Molly wondered if Angeline simply didn't like the idea of her as a stepmother but as the evening progressed she felt it was more than that. She resolved to have a quiet word with John at some point and ask if he had noticed anything. His daughter was growing up fast and with no mother to talk to about intimate matters, it might be that the girl was struggling. She had certainly lost her spark and seemed uncharacteristically downcast.

John and the children left just after ten o'clock. Molly stood on the doorstep waving them off. The night air was warm and soft and she continued to stand there for some minutes after they had gone. Somewhere in the distance an owl hooted but otherwise it was quiet and still.

She wondered if anyone in the world had ever been as happy as she was right at this moment. She was going to Buttercup House for dinner the following evening but already she was aching to see him again. When he had presented her with the engagement ring the day before he had told her he wanted to get married soon and she had agreed. No doubt a short engagement would cause further scandal, but then, people would gossip anyway.

She wanted to be with him on nights like this, properly with him as his wife. They both felt they had wasted so much time already.

She walked across to the paddock as she did every evening to say goodnight to Gracie. She'd had a shelter built in the paddock where Gracie could take refuge if it was rainy or particularly windy, but most of the time if the weather was a little inclement the horse seemed to prefer to stand under a great oak tree.

Docile and sweet as the small mare was, she had a mind of her own and Molly liked that. She felt that she and the horse had a bond now and that they understood each other, and in the last months when it had been just the two of them Gracie had provided love and companionship that had got her through days when she was feeling low. She would always be grateful for that.

She stroked Gracie's soft muzzle gently, wondering for the umpteenth time how Mr Stefford's friend could have parted with her. She knew she never would. Gracie was hers now and would remain safe with her. She hoped the little horse would have a long and contented life and die of old age.

She stood for a few more minutes, drinking in the peace and quiet of her surroundings as the birds settled down for sleep in the trees and hedgerows, and then walked back to the cottage. Once in her bed, she fell into a deep sleep and her dreams were good ones. For the first time since the loss of Matthew and Enid, she was truly happy.

* * *

It was Saturday afternoon and at Havelock Hall the first of the officers who were being housed there had arrived from the training camp; but it wasn't that which had Cuthbert beside himself with anger. A few minutes ago he had seen John Heath driving away with his daughter beside him in the horse and trap, and when he had enquired of Rebecca why Angeline was leaving so early, she'd told him Angeline had to get home as Miss McKenzie was going there for dinner.

'Miss McKenzie and Angeline's papa are going to be married,' Rebecca continued, blithely unaware of the effect her words were having on her father, 'and he's given her a beautiful ring. Angeline saw it last night. She said it sparkled like stars. And she's going to be a bridesmaid—'

'Married?' Cuthbert's face had flushed to a deep red. 'Don't be ridiculous, Rebecca. Angeline's teasing you.'

'She is not,' Rebecca retorted, affronted by her father's disbelief. 'Her papa only told her and Oliver last night but it's true. She's going to be a bridesmaid and Oliver is going to be his papa's best man. No one else knows yet but Angeline said it's not a secret. Her papa just wanted to tell her and Oliver before anyone else. It's not fair' – Rebecca's voice took on a petulant note – 'I've never been a bridesmaid and—'

She was talking to thin air. Her father had stormed off into the house, leaving Rebecca on the terrace where she and Angeline had been painting a picture of the grounds before John had arrived to collect his daughter.

Cuthbert was beside himself. He'd purposely avoided

speaking to John because of what he saw as the other man's disregard of his feelings over the matter of Havelock Hall being turned into a 'hotel', as he termed it. Gwendoline had been all for the idea but then she would be if he was against it, he thought furiously.

He had discussed the matter with several friends and one of his more forthright acquaintances had reminded him that everyone should 'do their bit', and that opening up his home to the army was nothing compared to fighting in the war. 'You're well over the recruitment age,' this fellow had said, 'but this is a way you can contribute, old man. It'd be bad form to refuse.'

He had brooded for days after that, but eventually had conceded and of course his dear lady wife had rolled out the red carpet for the officers who had been assigned to them. This did nothing to improve his temper when he burst in on Gwendoline, who was in her sitting room.

'I take it you're aware of the latest?' he snarled, slamming the door so hard it shook the papers on her writing bureau.

Gwendoline raised her head. She was deciding on the menus for tomorrow's lunch and dinner. There were going to be many more mouths to feed every day now the army officers had arrived but she was looking forward to having them around. The ones she had met thus far had been extremely genial and grateful to be accommodated temporarily in such comfortable surroundings. She raised her eyebrows at Cuthbert but didn't reply, knowing that would aggravate him further, but she didn't care.

'How long have you known?' he growled, standing with his legs slightly apart and glaring at her.

'As I have absolutely no idea what you are talking about I cannot answer that, Cuthbert.'

'Her. I'm talking about her, of course.'

'Half the population are females. Could you be more specific?'

He'd swing for her, so help him. 'Your bosom friend, the McKenzie woman.'

Behind her composed facade Gwendoline's mind was moving swiftly. Clearly Molly had done something or other that had caused this explosion, but what? The last time they had spoken, over a week ago now, there had been nothing untoward as far as she knew. 'Cuthbert, if you continue to talk in riddles I see no point in continuing this conversation.'

'You didn't see fit to tell me that she was marrying John Heath? After all that little trollop has put me through?'

She stared at him in amazement but recovered almost instantly. 'Miss McKenzie has put you through nothing, as you well know – the boot is on quite the other foot.' *Molly and John Heath?*

'You're two of a kind, I see that now. Cunning and manipulative. Don't think I don't know that you encouraged my house being turned into a barracks for every Tom, Dick and Harry.'

'It is *our* house and I was in favour of offering our hospitality, yes. I have never tried to pretend otherwise. I feel it is the least we can do when every day our soldiers are sacrificing their lives on the battlefield for their country.' Gwendoline spoke quietly but part of her mind was struggling to absorb what Cuthbert had told her. She felt slightly hurt that Molly hadn't even hinted that she and John were becoming close, although of course it was none of her business, she told herself firmly.

'Well, the girl has played Heath like a violin, stupid fool that he is. She was obviously angling for marriage all along. Give a wolf a taste and then get him sniffing about for more.'

'I hardly think anyone in their right mind could refer to Dr Heath as a wolf,' Gwendoline said coolly.

'She thinks she'll be accepted into polite society after graduating from mistress to wife, does she? Not if I have anything to do with it. Her and her damn houses.'

'Miss McKenzie is doing an admirable thing for the local people hereabouts and you have absolutely no proof that she was ever Dr Heath's mistress.'

'Oh, for crying out loud!'

She watched his cheekbones push out against his coarse red skin as he bellowed at her, his face contorting, and the fury his whole body expressed caused her hand to go to her throat. *He's unhinged*, she thought, as he bent towards her with a demonic expression.

'Can't you see what she's done?' he yelled. 'Even now when it's staring you in the face? Heath isn't the only one she's played for a fool, you stupid damn woman. Writing that letter was the beginning of it, and you went right along with what she told you to do and then compounded your betrayal to me by letting it be known you favoured her as an acquaintance. Her, of all people. A servant and a whore into the bargain. Have you no shame?' His voice was almost a scream now.

She stood to her feet, her body stiff, and her own voice ringing now, she cried, 'You? To talk of shame! You have brought dishonour to the name of Havelock in words and deed. You are a disgrace with your drinking and womanizing and debauchery, everyone knows it. You are disgusting, do you know that? My flesh creeps when I look at you. Molly McKenzie is a fine upstanding woman of great integrity but of course you wouldn't see that—'

When his fist shot out and caught her between her eyes she fell backwards over the chair she had just vacated, in the same moment as the door was flung open. Winters, followed by one of the army officers, rushed into the room and it was this same officer who, taking in the situation at a glance, manhandled Cuthbert out of the room and once in the hall delivered an uppercut to his chin that sent him sprawling against the far wall, to land in a heap on the polished floor. The housekeeper and one of the house-maids had also come running at the commotion, along with several other officers who had been drinking in the drawing room.

Gwendoline was aware of none of this, nor the fact that she was lying in Winters's arms on the floor as he cradled her to him, saying, 'Oh, ma'am, ma'am,' tears running down his face.

* * *

It was two hours later. Both John and Molly were with Gwendoline in her bedroom suite; Molly had just arrived at Buttercup House when the messenger from Havelock Hall had banged on the front door, requesting John's services. On hearing the man's garbled and shocked account of what had occurred, Molly had insisted on accompanying him to the Hall.

The house was subdued and silent. The officers had gathered in the dining room for their evening meal but none of them had much of an appetite after the day's happenings. Lieutenant Radlett, the officer who had struck Cuthbert, was still shaken. As he had said to his companions, it was one thing a man having a heated argument with his wife, but to use his fists on her was something else entirely. And she was a lady at that, a high-born lady according to the butler.

Cuthbert had disappeared shortly after the fracas. According to the chauffeur the master had ordered that he be driven to the railway station, where he was catching the evening train to London.

Winters had been in the kitchen with several of the staff when he had heard of the master's departure, and the enormity of what had occurred had dawned on each one of them when the old retainer had said bitterly, 'And good riddance to bad rubbish.' It was the first time in living memory that Winters had criticized any of the family and to speak thus of the master was doubly shocking.

Now, as one of the housemaids came into the kitchen

carrying a china wash bowl and bloodied towels, the cook said, 'What news of the mistress?'

'Oh, you ought to see her poor face, Cook. He's broken her nose and it's bled something terrible.'

'Is she conscious?'

'Aye, and the doctor and Miss McKenzie are sitting with her.' The housemaid lowered her voice, although it was only the cook and kitchen maids in the kitchen. 'From what I can gather Dr Heath and Miss McKenzie are engaged to be married,' she whispered.

They exchanged a significant glance. Everyone knew that Miss McKenzie had been Dr Heath's mistress before she had left him and started this building-houses lark, and that Dr Heath had been like a lost soul ever since. They'd all been agog earlier when the footman had reported that Miss McKenzie had accompanied the doctor to the house.

'So, she pulled it off then,' the cook said, and when one of the kitchen maids said, 'Who's pulled what off, Cook?' she swung round and said sharply, 'Nothing that need concern you, Peggy. Get on with what you're doing.'

'It's only just happened because Miss McKenzie was explaining to the mistress that's why she hadn't been told. They seem right pally, the mistress and Miss McKenzie,' the housemaid murmured.

Again they stared at each other before the cook said, 'By, the things that go on in this house. If it's not one thing it's another. It was never like this in the old master's day.'

Two of the housemaids who were attending to the guests in the dining room came into the kitchen carrying trays and for a few minutes the cook bustled about preparing the dishes for the main course. Once these had been sent through, she said, 'I'll do some sandwiches and pastries to go upstairs for the mistress or perhaps an omelette or soufflé would be better. Go and ask Dr Heath what he thinks she could best manage, Bernice. Is Mrs Lyndon still with her?'

Bernice nodded. Mrs Lyndon, the housekeeper, hadn't left the mistress's side since it had happened and Mr Winters was now sitting outside the door to the suite of rooms like a sentry on guard, having left the head footman to oversee the serving of dinner.

'Have a word in Mrs Lyndon's ear and find out if the mistress has been told that the master's hightailed it off to London. It'd put her mind at rest a bit if she knows he's gone.'

Bernice nodded again. She could still hardly believe what had occurred. In the mining village where she came from it sometimes happened that a man gave his wife a black eye when he was drunk, but for the master to raise his hand to the mistress, and him a gentleman . . . That was something else.

Upstairs in Gwendoline's bedroom, John was saying the same thing to Molly. He had given Gwendoline a strong sedative and in the last few minutes she had fallen into a deep sleep and now, as they prepared to take their leave, he glanced again at the bed. 'I'm finding it difficult to take in what's happened,' he said softly. 'A few of my patients allegedly walk into doors, especially on a Friday night when the men get paid, but for Cuthbert to do what he's done is unforgivable.'

Molly nodded. Even knowing what she did about Gwendoline's husband, the attack on her friend had shocked her terribly.

'He must be deranged,' John muttered as he inclined his head at the housekeeper; she had moved closer to the bed as they'd stood up and walked across the room. He had told Mrs Lyndon he didn't want Gwendoline left alone at all during the night and the housekeeper had assured him she would see to it that there would always be someone with her mistress.

'No, he's not deranged,' Molly said as they walked through into the small sitting room beyond the bedroom. 'He's just a thoroughly nasty individual who turns violent and aggressive if he doesn't get his own way. He's the worst kind of bully.'

John stopped dead, took her arm and turned her to face him. 'Tell me,' he said quietly, his grey eyes narrowing.

'Tell you?' she prevaricated, wishing she hadn't said anything. She hadn't told him about Cuthbert's attack on her and had never intended to.

'Molly, I'm a doctor and I deal with people every day of my life. I've developed a sixth sense and I know when something is said that means more than the actual words. Has he said something to you in the past? Done something?'

Just at that moment the housemaid who had helped John bathe Gwendoline's face entered the room and Molly had never been so pleased to see someone in her life. 'Dr Heath? I'm sorry to bother you but Cook wondered what the mistress should eat today? She thought perhaps a soufflé or something of that nature?'

John dragged his gaze away from Molly's face with some difficulty. 'I've given Mrs Havelock a sedative that should keep her asleep until morning,' he said, 'and I would prefer her not to be woken. Mrs Lyndon has details of her medication and so on, but I'll return tomorrow morning anyway and see how she is doing.'

'Very good, sir.'

Molly was aware of the girl's bright eyes as she looked at them both and sighed inwardly. She was in no doubt that within a very short time there wouldn't be a soul for miles around who didn't know about their engagement. Not that that mattered, and compared to what poor Gwendoline had gone through a little gossip was easily endured. She was used to it if nothing else.

She'd been horrified when she and John had first seen Gwendoline lying on her bed. There had been blood splattered down her silk dress and a towel with more blood pressed to her face. The housekeeper had been distraught and the butler, who'd been standing at the foot of the bed and who had left when they had arrived, had said in passing, 'He wants locking up, sir.'

Gwendoline had been lying with her eyes shut, the blood making her white face seem even more deathly, but when Molly had whispered her name she'd opened her eyes and reached for Molly's hand. Once Gwendoline was cleaned up and in a fresh nightgown after John had examined her, Molly had explained how the engagement had come about, not wishing her friend to think that she had kept anything from her. Gwendoline had smiled, even though her eyes were already so puffy she could barely see. 'I'm so happy for you both,' she'd murmured, and then had held Molly's hand while John bustled about sorting out the medication.

As the housemaid disappeared into the bedroom, Winters, who must have heard them talking, called from the doorway, 'How is the mistress, sir?'

They joined the old retainer on the large carpeted landing where he'd been sitting on a straight-backed chair one of the footmen had brought for him.

John patted the butler on his shoulder. 'Don't worry about Mrs Havelock,' he said gently. 'She will be asleep until morning now and will feel better when she wakes up. The shock is always a factor initially in things of this nature. I suggest you go and have a hot drink and a word with the other servants. With the guests you have at present I think the staff will need your direction to keep things running as smoothly as Mrs Havelock would like. Mrs Lyndon or one of the maids will be with Mrs Havelock throughout the night and there's nothing you can do here.'

'Very good, sir.' Winters seemed glad to be told what to do for once. It was clear that the whole episode had knocked the stuffing out of him.

As they came down the stairs Lieutenant Radlett met them in the hall. 'May I ask how Mrs Havelock is?'

'Of course. She's resting now and will sleep till morning.' John smiled at the army officer. 'I heard how you dealt with Mr Havelock – I couldn't have done better myself.'

'Obnoxious individual.' The lieutenant shook his head. 'Why is it that the finest of women are duped into marrying such men?' he said grimly.

They talked a little more with the officer before leaving the house, but once seated in the horse and trap, John looked at Molly. 'Well?' he said quietly. 'There's something with Cuthbert, isn't there. We're not leaving until you tell me.'

The sweet smell of freshly cut grass and the fragrance of summer flowers was in the air. The lovely day seemed all at odds with what had happened to Gwendoline and what she had to tell him. 'Cuthbert tried to force his attentions on me,' she said without preamble. 'That is how Gwendoline and I became acquainted.'

He froze for a moment and then swallowed hard. 'Tell me.' He took one of her hands in his. 'From the beginning.'

She did as he asked, starting with the incident at Buttercup House in the early days and finishing with the attack on her person in the lane near Lilac Cottage. When she became silent she wished he would say something, anything. But when his voice came low, the words that it spoke filled her with foreboding, for he said, 'I'll kill him.'

'No, John.' She clutched at him but he kept his gaze

concentrated straight ahead and she had to raise her hands to his head and make him look at her. 'Please, don't do anything foolish. It would spoil everything, don't you see? Everything that's in front of us now. You must let this matter be consigned to the past. Please, if you love me, promise me you won't do anything.'

'I do love you, more than words could express, but I'm sorry, Molly. I can't promise you.'

'You must.' He had to. Knowing what sort of man he was, she had to make him give his word that he wouldn't go after Cuthbert. 'If you seek him out, if you harm him in any way, he's won. Don't you understand? It would for ever be there between us even if no one else knew. And nothing happened, not really. I was frightened but that's all.'

He flinched. 'And where was I in all of this? Not protecting you as I should have been. I left you at the mercy of creatures like him.'

'That's ridiculous and you know it. I dealt with it, didn't I? John, I'm not a fragile butterfly of a woman who has the vapours at the drop of a bonnet.' She pressed her lips to his, careless that someone might be watching from the house. 'It was unpleasant but no harm was done, not really. In fact, good came from it. I met Gwendoline, after all. And now both you and I have to be here to support her after what's happened. I don't know what she will decide to do but I can't see them being able to live in the same house after this. At least there are lots of witnesses to testify to what happened.'

John rubbed his hand across his mouth in a gesture that reflected his inner turmoil. 'I'm sorry, but I can't think of Gwendoline right now, only you, and I still want to beat the living daylights out of him. That he dared to so much as—'

'Stop.' She put a finger on his lips. 'Cuthbert will get his just deserts for all the misery he's inflicted on so many people, if not in this life then in the next.'

He shook his head. 'I wish I could believe that.'

'I'll believe it for both of us.' She slipped her arm through his. 'Remember the evening you called on me after we'd confessed our love?' she said softly. He'd turned up on her doorstep as a gentle violet dusk had begun to fall, and they had walked arm in arm together in the scented night, their words and endearments punctuated by kisses and laughter. She had felt heady with the joy of loving and being loved, and she wasn't going to let a man like Cuthbert Havelock take that away from her. If John sought him out, if there was a fight or worse, it wouldn't end well for anyone – these things never did.

'I want more evenings like that,' she said, kissing the corner of his mouth. 'I want to go to sleep at night in your arms and wake up in the morning next to you. Don't do anything now to jeopardize that, my love. If you confront Cuthbert the way you are feeling, who knows what could happen?'

They had driven to Havelock Hall in John's horse and trap, and now, irritated by the fact that they had mounted the vehicle but remained stationary, the animal was becoming restless.

'Dobbin is telling us that he wants to go home,' Molly whispered as she kissed him again. 'And so do I. Promise me that you won't seek Cuthbert out and confront him and that you won't do anything foolish, John. I know how you must feel, truly I do, but the truth of the matter is that he hasn't the power to hurt us now unless you give it to him.'

He hugged her close, kissing her long and hard, and for a little while her anxiety faded. But she was to remember her last words before they left the grounds of the Hall, and wonder if a malicious sprite had been listening and had decided to teach a mere mortal a lesson.

When they arrived back at Buttercup House they had to field a host of questions from the children. Angeline in particular was agog as to what had happened after she had left Havelock Hall earlier that day.

John and Molly had decided to say that Gwendoline had had an accident and fallen and broken her nose. This was the same version of events that Rebecca had been told. Because the child had still been engrossed in painting her landscape on the veranda when the altercation between her parents had flared out of control, she'd heard nothing. Winters had had the presence of mind to instruct the other servants and the resident army officers to keep the true facts of the matter from Rebecca.

Mrs McHaffie had kept the dinner ticking over in

the range, and once John and Molly and the children had eaten, it had been decided they would sit outside for a while in the peace and quiet of the sleeping summer night. Almost immediately, Oliver engaged his father in a conversation about the progress of the war. Angeline grimaced at Molly, and smiling, she suggested that she and Angeline move their chairs a little way from the menfolk. They talked about the wedding and the colour and style of the bridesmaid's dress Angeline would like, but after just a few minutes Molly felt the same sense of disquiet she'd experienced on other occasions. Something was wrong with Angeline and she couldn't put her finger on it.

Deciding to take the bull by the horns, she leaned forward and said softly, 'Is anything troubling you, Angeline?'

The girl looked startled. 'Troubling me? No, no, I'm all right. It's just – No, I'm fine.'

'I don't think you are.' Hoping she wasn't spoiling whatever rapport she had with John's daughter, she said even more quietly, 'I don't want to pry – I mean that – but sometimes a trouble shared is a trouble halved. If I can help in any way I'd be glad to.'

Angeline stared at her for a full ten seconds. Her blue eyes were dark in the shadowed night, large and deep-socketed as they searched Molly's, and then she said very quietly, 'I – I don't know what to do, that's all.'

'About what?'

'Charlie. Charles Havelock.'

Molly felt her stomach muscles tighten but her face

and voice betrayed nothing of the sudden fear the girl's words had prompted. 'In what way, Angeline?'

'He' – Angeline glanced apprehensively at her father and brother but they were engrossed in their own conversation – 'he says he likes me and I like him, but the last time he was home for the Easter holidays he tried to . . .'

'What did he try to do, Angeline?' Molly asked with a calmness she was far from feeling.

'He tried to put his hand up my dress.' Angeline looked at her, her gaze begging for understanding. 'He – he's kissed me before but he says he kisses Rebecca too and I thought – I thought that was all right.'

It was taking all Molly's self-control to remain composed. Angeline was thirteen years old and an innocent. Charles Havelock was Cuthbert's first-born and several years older than John's daughter.

'We were at the lake in the grounds,' Angeline said, her words coming faster now as if a plug had been pulled. 'The four of us – me and Rebecca, and Charlie and Vincent. There's a rowing boat but I can't swim and I was frightened to go out on the water but Vincent and Rebecca went and Charlie said for us to sit and watch them. He started kissing me but this time it' – she shook her head – 'it wasn't the same. And then he pushed me so I was lying down and his hand went right up my dress. I – I didn't know what to do. I tried to get up and he laughed and said I was being a silly little girl and didn't I like him? And then Rebecca and Vincent had an argument and came back . . .' Her voice trailed away.

'Have you seen Charles since?' Molly asked quietly.

'No, but he'll be coming home with Vincent for the summer holidays. He – he was talking about enlisting when he turns eighteen at the end of July.'

Molly hoped he did. 'And he didn't apologize? After the event?'

Angeline shook her head.

'Even though he knew he had frightened you?'

'No. He said if I wanted to be his sweetheart then that's what folk did.'

'And do you want to be his sweetheart?'

Angeline hesitated. 'I thought I did but no, not now.'

'Good, because he wasn't telling the truth, Angeline. That is not what someone does when he asks a girl to be his sweetheart. It was disrespectful and wrong. You felt that yourself, didn't you, which is why you have been upset about it?'

Angeline nodded. 'He's very good-looking,' she murmured, 'and Rebecca says he has lots of girls setting their caps at him.'

And she had been flattered. After all, she was just a child. 'Angeline, I need to talk to you a little about what behaviour like that can lead to for a girl. It can be disastrous and ruin her life, all right? Do you know anything about how your body will begin to change for you to be a woman?'

Angeline shook her head, her eyes wide.

'It's nothing to worry about, it's completely natural.' Molly drew in a long breath and went on to give a short and sensitive explanation about the birds and bees. As yet Angeline's breasts were still flat and her shape that of a prepubescent young girl but within months that might well begin to alter. 'So you see, it's very important for a girl to keep herself for the man she will love and marry,' Molly finished, a little flushed, 'and if a boy has genuine affection for a girl he won't ask her to do anything she doesn't want to do.'

Angeline nodded. She hadn't seemed in any way concerned or embarrassed by their little tête-à-tête, merely intrigued. 'So this monthly occurrence is in preparation for when a woman wants to have a baby,' she said thoughtfully.

'Yes, that's right.' Molly smiled. 'But that is a long, long way in the future for you and you don't need to think about it now. Just remember what I've said about being careful not to put yourself in a position where the wrong sort of suitor would take advantage of you.'

'Like Charlie.'

'Exactly like Charles Havelock. If he really cared for you he wouldn't have tried to do what he did.'

Angeline nodded. 'I saw him lose his temper and try to kick his dog at Easter,' she said, a note of finality in her voice which told Molly Charles Havelock was now history.

'There you are then, he's not a nice individual at all, is he, besides which you are far too young to think about beaus at the moment. That time will come and you will have lots of suitors beating a path to your door.'

'Do you think so?' Angeline asked wistfully. 'Rebecca is much prettier than me.'

'She is most certainly not.' Molly leaned forward and took John's daughter's hand in hers. None of them had allowed for the fact that Angeline was at a vulnerable stage of her life where the input of a mother was crucial. 'You are beautiful and you have to value yourself, Angeline, as a person too. It's not all about how you look on the outside and having pretty dresses and nice things, but how you are on the inside too. Kindness and gentleness are important attributes but so are strength and determination, especially for a woman.' And when the girl's eyes opened wider, Molly said, 'Oh, yes, believe me, a woman has to be stronger than a man in this world. It is she who makes a home and bears children and raises a family while supporting her husband and maybe even taking a stand on certain issues like women having the vote and being heard in their own right.'

'I don't know anything about things like that.'

'You could always learn,' Molly said gently.

'Is that why you built the factory and are going to build houses? To show people that women can do such things?'

'Partly, but also because I wanted to. I didn't see why my being a woman should stop me doing what I want to do in life. Do you?'

Angeline thought for a moment. 'What if a girl, a woman, just wants to get married and have a nice house and a family?'

'Then that's fine as long as she isn't doing it because that is what is expected of her rather than what she really wants. It's all about choice, Angeline. Enabling women to have the opportunities in life that are often just reserved for the male sex. Do you see?'

Angeline didn't answer this; she was feeling strange. When Miss McKenzie had first come to live with them she had been pleased. Everything had seemed to get better overnight and happier. Papa had been nicer and Oliver had changed. He had really liked Miss McKenzie and so had she. She still did, but then Miss McKenzie had gone to live in the little cottage and built her factory and Rebecca and her brothers had been horrible about her. Well, not horrible exactly, but they had looked down their noses at her; and when she had told Rebecca that she and Oliver had gone to visit Lilac Cottage, Rebecca had asked what on earth was she doing visiting a servant? And she had felt ashamed, as though she had done something unseemly. She'd told Oliver what had been said and he had been furious and told her to tell Rebecca to mind her own business and that Miss McKenzie was worth ten of her, but she hadn't. Because she had thought the Havelocks were wonderful with their huge mansion of a house and umpteen servants and carriages and a car, and the fact that she was Rebecca's best friend had given her a prestige she'd not have had otherwise at school.

She bit hard on her lip, feeling as though she was looking into a mirror and not liking what she saw. She wanted to say she was sorry for not standing up for Miss

McKenzie but how could she when to say that would mean Miss McKenzie would know people were looking down on her? She recalled the look on her best friend's face when she'd told Rebecca that her papa and Miss McKenzie were getting married, and again she felt a wash of remorse that she hadn't challenged her. Instead she had quickly talked about bridesmaid's dresses and ignored the scorn and derision.

Her voice very small, she murmured, 'I'm glad you are marrying Papa, Miss McKenzie.'

'Call me Molly like Oliver does.'

'I'm sorry that I haven't been – That I didn't—' She wasn't sure how to go on. 'I'm not a very nice person, am I.'

'I think you are and so do your papa and Oliver.'

'Oh.' Her voice broke as she whispered, 'I'm not.'

'Your mama died when you were very young and I think you have coped admirably since. It's not been easy for you and Oliver, I know that.'

There was a great lump in Angeline's throat as she said, 'If we have coped it's because you came to live with us.'

Molly didn't say anything more. She simply put her arm round the girl's shoulders and, as Angeline nestled in to her, she thought, *Thank you, God. In a day of such unpleasantness, You have provided a silver lining. We can build on this and become a real family in the future.*

Chapter Twenty-Seven

Cuthbert Havelock swigged the last drops of the brandy from his hip flask and clambered to his feet. He had been sitting with his back against an oak tree for the last hour, surveying Lilac Cottage from a vantage point at the back of the dwelling. This was at the top of an incline where the wooded area began. He had watched John bring Molly home, his temper rising as they had exchanged long lingering kisses on the doorstep before John had walked back to his horse and trap and driven off.

His fingers curled round the box of matches in his jacket pocket and he smiled. He knew exactly what he was going to do. He had known it even before he had left Havelock Hall earlier that afternoon and ordered the chauffeur to take him to the railway station although he'd had no intention of catching the train to London, at least not before he'd carried out his plan. Once that was accomplished he'd take the train to the capital and stay in the city for a while before returning to the country and dealing with his wife. His eyes narrowed. He'd make Gwendoline wish she had never been born.

There was only a skeleton staff at the house in Kensington now due to the war, he thought with some satisfaction, and the housekeeper alone slept on the premises, which suited his purposes perfectly. Mrs Johnson was paid well and knew which side her bread was buttered; she'd swear black was white for him if need be rather than lose her job. If any questions were asked, he would say he'd arrived at the London residence late that night and gone straight to bed and he'd make sure Mrs Johnson collaborated with him and confirmed that story. A nice little bonus to her wage would do the trick.

Those damn letters. He ground his teeth, the rage that always consumed him when he thought of the hold that the McKenzie woman had over him rising up in a black wave. He still wasn't sure if they existed or if it had been merely a bluff on the women's part but, nevertheless, the threat had served its purpose and kept him from showing his hand against Molly McKenzie. Openly, at least. He'd had to resort to other methods, like hiring those two buffoons to intimidate the builder and his lackey, and that had nearly backfired. It was fortunate he'd made sure they weren't from these parts, even though it had taken some effort to find someone to do the job when he'd enquired in Newcastle. But with enough money you can buy anything – or anyone. Except her.

He glared down towards the cottage. The sky was clear and the full moon lit up the countryside, making deep black shadows and other areas where it was almost as light as day.

She had been like a canker eating away at him from when he had first set eyes on her, and at one time he had imagined the craving could only be assuaged by having her, but that had passed. He didn't want her, not physically, not any more. What he wanted was to destroy her – her and those damn houses. He was blowed if he'd see her married to John Heath and lording it over folk, thinking she was so clever with her little schemes and her blackmail tactics.

He began to make his way towards the cottage, swearing when he stumbled once or twice. He had been drinking consistently all day before the scene with Gwendoline and the hip flask had topped him up so now he was unsteady on his feet, but no matter, he told himself. He'd managed to get a lift on a carrier's cart bound for Cresswell shortly after leaving the station and he'd make his way back somehow. The gods were with him in this.

Once on more even ground he skirted round the paddock where a small horse came ambling towards him before stopping and neighing. He glanced in the direction of the cottage, hoping the sound didn't alert the occupant, but all remained quiet and still. 'Lucky for you you're out here and not in the stable, 'cause that and the barn'll be cinders tonight,' he growled at the animal, and as though sensing his intent, it neighed again and then trotted away towards where it had been standing under a large oak tree.

He passed an old disused hen house and run and opened the gate into the paved yard, which he saw held a privy and a wash house along with a coal bunker. His upper lip curled. The cottage and yard would easily fit into his drawing room with space to spare and yet she adopted such airs and graces. And to think his wife had been visiting here; where had her sense of decorum gone, to so lower herself? But it was that witch in there, and indeed he wouldn't be surprised if McKenzie *was* a sorceress, the way she cast spells on folk. First John Heath and the people in the village, then his own wife and now umpteen women who happily worked for her, not to mention the builder and his lackey. Well, witches were burned at the stake not so long ago and if he had his way this one would go the same. No one had ever treated him as she had and it had all been due to her that he'd lost his temper with Gwendoline.

He fingered his jaw that was still aching from the blow he had received from the army officer, which had been an added humiliation. One of his teeth was wobbly and he winced at the pain as he probed it. He'd make sure that the man was hauled over the coals by his superiors if it was the last thing he did.

He tried at the back of the property but the stout wooden door appeared to be bolted from the inside. Nervous, was she? Well, she should have chosen to live in the village with neighbours at hand. There were cottages scattered along this road and a farm or two, but nothing within a few hundred yards or so.

He walked right round the exterior of the dwelling, checking the front door, which was also securely fastened.

A bedroom window at the back of the house was open a crack but he wasn't about to risk life and limb by trying to climb up there, even though the wisteria which covered the stone walls looked to be as thick as a man's wrist and might have borne his weight. He'd hoped to start a fire inside the cottage as well as setting the thatched roof alight, but that might still be possible. First he needed something more substantial than his matches to create a blaze.

Retracing his steps, he left the yard and walked towards the barn and stable to the left of the enclosed paddock. The barn held a stack of chopped logs and several piles of kindling, along with bags and sacks of various types of horse feed and other bits and pieces. The light two-wheeled trap stood just within the entrance, a some-what flimsy affair, he thought, but one that would suit a woman on her own.

It was in the stable that he found what he needed. On a shelf holding grooming equipment for the horse was a pile of rags. He sorted out several large pieces of cloth that would burn well, smiling in satisfaction. There were a couple of bales of hay in one corner of the stable and he extracted a fat wad and set about constructing the first torch he intended to use. Wrapping a piece of cloth round the hay, he tied the ends tight and then found a reasonably substantial piece of kindling that he pushed up through the material and into the hay. He soon had several torches. Due to the hot spell of the last few weeks everything was tinder dry, which would help the proceedings.

As he left the stable he heard the loud, shrill shriek of an owl close by and the next moment it appeared, ghostly white and silent. A barn owl. He shivered. His nanny had been a country woman full of old sayings and superstitions and as a child he had been brought up on them. She had told him the bird had supernatural powers and its feathers were the main ingredients in witches' brews and potions by those meaning others harm. '*If you've mischief in your heart and you see a barn owl you can be sure it's a warning that your wrong will come to haunt you,*' she'd told him on more than one occasion, often when he had committed some misdemeanour or other. '*They are the guardians of the church and all things sacred.*'

As he had grown up he had realized that the bird's eerie reputation was less to do with the supernatural and more that the owl's traditional nesting site was in church towers, but even now just hearing an owl – let alone seeing one – gave him the jitters.

'Pull yourself together, man,' he muttered to himself. 'It's all poppycock.' The owl was just a bird, not a winged messenger from a higher authority.

Walking to the front of the cottage, he gazed up at the thick thatched roof above him. It was shaped so that it lay low over the mullioned bedroom window.

Was that the room where she slept? he asked himself. Not that it mattered. He would set the thatch at the back of the place alight too, but first he would see if he could ease a window open. Just a few inches would do, enough to drop a lit torch onto the floor. He reached into the inner pocket of his jacket where he kept the small thin box holding a silver knife which he used mainly to slice fruit if he was travelling anywhere. The box was an exquisite thing in itself, being made of papier mâché and decorated with a courtesan in a landscape, the sides with portrait roundels and hunting scenes, and the knife was engraved with tiny feathers and what appeared to be thistles. It had been his father's and had been presented to him by a Japanese friend decades ago. As a boy he had never been allowed to handle it and had once received a good thrashing from his father when he had disobeyed this order; consequently he always experienced a perverse pleasure that it was now his.

Taking the knife out of its box, he slid it carefully between the window frame and the somewhat frail catch. It gave way almost immediately and he was able to open the window with little effort. Peering inside, he saw a small sitting room in the dim light, and again his lip curled. She had refused him for this?

He was about to light one of the torches he had made and drop it through the window when his curiosity got the better of him; that and a need to invade her privacy and violate the space she had made hers. He could make sure her exit route was blocked, too, if he got the downstairs well and truly blazing along with the roof. He didn't want her running down the stairs and out of the house.

He rubbed his face hard; the amount of alcohol he had consumed had made him feel a little befuddled but also given him a reckless edge. Prising the window wide open, he wondered if he could squeeze himself through it; his girth had ballooned in recent years. Aware of the need for silence, he first dropped a couple of the makeshift torches through the window and then attempted to climb through the gap. It took some effort but finally he was standing inside the cottage, damp and sweaty under his armpits and his face moist.

Once his eyes had got accustomed to the near-total darkness inside the house he glanced about him. There was an armchair on either side of the open fireplace, and he picked up the book lying on one of them, walking over to the window where a shaft of moonlight enabled him to see what it was that she had been reading. *Poems by Currer, Ellis, and Acton Bell*. He sniffed. It meant nothing to him and he flung the book back on the chair so that the pages fluttered in protest.

The armchairs should burn well, he thought, along with the wooden furniture in the room and the thick clippy mats and curtains. He emptied the contents of an oil lamp that had been standing on a small table next to the chair over the upholstery before walking into the kitchen where he found another lamp and, much to his delight, a can holding more fresh oil. After sprinkling it over the kitchen table and the two rocking chairs he walked to the foot of the narrow, steep stairs. All was quiet. He went into the sitting room and brought the thick cushioned pad from the top of the oak settle and placed it on the stairs, followed by one of the clippy mats.

Then he ripped to pieces the book he'd found on the armchair along with a couple of others that had been on the shelves of a corner cabinet, and positioned the papers under the pile he had made on the stairs before tipping oil over it all.

He was enjoying himself and for a few moments stood just anticipating the moment he would light a few matches and set her home ablaze. He had noticed that the front door was bolted and had already decided that rather than trying to wriggle out of the open window, which had been a tight squeeze, he would simply slide the bolts and walk out of the door once things were burning well and he was sure that her exit was blocked. Lighting a few of his handmade torches and throwing them up onto the tinder-dry thatch would be no problem once he was outside.

He raised his gaze to the ceiling, his eyes narrowing. *Assumed you'd got the whip hand, didn't you*, he thought grimly, *but in a few minutes you'll realize how wrong you were, my fine lady. No one tries to blackmail me and gets away with it.*

He stood a moment or two more in the shadowed darkness, the feeling of power more intoxicating than anything that came out of a bottle, and then walked through to the kitchen where he lit the first match. Once flames were taking hold he repeated the procedure in the sitting room and then the pile on the stairs, which flared up immediately. Smoke began to billow and fill the downstairs and after putting his handkerchief across his nose he walked to the front door and slid the bolts. The door still didn't open. Pushing harder, it was a few seconds before he realized it had been locked as well as bolted and the key wasn't in the door.

It was getting more difficult to see and breathe now and after fumbling around for a few moments for the key he gave up and made his way into the sitting room, to be met by a small inferno. Coughing and choking, he made for the open window even as flames began to lick at the curtains. Heaving himself up, he tried to force his body through the small space, panicking as the intense heat made itself felt and only succeeding in wedging himself with his head, chest and arms outside the window and his big stomach, buttocks and legs inside the sitting room. The relief of being able to gulp fresh air into his lungs was only momentary. The fire was hungry and it was no respecter of persons. When the flames took hold of his legs he began to kick wildly as his body became shot with agony and he screamed like an animal caught in a trap, the sound piercing and terrible in the sleeping night. The fire was consuming the lower part of him and he was being burned alive, but wedged as he was he could do nothing to help himself. The flames were hissing and crackling and now his genitals and buttocks were on fire. He continued to scream and writhe as unimaginable pain engulfed him but his efforts were futile. The monster he had created wanted its pound of flesh.

* * *

Molly had been jerked from a deep sleep by the sound of the first scream. For an infinitesimal moment she lay still, her heart thudding, but then the sound came again and she jumped out of bed, becoming aware of the smell of smoke at the same time as she screwed up her eyes against the horrendous screaming.

What on earth was happening? Terrified, she ran to the door of the bedroom, but on opening it a wall of flame and smoke met her and she slammed it shut again, choking and gasping. *The cottage was on fire.*

Now the smoke was curling under the closed door but it was the sound of someone in mortal agony that froze her thought processes for valuable seconds before she told herself she had to escape. It was no use trying to go down the stairs so the only option was the window. She had left it slightly open when she went to sleep and now she ran and flung it wide, the terrible wailing and screaming from somewhere below her seeming to fill the night.

The moonlight was bright. As she peered out of the window it looked a long, long way down to the ground. Would she survive if she jumped, or perhaps be badly injured? Fear gripped her.

Glancing back into the room she saw black smoke rising between the floorboards and flames were licking all round the thin gaps of the door and at the top and bottom of it. Was the thatched roof on fire? She leaned out of the window as far as she dared but could see no flames above her as yet, although she knew it would only be a few minutes at best before it caught alight.

Whimpering, she pulled her dressing gown over her thin lawn nightdress, but still she hesitated to jump. The unearthly shrieking below her would have alerted anyone within earshot but now she added her cries for help to the screams, hoping against hope that someone would appear although in her heart she realized she had to save herself before it was too late.

'John, oh, John,' she moaned softly, the acrid smoke making her cough. It couldn't end like this when they had only just declared their feelings – it was too unfair.

The paved yard was directly below the window and the stone slabs would be unforgiving on flesh and bones. She leaned out of the window again and then the sight of the old, twisting tree-like wisteria caused her heart to leap. If she could ease herself out of the window and use the wisteria to climb down the stone wall, she wouldn't have to jump. It might give way but it was worth a try.

There was a mighty crash outside the bedroom door and she realized the wooden staircase must have collapsed. She had no option but to get out now, she thought, the heat and smoke overpowering.

Feeling with her bare toes, she found a thick wedge of gnarled wood just below the bottom of the window. For a moment she remained perched with one leg outside and the other on the windowsill, her fingers desperately gripping the flaking wood of the window frame. Above her the thatched roof was now beginning to smoulder and smoke. Any moment and it could burst into flames.

Feeling as though her chest was being squeezed by a

giant hand, and her eyes streaming and smarting so much she couldn't see clearly, she climbed out of the window. Her fingers clawed at the ancient wisteria as she prayed the plant would hold her weight. The sounds from somewhere below her had changed into an eerie high-pitched whine that made her blood run cold, but telling herself she had to concentrate on what she was doing she found a resting place for her other foot below the first, and then clung on tightly, unable to move as a bout of coughing rendered her helpless.

She had only climbed down another couple of feet when a further spasm of uncontrollable coughing and choking caused her to lose her grip. She felt herself falling backwards and pain shooting through her whole body and head as she made contact with the stone slabs beneath the window. She lay stunned for a moment, the searing heat from the burning house telling her she had to crawl away, but when she tried to move excruciating pain caused her head to swim. Just before she lost consciousness she wondered what was different and then she realized. The spine-chilling sound had stopped.

Chapter Twenty-Eight

John was never to forget the next twenty-four hours. He felt they would be engraved on his soul for all eternity – a horrific series of events that had begun when there was a frantic pounding on his front door in the early hours of the morning.

He had stumbled downstairs more asleep than awake, having only drifted off half an hour or so before. When he had first gone to bed he had lain awake, seething over what Molly had confided about Angeline and the Havelock lad. Initially he had wanted to commit murder, but Molly had assured him that Angeline had been more frightened than anything else, and that although the episode had been unpleasant it had been a salutary lesson to his easily led daughter to not allow herself to be put in a compromising situation again. They should speak to Gwendoline about it, Molly had suggested, and she would deal with her son. In the meantime there was no reason why Angeline's friendship with Rebecca couldn't continue, although visits to Havelock Hall would be limited to when Charles was not at home.

'We had a little woman-to-woman talk,' Molly had added, 'and hopefully you'll see a change in her. She needs guidance, John, but not a heavy hand.'

He had deferred to her wisdom although he had still wanted to get his hands on Charles Havelock, along with giving his daughter a good talking-to. When he thought what might have happened he felt sick to his stomach. Angeline was still only thirteen although she would be fourteen in October, but Charles Havelock was virtually a man. Like father, like son, he had decided grimly. The next time he saw Charles he would make it abundantly clear that if he so much as looked at Angeline he would swing for him.

As he opened the front door he was half-aware of Oliver coming down the stairs after him and Mrs McHaffie emerging from the end of the hall, resplendent in a long dressing gown of an indistinguishable colour and her hair entwined with strips of rag.

'Dr Heath?' The youth on the doorstep was tousle-haired, smudges of dirt on his face and his clothes emitting a strong smell of smoke. 'You must come at once, sir. A fire, a terrible fire.'

'Where?' John could see the fellow was in a state.

'Past the village, sir, on the way to Cresswell. A cottage, Lilac Cottage.'

John had heard the expression of one's heart missing a beat but he had never experienced it before. Oliver had come alongside him and it was he who said, 'The lady who lives there, Miss McKenzie? Is she all right?'

'No, no, you must come at once. I've got to get back, me da and our Mick an' George are trying to save the barn an' stable but there's sparks flying everywhere from the thatch.'

John was already running up the stairs to his bedroom, closely followed by Oliver, and his message having been delivered the young man ran to where he had tied his old nag of a horse and after vaulting onto its back persuaded it into a canter.

Lotty had now joined Gladys in the hall – Angeline was the only member of the household still asleep – and she had John's black bag ready for him when he thundered down the stairs again after throwing on some clothes. Oliver followed a moment later. 'I'm coming with you,' he said to his father and John didn't argue.

Running round to the stables at the back of the house they urged a reluctant Dobbin into his harness and once in the trap John took the reins. Oliver glanced at his father. John's face was as white as a sheet, his eyes dark pools in the shadowed night. Once on the road they didn't speak, each lost in his own thoughts of the woman who had captured both their hearts in different ways.

They saw the glow of the fire when they were still a good distance away and could smell smoke in the air shortly after they had left the village. When they turned a corner in the lane and the cottage – or what remained of it – came into view, John groaned out loud. He could see several folk standing on the bridle path but as they jumped down from the trap and raced over it was the sight of the thing hanging out of the sitting-room window that made him want to vomit. The blackened burned remains were obviously human, and it was only Oliver saying, 'It isn't her, Pa, it isn't Molly,' that choked the scream in his throat. Then he saw her lying a short distance away on a blanket someone had obviously provided, two women kneeling by her side.

When he reached her he thought he was too late. There was blood on the blanket that was clearly coming from the back of her head, her eyes were closed and she was as still as a corpse. He crouched down and reached for her pulse, his professionalism taking over.

'She was like this when we got here a little while ago, Doctor,' one of the women said. 'She'd fallen from the bedroom window, perhaps, or jumped. Me husband and our lads carried her away from the cottage an' I sent our Cecil to bring you.'

She had a faint pulse. Weak with relief, it was a moment or two before he could say to Oliver, 'She's alive.'

'We live up yonder.' The woman flicked her head in the direction of Cresswell. 'The first cottage after this one. I've always bin a bit of a light sleeper and I heard these screams, terrible they were, Doctor. Never heard anything like it and I don't want to again, on an' on they went. Anyway, I woke Jacob and we roused the lads an' when we got here we found her lying on the slabs at the back of the cottage. Just in time we were an' all 'cause it was only seconds after we'd moved her that some of the thatched roof fell just where she'd bin.'

She turned and looked briefly at the blazing house before continuing, 'We couldn't do nowt for that poor soul, whoever he was. There was no getting near him but we could see it was a man and he'd already breathed his last. Merciful release it'd have been too. The lass isn't burned from what we could make out but landing on them slabs . . .' She shook her head. 'Can't have done her any good, could it.'

'I need to get her back to my house so I can examine her properly. Is there a vehicle, a cart or something in which she could lie down?' he asked the woman.

'Aye, we've got a cart. My Jacob's a carrier, see. He'll drive you back, Doctor. It's Buttercup House, isn't it, in the village so not too far. We'd be glad to help. I'll go and get Jacob and tell him.'

So saying she bustled over to a small, bald man who had just emerged from the direction of the paddock. After a quick word he came hurrying over, his face grave. 'Just seeing to the horse,' the man said in greeting. 'Right skittish she was with the noise an' fire an' all.'

John nodded but didn't comment. He didn't care about the horse, his sole focus was Molly. 'You've got a cart we can use?'

'Aye, that's right, Doctor. I'll bring it here.'

The roof of the cottage had fallen in, causing a great explosion of flames, and Oliver turned to look, his gaze drawn by the macabre blackened figure hanging at the window. The carrier's family had said it was recognizable as a man when they had first arrived, although not now.

What a ghastly death, he thought, swallowing hard as bile rose up in his throat. Had the person, whoever it was, tried to help Molly and lost his life in the process? He had obviously been trying to get out of the cottage, though, rather than in.

His gaze returned to his father and Molly and he said softly, 'Will she be all right?'

'I don't know.' John drew in a long, deep breath. 'Where's that damn cart?'

It trundled up in a few minutes, drawn by a young shire horse. They carefully laid Molly on a bed of sacks and blankets, her body limp and unresponsive. The hair on the back of her head was matted with blood and her face was as white as lint.

'I'll drive the trap back,' Oliver said to John, 'and you sit with Molly.' John didn't argue, climbing into the back of the cart.

Once they were ready the carrier clicked to the horse and it plodded off at a steady pace. Even so the cart jolted over holes and bumps in the country road and John tried to protect Molly from the worse of the jarring. He was afraid, terribly afraid, she wouldn't survive the journey.

Oliver had ridden on ahead and by the time the cart reached Buttercup House, Gladys and Lotty were dressed and waiting. The carrier helped John and Oliver carry the unconscious patient upstairs to one of the bedrooms before he left. In the process Angeline awoke, so Oliver took his sister downstairs to explain what had happened.

Gladys helped John remove Molly's dressing gown after they had laid her on some thick towels on top of the coverlet so he could examine her, and Lotty brought hot water and more towels. Gladys winced when she saw the wound at the back of Molly's head but John was very much the doctor now. After ascertaining that Molly had a broken arm as well as the head wound, he began to clean her scalp with a solution of hot water and antiseptic. 'I'm going to have to close this with sutures, Mrs McHaffie,' he said grimly. 'Are you squeamish? Because I need her held in a certain way. I can call Oliver if you like?'

Lotty went green and made herself scarce but Gladys was made of sterner stuff. 'You tell me what to do, Doctor, and I'll do it,' she said stoutly.

Once they'd finished and John had seen to the broken arm too, the bloody towels were removed and they got Molly into bed. How much blood she had lost John didn't know. The blanket she had been lying on at the scene of the fire had been soaked with it under her head and it had continued to bleed on the journey to Buttercup House. His trousers and shirt were heavily stained. Whether she had damaged her spine in the fall he wasn't sure.

Now that he had done all he could for the present, he suddenly felt most peculiar. His head swimming, he put out a hand to steady himself.

Gladys, ever practical, pushed the straight-backed chair at the side of the bed under his knees and he was glad to plump down on it. 'I'm going to get you a large glass of brandy, Doctor.'

Her voice had been firm but he wouldn't have had the strength to argue with her anyway. Had he been about to faint? he asked himself as his head continued to swim and he shut his eyes. It was only ladies that fainted.

Gladys was back within moments. 'You get this down you, you're in shock,' she said, her voice verging on motherly. 'Once that's done its work I'll sit here with the lass while you get cleaned up and changed. You'll give her the fright of her life if she wakes up and sees you covered in blood.'

He hoped she did wake up, he thought, fear paramount and causing his hand to shake as he drained the glass, but almost at once the neat alcohol cleared his head as it beat a fiery path down his throat and into his stomach. He could smell the smoke on his clothes and when Gladys said again, 'You get yourself cleaned up, Doctor, and I'll stay with her,' he nodded.

He stood up and, looking at his faithful retainer, who he realized had been something of a rock in this household since Christabel's death, said quietly, 'I couldn't live without her, Mrs McHaffie.'

'What sort of talk is that? You won't have to live without her, now then. She might look fragile and willowy like most ladies do, but have you ever met someone so determined and strong as her? She'll pull round, never you fear, Doctor.'

She patted him on his arm and now, ridiculously, he felt he wanted to cry. He hastily left the room but as he did so he was thinking, *Yes, Molly is strong and she is certainly determined but that is in her mind. Her body is as vulnerable as the next person's and it doesn't look good. It doesn't look good at all.*

Molly lay for three days oblivious to where she was or what was going on. She wasn't left alone for a moment. One of the comfy armchairs from the bay window in the bedroom was moved to beside the bed, and here John sat, slept, ate and drank. The only time he left her side was for visits to the bathroom and to wash and change, but he kept these to a minimum. Either Oliver or Angeline took over for a few minutes when John left. Both of the children had refused to go back to their schools until they knew Molly was going to be all right.

Gladys's way of comforting the family was to ply everyone with constant food and snacks as well as encouraging words, but in private she and Lotty shed a few tears as time crept on and there was no sign of Molly returning from whatever world she inhabited.

John, whose medical experience made him well aware of the worst that could happen, was suffering the torments of the damned. In spite of that he tried to be positive and confident when he talked to his children, both of whom were totally distraught. The extent of their distress touched him deeply. He would have expected Oliver to be upset – he knew Molly and his son had become close – but he hadn't realized Angeline was so fond of her.

He and his daughter had several heart-to-hearts in the quiet of the bedroom, and Angeline opened up to him about Charles Havelock and the way she had been feeling. He realized he hadn't been fair to his daughter over the last months when she had irritated him at times. Christabel had been a coquette and a somewhat kittenish kind of female but the qualities that had attracted and captivated him as a young and ardent suitor had proved irritating and annoying as a husband. That was his fault, he realized. Not hers. Christabel had continued to be what she had always been; the mistake in thinking that a marriage between them could work had been all his. And when Angeline had displayed somewhat mercurial characteristics he had immediately decided she was the same as her mother, rather than appreciating that she was a confused young girl on the brink of puberty, with all the anxieties and hidden self-doubts adolescence brought with it. She had been like a lamb to the slaughter for someone like Charles Havelock and he could only thank God that she had talked to Molly and the whole thing had been nipped in the bud.

He did a lot of self-searching when by himself at Molly's bedside and made a lot of promises too, mainly to God begging Him to grant him a second chance at being a husband and better father.

On the third morning of Molly's inertia, he knew he couldn't ignore the demands of his practice any longer. There were patients he needed to see regardless of his own misery and consequently he took his morning surgery and made some home visits before returning to Buttercup House at midday. Two police constables were waiting for him. Gravely they told him that the body found at the cottage was almost certainly that of Cuthbert Havelock. A small knife found at the scene had been identified as belonging to him, and contrary to what people had been led to believe, he hadn't gone to London on the evening of the fire.

It had been Mrs Havelock who had been suspicious as to her husband's whereabouts after hearing about the fire at Miss McKenzie's cottage, one of the constables had explained. Mr Havelock had apparently been guilty of victimizing the lady in the past and had made threats against her. It seemed likely that he had gone to the cottage with the sole intention of breaking in and starting the fire which had ultimately killed him. Quite what had happened no one would perhaps ever know unless Miss McKenzie could shed some light on what had occurred, but from the position of Mr Havelock's body it would appear he had been trying to climb out of the window in the sitting room and become stuck fast. The constable shook his head. 'No one deserves to die like that.'

John looked at the policeman. 'All I can say is that if what you suspect is true then he fully deserved it and I hope he continues to burn in hell.'

Shocked, the young constable stammered, 'We – we will need to speak to Miss McKenzie when she regains consciousness, Dr Heath.'

'*If*, Constable, if,' John said grimly. 'Miss McKenzie is fighting for her life because of the events of that night and your sympathies should be solely with her.'

433

'Yes, sir. I didn't mean—'

'I'm sorry.' John knew he had been unfair – the policeman was only doing his job and his comment about Cuthbert's manner of passing had been natural in the circumstances – but he had meant what he said. Doctor or no, he'd meant it. 'I'm tired,' he said quietly, 'and it's been a long three days.'

'Yes, sir. Of course. I understand.'

It was clear that all the policeman wanted now was to escape, and once the pair of them had left John went upstairs and resumed his vigil at his beloved's side.

Chapter Twenty-Nine

As Molly came out of the deep depths of unconsciousness, she was aware of a bird singing. It was a sweet song made up of many notes and somewhere in her mind she said to herself, *That's a blackbird*, before the pain in her head caused her to moan. Immediately she heard a voice – John's voice – say, 'Molly, Molly, my love, can you hear me?'

She wanted to reply, she wanted to open her eyes, but she was falling into the black void again and such was the pain in her head that she went into it gratefully.

The next time she surfaced she sensed it was different; there were no birds singing and all was quiet and whereas before there had been gold behind her closed lids, like sunlight, now there was just a velvety darkness which was soothing. She ached, the whole of her ached, but it was the jabbing knives in her brain that caused her to moan again and like before she heard John say, 'Molly, my love, can you hear me? I'm here and you're safe. There's nothing to worry about, you are safe.'

Why was he saying she was safe? Had she been in danger of some kind? She wanted to ask him but it was too much effort and again she allowed herself to sink into the soft blanket of nothingness.

It was on the morning of the fourth day that she properly came to, and again a blackbird was singing outside the partially open window of the bedroom. She lay still without opening her eyes, a sense of well-being enveloping her. The grinding pain in her head had gone and just a headache remained but nothing like before, and she could feel a soft breeze on her face perfumed with the scent of roses. She forced her heavy lids open and could see something white fluttering, a muslin curtain.

She turned her head carefully on the pillow, wary of causing the excruciating pain to take hold again, and there was John fast asleep in an armchair just a foot or so away. She gazed at his dear face and she knew in that moment that that was all she wanted to do for the rest of her life. The factory, the houses and her plans for the estate were important, but nothing was as important as him. He was her life, her future.

Her eyes were aching and she closed them again, although this time instead of falling asleep she lay thinking. She was in one of the bedrooms at Buttercup House, but why? Why did she feel so tired and why was John sitting in a chair beside her?

The fire. Now her eyes sprang wide open and she winced as her mind slowly filtered through the information it had been holding back until she was ready. Lilac

Cottage had been on fire and she had been trapped. She had fallen—

'Molly?'

John's voice was soft and had a slight tremble in it as he bent over her. She smiled and lifted her hand to touch his face, surprised how heavy her arm felt. 'Hello,' she whispered.

'Thank God.' He pressed her to him but gently, as though he was afraid she would break. 'Oh, Molly.'

'I'm all right.'

He made no answer to this but closed his eyes tightly for a moment.

'Gracie?'

He swallowed hard before he could say, 'She's fine. She's with Dobbin and they seem to be getting on very well although I'm sure she's missing you.'

'My cottage?' It had been burning and Matthew's little boat had been on the mantelpiece in the sitting room.

He hesitated.

'It's gone, hasn't it.'

'Darling, we'll talk about things later. You need to concentrate on getting well.'

It had gone. And Lilac Cottage hadn't just been a house, not to her. It had welcomed her the first moment she had stepped inside like a living, breathing entity, wrapping its aura around her. She knew a moment of acute grief, almost as though a person had died whom she'd loved. And Matthew's boat . . .

'Rest now, beloved.'

He had taken her hand in both of his, bringing it to his lips, and although she wanted to ask more the headache was becoming insistent and the light was hurting her eyes. She shut them, thinking it would be for just a moment . . .

Over the next days she slept almost constantly but now it was a restorative slumber, enabling her bruised mind to heal. Gwendoline came to visit her briefly, her poor face still varying shades of yellow, blue and mauve, and although she only stayed for a few minutes Molly found she was exhausted when her friend departed. They didn't talk of the man who had caused both their injuries although each of them knew they would have to in the future. For the present it was enough that they were alive and their friendship was even more precious because of what they'd gone through.

It was another week before John considered her well enough to come downstairs and even then he insisted she sat with her feet up either in the garden or the drawing room. It was a beautiful July, the weather hot but not fiercely so, and the air was heavy with the scents of summer. In the evening the countryside echoed to the cries of swallows hawking airborne insects, and the garden was full of brightly coloured butterflies seeking sweet nectar and competing with bees buzzing lazily as they flew from flower to flower. It was better than any medicine and as Molly's strength returned, so did her desire to take up the reins once more, although her arm was still painful.

Mr Weatherburn, accompanied by Nelly, came to see her three weeks after the fire to report on the progress of the building work and assure her all was going smoothly. If they had imagined their visit would give her peace of mind, it did exactly the opposite. It brought home the fact that she had been away from the site too long. It was *her* dream, *her* baby, and however well things were going – and she didn't doubt they were – she wanted and needed to be in the thick of it again.

After dinner that evening when she and John were having coffee in the drawing room with the big doors open to the garden, she informed him of her decision. 'But first there's something I must do,' she said quietly. 'I have to go back and see Lilac Cottage.'

He shook his head. 'That's not a good idea,' he said softly. 'Trust me, my love. You're doing so well and it will be upsetting—'

'John.' She put her hand over his. 'You can't wrap me up in cotton wool, I'm not that sort of woman. I know I'll be upset but you can't protect me from heartache in life. What you can do is to face it with me. Whatever we encounter from now on, we do it together. Yes?'

He surveyed her for a moment and then a wry smile twisted his mouth. 'We'll go tomorrow morning.'

It was even worse than she had expected. She stood staring at the blackened shell that had been her home – although 'home' was too mild a word to convey what the cottage had meant to her. It had stood for decades, been loved and cared for, and one man's madness had destroyed it in just a couple of hours. Her eyes went to the gaping hole that had been the sitting-room window and she shivered in spite of the warm sunshine. John had told her, as gently as he could, what Cuthbert had done and the manner in which he had died, knowing she would hear it from someone sooner or later and preferring it to be him.

They were standing together outside the little front gate, his arm round her, and now he said softly, 'At least Gracie wasn't harmed.'

Molly nodded through her tears. Gracie, in fact, was thoroughly enjoying her new quarters with Dobbin and the two of them were becoming inseparable. If ever there were animal soulmates, those two were it.

She drew in a deep breath. 'It – it looks – beaten.'

John's arm tightened round her. 'Looks can be deceptive. I've got an idea.'

She glanced up at him but for the moment was unable to speak. The cottage had welcomed and loved her from the first moment she had stepped inside it – although that might sound fanciful she knew it was true – and it was because of her that it was now in this sorry state. If anyone else had purchased it from Mr Stefford, it would be as it had always been.

'We can restore it, Molly, using the old stones, but add to it, perhaps with two extensions either side of the original structure and maybe one at the back too, overlooking the fields and wood. It would make it a real family home, our first home together. I know how much you loved Lilac Cottage as it was but for us to have lived there it would have needed extending. There are Oliver and Angeline, after all – and maybe more children in the future,' he added softly.

She stared at him through misty eyes. 'But Buttercup House?'

'Would you ever have truly felt you were mistress there?' he asked gently. 'Could you have been happy?'

She was amazed at his perception. Christabel had put her stamp on Buttercup House as had been her right, and it wasn't only the morning room where her presence remained. It was a beautiful house but she would always have felt as though she didn't belong, that she was an interloper.

'The thing I have to know is whether you would want to live here again after what happened?'

'You mean Cuthbert dying?'

He nodded, his eyes tight on her face.

She looked at the cottage again, shafts of sunlight touching the mangled remains and glancing off the blackened wood. 'He's not here,' she said softly. 'I don't know where he is but he's not here. This is a good place full of love, and evil has no hold on it.'

'Shall we begin the process of getting plans drawn up?'

'I'd like that,' she said, her eyes looking into his.

'You're sure? I only want you to be happy.'

'I know that.' She was loved and she would go on being loved and loving in return. Turning in to his embrace, she stood on tiptoe to reach his mouth with her lips, and as her body became lost in his she knew that whatever happened in the future, this was the one real solid thing in an uncertain world.

The next weeks were hectic but now she was feeling fit again Molly relished them. Work on the housing estate was going well. Mr Weatherburn had been heard to say that he wished some of the men he'd known in the past worked as hard as the women, and this sentiment seemed to be echoed nationwide. It was reported in the newspapers that the new women factory workers were twice as good as men; one survey estimated that some factories were now two and a half times more productive. Foremen, who were reluctant originally about taking on females, were now praising the women's energy, punctuality and willingness. In munitions production many thousands aged between fourteen and middle-age were toiling twelve hours a day, seven days a week to meet the ever-increasing demand for arms and ammunition.

Molly's site was a happy one and now there was a small army of women working on it. Lonnie had had a chest infection that didn't seem to clear and had decided not to continue working, and Molly had appointed Nelly Parker as forewoman under Mr Weatherburn. The forthright northerner was a good choice. Her work ethic was second to none and she appreciated Molly's trust in her. Furthermore, she wouldn't stand for any gossiping about Molly living at Buttercup House with John before they were married, declaring that it was nobody's business but their own. This didn't stop the rest of the village raising their eyebrows, however.

Molly knew folk were talking about her and that they had assumed the worst – that she was living in sin. It only confirmed, said a lot of righteous souls with a shake of their pious heads, that she *had* been the doctor's mistress all along. She wasn't about to explain to anyone that she and John had separate bedrooms, a decision which had been his rather than hers. He'd told her that the first time they came together would be as man and wife. 'You'll be my wife, the mother of my children, and I want our marriage to begin right, my love,' he'd explained once she was well again. 'Our wedding night will be special – that's how it should be.' He had shrugged his broad shoulders ruefully. 'I love you too much for it to be any other way, even if I do spend half my nights thinking about you being just yards away.'

But now it was the end of October and the wedding was just days away. She and Angeline had been on a trip to Newcastle and chosen their dresses: pale pink silk for Angeline and white lace for her. Gwendoline had insisted that as her wedding present to the happy couple she would hold their reception at Havelock Hall, providing the ballroom for all the guests with a buffet meal and drinks. It was enormously generous and with Gwendoline's encouragement had meant they could invite all the women and their families who worked at the site as well as other friends and family from John's side. Ruth and Ivor and their children were coming, along with Mr Weatherburn and his wife; it was going to be a lavish affair, and dear Mr Weatherburn had agreed to walk her down the aisle.

Gwendoline had asked her, a little shyly, if it would be all right for Lieutenant Radlett to come to the reception if he could get leave. They had apparently been writing to each other once he'd left for France. Molly was thrilled and hoped their burgeoning relationship would bring her friend some happiness in the future. Mark Radlett was the very antithesis of Cuthbert and clearly smitten with Gwendoline, and she seemed like a different woman since Cuthbert's death.

The October day had been cold with a keen north-east wind, and after dinner Molly and John had retired to the drawing room where a roaring fire was burning. They were discussing the memorial service for Edith Cavell which had been held the previous day in London. Ten thousand people had made the journey to St Paul's Cathedral to mourn the British nurse. She had been executed in Brussels earlier in the month by a German firing squad for treason, despite the fact that she and her fellow nurses had treated the wounded of both sides. Her even-handed humanitarianism had seemed to win the respect of the occupying forces but it hadn't been enough to save her life. She had been charged with harbouring Belgians of military age and with helping young English and French soldiers escape to safety across the Dutch border.

'It says that an English clergyman who visited her death-row cell shortly before she was executed said she was admirably calm and well aware that she was guilty under German law,' Molly read from the newspaper, 'but happy to die for her country.' She sighed. 'I wish I could have been out there doing that sort of work.'

John looked askance. 'Well, I'm extremely glad you're not. You would have been the first to spy against the enemy or something along those lines and get yourself shot.'

Molly raised her eyebrows but didn't protest. She couldn't. He was right.

'Anyway, look at what you are doing for the community here at home, which is just as worthwhile,' John said firmly. 'You're making an enormous difference in people's lives, Molly. Some of the men whose wives work for you, along with mothers and sisters and sweethearts, will return to these shores broken in body and mind, and the difference it will make to live in a decent house and know that their families are not going to be turned out on the road will mean everything. Poor beggars . . .' He shook his head sadly. 'Even if we win this war, life's going to be hard. The country will never be the same again.'

Molly nodded. That was why she intended to build a row of shops on the estate once the houses were completed. They would sell good produce or in the case of cobblers and the like offer a good service but at reasonable prices, not selling at extortionate mark-ups like some of the colliery stores. She considered such premises operated a form of blackmail and the inflated prices meant mining families were for ever in debt to their employers. She wanted to build a community hall too, even a school, but that would come later. The first row of houses was nearly ready for occupation, and they were all working towards getting the next row watertight before the bad weather set in. Northern winters were invariably hard and tough.

When the doorbell rang, she sighed. Another call-out for John. Today was a Saturday and every night this week he had had to go out; she had been hoping tonight would be different.

Lotty tapped on the door and then came in and shut it behind her, which was unusual. Normally the maid just poked her head round and said who it was. Walking across to where they were sitting on a sofa pulled close to the fire, she almost whispered, 'There's two men in the hall who want to speak to you, Miss McKenzie.'

'Men?' John sat up straighter. 'What men, Lotty? What do they want?' There had been no more incidents like the one with Mr Weatherburn and Lonnie since, but he was always slightly on edge that some numbskull would object to what Molly was doing. Not that they'd be so foolish as to call at the house, he thought in the next moment, but nevertheless.

'They wouldn't say, sir. Just that they needed to talk to Miss McKenzie. They're in uniform, I think they might be from the training camp.'

'Their names?'

'That's the thing, sir. I asked but the tallest one just kept saying he wanted to speak to Miss McKenzie.'

'I'll deal with this.'

'No, John.' As he made to stand up, Molly caught his arm. 'Let them come in. You're here, I can come to no harm.' Looking at Lotty, she said, 'Show them in.'

'Funny kettle of fish not giving their names.' John stared at her and she nodded. It was strange.

When the door opened again and Lotty stood aside to let two men in army uniform through, they both stood up, John moving so he was slightly in front of her. For a moment she thought they were strangers and then as the tallest man said, 'Molly?' she knew.

'Fred?' She felt light-headed.

'Aye, an' this is Caleb. Didn't know if the Miss McKenzie I'd heard about was you, lass, but—'

She didn't hear the rest of what he said as the light-headedness became a near-faint. She was aware of John catching her and lowering her back on the sofa and saying, 'Pass me a tot of brandy, quick. There's a bottle and glasses in that cabinet there,' and then him holding the glass to her lips as he urged, 'Drink some – it'll help, Molly.'

It did. She gasped and choked a little but the faintness receded. Pushing the glass away, she said again, 'Fred? And that's you, Caleb?'

They were standing, running their caps through their fingers and looking extremely uncomfortable. Finally it was Caleb, a good six inches smaller than his brother, who said, 'We didn't mean to upset you, lass, but if you were the Miss McKenzie we thought you might be we didn't know if you'd want the maid and folk to know we were related, now you're a lady an' all.'

447

Now she got up and flew over to them, putting her arms round their necks and half laughing, half crying as she hugged them, saying, 'Not want people to know? You're my *brothers*,' and then they were hugging her back and all their eyes were wet by the time they drew apart. John had joined them, holding out his hand to first Fred and then Caleb as he said, smiling, 'We haven't been formally introduced but I'm John, Molly's fiancé.'

'Aye, you're a doctor, right?' Fred's voice was gruff as he tried to pull himself together.

'That's right, yes. Come and sit down and I'll get us all a drink. I could do with one, I don't know about anyone else?'

Molly hugged them both again and it was some minutes before they were all sitting down, Fred and Caleb still looking a little awkward as they gazed about the lovely room, clearly somewhat overwhelmed. 'How have you come to be here?' Molly asked softly, gazing into Fred's face which was still familiar, merely an older version of the brother she remembered. Caleb, on the other hand, had altered significantly. 'You're in the army?'

'Aye, volunteered a couple of weeks ago,' Fred answered, smiling as he added, 'Thought we'd jump afore we were pushed if you know what I mean.'

John and Molly nodded. There had been plenty of rumours about conscription over the last months and the subject seemed to be splitting Parliament. Some MPs insisted that voluntary effort was not enough to win the war and there must be pressure on those deemed to be shirking their duty, and others were adamant that compulsion was wrong. Posters appealing for young, single men to go to war were everywhere.

'They sent us to the training camp two or three miles hence and some of the lads were talking about a lady builder,' Caleb put in, grinning as he added, 'You're famous round these parts. A woman with her own business and young an' bonny an' all.'

Molly could imagine it wasn't just that she was famous for. The lads from the training camps drank in the local public houses and heard all the village gossip.

'We had to come and see if the McKenzie lass they spoke of was you,' Fred said, his voice still thick with emotion. 'I never forgave meself for you running away like that. I should've done something.'

'He looked for you for weeks,' Caleb said, his face straight now. 'Got in a fight with our da about it. First time Fred ever went for him.'

'In the end we thought you'd—' Fred shook his head. 'You know. There seemed little chance a wee lass could survive with winter coming on. I – I've had it on me conscience ever since.'

'But it wasn't your fault.' Molly reached across and took one of his hands. It was big, a man's hand, and one that had known hard work from the callouses on it. 'It was his, and our mam's too,' she added, unable to keep the bitterness out of her voice. She took a deep breath before she could bring herself to ask, 'How – how are they?'

'Mam an' Da? Oh, they're dead, lass. The pair of 'em.'

'Dead?' She was shocked. The monster she remembered had always seemed indestructible in his terribleness.

'Aye. Da was set on one night about a year after you'd gone. A bunch of blokes lay in wait for him in the dark and gave him a right good pasting. He'd upset a lot of folk in his time, had Da. They left him for dead and it'd have been better for him if he had died there an' then 'cause he had a broken back among other things. He couldn't use his legs or control his bowels and he used to scream for hours with the pain, begging Mam to put him out of his misery. Anyway, one night me an' Caleb came home and there they were. She'd slit his throat an' then her own.'

Molly gave a little gasp, jerking back in her seat, and John put his arm round her.

'After that me an' Caleb took off, getting work where we could before we settled on a farm up north. Bin there for years till we joined up. They were good folk, the farmer an' his wife. Let us live in a room above the hay barn and kitted it out for us with beds an' stuff an' we had our meals with them. Different to most farmers. Mrs Hartley cried when we left an' said we'd got a place with them after the war. She was more of a mam than ours ever was.'

Molly nodded. There had been nothing normal about her mother's obsessional idolization of their father.

'And you, lass? What happened to you after you left that day? You were more dead than alive.'

She told them her story right up to the present day, keeping nothing back including the manner of Cuthbert's death.

'Seems to me the blighter got what was coming to him,' was Fred's comment.

'Couldn't agree more,' said John grimly. He was finding he liked Molly's brothers. They were rough and ready but their hearts seemed to be in the right place.

The four of them talked some more before Fred said they had to be getting back to the camp. On the doorstep Molly hugged them again. 'We're getting married on Friday. You'll come, won't you, and to the reception afterwards?'

'Lass, you don't have to ask us,' Fred said awkwardly. 'We won't fit in with the sort of friends you've got now.'

'Fred, I can assure you that you'll fit in just fine,' said John warmly, 'and it would make Molly's day. Mine too. Most of the people there will be village folk, salt-of-the-earth men and women we're proud to call our friends.'

'Well, I'll have a word with the sergeant and see what he says.'

John nodded, making a mental note to contact the camp's commanding officer and make sure the brothers were given permission.

'You'll write to me too once you leave the camp?' Molly said huskily, fighting back the tears. Now she had found them, she didn't want them to go, and the thought of what they would be facing when they entered the war properly was terrifying.

Fred rubbed his nose sheepishly. 'Lass, me an' Caleb never learned to read an' write but I promise you this, once we're home again we'll come an' see you. How's that?'

Again, John made a mental note to have a chat with Fred when Molly wasn't present and to tell him to make her next of kin so at least she would be notified if they were injured or worse. It was the best he could do because he knew that for Molly not knowing would be unbearable.

The two men refused a lift back to camp and Molly and John stood on the doorstep, watching them stride down the drive. They waved before disappearing out of sight and it was only after that that Molly let her tears flow. 'I don't want them to go to war, not when we've just found each other,' she sniffed as John handed her a handkerchief.

'I know, sweetheart. I know.'

'I could have given them a job on the site doing something, and one of the houses.'

John was wise enough not to say that he doubted if Molly's brothers would accept what they would almost certainly see as charity. It might be different if Fred and Caleb survived the war, but they'd have to see. Who knew what the country would be facing then?

'Do you think they'll come to the wedding?'

He'd move heaven and earth to make sure of that. He kissed her. 'Yes, I think they'll come to the wedding,' he said gently. 'Now dry your eyes and come inside and go to sleep dreaming of walking down the aisle to meet me.'

She smiled. 'I love you.'

'And I love you.'

* * *

The wedding day dawned bright and sunny but bitterly cold. The first frost of the season had turned the ground white and decorated the bushes and trees in glittering fronds. Molly and Angeline had slept the night at Havelock Hall as it was considered bad luck for the bridal pair to see each other before the wedding.

Gwendoline fussed over her like a mother hen in the morning when Molly announced she couldn't eat any breakfast, eventually persuading her to have a soft roll and a little scrambled egg. Now the day was here Molly found she was a bag of nerves and she hadn't expected that. She found herself worrying about all kinds of things – had Ruth and Ivor and the children been comfortable at Buttercup House where they had spent the night? Would Fred and Caleb be in the church? Would Oliver – who was John's best man – keep the rings safe until the appropriate moment and not drop them? Had the decoration of the parish church – which Nelly and the other women had insisted on doing themselves – gone smoothly? Would she stumble or trip over her own feet as she walked down the aisle to John on Mr Weatherburn's arm?

After breakfast she slipped out of the house to have a walk in the grounds by herself for a few minutes. She needed to restore her equilibrium. The thick frost was still holding fast and everything looked new and clean and beautiful. As she wandered along it felt right that nature had put its seal of approval on what was going to be a fresh beginning for her as a married woman.

The sky was a cloudless blue and spiderwebs sparkled on bushes, their intricate lace designs reminding her of her wedding dress. Suddenly an enormous sense of well-being quietened her mind. She breathed in the crisp cold air and shut her eyes for a moment, thanking God that she was alive on this exquisite morning and was going to marry the man she loved with all her heart.

By the time she returned to the house to get ready she was herself again, and it was she who calmed Gwendoline down from panicking about last-minute details. 'I want everything to be perfect for you,' Gwendoline said anxiously as she and Angeline helped Molly get into her dress.

'It is.' Molly reached out her hand to her friend and smiled. 'I've got the people I love around me today – what could be better than that?'

And later, when Gwendoline's carriage and horses deposited her and Mr Weatherburn at the church and she saw the crowd of people gathered outside, greeting her with beaming smiles and oohs and aahs over her dress and veil, she again felt blessed. Angeline was waiting for her dressed in her pretty pink dress and carrying a miniature version of Molly's bouquet of pink and white roses, and Molly thought how beautiful the girl looked. They had grown closer and closer over the last weeks and Angeline had blossomed in confidence.

Angeline arranged the long veil over the back of Molly's dress. Then there was a movement inside the church and someone said, 'Ready?'

She nodded, taking a deep breath as the organ swelled into loud chords and Mr Weatherburn patted her arm. 'All right, lass?' he murmured, and then they were inside and walking down the central aisle that was warm after the cold day outside. Her high-heeled shoes felt strange – she never wore heels normally – but Mr Weatherburn's arm was solid and secure. She was aware of people turning to look at her and as she neared the front of the church she saw Fred and Caleb grinning at her, but it was the tall man who had moved to stand in front of the vicar who filled her vision as she got nearer to him. And then she reached him and Mr Weatherburn gave her hand to John, and as she gazed into his deep grey eyes they had a message for her alone that caused her heart to soar until she thought she would swoon with the joy of it.

As one they turned to face the vicar.

Epilogue

1965

Gwendoline sat comfortably in a big easy chair which was set at an angle to a roaring fire and her husband was sitting in its partner just a foot or so away. They had just finished breakfast and, as was their custom, had come through to the sitting room to read the newspapers which were delivered to the house each morning. It was one of the many little habits they had that Gwendoline treasured in her heart. Since she had married Mark Radlett a year after the war had ended they had never been apart for even a day. On her wedding day she had left the opulence of Havelock Hall – which her eldest son now ran as a luxurious hotel – for the little detached house she and Mark had bought together, and she had never regretted it for a moment. From having a houseful of servants at the Hall they now employed just a cook and a maid who had become part of the family.

She was reading an article in the paper and it had brought a tear to her eye, which was silly, she told herself – hadn't she and Mark gone to the funeral? But seeing it in black and white emphasized her loss all over again. She reread the words:

It was with sadness that the people of Ellington and those further afield said a last goodbye to Mrs Molly Heath yesterday. Mrs Heath, who died on the seventh of December, would have been gratified at the number of folk who attended her funeral and the heartfelt tributes made in her honour. Her late husband, Dr John Heath, who passed away only two months ago, was also greatly respected in the community. Mrs Heath was well known for her extensive housing estates which stretch as far as Newcastle and Berwick-upon-Tweed, and for her ceaseless championing of women in the workplace. She was also an avid supporter of education for the masses, and particularly higher education for girls. Her slogan, 'We are all created equal under the sun', has caused a headache to many a politician who dragged his heels on equality for women. Mrs Heath has, with good reason, been hailed as an entrepreneur and formidable businesswoman, but to her devoted family she was simply a wonderful mother and grandmother. Both Dr and Mrs Heath were greatly beloved by their children – Oliver Heath and Mrs Angeline Lindsay from Dr Heath's first marriage, and their sons David Frederick Heath and Luke Caleb Heath, and two daughters, Mrs Kitty Hammond and Mrs Violet Upton.

A coal shifted in the fire, sending a shower of sparks up the chimney and causing Mark to raise his head. He glanced at Gwendoline and immediately reached out and took her hand. 'Hey, what's this? Tears?'

'I'm just being silly.'

'You are never silly, my darling one.'

'I'm just going to miss Molly so much, Mark.'

'Everyone will. As it was said at the funeral, Molly building that library on her first housing estate and arranging lessons for any men and women who'd missed out on their schooling and wanted to read and write set a precedent. She opened up new worlds for the ordinary man and woman and that will never be forgotten in these parts. She was an unusual woman in every respect, was Molly Heath.'

'Yes, she was, but it's strange, in my mind I've always thought of her as Molly McKenzie rather than Molly Heath.'

Mark smiled. He had heard how Molly had set tongues wagging when she had first come to work as a housekeeper to John, and about all the trouble that had followed, but then she had continued to cause a stir all her life in one way or another. Perhaps it was always like that for strong, outspoken women who challenged the wrongs in life wherever they found them? One thing was for sure,

Gwendoline's dearest friend had never been afraid to stand up and be counted.

He patted his wife's hand. Yes, she would miss Molly, they all would. God had broken the mould when He had made Molly McKenzie.